THE RAINBOW SWASTIKA CONSPIRACY

D1447279

By Anthony Padgett

Published by
The Auditors of God

First Published 2009
Copyright Anthony Padgett 2009

ISBN 978-0-9561587-0-3

DISCLAIMER: The characters in this book are purely fictitious and any resemblance to real persons is purely coincidental.

PREFACE

Anthony Padgett has a BA in Philosophy, a PGDip in Stone Conservation, a PGCE in the Teaching of Religious Education, and an MA in the Theory of Contemporary Art and Performance.

The first half of this book is based on his own experiences which include his award winning sculpture "Zoroastrian Icarus", his work for the Palestinian Department of Antiquities, his art experiments in Jerusalem on Millennium Eve, his performance art and dance teaching and his 2 year Employment Tribunal case against Mr Tony Blair and the Trustees of the Tate Gallery.

The second half of this book is based on prophecies he made on July 7th 2007 about financial corruption and global conflict.

"And birth they do not use
Nor death on Betelgeuse,
And the God, of whom we are
Infinite dust, is there
A single leaf of those
gold leaves on Betelgeuse."

The last verse of "Betelgeuse" 1925, Humbert Wolfe (1886-1940)
Poet, civil servant and great, great uncle of the author.

THE RAINBOW SWASTIKA CONSPIRACY

Part I – The Prophet of Art

Part II – The Auditors of God

By Anthony Padgett

Part I – The Prophet of Art

1. Hitler's Bunker

The squeak and thud of leather jackboots echoed through the hallway. The officer's SS lightning runes were on one black lapel, the death's head scull on the other.

In the hallway behind him was the dominating portrait of Herr Hitler, in a visionary pose. The brown jacketed Fuhrer did not deign to look down upon the passing of mortal things. Beneath the slicked hair and above the tightly cropped moustache, his eyes stared into a promised future, now as unreal as the painting itself. Germany lay in ruins, its railways and bridges destroyed by the Nazis to stop the allies from taking the country.

The Nazi officer placed his cap onto the desk. The eagle, wings outstretched, talons holding onto a circular wreath, in which was the swastika, beneath a skull rested upon two bones.

Above him was the broken rubble of the Reich Chancellery building, the heaped brick of family homes and the piled bodies of troops and civilians. It was a shroud for a defeated nation.

The red Nazi flag bristled in the occasional wind, its black swastika unfolded its arms in a white circle then collapsed, hiding in shame. The Third Reich was at its end.

Hidden from the brutal shrapnel, smothered beneath 6 metres of reinforced concrete, sat "Adi". His exhausted troops, his Hitler Youth, and his elderly civilian militia were outnumbered by Marshall Zhukov's Red Army 15 to 1.

He sat stiffly, with clenched fist. He was dressed in a grey tunic, emblazoned with the Gold Party Badge, the Iron Cross and the Wounded Badge of World War I.

His black tie contrasted with his white shirt and bright red face. The fury in his pupils echoed in the small moustache above his ranting, scarlet mouth.

Beside him sat his new wife, Eva Hitler, listening, to her husband in full rage. Excusing him for his outburst because he was a genius and, to many, was a god.

She dressed as if staying at the Berghof, their retreat in the Bavarian mountains. The sun was kind on her face there and the views were breathtaking. Now they were cramped in a stifling dungeon, in "The Fuhrer's Suite" of the Chancellery Air Raid Shelter.

She wore a black dress with red appliquéd roses, one of Hitler's favourites. Her brightly coloured high heels complimented the roses. As did her lips and cheeks. Her hair was freshly washed and beautifully coiffed.

Hitler sat on the left side of a sofa and Eva sat on the right. The white sofa was patterned with blue deer and German folk, dressed in traditional clothes.

Beside him, on a small table were his mother's photograph and a vase of tulips and daffodils.

Eva admired her new wedding ring. They had married at 2am that morning, the 30th April, 1945, in the Map Room of the bunker. Hitler had struggled to control the trembling fits in his left arm and leg as he put the ring upon her finger. The black silk dress that she had worn was the best dress that she could find. It was not the traditional white and nor was it the nation's finest state wedding, but she had always wanted to be married.

Now in "The Fuhrer's Suite" with its steel, fire-proof, gas-proof and sound-proof door, the yelling would soon start.

In front of Hitler, on the wall, was a painting of a uniformed figure in a wig whose hard, sombre jewels and penetrating eyes had an uncanny resemblance to Hitler's. He turned to Eva. 'Frederick the Great was the last King of Prussia, from 1740 – 1786. He was revered by Napoleon just as I shall be revered. He was a tactical genius and a hero.' Hitler continued as he looked down at his Iron Cross.

'I leave this painting to my pilot, Hans Baur. The one man I can still trust not to sell it for a shekel.' The veins on Hitler's temple were becoming visible under his red skin.

Eva tried to sooth Hitler, placing a hand on his shoulder. 'Poor Adi, deserted by everyone, betrayed by all. Better that 10,000 others die than that you should be lost to Germany.'

'Eva, I die with a joyful heart knowing the immeasurable achievements of our soldiers, women, workers and their unique contribution to history. From our death will spring the seed of a renaissance of the National Socialist Movement.'

'This war was provoked by foreign powers led by Jews. The same Jews that rejected me from their Academy of Fine Arts.' Hitler thumped his fist onto the chair arm. 'I did not blindly follow their degenerate expressionism and surrealism. But I still earned my living selling watercolours and oil paintings of scenes of Germany. And my legacy will always be greater than theirs.'

Hitler's held his shaking left hand by his thigh.

'My rallies in Nuremburg were like opera, equalled only by Wagner. 140,000 brown shirts in 6 columns, waiting to hear their Fuhrer speak. 300 searchlights turning the clouds into a roof of blue. I marched between them, with gold and red standards, in a triumph of strength and beauty!' Hitler thrust his fist upwards with left thumb and forefinger extended, pointing, shaking.

His hand fell as he sat back, considering. 'It is my legacy that will last forever. Not the degenerate art of the Jewish Modernists whose work is against beauty. These rotten cretins were half blind, that is why they painted such unskilled worthlessness. They are art criminals and their Jewish press, with its so-called art criticism, is full of mendacious claptrap and jabbering. They always want what is new, the latest fashion for the "art initiates". But true

"German Art," the art of heroes and landscapes, expresses the essence of the German people, and, like all true art, it is eternal.'

His thoughts turned back to Eva. Aware of the sadness in her face, he feigned intimacy, 'I am sorry my dear, I am lecturing you.'

Attention was all that she needed. 'Oh no Adi, I love it when you talk. I love your passion. You give the German people their nobility again.'

He continued, 'These are my three great loves, Germany, Art and you, Eva. You are the perfect example of our German race and the way we end our lives will be our final, glorious sacrifice.' Hitler looked at her gracefully formed face, her gently toned form. He did not lust for her. He stared past, to the painting. 'In time a new Wagner will write an opera to us both.'

Eva held Adi's hand. He did not notice the pretence of enthusiasm. Instead he was encouraged. 'One Opera of Wagner is greater than all of the degenerate Jazz music of the Negroes. That racket of sound is proof of their inferiority. Like the Jews, they have produced no single great artist or philosopher. The money hoarding Jew could never see Wagner's spiritual purity.' He had begun to rage again.

He rose from the couch and nearly fell back down. But he refused to accept that he felt dizzy and sick and that his legs were trembling. 'I am sorry my dear, I am shouting.'

Eva was quick to reply. 'No, it's alright.' She should listen, it was her duty. Besides, since the operation on his vocal chords his shouting was not so severe.

He continued to stare at the painting and with the lull in conversation Eva built up her courage. She took the chance to ask what she needed to know.

'I can't understand how we can be losing, has God forsaken us? Did we make a mistake?'

With alarming acuteness Hitler's eyes pierced her. His face went as white as a sheet and he clenched his jaws. 'Germany is the only God I know!'

The reply had not answered her fear. She looked into his pupils. 'Don't you still believe in Jesus Adi?'

He began to explain, as if to a child. 'Christ recognized the Jews for what they were. He heroically used a whip to drive the money grabbing Jews from the Temple and for this he was nailed to the Cross. We are like the original Christians, true Aryans, who were opponents of the Jews. But the Jews took over Christianity and turned it into a religion of meekness and flabbiness? This is why I showed our people that true Christianity is the "Blood and Soil," the Land and Volk of Germany!'

As the veins rose on his forehead and his eyes popped out of his head Eva pleaded 'Please Adi, Please!'

Hitler turned and sat back into the sofa, breathing deeply. 'I am sorry.'

'I need something to believe Adi. I'm afraid. I don't want to go to Hell!'

'This is Hell Eva!' As he snapped he saw the panic in her eyes. He needed to give her courage. 'We are Aryans from Thule, in the North, but we are originally from the stars. I know you are afraid. But we must obey the Higher Powers. When I was in the Thule Society, the group that established the Nazi party, I gave unquestioning obedience to my spiritual "Master." He gave me the power to lead the crowds, he guided me to lead our Aryan race to the next level of evolution of mankind, to become a pure race of "Supermen." I have seen one of these new men. He was free of conscience and morality, ready to make hard decisions for the good of humanity.' Hitler was ready to scream at her but dread in her face stopped him. 'I was afraid of him just as you are now afraid, but we must be a willing sacrifice.'

'Why do we have to do this?'

'Our Aryan Masters will lead the herd in the "Thousand Year Reich" against the Bolshevik Jews. They are the cosmic enemy, a vermin to be swept out with an iron broom. Our deaths will take us to our place in the heavens, a place where we can help with this. I have chosen this day Eva.' Adi now held her hands. 'It is the eve of the Druidic feast of Beltane. We were consecrated in our marriage, you as the Earth and I as the Blood, and our deaths will be an honourable act, a ritual where we will be reborn through our Aryan children.'

Eva was silent, he eyes filled with disappointment. 'You mean you only married me to make this ritual?'

'No, no, Eva. I married you out of love.' The words tumbled from his lips, onto the floor. His ambition had long since destroyed any real ability to love.

'Adi, I'm afraid. This is black magic.'

'No!' the veins rose on his temple. 'Our sacrifice will help the German Nation!'

'Adi! You are always shouting!' She turned away sobbing into the corner of the couch.

He grabbed her shoulders. 'I am the Fuhrer and you are the Fuhrer's wife! Do not dishonour me with cowardice. You will bite the capsule that I give you and invoke our beloved motto, "One Reich, One Folk, One Fuhrer." Do you understand?'

Crying, Eva nodded.

'Do you understand?' He shook her.

'Yes.' She sobbed.

He collapsed back into the sofa, breathing deeply until he regained his composure, then drew close to his wife. 'Come here, I'm sorry. Please believe me.' He put his arm around her shoulder. 'Do you remember the Berghof?'

'Of course.' Her tears soaked into the couch, her mind drew to the magical events at their county retreat in the Bavarian mountains. She did not want to argue, she only wanted love. She drew her legs up under herself and onto the sofa to snuggle-up. Her shoes fell to the floor. It was like when they would sit with their two black guard dogs at their feet.

'I love you Adi,' sighed Eva. 'Can I have one last kiss?' She could barely ask for fear of being refused. Her full red lips touched his thin mouth. 'Will it hurt?'

'No.'

'I don't mind dying a heroic death, but it mustn't be painful.'

'Don't worry. Your heart will beat fast and strong, then in less than a minute it will be over.'

'I'm not afraid.'

'You will be brave.'

Hitler took a 6.35mm Walther pistol out of his left pocket. 'If you are in pain then I will end it quickly.'

'No Adi, I do not want everyone to come in and see me...'

'Don't worry, I won't spoil your beauty. I want to see you perfect when I go. I only want that you do not suffer. I will only use it if I must.'

He opened his hand and Eva took a brass pellet. She opened it. Inside was a glass ampule.

Staring into Adi's eyes she slowly and deliberately recited each word. 'One Reich, One Folk, One Fuhrer.' Then bit the cyanide capsule.

Her breathing grew quicker then she started rasping. Her face and body began to convulse in pain, she stared in panic, but it eased as her breathing slowed and finally stopped. The poison had paralysed her respiratory organs and then her heart.

Hitler let the pistol fall from his hand.

Her body lay on the couch like a statue. A yawning, silent emptiness filled the room. Then as he prepared his own 7.65mm Walther pistol a movement caught the corner of his eye. He sharply turned from Eva to the side of the portrait.

It was a figure, black as shadows.

The blood that had filled his raging face with life now rushed to his stomach and limbs. He jumped up from the couch. 'Who is it?'

His forehead dripped with the sweat of panic. 'Eva!' He cried out loud. 'It's him, its him, he's here.' His face turned a pallid grey and his lips turned to blue as he recoiled back onto the sofa. Alone, terrified, a voice in his head mocked, repeating again and again. 'One Reich, One Folk, One Fuhrer. One Reich, One Folk, One Fuhrer. One Reich, One Folk, One Fuhrer.'

'One Reich, One Folk, One Fuhrer!' Hitler screamed as he placed a cyanide capsule in his mouth and bit. At that moment he also fired his pistol.

The blood trickled over his face and dripped onto his gold party badge. Its imperial eagle, wings outstretched, tightly clutching the oak wreathed swastika.

2. Cherubim at the British Museum

2 large, winged bulls flanked the entrance to the Babylonian collection in gallery 6 of the British Museum. Above them was a carved solar disc, flanked by outstretched wings. In the centre of the disc was a bearded man, holding a hoop.

David Wolfe was a sculptor, with a joyful smile and sparkling eyes. His wild mass of thick hair swept back above his handsome Jewish face. It made the back of his head seem extended, as if belonging to an ancient Egyptian king, divinely appointed as the holder of sacred mysteries. His full lips held tightly together as his curved nose cut the air, as if to sniff complexity. He had a mark, a ring shape of the Hindu spiritual Third Eye, indented between his intelligent eyes, eyes which calculated with sublime perception.

But for now he wore a white lab coat over his fashionable black jumper and shirt as he waited to be shown the Babylonian Alabaster relief he would be cleaning for the conservation department. He had to do this work to make a living, until his art was recognised.

As he stood, staring upwards, the curator Dr. James Rockschild, came to his side. This short, plump American professor in his late fifties was smartly dressed in a check shirt. He was from a wealthy banking dynasty and had chosen to use his inheritance to pursue a career in culture and history. With a smile he gave a firm, if somewhat sweaty, handshake, then with a thick, nasal accent he asserted his knowledge. 'The disc of the Assyrian sun God, Shamash. A symbol of divine royalty.'

David nodded in interest and looked at the human headed, winged bulls. 'And what about these?'

'Assyrian Guardian Angels, from the palace of Nimrud, dating from around 865 to 850 B.C.E. They guarded doorways to scare away evil spirits. The Jewish scriptures named them Cherubim and placed them as guards of the Tree of Life in the Garden of Eden.'

David raised his eyebrows. 'I thought they were Babylonian. So, where exactly was Assyria.'

'The history of the Ancient Near East, Mesopotamia, is confusing. It was made up of Assyria, Babylon and Persia, what are now North Iraq, South Iraq and Iran. They had many common beliefs. For instance each nation had its own high bull God of the sun, Assur for the Assyrians, Marduk for the Babylonians and Ahura Mazda for the Persians. And each God had 7 aspects, 7 lesser divinities that they ruled over. Marduk had serpent spirits, Ahura Mazda had winged men and Assur had both.'

They moved over to a section of metre high relief carvings. 'But you'll be working here, in Gallery 7, on this alabaster frieze from the North West palace at Nimrud. It is a protective spirit sent to teach mankind wisdom. You can see how the spirit sprinkles water from a pine cone onto a date tree.'

David admired the detailed artistry of this half-life sized man whose wings showed each feather and whose hair and goatee beard were formed of tight rings. He wondered at the meaning of the triangles of cuneiform writing that filled the side of the relief. The thick metre high piece of dark brown Alabaster, Calcium Sulphate, a large mass of salt crystals, would have been soft to carve, easy to damage. It was amazing that it had survived 2,500 years.

'The carvings would have been mounted besides the steps of the towers, the ziggurats. All the figures facing in the direction of the King so that as his subjects walked, they would know who ruled over them. And these Kings were also the state high priests.'

David nodded in interest. 'A King-Priest, a bit like the Jewish idea of the Messiah?'

'Exactly, and performed all the major sacrifices, including the annual fertility sacrifice of the Bull God.' Rockschild looked at David's face to find the reason behind the question. 'Are you Jewish?' David nodded. 'So you will know how Nebuchadnezzar captured Jerusalem in 586 B.C.E. and marched our people in chains to Babylon. But did you know that this is where we got Monotheism? But not from the Babylonians, from the Persians after King Cyrus conquered Babylon in the 5th century B.C.E. Cyrus allowed us to rebuild our Temple back in Jerusalem but under the influence of Zoroaster's religion.'

'Zoroaster?' enquired David.

Rockschild smiled kindly. 'Yes, the prophet of Ahura Mazda, the God of Light, who created the world and was in a cosmic battle with the evil God of darkness, the serpent Ahriman. They were twins under their father Zurvan, the god of time. Unfortunately I can't show you any artefacts because they had no images of their God in the Temple. Again, like Judaism.'

David tried to interrupt, to ask about Zurvan, but Rockschild did not allow him. 'But the Persian religion's influence was even wider. In the 4th century B.C.E. it was spread through the Ancient World by Alexander the Great. He believed that he was the incarnation of Mithras, the greatest of the 7 aspects of Ahura Mazda. Mithras was the aspect of fire that came to earth and Mithraism later became the warrior religion of the Roman Empire Every town, city, military garrison and outpost from Syria to Scotland, had a Mithraeum and priest until around 300 C.E.'

'So what did they believe?'

'Little is known because most of the evidence was destroyed by Christian zealots. But, basically, Mithras slayed the bull God in a cave and created the world from its body. His followers would sacrifice a bull and share its body and blood in a ritual meal. The start of this religion marked the end of the Age of Taurus, the bull of nature, and the beginning of the Age of Aries, the ram of war. Alexander was a great warrior and each morning, like Mithras, would sacrifice a bull to the sun.' Rockschild noticed that David had stopped listening closely at this point. 'Mithraism is now a dead religion and Zoroastrianism has only a small number of followers today but it had a major influence on the 20th century, through the Nazis.'

David turned sharply.

'In the 1870's the archaeologist Heinrich Schliemann discovered the swastika symbol in the site of ancient Troy. The Nazis linked it with the swastikas found on ancient German pots and created the myth that there was a unity between Germanic, Greek and Indo-Iranian cultures. They believed that an "Aryan" master race originated in northern Europe, and migrated down, through Mesopotamia, into India and Tibet. The Nazis believed that their Aryan ancestors brought the Swastika of their Sky God, throughout this region. But there is almost no archaeological evidence of the swastika in Mesopotamian art. The Nazis couldn't explain its absence. But the reason is that the swastika is a symbol of the Earth Mother and its association with the Sky God was just a Nazi myth.'

Rockschild continued speaking as he backed up the corridor of carvings. 'They also latched on the writings of the German philosopher Friedrich Nietzsche, who had promoted the idea of a Master Race in his book from the 1880s, "Also Spoke Zarathustra", another name for Zoroaster. He argued that the religion of the Jews and Christians was too stifling of evolution. He wanted to replace it with human strength, creativity and will power, the qualities of the new Ubermensch, the Superman. Because Zoroaster was the first prophet of Monotheism, Nietzsche used him to replace Monotheism with his new system of a belief in the Ubermensch. Hitler misinterpreted this and saw himself as being like Alexander the Great a semi-divine incarnation, like one of these Ubermensch. He mixed up a cocktail of lies that ended in the Holocaust, the Nazi genocide of the Jews.'

David could see that Rockschild had taken a liking to him. Maybe he saw him as some kind of protégé. But Rockschild had checked his watch and now looked impatient, as he turned to inspect the relief. 'So, this carving is dirty and out of keeping with the other exhibits. How should we clean it?'

David scrutinised the surface. 'Alabaster is soluble in water, so I'll need to clean it with a non-ionic liquid.'

'How long will it take?'

'It's only a short job, just a few days. So it's not worth removing from its steel fixings on the gallery wall. But we'll have to close off Gallery 7 because of the fumes. But the delay should be minimal.'

'Fine. Work here in the morning and late afternoon and we'll open the gallery as normal at peak times.'

-

David began the slow, patient process of conservation. He was careful not to remove too much grime, lest the antiquity became too clean.

He used solvents so as not to remove any of the surface of the water soluble alabaster. So he wore a mask to protect him from the fumes and latex gloves to prevent his skin from drying and cracking. He wrapped cotton wool around a cocktail stick, applied the solvents and began to clean the figure. Each groove in each feather needed careful swabbing. Each corner of the triangles of cuneiform writing needed cleaning out.

Over the painstaking days his mind began to wander.

The scenes around him included the killing and enslavement of men. He thought of the cruelty of their tortures and the way that religion was used by rulers to dominate their subjects. David believed in no Gods. And these scenes drained him empty, until he believed in nothing and grew depressed within his Nihilism.

But he couldn't accept that there was no purpose behind the Universe? He needed some kind of belief. But how could there be a God, why should that God be Good. And why should God be bothered about human beings. He was more confused than ever. He was searching for truth but what he desired, what he needed, most of all, was to meet a beautiful girl. But he couldn't talk to girls, he couldn't even look them in the eye because he was too wrapped up in thinking about the meaning of life.

He wanted to sit in the conservation workshops with the pretty, young, cashmere wearing girls. On their well-lit benches were large magnifying glasses, trays of fine tools for cleaning and scraping, and plastic bottles with long curved tubes. They would sit in lab coats all afternoon, chatting, drinking tea and listening to the afternoon play on BBC Radio 4.

He had a crush on the girl who conserved ceramics. She smiled and laughed with perfect teeth and stood tall and confident. He longed to be in her company. But he didn't know her name, didn't know how to speak with her and when he collected his materials in the morning she just ignored him.

Maybe, if he expressed some monumental truths in his art, then she would love him.

He returned to analysing again. He never understood how God could allow famine, drought, floods, storms and earthquakes. But the Zoroastrian faith made sense of a world full of pain, lust and hate because its' God, Ahura Mazda did not create them, They were made by Ahriman, the Devil who he battled against. Each struggled to control the world. This made sense, but it was not Monotheism like Rockschild had said it was. It was two Gods, not one, it was Dualism.

David could not shake the Jewish belief that there was just one God, supreme and without equal.

As he continued to work the hierarchical palaces of Assyrians society gave him key. They offered no freedom and the Jewish slaves in Babylon knew the importance of freedom. So what made the Jewish God unique, what made him closest to humanity, was that he was free and gave freedom to the lowest slave, to the Highest King, and to the Angels themselves. This God was free to choose goodness and be worthy of worship but was also free to make mistakes and be a terrible God. This God allowed evil in the world because he was free, because sometimes he was evil, and he had created angels and mankind to be free, to be evil as well.

-

That Friday, at the end of the day, David walked, back from Gallery 7, to reach the stairway that led down to the conservation laboratory. He passed through rooms of marble sculptures, from Ancient Greece and Rome, to get to Gallery 7. Their pure, white, muscular bodies were an ideal that he wished he attained himself. Their faces were superhuman, Gods incarnated in marble. Like the beautiful people who adorned the London advertising boards, they had a physical perfection that masqueraded as moral perfection.

As he stumbled around a corner, past a security guard who seemed almost mummified, he bumped into an elderly couple. They had turned away from their tour guide to look at a large glass case of coins. 'Sorry,' he mumbled, as he squeezed past them then weaved his way through a group of school children.

Then he stopped in gallery 69.

Till now he had taken no notice of the statue of a soldier slaying a bull. But this robed figure took on meaning as he realised it was a depiction of the God, Mithras, defeating the cosmic bull.

Mithras stood over the beast, pulling its head back and piercing its neck with a sword, releasing its vital essences. The apparent ease of the action seemed unconvincing as the bull strained and stretched at its ropes, ready to explode and bellow. A snake drank the blood pouring from the open wound.

He read the sign on the plinth. "Mithraism flourished until it was replaced with Christianity by Constantine the Emperor of Rome, in the 4th century C.E. Like other Greek and Roman "Mystery Religions" the priests of Mithraism believed that they could rise to the heavens, through blood sacrifice to help them purify their souls."

The sculpture was cracked and badly repaired. The bull's leg was coming apart and a large flake was spalling from its rear. As he inspected the statue everyone walked around him as if they owned the museum. Japanese tourists gathered and their camera flashes bounced off the display cases. A shapely Mediterranean girl, who wore sunglasses on her head and whose boyfriend wore a jumper on his shoulders, wanted to know what excited David. She read the sign then turned away, bored.

Guessing that it was time to go he asked the stout, museum attendant for the time.

'5.30,' he replied.

David bounded down the West stairway, three at a time, hoping to get to the conservation department before the girl left, hoping that she would be working late, so that maybe he could ask her out on a date.

On the way down the steps he saw a meandering mosaic that lined the walls. Its design was a swastika, the symbol of the Nazis. Why was it here. He slowed on the corner. The sign read. "Mosaic Fretwork of the Parthenon in Athens, the Temple to Athena, the Greek Goddess of Wisdom." He continued bounding down.

By the time he got to the workshop the girl was just leaving with her tall, well dressed, boyfriend. He had no idea. David said 'Hello' as he passed them both, whilst looking at the floor.

-

Back at his Islington studio David contented himself to carve subtle lines and smooth planes. Art was his substitute for love. He searched for perfection in the geometries of the body, expressing their sensual curves. The complexity of the human form held a fascination surpassed only by his need to discover a deep truth. But the art created in his hands was a way to find a truth that lay beyond the powers of his reason.

An untouched block of Portland limestone dominated his studio. This was the type of stone used on the finest buildings in London, shaped into sculptures and stones for buildings like Saint Paul's Cathedral. It was quarried, hewn, from a rock face. The grand and imposing city rose as a mountain of these blocks, wiping away any trace of the nature from which they came. He was full of hope but did not know where to start.

Images of the statues from Persia, Greece and Rome were stored in his mind as he began carving, cutting a figure straining to hold an unclear idea of God.

He chiselled away, head down.

The floor began to fill with rubble and the air clouded with dust.

The ring of his tungsten tipped chisel reassured him that there were no flaws that might split the stone. He gouged the surface, exposing the shells of ancient sea creatures. These tiny exoskeletons, compressed on the sea bed millions of years ago, were revealed for the briefest of moments, then destroyed by another carefully placed blow.

He breathed in the dull, burnt smell of the dust and entered a communion with the freshly cut limestone which he shaped. The chisel was a tool in David's hand and he hoped to be a tool in the hands of timeless truth and beauty. He loved the craft of stone carving. He had learnt his skills in the Mason's college in Portland and could understand how the Masons had come to see their art almost as a religion.

The Masons were technicians, commissioned to construct the Catholic Cathedrals of Europe, saw God as the Master Builder and with their expertise they grew rich and powerful. They had helped to begin the expansion of western learning that led to the Renaissance and their knowledge was not just technical, it was spiritual. But when, in the 16th century, the Protestants broke from the Catholic Church in Rome, many of the Masonic Lodges were destroyed, and their finances seized. It was after this that Freemasonry began. Instead of being a trade organisation for stone masons it was open to merchants and businessmen who were interested in the ancient spiritual truths and symbols of Masonry, like the square, compasses, level, plumb-line and the chisel and used these in secret ceremonies and rituals.

Now with inspiration and intuition David was trying to get back to the source of those secrets, back to the stone itself, and as the piece progressed the ideas took shape.

The body of a bull-man began to form, with the legs of a bull and a lion. Its arms were wings to soar above this animal nature and reach a higher consciousness. The elements were like those of the Cherubim, at the British Museum, but this was more man than a bull.

It was like Icarus, the son of Daedalus, from the Greek myths. Daedalus had built a labyrinth for the Minoan King, who had placed a Minotaur, half-bull and half-man, within the labyrinth. The Minoans worshipped a Bull God of nature and their Minotaur would devour human sacrifices. Daedalus fell out of favour and was imprisoned along with his son. So he created wings from feathers and wax so that they could escape. He warned Icarus not to fly too close to the sun but Icarus disobeyed his father and flew higher and higher. His wings melted, and he fell to his death, like an angel cast from heaven.

Eventually the Minotaur was killed by Theseus, the king of the Greek city of Athens, symbolising the way that the Olympian Gods of Greece, conquered the older, Minoan Gods of Crete. It symbolised how the philosophers of Athens led a new dawn of human reason and David's sculpture symbolised his attempt to master animal nature, to reach nobility and truth.

But the sculpture's head remained unformed.

-

Months later, the body was finished, supported by a lion's leg, that curled and pushed at the rear, and by ox legs at the front, propping against the lion's force. The sculpture strained with energy and power whilst the wings reached and bent, trying to embrace something too big to grasp.

The head was now fixed and proud, defiantly rejecting degeneracy. Its hair and beard were tight rings. In the midst of these were smooth cheekbones, a strong nose and a steady graceful brow, all connected to perfection. David rubbed the face, lovingly, with sandpaper. This was the ideal face of an Ubermensch, a superhuman, a Divine being, a Cherub, incarnated in art.

The sensual upper lip, cut with two perfect curving lines met in a ridge. The lower lip was rounded and trammelled like a fine architectural corbel. David could kiss those lips. He blocked the thought.

As he carved and rubbed, his mind wandered to the statue of Mithras, whose face was a perfect form, cut in marble but eternally lifeless. Its only character came from the corruption of time, from the rain and wind, from being buried in the earth, and from being broken and smashed.

David's angel was without vision. It needed life breathing into it. He gouged deep into the eye sockets of the head. Then left them empty like the bronze sculptures of antiquity that were filled with glass eyes, to give life to the work. He chiselled deep with his finest tool. A fire should be in the eyes but there was nothing. They were blank above a curled nose and expressionless mouth. Inside these hollows were no deep prophecies.

Like Icarus the figure was trying to reach something that should not be in his knowledge. Unless it was careful, this "Zoroastrian Icarus" would surely crash to the ground.

With the final mallet stroke, he forced his last path into the virgin material and ended with a sigh.

3. Christian Matchmaker

David had been invited to the church in Islington by his friends, Sebastian and Paul. Sebastian, a well dressed, good looking man, with the appearance of a 1920's dilettante, was an artist and an interior designer who had found God after being beaten up in an alley, just for being bisexual. Paul was an unemployed, sensitive hippie with long hair, who had become confused about his sexuality. The two of them had met on the dance floor of a gay club. In the thudding disco they had both resolved to change their lives.

So they joined the Islington Christian Fellowship. This was part of the House Church movement, led by the Charismatic American Evangelist Jerry Fulwell. Each church had a Pastor but they rejected the religious ritual that had developed around Christianity and sought to return to the ways of the early church, so church members would meet in small, informal, prayer groups in each others houses.

As David stood in the giant church Hall, the young congregation stood with arms reaching into the air. A small band, with drums and electric guitars, stood at the front, singing from words projected onto a screen. 'He is worthy, He is worthy, He is worthy, of our praise.' They repeated, the words, priming themselves for the sermon by Fulwell, their visiting founder.

Paul was a steward on the door. He had combed his long straggling hair and wore a crimpled grey shirt in an attempt to look smart. Eyes closed, he held a grateful, yet expectant smile, his hands and face receiving the blessings that descended upon them.

David didn't share the sentiments but tried to enter into the uplifting spirit of the hymns. Then, as the music ended, the slick, black haired Fulwell, in an expensive suit and open shirt called for everyone to receive the blessing of the Lord.

'Hallelujah! He is risen.'

Fulwell looked like he was making a statement about his machismo, that he was living a hard-working life, and that in return he was gifted with God's abundance.

'Christ's body is the Temple, the Temple that he rebuilt with his resurrection after his crucifixion. He ascended to Heaven but Luke 21:24 tells us that he will return after the "times of the Gentiles." These are the end times as prophesied, when Jerusalem will be under Gentile control of non-Jews. A time that began with the first conquest of Judah by the Babylonians in 605 B.C. But before Christ returns there will be the Rapture, when 144,000 true Christians will be lifted to Heaven. Meanwhile, on earth, there will be chaos as a new world leader, the Anti-Christ, will arise out of a new Roman Empire.'

The congregation hung on every word.

'This Anti-Christ will make a covenant with Israel and rebuild the Jewish Temple. Babylon will fall and Israel will be invaded from the North but the Anti-Christ will defeat the Northern army. He will receive a death blow but will recover and reveal himself as the Beast, whose number is 666. Aided by a false prophet, his image will be set in the Temple and he will demand to be worshipped as God.'

As David looked around the only decoration in the hall was a patchwork banner showing a grapevine. There were no crucifixes, no statues. This House Church movement inherited the 16th century Protestant Christian tradition, which rejected the Catholic use of pictures of Christ, elaborate rituals or fine vestments. Instead they wanted a simple, immediate relationship with Christ.

'The remaining church will be destroyed and many, including Israel, will be martyred for refusing to worship the Anti-Christ. This time of the Gentiles will only end with the second coming of Christ. Then the kings of the Orient will invade Israel at the battle of Armageddon. The Anti-Christ and the false prophet will be cast alive into the Abyss, the lake of fire, and Israel will finally receive Christ as Messiah. He will establish the kingdom of God in Israel and the earth will bask in his glorious reign.'

Fulwell now looked David in the eye. 'We will be judged on how we treat God's covenant people, Israel, during the end times and we are heading to these times right now.' He paused. 'Let us unite in Christ.'

The group began to pray, then sang again. 'He is worthy, He is worthy, He is worthy of our praise.' They all stretched up their arms to received blessings.

A gentle strumming of the guitar continued as they lined up, row by row to form a queue. With contrition they bent and took a small piece of dry bread, followed by a sip from the chalice of wine. Returning to their chairs many still had their hands clasped together, keeping the forgiveness close to their hearts.

David did not take the Eucharist. He wanted to be together with his friends, not always on the outside, but he was not allowed to share in the blood and body of Christ, without being committed. The hymns continued, more upbeat, 'Our God is a Mighty God, Our God is an Awesome God.'

The service ended, with a final prayer, and each person shook the hands of those around them, wishing them peace. David shook hands and mumbled 'Peace be with you,' but he couldn't look anyone in the eye.

As they drank orange juice Fulwell stood, flirting with the young women that surrounded him. The only people David felt confident to speak with, were some elderly believers who repeatedly advised him that he had to open his heart and "experience" the truth of a personal relationship with Christ.

-

David sat in Sebastian's living room. The low, art deco armchair rose up from the plush carpet. He stared, full from his evening meal, past the bamboo leaf design of the wallpaper, to the dark green ceiling.

Kirsten, Sebastian's wife, sat next to David under a large lampshade. She was young, pretty and slightly plump. She had rebelled against her divorced parents, her wealthy American father and her hippie mother, by becoming a teenage pregnancy statistic, then becoming a Charismatic Christian and marrying Sebastian.

'I think that He's got His hand upon you,' said Kirsten. 'Just accept Jesus as your Saviour and you'll have all you need.' She poured David a cup of tea. 'I've been reading a book by Peter Kwashi, the Archbishop of Nigeria, who says how a man in his Church asked God for a bicycle and didn't get one. Then the Holy Spirit told him that he wasn't being specific enough. So he prayed for a red bicycle and got it! I'm praying for a fridge and a washing machine.' She laughed, exuding confidence. 'That's what it means to get back to the original Christianity, to the real power of prayer. The Holy Spirit brings signs, prophecy, speaking in tongues, and healing.' Then she added, without irony, 'Though women no longer have to cover their heads in church, which I'm quite glad about.'

David shook his head. 'No one knows what the original Christianity is. The final version of the Bible wasn't even decided upon until the 4th century C.E., by the Holy Roman Empire.'

'You analyse too much. The Bible is the word of God. And our faith has all the features of the early church in the Acts of the Apostles.' Kirsten wanted David to accept her belief. 'If you don't believe me then listen to my "Witness". Last year I was diagnosed with cervical cancer, then, 6 months later, with the power of prayer, I was cured without treatment.' She was giddy with excitement. 'Praise the Lord.'

He knew there was nothing he could say to shake her from her conviction and her need to convert him. He pulled back as she reached out and ruffled his hair. 'Sorry, it's too precise.' She studied his face and smiled. 'I know just the girl for you, the pastor's daughter. She is "Spirit-filled." And you both have lovely brown eyes.'

He knew the condition was that he became a Christian. 'No, I know who you mean, but she's not suitable.'

'Why not?' she enquired, as if the decision had already been made.

'She just isn't.' He didn't want to go into a lengthy explanation. 'She wouldn't be interested in me for a start.'

'Of course she would be. Sebastian told me you are a talented sculptor. I could arrange for you to meet her at our House Group.'

David picked up a Bible and turned to the New Testament for help. 'I can't find it, he said, flicking through, but Paul says that it is better to be without a partner.'

Kirsten frowned, annoyed. 'Yes, I know, but he also says that if you burn with passion you should marry. Besides, even if you don't burn with passion, righteousness only comes from Jesus, not from your own efforts.'

Sebastian had overheard the conversation as he entered the room with Paul. They sat with drinks, sharing a couch beneath a large wall mirror. 'You keep telling me that you long for a partner,' said Sebastian, 'it's just what you are looking for. But why don't you come to our House Group anyway? We worship together then share a meal. It's not anything you wouldn't feel happy doing.'

David couldn't answer this. It was true, he was lonely. But the church was not the place he could be at home. He just didn't believe. As he listened he picked up the delicate fragrance of Sebastian's aftershave. Sebastian burned with passion for both David and Paul, but believed that God understood and forgave his sexuality.

Sebastian began his well rehearsed lines. 'You say you're open to the truth, but you'd believe anything, as long as it is not The Truth,' said Sebastian, leaning forward in his chair. 'Just put your faith in Christ and he'll show you that he's the Truth.'

'I would be more open to Christ,' said David, with wide eyes and open hands, 'if it wasn't for the doctrine of the Trinity. How can God be the Father, the Son and the Spirit at the same time?' He had made this reply so many times before.

'God can do anything. His Truth is beyond complicated reason because it has to be simple, open to everyone, otherwise he would be too exclusive.' Sebastian looked triumphant in his reasoning.

Paul sat back, with the same confidence in unshakeable beliefs. 'The Trinity is beyond human logic, as 1 Corinthians says, "Has not God made foolish the wisdom of the world?" All you need to kow about the Trinity is that God became Jesus, the Son, so that he could pay the debt for the sins of the world by this death on the cross.'

David put his head in his hands. 'I can understand how Jesus' forgiveness could be an example to humanity, but not how his death on the cross could pay for our sins.'

Sebastian furrowed his brow and put his drink on the side-table under the lamp. 'Jesus isn't just "an example," He is God, and the only way to salvation. We are all sinners but Jesus was perfect and can save us because his sacrifice paid for everyone's sins.'

'Surely Christ's message was that we must try to be good to people even when they persecute us? You can't just do whatever you like then ask for forgiveness on Sunday. You can't say that people who help others are only good if they accept Christ.'

Paul changed the approach. 'Look, we're going round in circles. You are looking for answers to the meaning of life and whether God exists. Well we have all these answers, that is why we have a deep peace. Isn't this what you want?'

'No, I don't want peace by believing a set of contradictions,' replied David.

Paul shook his head, smiling. 'They are only contradictions to your limited mind.'

Kirsten had her arms folded. 'You need to be careful that you aren't deceived by "The Dev".'

David looked up blankly, Sebastian clarified, 'The Devil.'

David was tired of the bombardment. He returned his head to his hands and looked at the floor. He loved his friends but needed them to show more of the love of which they preached. He needed them to love him for who he was, even for not being able to accept their God.

As his friends prayed, asking Jesus to come into David's life, the evening extended into the night and followed a predictable route of theological bullying. It ended with David's friends making a final statement. 'You need to open up to God. All you need to do is pray to Jesus and he will come into your heart.'

But how could he pray to Jesus unless he already believed in Him?

4. Maitreya Institute

David had to get away from London's drab, dirty, dusty streets, away from its tower blocks, broken factories and empty warehouses. Even the fine churches and pristine Neo-classical mansions around the city gave no relief.

He decided to retreat, for a month at the Maitreya Buddhist Monastery, just to the south of the Lake District. It was in the grounds of a run down neo-gothic mansion, by the side of Morecambe Bay. Here he hoped to learn more about Buddhism, to find inspiration in the mountains and to commune with the grandeur of nature.

His room was on the first floor in a slate-built, Victorian, terraced annex. The room was large, with dark green walls, golden borders and a white ceiling.

As he got changed into shorts and trainers he admired the framed print on the wall. It was of the 1818 painting "Wanderer above the Sea of Fog", by the German Romantic artist Caspar David Friedrich. It was a timeless vision of a lone figure, dressed in a knee length coat, standing on top of a mountain, looking across a sea of clouds from which peaks arose. The figure had his back to the viewer and was ready to merge into the horizon, into the home of the Gods.

David cast a final glance at the painting and set off to run on the fells.

The ground was soft beneath his trainers on the hill tops. He headed for the peaks and as he approached a small mountain lake, a tarn, a flock of birds took to the air in startled unison. He regretted the intrusion but continued his run, stepping on the airy grass which sprang him upwards.

He sweated in the sun but, as he removed his shirt, the fresh wind blew his body. It was a pleasurable balm. He was remote from the gaze of man, in harmony with the hills around him. He was no observer, he was a part of the mountain and its crags. Roaming, like a wild, free animal, within a miniature Cosmos. As he ran over the hills, his near naked, youthful body was in harmony with its surroundings, absorbed in all that was around, cutting a path through the mountains, transforming himself. He was no leisurely wandering poet, he was a prophet.

Shadows of cloud passed over as the sun bathed hills and the wind softly stroked the grass, creating rippling waves.

On reaching the summit, David could see the plateaux undulate for miles, to the distant mountain peaks beyond. He felt that this beauty could only be made by God, but quick to gain control, he denied the feeling. It was an unproven superstition, a personification of the forces of nature, a lie. But the lie came from somewhere deep within his very soul.

He stood in awe, and admiration of the scene. The sweat cooled upon his back and cloud began to fill the sky, obscuring the sun. The sun struggled to break through and suddenly it began to rain. The peaks now took on a different mood, reminding him that they were formed of rock, rudely cast forth from a timeless, volcanic brutality.

The divine had taken on a sinister presence. He set off over the wet grass, making his way down the steep sides, controlling his fear. The rain stopped and a mist began to rise. He continued, then soon realised that he was lost.

He stopped to listen. He thought that he heard his name being called. A patch of mist began to clear and he was shocked to see that he stood at the edge of a sheer drop into the valley. He stared into the sublime abyss in fear and awe. He fell backwards, against the damp hill, then edged his way back up the ridge. He now began to panic. He might be stuck up the mountain. 'Please help me God.'

On the ridge he desperately searched for a familiar landmark, a familiar cairn, a pathway down. There were none. He had to do something. He turned off the ridge-way, following a sheep trail down the side of the valley. As he prayed again he glimpsed life's purpose, its meaning. It lay in choosing the right path, to follow good rather than evil. But how did you know which was the right path.

Fear kicked in again as he slowly climbed down the siding. The grass gave way to scree that slid under his feet. As he scrambled down the rise he wondered if this would lead to another cliff edge?

Relief surged through his whole being. He had reached thick bracken on a banking that rolled down into trees. The sweet smelling leaves brushed against him, sending cascades of cold water on his arms and legs, it was refreshing, life giving.

Halfway down the bank the trees now surrounded him as the sky darkened with full storm clouds and a cold wind rustled the leaves. He glanced around then shot through the trees. He could not tell if he was being scratched, cut or stung as it began to rain. It was a downpour by the time he finally he descending from the crags and reached the road. He pounded, in soaking trainers, the last stretch until he turned into the back yard of the monastery.

The Lakeland Mountains surrounded him with their cold, grey presence.

-

David lay on his bed staring out of the window, at the mist, suffused by the moon's pure glow. He soon fell asleep in the warmth.

He dreamed that the fells and mountains were half engulfed in vast waters and he was on a narrow walkway between two peaks. Bright stars shone in the night air above but in front of him stood a tall figure, robed in black. He could not see its face, but behind its head was a nimbus that shimmered and crackled, like the sun on rippling waters. The shards of energy showered twisted malevolence. It was the Devil.

'I'm not afraid of you,' said David, 'do your worst. I still won't be afraid.'

The instant the words left his lips the figure and the waters vanished.

Cold air rushed up from the gaping chasm beneath the walkway. He was terrified he would fall into the abyss, that his soul would be annihilated.

He bolted upright only to see the silhouetted figure at the foot of his bed. Naked and afraid of the dreadful vision he knew that he must break the its power.

With a decisive swipe his arm cut through its torso and the figure disappeared.

He lay back, sweating, staring at the ceiling. His belief in the Devil slowly leaving as his terror subsided.

-

The weather had cleared by morning and David walked in the grounds of the Maitreya Institute. Its gardens edged out onto the sands of the bay. They were a blend of wild plants and carefully cultivated flowers. Their growth and decay in a natural rhythm, like the sea lapping up to the foliage, slowly eroding its soil.

He stared across the bay at mountains that moved from between sun and shade. The sky was sharp blue and the clouds bright white. Beams of light cut down, as if the buttresses of a colossal Cathedral of the heavens, and the wind blew the sea into quickening shapes whilst birds sang in the fresh, cleansed air.

On the beach he reflected, wondered how Buddhism could help keep his mind from thoughts full of lust. He wanted to replace his carnal longings with pure and perfect truth, with an inner transformation.

Passing back, through the stone entrance to the mansion, he was greeted by Jane, a slim, intelligent lady with henna coloured hair, in a loose mohair jumper, in her mid 40's. She was a lay member of the Buddhist community, whose role was to instruct visitors in the basics of its teachings. A group of students had congregated around her and she led them into a heavy oak panelled room. Rich, ladies, with perfect hair, dressed in cashmere jumpers, mingled with middle aged men in perfectly ironed shirts and blazers.

She moved to a leaded window and began to explain. 'Buddha lived in 500 B.C.E. and renounced his life as a prince in order to search for the truth. For many years he tried different philosophies and teachings in his quest for Enlightenment, Nirvana. He only found this when he gave up all the other systems and created his own, whilst sitting under a Bo tree. It was then that he ceased to be a slave to his desires and freed himself from the need to be reincarnated. He realised that all of reality has no permanent essence. That even the idea of "self" is an illusion, that the only thing that lasts forever is Nirvana, and we experience its "Oneness" when we realise that all just is what it is, without any deeper essence.'

David struggled to follow, wondering if it could have any practical effects for his life.

'The monks here are from the New Kadampa Tradition,' said Jane. 'It is one of the Mahayana (Greater Vehicle), schools of Tibetan Buddhism and is dedicated to the Bodhisattvas. These are Buddhas who gain Enlightenment but choose not to extinguish themselves in complete Nirvana. Instead, they become almost like gods and stay to help other beings attain Enlightenment.' She swept her hair behind her ear and smiled. 'But, personally, I see Buddhism and meditation as a kind of therapy. You could say that Buddha was the world's first psychoanalyst.'

It seemed a sweeping statement, David wanted clarification. 'So how does Buddhism relate to Freud and Jung?'

She raised an eyebrow. 'Jung believed in a shared mystical truth behind all religions, and Buddha gives us the way to experience that truth. Buddha freed his mind from attachment to desire and dwelled in the perfect moment, in pure consciousness in unity with "God." Freud, by contrast, did not believe in this united consciousness. He held that humans were driven by a creative sex drive, Eros, and a death drive, Thanatos. He thought that Nirvana just came from the death drive. But he didn't understand that Nirvana is beyond opposites like life and death, opposites imposed by our limited, rational minds.'

'So what did Freud think religion was about?'

'He thought that religion began with hunting tribes that were dominated by a single male. The male children would fight their father for supremacy and the tribe would eat him if he was killed. But as humans moved into agriculture they formed societies where fathers were revered as spirits and were worshipped with statues. These ancestors became animal Gods, who were sacrificed and eaten in fertility rites to promote a good harvest but also as a way to control the unconscious instinct to kill the father.'

David looked at Jane, comparing her to the gleaming, golden chested statue through the doorway behind her. He felt ashamed to think it, but this Bodhisattva seemed more beautiful and held more promise than the touch of a woman.

She paused a moment, noticing where his attention had shifted. 'Freud saw the worship of religious Totems as worship of the phallus of male power. But here we just use statues to help us focus on Buddha's teachings.' She led the group out of the room.

Almost too big to occupy the hallway of the mansion, competing with a sweeping staircase, sat the golden statue. 'Maitreya is the Buddha of Compassion and Wisdom. He will return as a saviour of the world in the coming Age. He will teach the unity of the Universe.' Serenity filled the statue's face. The plump roundness of his skin echoed in his limbs and body, its smoothness expressed harmonious oneness. His right hand was held, palm facing forwards, in a blessing of peace and wisdom. His left hand rested on his lap.

David admired the statue, but something dark also repelled him. On its chest was a swastika. If all reality was one, did this mean that good and evil were one?

'Now, we'll go to the meditation hall. Remember, meditation is a system to control your cravings. You can do this by simply watching your desires arise and pass, without attachment to them. Simply observe your desires, then let them pass away, without feeling that they belong to you.'

The group took off their shoes as they followed Jane into the warm, airy hall. It was carpeted in red and brightly coloured paintings of Buddhas adorned the walls. They sat on rows of cushions and David fidgeted as he found a comfortable position for his crossed legs.

He could now get a good look at everyone, but he didn't want to. He no longer cared about what people looked like. The middle aged seekers had started to still their minds and quieten their thoughts. A small bell rang. He closed his eyes and began to drift off.

In a clear vision of a star filled universe, an infinite, eternal expanse, where all of reality was one. Everything was equal and nothing was more important or more significanct than anything else. All just was what it was, of the same, fundamental, ordinary nature. All was beyond meaning and meaninglessness, beyond good and evil.

As he became self-aware of his Enlightenment the experience faded away. The more he concentrated on it the further away it went.

He couldn't will it back, but he didn't want to. 'Is that all it is,' he thought. All the claims that Nirvana was of great significance when it was neither meaningful nor meaningless. It was just ordinary, just a retreat from the struggle to be good, just an escape. And how could Buddhism be good when the Bodhisattvas weren't concerned with helping people fill their bellies or get a roof over there heads, they were just concerned with helping them attain this "Enlightenment."

David didn't want to dissolve his problems into a transcendental nothingness, into a reversion to the womb. It was his duty to be good, and to struggle against evil in a moral Crusade. He wanted to be a visionary in the world, not a mystic beyond it. It now seemed as though the people sitting around him did not want to be fully alive. They were destroying their wills, losing their egos in an ocean of mystical forgetfulness. They wanted to sink back into some primal, mythical waters of time.

The Enlightened consciousness that they sought was beyond good and evil, beyond even God Himself. This was Hubris, a pride, like that of Prometheus, who stole fire from the Olympian Gods, to give it to mankind. For which he was eternally punished by Zeus.

5. Sugar Gallery

Back in London David glanced at women as he travelled in a tube train on the Northern line. They were the idols of his desire. He was possessed until the fire subsided and he came to his senses again.

Would he bother searching for the meaning of life if he could make love with these beautiful women. Was his religious quest just compensation for not finding love. It was easy to choose charity and poverty when he had no power or riches to renounce.

He searched his soul. He wanted to believe that his calling was too deep to let sex or money control him, to believe that the question was not whether he would be religious. But in what way.

The night before, after spending many hours discussing theology and art in Sebastian's lounge. Sebastian was finding it hard to reconcile his Christian faith with his style of painting. Since becoming a Christian his sales had gone down. Now his main income came from interior design. He'd begun to smoke again, cigarette after cigarette, and after drinking a bottle of red wine, a strange change had come over him. He had spoken abruptly, directly. 'I'm hungry.' There was a long pause. 'Hungry for sex.'

David was not stunned by the proposition. It was almost a relief to hear Sebastian say what he'd been communicating with his eyes. David's loins stirred, but he violently shook off the feelings. He hated them and blamed Sebastian for imposing them on him. But he was desperately lonely. He needed Sebastian's company.

'You'll have to stay hungry then,' was all he could reply. 'It's late, I have to go. I'll see you at the Sugar Gallery tomorrow.'

Despite the yawning hole in his life his sight was clearly fixed on striving to be good. What that goodness was he didn't know, but he knew, clearly, that it was not the calm, soft comforts of Sebastian's embrace. He rejected the feelings again, with greater passion.

-

Drawn, yet repelled, he met Sebastian at the steps of the Sugar Gallery at Millbank, across the road from the Thames. Sebastian walked in front, with the expectation that David would follow. 'I want to help you. You won't get anywhere in this town unless you understand modern art, but I don't have too long. I forgot that I arranged to meet a dealer this afternoon.' They passed between the limestone entrance columns of the neo-classical building. 'Your sculptures are too traditional,' said Sebastian. 'You need to take on modern influences.'

David raised an eyebrow at the comment. At the moment his friendship was too delicate to begin an argument. But he couldn't help himself. 'Modern art is meaningless, it has no moral purpose.'

'It's not meant to have a moral purpose,' said Sebastian, shaking his head. 'It's art for art's sake.'

The sculptures in the tall, white rooms and the paintings on the long walls and corridors were arranged in historical sequence. And as David walked between the works Sebastian pointed to a painting that reached up and across the wall. 'Look, Pablo Picasso's 1907 "Les Demoiselles d'Avignon". These three naked ladies have angular faces copied from African tribal masks. Picasso used them because of their essence, their wild energy. His new system of Cubist painting analysed and abstracted objects into different elements, different viewpoints, then put them all back together in one work. It encapsulated the dynamism of the age into a new way of looking at beauty and painting.'

David's eye was drawn elsewhere, to an attractive blonde with bright red lips. She was looking at the last work in the room. Dressed in an open white shirt and cream woolen skirt her beauty was far more convincing than any of the works. He wasn't sure if she was deliberately ignoring him, teasing him. Then he frowned as he noticed her gaze land on Sebastian, despite his conspicuous gold wedding ring.

Sebastian continued. 'The work has no moral purpose. But it's great art, regardless of whether you think it is moral or immoral.'

David nodded in understanding as he followed Sebastian out of the room, past the beautiful lady. He looked again, trying to get her attention. Fantasising that if he could become a famous artist then he might have women like this come after him.

Now, in the main exhibition space, they stood in front of a 1.5 metre wide, 1 metre high painting. Sebastian tapped his shoulder. 'This is "Number 3, 1949: Tiger" by the American Abstract expressionist, Jackson Pollock.' The complex interweaving and interlacing layers of primary coloured paint formed a battleground. Yet the colours balanced each other, held together with black lines that fixed the work like rigid markers. It was a piece of music to be listened to, rather than a story to be understood. 'His work developed out of the Surrealist technique of automatic drawing where the artist closed down his conscious mind so that he could express himself directly from his unconscious mind. Pollock painted as if possessed, making short, rhythmic strokes. It was a new way of working. There was no copying any objects that existed in nature. Instead he said, "I *am* nature" because his gestures of pure energy connected to the very forces of nature locked in his unconscious mind. He linked this way of working with a belief in Jungian psychology, ritual magic and tribal dance. I tend to steer clear of this kind of work. It's not very Christian, leaves you open to spiritual forces that we don't understand.'

David raised his eyebrows and nodded.

'But the real mystic was Mark Rothko.' They moved onto a large, rectangular painting dabbed and daubed in two main blocks of colour, orange and red. They blocks were like clouds, floating as a heavenly doorway. 'Rothko sought an unfettered expression of his Jewish mysticism. But it was tinged with the despair of the Second World War, the gas chambers, the atomic bomb. These had destroyed faith in science and technology. Mankind had sunk into a new barbarism and it was out of this despair that Rothko tried to transport himself into a sublime, a pure experience of truth.' Sebastian spoke with the drawl, of one who accepted the theory of why an artwork was great but did not experience it first hand.

There room was full of Rothko's dark and profound paintings. David was willing to merge with these sublime landscapes, but as he continued to stare the experience brought disappointment. He moved between the different colour combinations, but all seemed the same, like Rothko had just been cashing in on a style that worked.

David grew tired as they assembled in front of another Rothko. He began to fidget. He pretended to cast a critical eye as he positioned himself where he could watch the lady. But when she wasn't admiring the art she was looking at Sebastian. Sebastian put an arm around David's shoulder and the lady now cast a scathing look at him. Sebastian smiled at him.

'Rothko's art was an expression of despair. His doorways were clouded, and he never passed through them, to complete his vision of mystical union. He suffered a long period of depression that ended in suicide.' Sebastian breathed in deeply and fully straightened his posture.

He led David forward, past a painting of rows of red and white Campbell's Soup cans, and pointed to the next painting, a giant head of Marilyn Monroe. Her hair was lurid yellow, her face bright pink, and her lips and teeth were smeared with red. 'Rothko's search for deep meaning was replaced with a search for money in the 1960's by Andy Warhol. Warhol painted Campbell's soup cans to show how consumerism had become the most important force in American society. His "Marilyn" works are amongst his most famous images. They show how celebrities, women, death, art, everything, had been reduced to objects, to be bought and sold.'

David moved over to a giant print of the head of Chairman Mao of the Chinese Communist party.

'Here, in his portrait of 'Mao' 1974, Warhol showed how even communist imagery could be turned into a capitalist commodity, into a pop icons. "Mao" proved the point. Avant-garde artists once created shocking art to waken the bourgeoisie out of political complacency, but now Warhol used shock to thrill the bourgeoisie and make money. His paintings turned everything, even electric chairs, car crashes and skulls, into a commodity. The artist was now just a businessman with a factory where people made his artwork for him. This wasn't like the renaissance workshop of Michelangelo, it was a production line, churning out art.' Sebastian drew breath and looked at David, trying to read him. 'But do you think Warhol was religious?'

'No, from what you say I don't see how he could be.'

'Well his religious works from the 1980s is the largest body of religious works by any major contemporary American artist. Warhol was openly gay life but was secret about his Christian faith. It would have been bad for business. Even now galleries don't show works like his 1986 pictures of Christ's Last Supper. They like his pictures of electric chairs and car crashes, not his pictures of Christ mixed with adverts for Potato Chips, Dove Soap, and General Electric. Maybe his Christianity was just another form of consumerism but I like his work, it shows he was trying to make sense of his relationship with Christ.'

David now noticed that the lady played with the small silver crucifix around her neck as she eavesdropped.

'For a long time Rothko's abstract canvases were seen as more serious than Warhol's art. Maybe it was because New York art collectors came from a tradition of Protestant and Jewish simplicity, a tradition that rejected kitsch imagery. But eventually the collectors changed their focus. Why, because money now drove society more than religion and Warhol's art made icons of money and consumer goods.'

As they left the lady faced Sebastian square on. He walked past her, ignoring her. She turned to David but he looked away. He didn't like being second best. They marched out through the galleries to the sound of Sebastian's shoes echoing around Rothko's, Pollock's, and Picasso's art.

David sighed. He'd had enough. He hoped Sebastian might give him a new direction for his work. But he wasn't sure what he "should" think as these weren't works that he admired. 'Thanks for showing me around,' said David. 'I'm not sure how it makes me feel. I need to go for a wander, to look around a bit.' He needed to regenerate, to return to the art he preferred, to see some of the classics.

'That's fine. Like I say, I've arranged to meet a dealer this afternoon. So it was actually a bit awkward to meet this morning.' Sebastian reached out his arms. 'So, see you soon.' David smelt the aftershave and felt stubble on his face as they hugged, before Sebastian headed for the entrance.

-

In the galleries of eighteenth and nineteenth century oil paintings, the dark landscapes and rural scenes, mounted in large gold frames, felt rich and comforting. Marble busts of Victorian gentlemen and Victorian sculptures of Roman heroes seemed to condone his appreciation of the work. To emulate it was not enough. They said something true about the era in which they were created but now they were a testament   to history. He needed to be original, he needed to express his own truths.

As he walked between them he cast a desperate glance at the young ladies who passed the works. The glances were not returned.

He was about to leave but became curious of the glass doors to a dimly lit room. The light levels were low, to protect the works, and knowing this drew him inside.

On the wall facing him was a small pen and ink watercolour. Its distorted neo-classical figures contrasted and blended, almost child-like in style. They were aggressive monstrosities that stared out at him. Bathed in fire, a red dragon-figure with seven horned heads raged angrily above a Beast that rose from the sea. Between them was a creature with a sheep-like skull. Their colours and swirls were dynamic, powerful, and malevolent.

David read the caption. "'The Number of the Beast Is 666." by William Blake 1757-1827. Revelation 13 verses 11-12 & 18. "The Red Dragon and the Beast from the sea are joined by a Beast who comes up out of the earth. The Beast will have two horns like a lamb and will speak as a dragon. He will cause the earth and all who dwell therein to worship the first Beast and will make fire come down from heaven." "Here is wisdom. Let him that hath understanding count the number of the Beast, for it is the number of a man, and his number is Six hundred three-score and six.'"

The energy and vitality coupled with the uncompromising vision from the New Testament spoke directly to David. It seemed to be as relevant now, as then. It was timeless. He began to read more about Blake.

'Blake was a visionary artist who worked in a neo-classical style in prints and watercolours. He made his own mythology with two main characters Urizen and Los. Urizen (reason) who was like the Old Testament God, Jehovah, whose Laws and idea of 'sin' were oppressive traps to prevent people enjoying earthly pleasures. Blake believed that Los (imagination) could save mankind.'

David looked for another painting to help him understand. Nearby was a small watercolour, "The Ancient of Days" 1824. Here the hand of the bearded Urizen was making a compass that emanated golden lines. Like Jehovah he was setting out the creation of the Universe. The text explained. 'This design resembled the cover of Isaac Newton's scientific treatise, "Principia Mathematica". Blake believed that science, like Urizen, trapped men's souls in a prison of rationalism and materialism which only Los, imagination, could overthrow.' David continued reading. 'Los would bring man back into unity with the Divine through his son Orc, a serpent of revolutionary energy. Orc would help Los unite with his female aspects and eventually even unite with Urizen.'

David stared at the works. He liked Blake's images, at face value, as illustrations of the New Testament, but the text didn't make much sense. He was laying a message of spiritual unity, of Eastern mysticism over Western religious imagery.

But worse than this, Blake's vision marked the start of era when Western society began to trust artists, not priests and ministers, as the people with access to spiritual revelation. Artists now had the prophet's right to decree on issues of faith, and eventually they would proclaim that God was dead.

David's legs were tired. He crouched. Chin in one hand, elbow resting in another as he closed his eyes and began to see a balancing pattern developing between figurative art about the Gods and abstract art about Enlightenment.

He remembered the Greek statues in the British Museum. These sculptures directly depicted the Greek Gods, and the Modern art of Rothko and Pollock directly expressed the abstractions of mysticism. But this was a Western way of looking at art. Other religions had a different approach. The mystical Enlightenment, in Buddhism, could only be experienced by the few, so artwork with human figures was needed to help the rest of the followers understand its abstraction. In contrast the Monotheistic faiths, like Judaism and Islam, had a God who was a father figure, so its believers banned idolatry and rivals allowing only abstract design.

David opened his eyes. He was getting swept away by the idea.

A long time had passed. David steadied himself as he rose. With aching legs he hobbled until he could straighten them. He went through the combinations again and again, trying to make it work. Then it clicked as he made his way out of the Sugar Gallery.

Both the Greeks and the Modernists believed, above all, in progress through the use of reason. The Greeks sought to become like Gods, to steal their fire, through reason. But the Modernists used reason to kill faith in God and sought Enlightenment to fill the void, expressing their search in art like Rothko's.

David's step was light. He was soaring up, reaching higher and higher. He didn't like what he understood, but everything was beginning to make sense. The priests were no longer in control of faith and revelation, but nor were the artists. When the Modernist project failed, Warhol began the worship of new, human Gods and icons of consumerism, like Marilyn Monroe. And those now in control were the buyers of art, the men of money and power, the men who now acted like they were the new Gods.

6. Quaker Sign

That evening David still needed to clear his head. So he walked from Islington to Euston station, then down past Oxford Circus, down towards Trafalgar Square.

Passing a slow moving traffic queue on the busy Saint Martin's Lane he noticed, in a terrace of cafes and theatres, a sign to the left of double doors. It read "Quaker Art Gallery".

He peered through the windows of doors that opened into a small, empty, corridor. To the right of the entrance another sign read "Quaker Meeting House." His head turned as the idling cars edged past. How could a gallery also be a place of worship.

Beneath the sign was a paragraph entitled. "What We Believe?" He read.

"Quakers originated in the early seventeenth century. They were so named because they "Quaked" before no man, just God. They were pacifists who believed in simplicity of living and worship. They rejected the "Steeple Houses" and the rituals of religious hierarchy. Instead they believed that an individual's conduct was more important than what they believed and favoured charitable works to help their fellow man. Just like their forebears, Quakers today still hold their Meetings for Worship in silence and seek to be open to revelations from the Holy Spirit. Whilst Quakers used to be exclusively Christian they now accept anyone who follows their inner light and conscience, whatever that may be. Even Atheists are welcome to join Quaker worship."

-

On Sunday the dark wooden doors were opened and David entered a long narrow corridor. Nothing was hung on the picture rails and he passed through the space. It opened into a bright and airy room with high sky lights. Old floral cushions were crumpled into wicker armchairs and a patterned carpet covered the polished wood floor. They gave a feeling of calm and cleanliness, reinforced by the well dusted collection of books on shelves. It was like being at a grandparent's house.

'Hello Friend,' said a lithe, short-haired, bespectacled, fifty year old. He wore cycling shorts and was ushering people through heavy swing doors, into the main Meeting room. 'I'm Patrick.'

David exchanged the greeting and followed without hesitation and entered into an altogether different atmosphere.

The room was dim with dark, oak panelled walls and only a single skylight. High backed chairs, upholstered in leather, were arranged next to low chairs, upholstered in blue nylon, and benches, on which rested long cushions.

The congregation ranged in size   from small and plump to tall and thin. But in a quick inventory David saw no eligible ladies amongst the grey, shoulder length hair, floppy hats, brown sandals and long floral skirts.

David's friends had asked him to be open to Christ in prayer. Here was his chance. He could be open to the Spirit, whatever that might be, whether just his conscience or the Holy Spirit. He could speak to it and seek its truth. So, burying his head into his hands, he sat in silence, open. He didn't speak to God or Jesus. He just became receptive to inspiration, free from religious dogma.

He waited.

No voice spoke inside his head, but a presence filled his mind. There was something there, like the experience he had of God in the Lake District, only this time he didn't fight it, he didn't rejected it. He let his natural feelings occur and he began to believe in the existence of God.

-

He became a regular "attender" at the Meetings. The congregation changed from week to week. But there was a core of retired teachers, civil servants, charity workers, university lecturers and students. All professionals, all committed believers in ethical activism. They were not reclusive mystics, they campaigned for fair trade, abolition of world debt, world disarmament, and animal rights.

Speakers would occasionally stand, inspired by the Spirit to make a political, personal or spiritual statement. Then the silence returned. It was strange that the Spirit created such diverse, sometimes contradictory, opinions. But agreement wasn't necessary because they all accepted one Spirit. A Spirit that was without a definition, that was as varied as the assortment of chairs that filled the room.

He didn't like the high chairs, they seemed too magisterial, preferring the low chairs instead. He avoided the benches because he sometimes rocked as he prayed. He was aware that this might disturb the people next to him. He rocked because this was no quiet meditation, it was a battle to find the truth whilst fighting the lustful thoughts in his mind.

In the weeks and months of prayer he clasped his hands, seeking guidance from God. The direction slowly pieced together as he sat, with a pounding in his heart, in his favourite chair.

After the hour-long meetings everyone would go back into the reception room. There they would get a hot drink and a plain biscuit from the serving hatch. David would drop a contribution into a glass bowl, glancing around the room. His cup rattled on its saucer as he passed pleasantries with everyone, but he could speak in depth with no one. Then he would stand in the corner, hoping that he might meet a partner. There were rarely any girls here, but even when there were he was too shy to talk to them. Instead he idly browsed the book titles.

This Sunday he picked a heavy tome from the shelf. It was a new book on the history of Christianity. Checking with the highly amenable Patrick that he could take the book he headed home, on the Northern Line from Leicester Square tube station.

-

On the train he flicked through the heavy book, looking for topics of interest. It fell on a page about the Holy Trinity. He scanned the long paragraphs of complex argument and came to the bottom. It seemed that many Trinitarian influences came from Egypt.

The Egyptians had made Christ resemble their own ancient deities. Christ, the God King, born after God miraculously impregnated the Virgin Mary, was like Horus, the God King, born after the God Osiris miraculously impregnated the Goddess Isis. When Horus died he became Osiris, just as Christ became one with God. Isis was also venerated, just like the Virgin Mary, and this only ended when Emperor Constantine made Christianity the state religion of the Holy Roman Empire in 312 C.E.

Christianity had swept across Europe and Asia so Constantine had to accept Christianity to keep his Empire from falling apart. But he transformed it into a warrior religion, just like the Roman religion of the sun Gods Sol Invictus and Mithras. Instead of spreading Christ's message of "love your enemy" Constantine's Holy warriors would kill their enemies then pray for them afterwards.

To keep the Empire unified the worship of Mithras was banned and, at the Council of Nicea, 325 C.E., a single Christian doctrine was produced. The Council's Nicene Creed made the Holy Trinity, the unity of God the Father, the Son and the Holy Spirit, an essential part of Christian doctrine. And these Trinitarians, the bishops of the Holy Roman Empire, excommunicated, beat, intimidated, kidnapped, imprisoned and killed Unitarian and mystics for being heretics. They persecuted the Unitarians for believing that Jesus Christ was just a man and the mystics for believing that Jesus Christ was completely divine.

David was interested. He flicked to the end of the book to find a further reference to Unitarians. As he read their beliefs struck a chord. They believed in strict Monotheism, in the divine "unity" of God, just like the Jews and the Muslims. As a Jew Jesus he would have been brought up to believe in One God and many of the early Christian Jews would have been Unitarians, seeing Christ as a man, a prophet, not a divinity.

He closed the book and sat back, then closed his eyes, soothing them under the electric light. When he opened them he noticed the young lady opposite him had smooth waxed legs that looked cool to the touch. He felt shame but he couldn't help his imagination.

He wanted to feel close to God but couldn't because of his lust. Sex was an escape, but no, he had to battle against it, overcome it, and transform his desires.

'Oh God, please forgive me.' He prayed into his hands as he had done so many times at the Quaker meetings.

The words of his friends Paul and Sebastian came to his mind. 'Accept that Christ died to take on your sins. Then you will be forgiven.' But with forgiveness there was a risk that he was becoming corrupted, more accepting of his own licentiousness, excusing the flood of desire coming over him.

-

Back in his studio David took a piece of London Plain wood and prayed to God for inspiration, seeking to capture the essence of forgiveness in a sculpture of Christianity.

He sawed the section of log, cutting it to shape, then started to carve.

Chunks and flakes of wood surrounded where he sat as the sun began to sink, its light gently fading in the studio as he gouged.

Three figures battled their way out of the wood. A gnarled, roughly cut figure of "Evil" snarled, with sharp teeth, as it tried to pull down a rigid, angular figure of figure of "Good". "Good" punched back at "Evil" and reached up towards a smooth and perfect figure of "Forgiveness." "Forgiveness" had arms outstretched, like Christ, ready to embrace "Evil" and had its back towards "Good". The figures were connected, in fact, "Forgiveness" rose from the loins of "Evil," sublimating it into a higher, selfless love.

This captured David's own inner struggle. He was three people struggling in one, so why was the idea of the Holy Trinity still a logical contradiction, to him. Was it because he felt that God was perfect. That if Christ took on sin then God would become impure, but wasn't God free to choose evil, and wasn't the morality of the Old Testament questionable anyway.

In II Kings a group of children called Elisha "bald head" so he cursed them in the name of the Lord and two bears killed them. In Numbers 31 Moses was guilty of ordering infanticide and rape "kill every male among the little ones, and kill every woman that hath known a man by lying with him, but all the women – children, that have not known a man by lying with him, keep alive for yourselves." In Deuteronomy 22 the faithful are told to stone people to death for working on the Sabbath, for not obeying their father and mother and even just for stubbornness.

He was full of contradictions, of different beliefs, splitting him in two. He had to get out of the studio and walked into the night, through the deserted City of London. He needed to reconcile all these splits.

Car headlights sped past. He headed down the Strand, through Trafalgar Square, towards the London Bridge. He couldn't work out the link.

He walked along the South Bank of the Thames, past the Sugar Modern, then across Tower Bridge. He turned then headed up past Liverpool Street Station, past the run down dirtiness of Bethnal Green.

With all the fighting doctrines of religious belief, surely the person's essence, their spirit, their life, their free-will was what people all shared. The Quaker Spirit, "that of God within all of us", was the closest to that unity. It was no answer and God was stripped of detail but it was the start of a bridge to unite his divded psyche. Maybe even to unite the world.

With weary legs he arrived back in Islington.

-

David kept working on his sculptures whilst doing conservation work around the museums and churches of London. Months later he was still a regular attender at the Westminster Friends' Meeting House.

Only ten people entered and as each moved to their favourite, familiar seat the weather above the skylight begun to turn. David delved deep into prayer.

He was troubled by his conservation work. He was tired of working for a low wage on churches belonging to an Anglican faith that he did not believe in, tired of conserving civic monuments to the great and the good, working like a latter day serf for the landed gentry.

Was this where his life, his calling had really led him. He had wanted to work on religious buildings where people praised a God that he could believe in. He dreamt of working in a place where the buildings and objects were still venerated by society, still treated as holy. But he wanted an authentic faith, a real and relevant belief. This was the art and architecture of God that he was looking for.

Earlier that week he had been offered what seemed to be a good job, restoring Buddhas imported from Afghanistan. Maybe Buddhism was a developing religion in the West that might change society for the good. But these Buddhas were to be given "invisible repairs" then sold as if without blemish. He could earn half again as much money as he currently earned but this was faking, cheating. What was worse was that many of the sculptures had been illegally exported and the money raised from them went to purchase weapons for Afghan warlords.

No. David wanted to work on art that was a force to resolve conflict, not aid it. But how could art do that.

Then, in a feeling of utter doubt about his whole life, he lifted upwards a question to God. 'Why do we even need religious buildings?'

Lightning flashed and thunder cracked simultaneously above the Meeting House.

Rain began to pour on the glass skylight.

This was a sign. He had been wrong to think that places of worship were not important.

Coming out of the Meeting, into the library, a book titled "Jerusalem," by the modern architect Moshe Safdie, lay on a table.

This really was a sign.

Taking the book he exited into the rainy street. He would go on pilgrimage to the Holy Land. A place where doctrine created a real battle over buildings, territory and resources. Not like in London where followers of religions blurred and watered down their differences in interfaith events run by privileged Westerners.

7. Arrival in Jerusalem

David arrived in the new city of west Jerusalem by white taxi van. He queued at the bus station with khaki wearing, rifle carrying, Israeli soldiers. The bus took him past some of Moshe Safdie's domed buildings. He recognised it as modern housing that the Canadian Jewish architect had designed to echo the traditional architecture. As they headed towards the old city the land of the Bible, pivotal in Western History, was coming to life. The separation of fact and myth was blurring. David was excited as the bus stopped at the north west corner of the old city walls. The golden limestone cried out a sacred history.

Above the parapets the silhouettes of the domed mosques, with tall marble minarets, competed for the skyline against church towers and satellite dishes. But the whole city was dominated with the Israeli flag, a blue Star of David upon a white background, draped over the many gates of the old walls.

There was an underlying tension, a trace of terror and death in the stones of this golden city of Jerusalem, created by King David in 1000 B.C.E. after invading a Canaanite city that dated from 3000 B.C.E. It was then conquered by Assyrians, Romans, Muslims and Crusaders and each time the blood of innocents was spilled. Now, the stones were said to turn red at sunset, with the blood of all who had been slaughtered.

The sun beat down as David put on his hat and lifted on his rucksack. He squinted as the white paving reflected the light. He shifted his backpack to make it comfortable and began walking east, past the un-repaired bullet holes in the walls, down the hill, along the northern edge of the old city.

The 20th century had its share of Jerusalem's violent disputes. At the time of the First World War, 1914 – 18, Arab Palestine was governed by the Turkish Ottoman Empire and Jews made up only 1% of the population. The British promised the Arabs full post-war sovereignty for fighting the Turks who had sided with the Germans. However the Americans were also promised a Jewish homeland if they entered the war. So in 1917 the British Foreign Secretary, Lord Arthur Balfour, and Lord Lionel Walter Rockschild, a leading British financier, signed The Balfour Declaration, establishing a national home for the Jewish people in Palestine. After the war this was administered by the British as a League of Nations mandate. Rockschild also had claims on Palestine because Turkey owed him millions of pounds in unpaid loans.

As David descended he could no longer see over the walls. Cars rushed down the busy roads and he was soon at the impressive, crowded, Damascus Gate. He stopped at a taxi rank and looked across the amphitheatre of steps down to the defensive fortification. It was rebuilt, with all the walls, in the 16th century by Suleiman the Magnificent, and faced north to Damascus in Syria.

Across from him, at his eye level, an Israeli soldier leant, in the hot sun, against a parapet. He rested a gun, nonchalantly, on his knee and watched, through sunglasses, the Palestinians below.

Old ladies in headscarves and traditional dress jostled with young men in check shirts and jeans at the tall entrance. Widows in black sat, hands outstretched, selling a pile of herbs rather than just begging. It was Friday, the day of prayer, and the streets were busy with visitors heading to the Haram esh Shariff, the noble sanctuary, the third holiest site in Islam, location of the golden dome that he had read so much about.

Stall-keepers were keen to catch the morning trade, before the afternoon prayers. Like the cathedrals cities of Europe once had been, this holy city was alive, with the rhythms of a religious society.

He made his way past Damascus Gate and he was reminded by t-shirts and souvenirs that this place was not called Jerusalem by Muslims. It was called "Quds" and to Jews it was "Yerusalem." Ladies at the busy market stalls, around East Jerusalem bus station, were selling fresh vegetables and men stood at small stands covered in watches, magazines and music tapes, all featuring heavily coiffured, Middle Eastern, pop stars. Their high pitched sounds blared, momentarily, above the engines, horns and shouts.

He was in Palestinian East Jerusalem, crossing Saladin Street, named after the Muslim hero who defeated the Crusaders, heading, past the post office, towards the Rockschild Museum. This would be the base for his work with the Israel Antiquities Authority.

The imposing, fortress like tower of the Rockschild Museum came into view. It stood across from the North East corner of the Old City walls. It was designed in 1927 for J.D. Rockschild, who had an enormous oil and banking empire.

David showed his passport at the checkpoint, then was directed to the side of the building. He passed through a parched garden, where silver green leaves from groves of grey olive trees gave dappled shade and water from spinning sprinklers patted against his leg, before quickly evaporating.

Near the conservation centre Corinthian capitals and columns lay discarded and the sprinklers wet the hot path that led to its newly built workshops.

There the conservators repaired ancient mosaics and pieces of excavated masonry. The set up was familiar, as was the sharp aroma of resins for repairs and chemicals for cleaning. The main wall was stacked with dusty mosaics from archaeological sites.

Delighted to be there he removed his hat and took a moment to thank God for allowing him to come to such an interesting place.

Then, unsure of the protocol, he carefully attracted the attention of a bespectacled lady, wearing a headscarf, an Orthodox Jewess.

Almost gliding over she asked 'Ken?'

David knew that underneath her scarf was a shaven head. He lifted his rucksack down off his wet back. 'Jacov Sussman?'

'Ah'. The lady spoke some words in Hebrew then pointed past the main wall, to a doorway out of the workshops.

David started to leave when he saw, on wooden batons, propped against the wall, a damaged mosaic bordered with a swastika motif. The relic was half-hidden by a chest high mosaic of a Sun God in a chariot drawn by four horses.

'What is?' enquired David.

She smiled. 'Ah you only speak English. Why didn't you say?' She wiped the dust from the surface. 'It is the from the 5th century synagogue at Sepphoris, Lower Galilee, part of a Zodiac floor.'

She had the wrong mosaic but had still fired his interest. 'I thought that there were strict rules against figures in Jewish art.'

'Yes, but there have been many not so strict periods. In Solomon's Temple there were lions, bulls and cherubim. Then, after the destruction of the Second Temple in the Talmudic period, some synagogues were even ornamented with human figures. Nowadays the Hasidic Jews, the ultra-orthodox, are the strictest against figures, but they still have photographs of their leaders, like Rabbi Solomon Cohen, all around Mea She'arim.'

'But this isn't just a figure of a man. It's a God.'

'Like I said, there have been many not so strict periods.'

Clearly the Jews had absorbed more Roman ideas than she liked to discuss. David didn't press the point. He just headed to the connecting building.

There, in the cool, air conditioned office, architectural drawings lined the walls. The Director's secretary, Seema, offered him water from a large, inverted blue bottle. It glugged as he filled his plastic cup. He waited until Sussman was ready to see him.

-

The balding man sat in an open shirt behind a desk full of paper. He looked more like a lawyer or a businessman than an archaeologist. Behind him was a fresco of a lion, pouncing, biting the neck of a gazelle.

He greeted David with a handshake. 'Shalom.'

'You have a big team,' complimented David

'Yes, we have many Russian Jews who made Aliya, emigrated here, but it will be good to see how you British are working.'

There was a knock and the bespectacled lady that David had just spoken with put her head around the door. Words were exchanged in Hebrew then Jacov introduced her.

'This is Aliezer Scheffer, she is in charge of stone conservation. You will be working for her on a United Nations funded project, for the documentation of fountains in the Old City.'

Mutual recognitions were made but they did not shake hands. She smiled. 'I guessed that you were our new recruit.'

'We were just talking about where our conservators are from,' said Jacov.

'Yes, this is such an interesting of places to work. We have people from all over the world here.'

'So, where will you be staying while you are here?' asked Jacov.

'At the British School of Archaeology on Mount Scopus.' Scheffer raised an eyebrow at David's reply.

Aliezer's neck stretched forward. 'You're staying in East Jerusalem. You must be careful if you go through Damascus Gate. I know people who were stabbed.'

David nodded, bemused at the protectiveness.

'Aliezer will take you to her workshop and help you in any way.' Jacov shook his hand again. 'It is good to have you with us.' David left with Aliezer.

Outside the office David stopped as they passed the mosaics. 'Sorry, I meant to ask before, what is this?'

Aliezer stood, obscuring the swastika from view. 'It's the pagan Sun God, Sol Invictus, Apollo.'

'No, I mean behind it.'

'Oh that.' Her face was expressionless. 'It's from the 5th century synagogue at Maoz Haim in the Golan Heights. It's just a Roman design.'

He took a closer look. Set with small golden tiles, swirling on a dark brown background, bordered by red and black. They were unmistakable. It had been a surprise to see swastikas in a Buddhist Temple, but a swastika, a Nazi symbol, in a synagogue? 'But it's a swastika.'

Aliezer snorted. 'You can see a better example, with a single swastika is in the middle of the floor, at the 3rd century synagogue at Ein Gedi, near the Dead Sea.'

David understood that she had closed the matter forever as he followed her into her workshop. There she described his job. He would be making a full inventory and conservation assessment of all the fountains in the Old City.

-

With soldiers on all the main gates and streets a sense of conflict was never far away. Their presence was a threat but also a comfort as David was jostled by youths whilst heading to work, passing through the busy Damascus Gate. He turned sharp left, was elbowed roughly as he pushed forwards , then turned a sharp right before descending into the narrow streets of the old city market.

The cacophony of sounds was confusing. Clothes shops next to butchers, vegetable stands and hardware stores, bakers with fresh round pitta bread in plastic bags, the new sites and smells were exhilarating. Cries came as young boys pushed makeshift barrows, piled high with boxes, through the busy crowds over the slippery flagstone floors.

As he walked, in sandals, over the newly paved white limestone flags, he avoided the fish remains, washed down the central drains from the fish-mongers stalls. Then, heading straight down Suq Khan Ez-Zeit, he escaped the noise and took a quieter street. He headed through the cool, dark suq then realised it was the butchers' passage. Here the smell of meat, past its prime, was overwhelming. It came from sheep's heads and carcasses that hung half in his path. The necks of the upside down beasts slit and drained of blood, bled dry, Halal fashion, to ensure there was no chance of the believer eating any blood.

Holding his breath he turned away from the market and up the dirt streets and alleys around the labyrinthine city. The city was full of pockets of space where the people crammed together.

Boys would walk behind him, playing with wooden sticks, kicking small balls and practicing their English, saying 'How are you? How are you?'

In reply David would practice his Arabic 'Keefalaq?' 'Inta mabsut?' 'Ana Mabsut itha inta mabsuta!' 'I am alright, if you are alright'. The children liked him, he felt welcomed by them.

There was a stink of bad drainage as he passed the assorted bags of rubbish and rubble that lined the dirty passages. It was impossible to tell what where the earth ended and the trash began. The historic fountains that he drew and inspected once brought purity, the water of life, but now the dirt would get between his sandals.

A plump, moustached shopkeeper, stood behind a refrigerator full of meats, and stacked with bags of unleavened pitta bread. To his side were sweets, drinks and newspapers. The road was narrow here and the stones were dark in the shade. He watched David immediately across from him, as he completed the measurements for his first fountain.

It was set into the side of a wall on El-Wad Road, an arch above a trough, with the now dry hole in the centre of the back wall. The trough was blackened by fires and though he had emptied it the day before it was beginning to fill with rubbish again.

Most of the public fountains on his list to work on were like this one, Ottoman drinking fountains set into a wall. Others stood in squares, built for traders and their camels, but many had long since disappeared, under new developments. He got the feeling that this was a job that Aliezer had been glad to pass on. She preferred to work on the excavations around the Western Wall, the Wall was where the Jews prayed for the return of the Messiah and the restoration of their Temple.

Whilst on his break he had bought a copy of "Al Quds", the East Jerusalem paper, from the shopkeeper. It reported how pressure was being put on archaeologists to show the Holy Land as being Jewish. "Archaeological" excavations were only funded if they uncovered the layers of Jewish history and to do that they had to cut through years   of Palestinian history, eradicating any detailed knowledge of the Ottoman, Mamluke, Crusader, Fatimid, Abbasid, Umayyad and Byzantine presence. The selective approach was removing the Arab footprint and promoting the Jewish territorial claims.

David felt confused, because the paper also reported how ultra-Orthodox Jews had been protesting about the sacrilege that archaeologists were committing by digging up buried Jewish skeletons. It was because the Jewish state, that funded the archaeologists, was run by secular and Reform Jews.

Now he realised why Aliezer had requested that he record just those fountains that were over 100 years old. But the modern fountains in the mosques seemed to be as much a part of the history of Jerusalem as the older ones. So he decided that he should include them in the final survey.

As he turned to leave with his tape measure and sketch pad he saw two small boys playing up an alley. They were poking a stick down a snake like reptile's throat. It was clear that they had been torturing it. They held it aloft, by the stick, like a flag, as if seeking praise. 'La, La.' He protested, but they just turned from him and continued their sick game. He wandered over and raised his voice. 'La.'

They looked into his face, shook the snake from the stick, dropped the stick and walked away, resenting his intervention.

He had to put it out of its misery. Its internal organs ruptured. He raised his foot and stamped on its head. Taking his foot away, the creature continued to writhe. Was it a nervous reaction or was it dead. He stamped harder, crushing the skull. Finally it stopped twitching. How hard it was for animals to die.

8. The Jewish Faith

David wandered south, heading for the Western Wall, as young, religious Jews hurried past in open necked, white shirts and fedora hats. Tassels from their prayer shawls, hung down beneath their black jackets. These were Orthodox Yeshiva students.

He followed their flow towards the modern Jewish Quarter. Many of the buildings in this clean, spacious estate had been designed by the architect Moshe Safdie. But standing, in the middle of the uniform domes and arched windows, were the beautifully preserved ruins of a synagogue.

David stared and a plump, ginger haired gentleman said 'Shalom,' then asked, in a New York accent, 'Where are you from?'

'London.'

'Oh, you're British. I'm Rabbi Shmuel Jacobs, and you are?'

'David Wolfe.'

'Are you here on holiday?'

'I'm working with the Israeli Antiquities Authority, documenting historic stonework.'

'Good work and there's so much of it here. You could have a job for life!' Shmuel momentarily admired the ruins then turned. He paused a moment. 'I hope you don't mind me asking, but, are you Jewish?'

'I'm a Quaker by faith, but my mother is Jewish.'

'A Quaker, a Christian? But if your mother is Jewish then that still makes you Jewish. Here, take my card. I'm a Reform Jew. I run an Anti-Missionary Centre, here in Jerusalem. You are welcome to come to our meetings. I can explain to you things that the Quakers won't have told you about Christianity.'

'Well, I'm not a Trinitarian for a start. I'm more a Unitarian, like the Jews.'

Shmuel raised a hand to stem David's words. 'Very good, you have a keen interest in religion and philosophy. Come to our classes, you'll find them very illuminating.'

'I'll do that. I'd like to find out more about Judaism.'

Shmuel took a deep breath and looked around as he patted David's back. 'Listen David, have you ever had a Shabbat meal?' David shook his head. 'Shabbat is a time for family and friends. My son and wife are away in Haifa this evening so you are welcome to come to my home this evening.'

'Todah, thank you. I'd like to come, I'm vegetarian though.' Shmuel nodded that this was fine. They arranged to meet and David left holding up Shmuel Jacobs' business card, emphasising his eagerness. Shmuel turned to speak with a small group and David read the card. It stated that Shmuel was also a corporate lawyer, so his anti- Missionary centre must be a part-time passion for him.

David put the card in his pocket and continued his sightseeing, heading up shaded passages. A sign in a shop saying "Temple Institute" caught his eye. The window display was quite hard to see, but behind a metal grill, was a large, golden candelabra, a Menorah. Beneath this was a scale reconstruction of the Jewish Temple. Next to which was a tailor's dummy wearing the robes of a High Priest, including a golden breastplate, set with 12 jewels to represent the 12 tribes of Israel.

The Institute was closed but he read a history of the Temple in the window. It stated that the first was built around 1000 B.C.E. by King Solomon and destroyed by the Babylonians in 586 B.C.E. The second was allowed to be rebuilt by the Persian king Cyrus the Great around 516 B.C.E. and was renovated by Herod in 19 B.C.E. but this was then destroyed by the Romans in 70 C.E. When the US declared Israel a nation, in 1948, Jerusalem was still under Arab control. In the Six-Day War in 1967, the Israeli flag was temporarily raised beside the Dome of the Rock but control was given back to the Muslims in order to "keep the peace". The founders of the Institute thought that this was a mistake and planned to follow God's commandment to re-build the Holy Temple.

David peered through the glass at the model. It had a walled outer court for non-Jewish Gentiles, an inner court for all Jews, then one just for Jewish men. This last court led up steps to a high, square building with long double doors, flanked by pillars. Inside here was the Holy of Holies, where the Ark of the Covenant was kept.

Directly opposite this Temple model was a large, ornate box, with pole handles to carry it. The original would have been the size of a tomb but this copy was a half-scale. On top of it were two kneeling angels, Cherubim, which faced each other in prayer, their arched wing-tips touching.

The sign read, "This is the most beautiful reproduction of the Ark of the Covenant ever." It was followed by a quote: 'Make two Cherubim of beaten gold for the two ends of the propitiatory, fastening them so that one Cherub springs direct from each end. The cherubim shall have their wings spread out above, covering the propitiatory with them, they shall be turned toward each other, but with their faces looking toward the propitiatory.' Exodus 25, verses 18-22.

The Cherubim looked like his Zoroastrian Icarus. But his sculpture tried to find the essence of God, whilst these protected it. He wandered away, lost in thought, into a maze of tall, narrow alleys.

Weaving between the walls David finally came to limestone steps leading down through the new buildings. Here he gazed across the urban valley to the brilliant Dome of the Rock. It shone in the sun.

Here was the heart of Jerusalem. Here was the city he had dreamed of visiting.

As he headed down and around, the Dome disappeared from view, down and around again, it reappeared, larger, more vivid.

Getting closer he entered a stream of men, ladies, children. But they weren't heading towards the Dome. They were heading towards the Western Wall. To the last part of the Jewish Temple Mount, where Jews had continued to worship for centuries, despite being hemmed in by Arab houses. After the Six-Day war these old houses were demolished and Safdie had designed an open plaza in front of the Western Wall. The plaza was partitioned into a section for men and a smaller section, to the right, for women. The different periods of the Wall were easily visible. At the bottom were 6 foot long blocks of Herodian stone, 100 feet up the stones were much smaller, rebuilt by the Byzantines and Muslims after the Romans had toppled the giant ashlars when they destroyed the Temple in 70 C.E.

As the hot afternoon ended, Hasidic Jews arrived in long black coats and large black hats. Their beards and locks of hair made them look like they belonged to 18th century Europe. They had walked from Damascus Gate, through the Arab Old City, protected by the Israeli soldiers who sat, with semi-automatic rifles, at street corners.

There was a quiet buzz of reverential activity as the Jews prayed, rocking back and forth, praying, dwarfed by the Wall.

David wanted to touch the Wall, to pray at the Wall. He took a cardboard skullcap, from a pile, placed it on his crown and entered the men's area. Standing close he marvelled at how the massive stones had been so perfectly cut, "dressed," to within millimetres. Pieces of paper containing prayers were still stuck between the joints of this Wall, smoothed and darkened from centuries of the grease of touching hands. Higher up plants grew from large cracks.

Around him some of the devout men had Tefillin strapped to their heads, small black prayer boxes to remind them that God rescued the Jews from slavery in Egypt. David prayed. 'Thank you God for allowing me to be in this wonderful holy place. Please help me to do your will and not fall short.'

He returned to the plaza, relieved not to have caused anyone annoyance and wondered if he, as a non-practicing Jew, would have been allowed past the Court of the Gentiles. He imagined how the Temple would have looked, situated where the Golden Dome of the Rock now stood.

He imagined the two Holy buildings on the same site, next to each other, Jewish and Muslim. Then shook his head, knowing it could never occur.

The Wall and Dome were floodlit as the sun. A large crowd of students gathered in a circle on the plaza and began traditional singing and dancing. He wanted to stay and watch but he was late. He checked his map and set off to walk for Shmuel's house, outside the Old City's walls.

David placed a kippa skullcap on his head as he entered the ground floor apartment in West Jerusalem.

'Shabbat Shalom,' said Shmuel.

'Shabbat Shalom.'

'You found it, good. Please come in. I hope you like stew.'

David draped his coat over a chair. 'Vegetarian and Kosher?'

'Of course, I set a bit aside before I added the beef.'

'So, what makes your stew Kosher?' David looked genuinely bemused.

'The cow would've been slaughtered with the correct techniques, to drain the blood. And it contains no dairy products because we can't mix them with meat. It may seem strange, but eating kosher food is more important than eating health foods and we have dietary inspectors to oversee where food is produced and to give food a stamp of approval. But we digress.'

Shmuel gestured to a small table set with 2 loaves of bread, a bottle of wine, covered plates and a candelabra, a Menorah. 'We mark the Sabbath with a meal to remind us of the Exodus of the Jewish people from slavery in Egypt. First the wine, it symbolises the lamb's blood, dabbed above the Jewish doors so that the Angel of Death would pass over and kill only the first born of the Egyptian captors. I'm now going to say Kiddush over it.' He spoke in Hebrew, then translated, '"Blessed art thou O Lord our God, Ruler of the universe, who creates the fruit of the vine."' They rose their glasses and drank.

'The bread, the Challah, symbolises the manna that God sent whilst the Jewish people wandered in the wilderness after leaving Egypt.' He spoke in Hebrew then translated, '"Blessed art thou o Lord our God, Ruler of the universe, who brings forth bread from the earth."' Shmuel cut up the braided bread and gave some to David. They dipped their pieces in salt. It tasted sweet, eggy.

The ritual reminded David of the Last Supper, where Jesus said that the bread and wine were his body and blood, to be taken in communion, in remembrance of him. He wanted to find out more from Shmuel. 'So what else do you have to do on the Sabbath?'

'We have set prayers to recite but it's more what you don't do, because the Sabbath marks God's day of rest on the 7th day after creation. We cannot do any work so I leave the light switches on and I leave the stew on a low heat, because I'm not allowed to do any cooking. The Orthodox, though, have strict charts that give them the times for everything they do throughout the day, even for getting up and getting dressed. But all Jews must pray "May the Temple be speedily rebuilt in our own time" 3 times a day. And this is why the Sabbath is a joyful day, because it is a glimpse of the Messianic times, when the Temple will be rebuilt and every Jew will observe the Sabbath.'

Then they ate the stew. David tried to look as if he was enjoying it. 'So when do you think the Messiah will return?'

'No one knows, but the Religious Zionists think that it will be soon. This is why they encourage Jews to return to the land, in preparation for the Messiah. They also run organisations like the Temple Institute where they prepare for the rebuilding of the Temple.'

'I saw this today.'

'Yes, but most Jews don't expect the Messiah to return any time soon because it is said that He will only come when Israel is a light unto the Gentiles, at a time of peace. And this won't be soon because the Palestinians have said that they want to drive us into the sea.'

'And why don't you think Jesus is the Messiah?'

Shmuel breathed in his stew and coughed. There was a red faced silence.

'David, Christian ideas of the Messiah, his virgin birth and sacrificial death, are all pagan. Jesus was a Jew, but the whole of the religion created in his name comes from the Pagan Sun Gods. His holy day was Sunday, the day of the sun, instead of Saturday, the Sabbath, and he was even given the same birthday as the Roman Sun God, Sol Invictus and the Egyptian god, Horus, the 25th of December.'

David began to pick at the stew.

'The virgin birth comes from the Greek God of wine, Dionysus, who was fathered by a God. And the same parallels are there in the Crucifixion. Dionysus died a violent death then came to life again, as did Horus who was buried for 3 days before he rose again to enter Heaven. The same with the Roman God Mithras, who died a violent death for man's sins and descended to the underworld, then rose again into Heaven. The followers of Mithras even bathed in the blood dripping from a dying bull in order to rejuvenate and purify their bodies. Just like the Christians who take communion in the blood of Christ.'

David put down his spoon.

'Even the idea of a sacrifice to pay for sin has nothing to do with Judaism. Sacrificial offerings could be used for thanking God, for cleansing a person of ritual impurity or for obtaining forgiveness for unintentional sins. They could not be used to remove a deliberate sin. Not even the High Priest's Yom Kippur sacrifice of a bull in the Temple, to atone for the sins of the whole nation, could do this.'

David tentatively raised his hand to stop the flow. 'Like I told you this afternoon, I'm a Unitarian. I believe that Christ was just a man, not a God, and that his sacrifice was an example to mankind to be forgiving, even to the point of death.'

'That's an interesting way of thinking and would fit with the Monotheism of the Jews,' said Shmuel, 'but you don't know your scriptures, the New Testament clearly states that Christ is God.'

David continued. 'But the scriptures were only set in the 4th century when the Unitarian belief was declared a heresy at the Council of Nicea.'

Shmuel nodded in agreement. 'But unfortunately the pagan blood rites of won out and Christianity became another version of the old religions of Dionysus and Mithras.'

David shifted in his chair. 'So if you don't believe in Christ's sacrifice and forgiveness then how do you gain forgiveness?'

'The Jews never believed that the path to righteousness was through sacrifice. It is through following the Law and through the Kabbalah.'

'The Kabbalah?'

'Yes, the secret teachings encoded in the 22 letters of the Jewish alphabet. Each letter had its own number used in the hidden coding of the Torah.'

David shook his head. 'The New Testament warns that numerology is witchcraft and that false prophets will use it prior to the Second Coming of Christ. Besides, I thought the Kabbalah came out of the Renaissance.'

Shmuel smiled and raised his eyebrows. 'You know a lot and there is some truth in what you say. Scholars hold that the great Jewish thinker Maimonides introduced the Kabbalah to Europe in the Middle Ages. But its truths are eternal.' Shmuel pointed at the candelabra, its candles shone. 'Just like the Menorah's 7 branches were derived from the 7 Zoroastrian, angels of fire, the Kabbalah also came out of the Jew's time in Babylon and Egypt. Its 22 letters are "paths" between 10 "emanations," aspects of God, up the Tree of Life. This journey begins in the material emanation, Malkuth, but the goal is the top emanation, Kether. Maimonides believed that God created man as an angel with this consciousness. But mankind fell when his female side was tempted by the serpent, bringing knowledge of good and evil. Now forgiveness and righteousness come when we return to the original Oneness of God, to the absolute reality, where all opposites are united in balance.'

David sat forward on his chair, excited by Shmuel's ideas. 'That's a very Buddhist way of thinking, but if God is beyond good and evil. It's just Pantheism. I'm a Monotheist and I believe that God made a free choice to be good. And that's what makes Him Great.'

The Rabbi was pleased. 'You ask all the right questions. But God is beyond these limited ideas. If you look with your spiritual eyes then you will see that God created good and evil.'

By the time they had finished talking about mysticism the candles had burnt out. They recited grace after their meal and David left, unconvinced.

9. Church of the Holy Sepulchre

David wanted to take part in the rituals of the City and certain festivals, like Good Friday, the anniversary of the Crucifixion of Christ, had to be celebrated in Jerusalem. But Israeli female soldiers in tight trousers, whose rounded bottoms burst with ripeness in the hot sun, competed in his mind with the religious traditions.

David walked across the bright courtyard, through the high arched, double doorway of the Church of the Holy Sepulchre. It seemed eternally dark in the church, whose walls were still unfinished after centuries. In the fourth century Queen Helena, mother of Emperor Constantine, had named this the location of Golgotha, the Hill of the Skull, the place of Christ's death. Now most of the church dated from the Crusader period.

A sharp right from the main doors led upstairs, onto a green marble balcony, at the top of Golgotha. The floor was packed with Spaniards, Italians, Greeks, Japanese and Americans, all waiting before an altar. Sweet incense pervaded the air as David climbed onto the wide, flat banister at the back, raised above the jostling pilgrims and tourists. There he could see the priests lifting up an effigy of Christ crucified, a statue painted with all the detail of life.

Looking down, back towards the double doors, a procession of priests entered the church in gold, red and black robes, waving incense. They were led by a man in a gold braided uniform and a red fez, who banged a heavy staff on the floor. Its thud resounded through the church, commanding people to stop their frenzied pushing for position and to move out of the way.

The procession moved up the small stairway to Golgotha, crushing the crowd, forcing it to move aside, performing their rites as they pushed forward. Soon all he could see was their heads.

The dark, vaulted ceiling curved down into the hubbub of people and amongst it all, standing out, was the statue of Christ crucified. David absorbed the atmosphere as he prayed. But he could no longer put aside the tempting thoughts. Looking around he became intoxicated by the scantily clad young tourists, their soft and smooth skin, their dark hair and lush lips. He began to imagine their hot and sweating bodies. He didn't want to think this way, not here, but they were there, in front of him. He couldn't help it.

The crowd surged to get closer to Christ. One by one pilgrims disappeared, then re-emerged and moved away, down the side steps.

Eventually the crowd grew small enough for him to climb down from the balcony and join the end of the remaining queue. People would kneel and lean into a small marble hole beneath the feet of Christ. There they were kissing the rock, kissing Golgotha, the place of the skull.

He needed Christ's help but the wooden figure of Christ did not move. How could it help. It represented a man who worked in wood and ended his life nailed to wood. Jesus was a carpenter, a man who might have carved grapes, floral reliefs, even Cherubim in commissions to cut the decorations and designs of synagogues. He might have absorbed the influences of the latest techniques and styles, transforming the synagogue floors with the Roman signs of the zodiac. But one day he found that the Jewish God was not in the art of the Synagogue, He was in the scriptures, in his Holy Word.

David rested his hands on the hard floor and thrust his body forward. His neck was exposed, like a man awaiting execution. Nose against the floor he suspended his rationality and prayed out loud to the wooden Christ above him. 'Oh God, please help me, please keep me from a lusting heart.'

Retreating back to the banister David watched as the effigy was taken from the cross and removed from the empty balcony.

Below him, in the entrance, opposite the main doorway, a new effigy of Christ was being laid on a slab, the Stone of Unction. The crowd gathered round as incense burnt and it was anointed with oils, just like it was the real body of Christ. The power of ritual was clear, the religion had come to life, below him was Christ, sacrificed for all humanity.

The Romans brought their Gods to life by using statues in ritual theatre, in dramatic enactments of the stages of life. This was why the art of the Jews was too abstract for the Holy Roman Empire, it had no statues. So they converted the Jewish God into a Roman God by incarnating the Jewish God in the human figure of Christ in the doctrine of the Trinity.

David stepped down the flight of stairs and waited patiently, behind an elderly queue, as the effigy below them was lifted and carried around the corner, further into the church. He left the bitter sweet aroma of incense behind and headed to a Tomb, the Holy Sepulchre, in the middle of a huge, circular hall. It was a rectangular structure, topped with an onion dome and covered with candles and lamps. Above it was a dark, star-studded dome, with a circular hole from which light shone down.

As David queued his mind wandered back to his conservation work in London's Catholic Cathedral, an imposing neo-Byzantine structure in Westminster. He had worked on scaffolding around a giant suspended painting that dangled like an enormous stalagmite in the vaults of sooted brick. The thin figure of Christ was stretched out upon a blood red background, surrounded by a heavy, gold, cross-shaped frame. As David cleaned the Nimbus the gleaming gold reflected on his hand, in celestial splendour.

Below him rows of chairs, parted by an aisle led to the light of the entrance, but directly beneath him was the altar, protected with a burgundy and golden cloth.

He gently rolled swabs of cotton wool, slowly wiping away candle soot that contained a century of faithful devotions, revealing the gentle face of

Christ. He was cleansing the body of Christ of humanity's sins, so that Christ was ready to be seen again, in all His risen glory.

David was brought back to the present moment by a grey bearded priest instructing him to bow and pass through the small entrance to the Tomb.

Inside was a small space where he queued again, until ordered forwards, through an even smaller entrance.

He bowed and came into a tiny room where, on a marble ledge, was the figure of Christ, half size, lit by a forest of thin, brown candles. David had only a few seconds to pray. 'Oh Lord. Please help me follow your way. Please help my family and help the world to be a better place.'

'Come!' the priest brusquely ordered. David had no time to think. He quickly rose and banged his head on the low marble lintel as he exited. Leaving the Holy Sepulchre to another believer.

The service was now over and some of the crowd continued to sit and pray but most wandered, as tourists, around the church. David returned to the balcony of Golgotha. Here he watched the crowd gather below, arriving from the passages around the tight inner courtyard of the church. They were keen to get out and their numbers soon swelled.

When the doors finally opened, into the blinding, midday light, a group of Orthodox Christians began to push its way in. The pilgrims wore yellow hats with red Jerusalem crosses and the Orthodox priests wore high black hats and carried Icons of Christ.

This division between Catholicism and Orthodoxy began with the death of Emperor Theodosius the Great in 395, when the Holy Roman Empire was divided into Western and Eastern halves, each under its own Emperor, each with different rites and doctrines.

Both began with the same faith and also with a common art, derived from the widespread methods of making images in pagan Rome. The Holy Roman Christians revoked Jewish prescriptions against images of God because God now had a human form, Jesus Christ, so He could now be represented, like a Roman God. The problem that no original images of Christ existed was overcome when the first Byzantine Icon was created in the 4th century. This was taken from what was described as being a miraculous image imprinted onto a shroud of cloth that had been pressed onto Christ's wet face after his crucifixion. The Orthodox tradition kept the use of these Icons, flat images, but the Catholics began to create ever more elaborate statues and paintings.

The crowds surged into a maelstrom, 2 crashing streams, flowing inwards and outwards. David descended from the balcony and was carried by the current, within the Catholic throng, spilling out of the church, headlong into the warm air and the city's tributaries. He came out of the colour and ritual of the Church of the Holy Sepulchre and immediately began to lose any sense of certainty. He passed shops selling Orthodox and Catholic crucifixes, icons, prayer-beads, postcards, posters, olive wood figures, t-shirts, cups, satchels, carpets. The wares neatly arranged, overflowing into the street. But even they couldn't help him keep hold of any sense of faith.

There were too many conflicts here, too many beliefs and the original, small, Jewish sect, headed by James, Jesus' brother had been destroyed. It had been turned it into a pagan faith that had split into Orthodox and Catholic groups. This split had reached its high point in the Great Schism of 1054, when the Western, Catholic Church changed the doctrine of the Nicene Creed to say that the Holy Spirit proceeds "from the Father and the Son," not just "from the Father." This minor change created a split so great that in 1204 the Catholic Crusaders even sacked Constantinople, the capitol of their Orthodox brethren.

10. Dome of the Rock

Dazzling light reflected on the golden Dome of the Rock as David crossed the exposed Western Wall plaza. He headed up the ramp, to the right side of the Wall, towards the large metal doors, to the Haram esh Sharif, the Most Noble Sanctuary.

Israeli soldiers checked him for any weapons then, as he stepped through a small entrance in the iron doorway, David was greeted by a broken-toothed, elderly man with a moustache and heavy white stubble. The man sat, in a grey suit like robe and wore a white kifr on his head. Behind him was a garden paradise, where trees and marble fountains stood on a plateaux of limestone paving.

He took David's entrance fee, whilst passing a string of prayer beads through his fingers. He was reciting, 'Glory be to Allah', 'Thanks be to Allah', 'God is Great' as he counted the beads.

David strode forward and a cool breeze swept over him as he passed under the shade of the tall trees. Avenues of trees, stepped terraces and the grandly ordered gardens filled with brightly coloured flowers, all fed by black hose pipes, these were the art here.

In the Qur'an heaven is an oasis of gardens, rivers and trees. It is where men wear silk robes and lie on couches with an unlimited supply fruit and wine. To some it is also where each man has an almost unlimited harem. But this was Heaven itself, away from the chaos and grime of the old city.

David tried to apologise to the various guides that approached him, giving him a persistent, hard sell. He felt like he was invading their holy space so eventually agreed to be shown around by a short man with a black moustache, wearing a white shirt and grey pants.

'Many Jews do not want to visit this site. They fear they might stand upon the Holy of Holies.' He pointed up to the golden dome beyond the trees. 'A place they are not purified to enter. But first we look at Al Aqsa Mosque, the largest mosque in Jerusalem.'

They paused at a long, grey domed mosque, its entrance flanked by majestic columns. 'Some extreme Jews shot men whilst they prayed here, and recently some Christians tried to burn it down. They want to capture the "Holy Land" from Muslim rule, like the Crusades all over again.'

The man began to reel off his lines. 'In 1119 C.E. the Crusaders slaughtered everyone in Jerusalem, whether Muslim, Jew or Christian. Then they established their camp here, at Al Aqsa. They were supported with money from wealthy Europeans but still in 1187 C.E. the Muslim army of Saladin defeated them and took Jerusalem. The Crusaders continued to occupy parts of the land until 1291 but they were divided, split between the Genoese bankers who supported the Hospitallers, and the Venetian bankers who supported the Knights Templar.'

'The Templars won and the Venetians covered Italy and northern Europe with their modern banking system, lending money with interest. It was usury, forbidden by the church, but they sidestepped this with clever loopholes. They even began to issue paper money, loaning ten times more than the value of the gold they held.'

David glimpsed, in admiration, the golden panelling on the Dome of the Rock. He was lost in admiration of the architecture.

'Then, in 1305, the Kings of France and England rounded up their Templars, confiscated the Templar's wealth and charged them with Satanism. The Kings claimed that the Templars had found the secret teachings of King Solomon's master mason, Hiram Abif, a pagan from Tyre, under the Temple in Jerusalem, and has begun to worship the horned God of the Pagans.' The guide gestured, making his fingers like the horns. 'Meanwhile the Mamlukes began their glorious rule over Jerusalem.'

David had stopped listening. 'Is it alright to pray inside?'

The guide misunderstood the question. 'The Prophet said if you pray 5 times a day then Allah blots out evil deeds.'

David repeated the request and the guide looked surprised. He nodded then instructed him to remove his sandals and follow him to begin the Wudhu ritual of washing before prayers. They washed, three times for the hands, three times for the mouth, nose, face and ears, three times for the arms and three times for the feet. It soothed and cleansed.

When he had finished he was invited into the large, carpeted space. David stroked the stubble on his chin and stubble as he looked at its columns and high dome. They were made of green, red and blue marble, from the Roman ruins at Caesarea. The floor was covered with prayer mats, which all faced the Qibla, the direction of prayer, Mecca. Upon some of the mats young men were praying. Behind them, within a golden frame, was the word "Allah".

The mosque was free of images, statues and furniture. Here nothing detracted from the worship of Allah.

At the far end of the open space was a stepped pulpit, a Mimbar. Upon this stood the Imam, dressed in white, with a red Saudi Arabian headscarf. The Imam clasped his hands then held his arms outstretched. 'As Salaam Alaykum … Peace Be Upon You.'

The small crowd responded with 'Alaykum As Salaam … And Upon You Too.'

David could only guess what the Imam barked and thumped on the Mimbar. As he heard the guttural words, he began to stare, drifting into a daydream. Then he caught the ferocious gaze of the Imam, turned a burning red and looked at the floor, earnestly hoping that his desire to worship might be recognized as being genuine.

David's guide began to whisper a translation of the sermon into his ear. '30 years before the end of the earth will be the Day of Judgment. There will be a loud call from the sky and the Imam Mahdi, the "Divinely Guided One," will arrive from Mecca. No one can determine when this will be, but it is said that he will come after two thirds of the world have died - a third in a Great War and a third in the sickness caused by the war. His name will be Muhammad, and his character will be blameless. He will resemble the Prophet with a strong forehead and nose.'

The guide could not translate the next words. Then continued. 'He will convert many non-believers to Islam and along with the prophet Isa, Jesus, he will lead all Muslims to create a perfect society of Islamic justice and peace throughout the world. The Mahdi and Isa will bring an end to the worship of false idols and will defeat the Dajjal, the Anti-Christ, in the last days, before the Day of Judgment. But the Dajjal shall make a breeze from the south and will kill all the believers.'

The Imam pointed past the crowd, in the direction of the Dome outside.

'Then the dead will be resurrected at Bir el-Arwah, the Well of Souls, where they will be judged, by Mohammed and Jesus, for every action that they did and for every word that they spoke. Lying, corruption, unbelief, greed and selfishness will condemn you to Hell. But Allah is merciful and will grant forgiveness, to those that deserve it.'

The sermon ended and the men spaced out evenly in rows. Facing the Qibla they raised their hands to shoulder height 'Allah Akbar'. Placing their hands upon their chests they recited phrases in Arabic.

Then the first Surah of the Qur'an, Sura Fatiha, was recited. David recognized some of the words from the classical Arabic.

'In the name of God, the Most Gracious, the Most Merciful'

'Praise be to God, the Lord of the Universe.'

'The Most Gracious, the Most Merciful.'

'King of the Day of Judgment.'

'You alone we worship, and You alone we ask for help.'

'Guide us to the straight way,'

'The way of those whom you have blessed, not of those who have deserved anger, nor of those who stray.'

'Amen'

The words burnt into David's heart. They were perfect in their expression. They were all that he wanted to say.

He tried to keep up with the movements of the congregation as they bowed in unison. They rested their hands on their knees, stood upright, then knelt with their foreheads touching the prayer mat.

Lifting up their faces they said, 'O my Lord! Forgive me, and have mercy on me.'

They prostrated themselves again then all stood in personal prayer. David added his own words. 'Please Lord Forgive me. Help me to have the strength to follow your faith.'

They finished by turning their faces right then left, each time saying a salutation to the other worshippers. 'Peace is on you and the mercy of Allah.'

David felt a deep calm as the worshippers left the cool magnificence of the hall. He put on his warm sandals and entered the bright sun-lit courtyard. 'Oh, you are good Muslim now? Ha, ha,' said the guide.

David headed towards a marble fountain. 'I wish, but it's very hard to follow, very confusing.'

'You will learn.'

David was enrapt by the service but he couldn't make the commitment to give prayers 5 times a day. Besides he needed the freedom to explore other faiths and if he now took on Islam and then later turned away the Qur'an instructed that he should be killed.

Whilst they stopped to speak the Imam left the mosque with a crowd. The guide put a hand on David's shoulder. 'He is a Saudi, Sheikh Abul Qasim Muhammad. It is not good. He is trying to stir up trouble. We do not want this. We must learn from history. Everyone, Muslim, Christian, Jewish, must try to live together.'

The crowd neared them and the Imam greeted the guide. 'Salaam Alechum.'

'Alechum Salaam.' The guide then turned to David and spoke in a surprisingly brusque manner. 'Now you must become Muslim'.

The Imam did not look at David, just continued past them, up a stairway, through a row of four arches, to the shining golden dome.

David gazed up after the Imam and the crowd as it filtered under the arches at the top. They waited a while, then followed.

The simple, brilliant dome was built upon an octagonal structure, whose arched side walls were tiled with blue and white arabesque designs. The geometry of Dome of the Rock was a perfect symbol of how Mohammed unified the different tribes into the worship of a single God and its mathematical structure also reflected a puritanical sense of religious order.

The guide continued. 'The Jews say that this is where God tested Abraham, to see if he would sacrifice his son, Isaac, as a sign of his faith. At the last minute God intervened and gave Abraham a ram in place of his son. But the true story is that the son was Ishmael, ancestor of the Arabs, not Isaac, ancestor of the Jews. And it all took place at Mina, not here. But still, this is why the Jews built their Temple here.'

David nodded in interest as he listened.

'This place is important to us because in 621 C.E. Muhammed made his Night journey on a winged creature, with the angel Gabriel. It was here that he spoke with Allah and led prayers with Adam, Idris the prophet of Noah,

Abraham, Aaron the High Priest of Moses and Moses. He showed that he is the last true Prophet, the "Seal of the Prophets." Inside here is the mountain from which he flew. And beneath it is the Well of Souls.'

David admired the classically Islamic, decorative splendour but also how the economy of design would suit a modern architect.

'Inside you will not see any idols like in your Christian churches. We Sunni Muslims have a ban on idolatry. There are no pictures of the Prophet, surrounded with flames, on a winged beast. These pictures come from the east, from the Shia Muslims, who were influenced by the fire worshipping Persians.'

David began to take off his shoes, ready to enter.

'You are a Muslim now?'

David shook his head. 'I'm still deciding.'

The guide closed his lips together. 'Once a believer you must never stray again.'

David nodded as he backed away then turned to enter, through the ornate doors, into the dim light of the spacious dome.

The carpet was soft. As he walked over it he looked up, beyond the marble walls and columns, to the golden mosaics, the floral designs and the swirling Corinthian capitals. But the Arabic inscriptions, of the names of God and verses from the Qur'an, were the real artworks here. These were the Holy words, the poetry of the Qur'an, put into a visual form. The high stemmed letters, curved with small, tight, round consonants, to form shapes of divine beauty.

This was the only way that Allah, the most infinite being, whose greatness is beyond any depiction, could be shown.

At the far end of the building he descended steps to a small cave. This was the Well of Souls but he imagined that it was also the site of the Holy of Holies, the place where the Ark of the Covenant would have been kept. David kneeled and began to pray. 'Dear Lord…'

'La, La' a tall, fat, guard in dark blue robes, had followed him down the steps. He pointed upwards, out of the cave. There was no room for discussion. It was an order.

Stumbling to his feet David ascended back to the main area and moved to the wooden railings that encircled the enclosed mountain summit. The stone looked artificial in the glow of orange lights. He closed his eyes, and held his hands by his stomach. 'Dear Lord. Please help me to be a better person. Please guide me in…'

'La, la. Out. Out!' This time his guide came over with the guard.

The guide waved his arm angrily and called out, 'Go away, you are not welcome here.'

David raised his hands. 'I'm sorry, I'm sorry. I'm going. Salaam alechum'

'Yes, yes. Alechum salaam'

As David reached the exit he turned and looked a last time at the splendour of the vault. There he noticed a decorative band running above the cream and black arches. Ringing the inside of this Holy building, surrounding the top of Mount Moriah, were small swastika mosaics.

-

That evening, he sat in a warm breeze on the flat stone wall around the large, Jewish cemetery on the Mount of Olives. He looked west, across the Kidron valley to the Old City, whose buildings spread before him. The grey domed Al Aqsa mosque and the golden Dome of the Rock dominated the view. David's hands were heavy as they rested on his knees. The light from the sun, setting behind the clouds, made his eyes squint. He closed them briefly and felt his eyelids warming.

He opened his eyes and focussed on the eastern wall around the Temple Mount. In this was a gateway whose two arches were blocked up. This was the Golden Gate, through which the Messiah for the Jews, Christians and Muslims was supposed to arrive.

David turned his face to the sky, praising God as rays of light struck through the clouds onto the Holy Land before him. Once it all belonged to the Canaanites who worshipped Baal, the Bull God of the sun. He chased the remnants of the setting sun as he considered how the God of the Jews was different. More than just the sun, the moon and the stars, He was a sky God who ruled over everything.

David closed his eyes and opened his heart to God, asking for guidance. What should he believe when all the religions were fighting each other and twisting history to suit their own ends.

Each religion claimed that only they had the true scriptures and that the scriptures of other believers were wrong. The Jewish Torah, supposedly written by Moses about the One God, contained internal contradictions and was only collated many hundreds of years after Moses. The Christian belief that Jesus was the Messiah of the Jews and the son of God contradicted the Jewish beliefs about the Messiah. The Muslims then denied Christian beliefs about Christ's divinity, his Virgin Birth and the idea that he was a sacrifice to forgive mankind's sins. Mohammed also said that he was the fulfilment of the Jewish religion, which contradicted the Jewish beliefs.

A Quaker phrase fell from his lips, "The Spirit liveth, but the letter killeth". It was not the literal words that were important, but the Spirit. Yet this Spirit was too vague to give any guidance. He needed to make a commitment to God to get deeper guidance. But that commitment must be forever.

It would mean that he could no longer lust over the scantily clad Israeli, Arab and Western girls who walked provocatively around the city.

'It is too much God, I can't do it. I can't follow it. Not yet, not now.'

When he opened his eyes the sun had set.

That night he shaved, and in the days to come he developed a routine, a habit, of working in the evening but spending the afternoon sitting in street cafes. Beautiful, tanned Israeli girls walked past, the Sun God touching their swollen breasts and smooth buttocks. Their sweating bodies heaving in a light, soothing caress. Here was paradise. Here was heaven on earth. Why wait for the virgins when he was surrounded by them right now.

11. Burqin Church

Later that year David stood at the central roundabout in Ramallah. The call of the drivers at Damascus Gate still ringing in his ears. 'Ramallahramallahramallaaah." The white mini buses and Mercedes Benz 'Service' taxis were parked behind him. These were the quickest, cheapest way along the dusty roads and through the roadblocks to the acting Palestinian capital.

On the outskirts of Ramallah he had passed gaudy, kitsch mansions and half-constructed, concrete buildings. The chaos of the exposed steel and marble cladding was echoed by the city's fruit stalls, parked in front of shops that displayed ostentatious mirrors and brass light fixings. Behind the windows golden verses from the Qur'an mixed with paradisiacal scenes and framed photos of Palestinian pop stars. Pictures of cascading waterfalls, propped amongst silver pans and plastic water jugs. All made in China.

The project in Jerusalem had drawn to a close and David was to meet with Dr Hanan Hadawi, Director and Chief Architect for the Ministry of Tourism & Antiquities of the Palestinian National Authority. Its offices were just north of the central roundabout in Ramallah, located in a grey three-storey, 1940's, government complex that was shared with the police.

Hanan was a portly, balding, bespectacled gentleman whose kindly disposition was marked with the pressures of work. He welcomed David from behind his desk and offered him a small glass of tea with sugar and mint.

'We would like you to work on St. George's church in Burqin, a village in the North, just west of Jenin.' Hanan struggled to draw breath between each sentence. 'It is a very important church and part of the tourism development of the area so we want it to have the best conservation possible. It is the 4th oldest Orthodox Church in the Holy Land, after Bethlehem, Jerusalem and Jifna. It was established by Queen Helena, mother of Emperor Constantine, at the cave of the miracle. The story is in Luke's Gospel. It says how Jesus was on his way from Nazareth to Jerusalem, when he heard the cries of ten lepers from a cave. He healed them all, but only one, a Samaritan, returned to thank him.'

David took the tea from the round metal tray. It was too sweet, but he was thirsty so he sipped it.

'The church itself has four historical periods. The first was Helena's church, built around the cave. The second added further construction between the 5th - 9th centuries. The church was then rebuilt and enclosed within a wall in the Crusader period, in the 12th century. Finally the church was rebuilt again Ottoman period, in the 18th century. But now joints in the stone have been filled with concrete and the antiquities in the church have been covered in a layer of concrete. Salts are crystallising under the hard concrete and are destroying the softer stonework. We would like you to show our workers how to conserve the stonework. Is this of interest to you?'

David nodded his head, 'Yes,' he was excited. 'It would be a privilege to work there. I will make an assessment report and keep a full documentation of works. But to remove the concrete I'll need an air chisel.'

'Good, good. If you find this we will buy it for you.' Hanan stood up from behind his desk and smiled with a light in his eyes. He shook David's hand. 'Our Palestinian National Authority has no trained conservators so we appreciate your help. You are the first British person to help us.' David smiled, ignoring the smell of Hanan's sharp breath.

Back down in the street David was surprised when Hanan introduced him to a familiar short, middle-aged European.

'David Wolfe. It's good to see you again. I hear you'll be working for Dr Hanan at Burqin church.' It was Dr. James Rockschild. 'It's an important project so I trust you'll make sure it all goes well.' Rockschild handed his card. 'I'm now consultant for the Middle East with the Cultural Property Division of U.N.E.S.C.O., the United Nations Educational Scientific and Cultural Organisation. Just call if you need me.'

A white car with the blue number plates of the Occupied Territories pulled up. Rockschild's eyes had a sparkle to rival Hanan's as he commanded. 'On the horses boys!'

Hanan bit his lip as he got into the front of the car and turned to David. He spoke softly, raising an eyebrow. 'Now we will go to Burqin, where we will do some good work.'

They left, through newly built suburbs of the city, travelling on unfinished roads, and entered the hills of the West Bank. It was a landscape of bleached limestone outcrops and wind blown olive groves. But far from being a biblical desert scene the spring trees and grass were full and lush. They seemed to celebrate being alive.

Cool air blew in through the car window as they weaved round the contours of the West Bank. Hanan turned to speak. 'This land was known as Samaria, the land of the Northern tribes of Israel, the Samaritans. They believe that they have the true Bible, given by Moses, that the other Israelites, the Jews, have the wrong scriptures. They are now only about 550 people but they wait for the nation to be restored when their Messiah, the Taheb, will return.'

David nodded in interest and realised how little he knew about this country and its people. But, for now, all he wanted to do was just sit back to admire the view. His faith seemed to be returning. In any country this natural scene, of vibrant beauty, of valleys and sun lit clouds, would suggest that God had designed it. How much more so in the Holy Land, where even the dry stone walls, shoring up the earthen terraces on the sides of the hills, seemed to be a part of God's plan.

After an hour they neared a city. 'This is Nablus,' said Hanan.

'Known to the Jews as Shechem,' added Rockschild.

Hanan frowned, 'From here the Intifada against the Israelis began.'

As he spoke David noticed the Israeli tanks on the plains outside the city, under the light cover of a line of trees.

They approached a warren of white concrete buildings that covered the hillside. As they drove between them Hanan pointed to a hill which overlooked the city. He shouted over the sound of the traffic. 'That is Mount Gerizim. Up there are the ruins of the Samaritan Temple.'

They travelled further into the city where the green, black, red and white Palestinian flag hung from buildings whose walls were sprayed with slogans. They passed the bus station and a large, overgrown archaeological site. David did not ask Hanan about it. His attention was focussed on the young men, walking hand in hand down the street. It looked homosexual, but they were just channelling their sexual frustrations, into affections towards each other because they were not allowed to walk with girls until they could afford one, in an arranged marriage.

At the bottom of Nablus they turned right and headed north. They left, directly behind them, a giant Israeli motorway. It was still under construction, scarring the hillside, running straight, like a Roman road. The Israelis saw this as their land, promised by God to Moses, but were bulldozing its beauty in the name of progress.

The further north, into the West Bank, that they drove, the more he sat back and enjoyed the thousands of years of unspoilt land. It was God's natural beauty, undestroyed by developers.

Down from the hills they opened out onto the straights from Nablus to Jenin, towards the border with Israel, beyond which lay the Sea of Galilee. On the straight they passed a pyramid shaped mound in the distance. Hanan turned to face them, 'That is Tel Megiddo. Twenty levels of habitation from 7000 B.C.E. to 586 B.C.E. It is like a giant rubbish tip, each generation building on the ruins of the previous one. It was full of Palestinian artefacts but the Rockschilds excavated it in 1930s, confiscating everything they found, putting it in their Museums.'

Rockschild put his hand on the top corner of Hanan's seat and leaned forward 'It needed to go there to be protected.'

'We can look after things ourselves.'

'Like you do with your buildings?'

'Our craftsmen repair our old buildings in our traditional ways of working.'

Rockschild protested. 'But you have lost your traditional skills. Now you use concrete instead of stone. You are destroying your history.'

Hanan forced a smile, and turned to David. 'We will do good work in Burqin, In Shallah (God willing). My workmen will remove the concrete from the church walls. Then re-plaster them with lime, to let them breathe,' he gestured with his hand 'to allow the salts out. And David will work on the antiquities inside.'

Rockschild shook his head. 'I know you want to do good work here but you're using concrete everywhere else. It's idiocy.'

'We only have money for lime at the most important sites. If we didn't use concrete in other places the buildings would collapse.'

'But you're just ruining them, because you won't use the proper materials, because your corrupt government is misusing all the international funding for conservation. And you wont' stand up to them because you don't want to lose your job.'

Hanan shook his head but David remained silent and still after Rockschild's outburst. At least he would be able to do some good works in Burqin. In Shallah.

He looked out of the window, watching as they passed the hill, the Tel of Megiddo. It was Har Megiddo, Armageddon, where the New Testament prophesied, in the Book of Revelation, that the kings of the earth will fight against the forces of good, at the end of the world.

-

They drove through the small town of Jenin and parked by the side of a dusty valley road. To the right, a track headed into the limestone hills, where wild red flowers stood in olive groves. To the left, buildings rose on the steep outskirts of the village.

A tall thin minaret pointed into the blue sky behind them. David struggled to see the Church of St. George and his heart sank when he finally saw this world significant church hidden behind the frame of a new construction site, a four-storey concrete building. Now he understood Rockschild's concerns

As they climbed upwards Rockschild turned to David. 'This is how they treat the site of a miracle.'

They took a short cut through the building site, walking up its flights of concrete steps, then climbed back onto the hillside, reaching the high wall around the church. Large sacks of sand were piled beneath a white sign that proudly announced in black and red "Palestinian Department of Antiquities. Project funded with the co-operation of the Dutch Government."

They pushed open the stiff metal doors and passed under a cross into a wide, parched, earthen courtyard. In front of them was the church, set into the side of the hill. It had plain walls and a doorway under a well carved arch. A small bell hung above the whole church.

Two noble trees stood at either end of the courtyard. Beneath the nearest one a man sat on top of a mound of limestone blocks and rubble. He wore a white kifr and had a white moustache and stubble. He held a block of stone between his bare feet and cut this with a Shahutah, a toothed adze like tool.

'Salaam Alechum,' said Hanan.

'Alechum Salaam'. He measured the stone with a right angle, marked it with a pencil, then carried on his work.

An elderly man emerged from the church. He wore a suit and had a well clipped moustache. 'This is Abu Azmi,' said Hanan as the tall thin, man offered his hand. David shook it.

'Welcome, Welcome. I look after the Church here. I am also a teacher of English.' His English was stilted.

Hanan added. 'Abu Azmi is the Mayor.'

'And next Friday you will come to my house?'

David nodded. Hanan began talking in Arabic, cast a disapproving stare at Abu Azmi, then turned back to David. 'Come, look what the villagers have done.'

They stepped up into the church, through a single metal doorway, passing from the bright outdoors, into a cooling darkness and a damp, musty aroma. It took some moments for David's eyes to adjust.

A small cave in a cliff wall faced them and a stone Iconostasis stood in front of this. The floor of the church was covered in polythene and upon this were halogen lights mounted on yellow stands.

Hanan switched them on and the work area became visible.

The Iconostasis had three archways and above these was a balustrade, topped with a triangular pediment. All Icons and hanging lamps had been removed, to protect them. Hanan pointed to the concrete in the joints and the white salts mixed in with the crumbling corners of the stones. 'Come,' said Hanan. They stepped behind the thin Iconostasis. 'The biggest problem is this thick layer of concrete supporting the back. How do we do remove it without collapsing the whole structure?' Hanan smiled nervously.

David inspected the concrete. It was two inches thick and covered the whole antiquity. 'We'll be able to remove it with an air-chisel, section by section, repairing as we go along.'

Hanan nodded as David looked around the cave. In the centre was a rough altar, a single block of stone that had been hollowed out, with a stone slab put on top. David's hand touched its cool surface and he let his fingers tarry over its roughness.

Rockschild nudged David and pointed at a hole, at the back of the cave roof. 'A family have put their garden over that air vent. It causes terrible problems with damp but Hanan won't do anything about it.'

Hanan winced. 'We are doing our best to protect the church, but it is a sensitive matter.' He looked to David for understanding.

Rockschild continued. 'It's because if he orders them to open it then it would be seen as giving land back to the Christians. The Arab Muslims criticise the Jews for taking their land but they don't mind taking it from the Arab Christians.'

'We have already removed the concrete render from the ceiling,' said Hanan as he led them back to the main area and pointed upwards. 'Soon we will re-plaster.'

Rockschild folded his arms, looking up at the exposed coring. 'It's a disaster. The whole ceiling needs replacing. All of this mortar and rubble is just full of dirt and salts. It needs removing, but they won't do it.'

David refused to be drawn. His work was on the monuments. Instead he traced down from the vaulted ceiling to the line of the Crusader arches onto the springers, the base walls from where they began.

Hanan ignored Rockschild and put his hand on David's shoulders. 'Interesting isn't it. But look at this.' He led David to a large antiquity to the side of the Iconostasis. It was covered in plastic sheeting and was half set into the rock wall. 'It is a bishop's Throne.' Hanan uncovered the enigmatic object, its back cut from the rock fac, its sides and roof made of stone. 'We will remove the concrete and replace this pink marble seat with one that is more appropriate.''

David wasn't listening as he looked at its two arms. They stuck out. Each had the head of a serpent, mouth wide open. He couldn't understand it. Wasn't the serpent an evil Tempter that seduced Eve to bite the Apple from the Garden of Eden. 'What's the meaning of these serpents?'

'We don't know,' replied Hanan. 'There is nothing about the Throne in our records. But this...' David's attention was led to a picture in a stone frame cut into the cliff wall. It was a faded and flaking painting of Saint George, on a white horse, killing a dragon with his spear. '... is Saint George of Lydda, the 3rd century Roman Christian soldier, martyred in Palestine. George and Constantine, the future Emperor of Rome, were soldiers and friends.'

Rockschild saw David's interest and took over from Hanan. 'That's right. When George became a Christian he was tortured and executed because he would not follow the Emperor Diocletian's orders to persecute Christians. So when Constantine became Emperor in 306, he made the martyred George a Saint and the "Champion Knight of Christendom." He made him an icon for the new warrior Christianity that replaced Mithraism the old religion of the Roman soldiers. Then, when Constantine's mother, Queen Helena, rebuilt the churches destroyed by Diocletian she dedicated many of them to St. George.'

'What about the Dragon?'

Rockschild's mouth turned down as Abu Azmi, interrupted. 'Saint George killed the Dragon, the Devil, and brought people to Christianity.'

The conversation was broken as a curly haired, young man, wearing sun glasses and a "Yankees" baseball cap, entered the church.

'Ah, David,' said Hanan, 'this is Riyad, he will be working with you. He has an MA in mortar analysis from Athens University.'

Riyad took off the glasses and shook hands. 'Helloo David. I will be happy to learn from you.' David lent forward to hear the mumbled words. But Riyad's face dropped as he turned to speak to Hanan, in Arabic. Hanan nodded and both headed outside.

Rockschild put a hand on David's shoulder. 'You know the reason that they have neglected the church for so long?'

'No.'

'They believe it was used for Devil worship by the Templars during the Crusades.'

David raised an eyebrow.

'And they blame these Templars for the rise of the Jews. Supposedly the Templars started the early banks along with the Jews, causing wars in order to make profit. They claim that it was all led by my family, and our banking dynasty.' Rockschild sighed. 'They even think that charities like the Freemasons are involved in some kind of Global conspiracy with us. It's all just dangerous, anti-Semitic poison.'

'But aren't the Freemasons full of businessmen who make secret deals and conduct secret rituals?' asked David.

'All businesses make secret deals and the Freemasons' rituals aren't Satanic. They just dramatise the climbing of degrees, the learning of true knowledge.'

'So what is this true knowledge?' asked David.

Rockschild looked into his eyes. 'If you are interested then maybe you will join one day. The first step is to become an Apprentice. Later you can become a Master Mason, and that's where most Freemasons stay. But you can progress and earn titles like Temple workman, Israel tribesman, High Priest of the Jews, King Hiram of Tyre and Knight Templar. That's when it you learn the secret knowledge.'

Hanan appeared back at the doorway. 'Dr Rockschild, we must leave. We have more sites to visit.'

Rockschild embraced David. 'David I wish you well here.' Then he whispered. 'But take care, you are being watched.'

As David stepped back, confused whether he meant by the Palestinians or the Israelis. Hanan shook David's hand. 'Keep in touch. You have my number. Salaam Alaykum.'

'Alaykum Salaam.'

-

The days passed as David worked in the cool, musty church to the sound of Abu Walid cutting stone outside and Riyad removing concrete from the walls with a group of villagers.

David took photographs of the monuments and used architectural drawings to make condition reports, recording the surfaces, documenting the presence of damp and salts, highlighting the areas that needed repairs.

He collected fine chisels for removing the concrete joints, spatulas for re-pointing them with lime mortar, syringes for grouting into recesses and the clay poultices to remove salts.

When he grew tired he took breaks in the warmth of the doorway. He scratched his newly grown beard and watched the wizened Abu Walid. The old man's expression fixed into furrows by the sun, his cracked face like the trunk of the tree under which he sat. Even his eyes seemed hardened.

Riyad came over and smiled. 'David, when can we begin with the air-chisel?' He made a drilling action.

David shrugged. 'As soon as I finish the reports.'

At the end of the day's work David and Riyad headed up to the village, up a snaking alley, past the white washed walls. Large, elderly ladies sat, in traditional red and black robes, in the recesses of doorways, shelling chick peas. They watched and smiled. Small children ran around calling 'Hello, Hello,' to David

A donkey stood, tied to a post, staring at the floor. Its thin, dusty, old body was completely still.

The alley opened onto the village square, overshadowed by the minaret of the village mosque. The large expanse of dust and rubble had a road skirting its sides. At the far end were a couple of shops, selling food and hardware. Next to these the battered blue and white bus to Jenin was waiting. David bought the evening meal and a bottle of chilled water. It was wet to the touch. He drank and his throat relaxed. Then they headed across the square to David's ground floor apartment. Two old cars drove by and left dust that lingered in the hot Palestinian air.

Up a side street from the road to Jenin was his simple accommodation. The marble floor cooled the room and a fan brought added relief.

'David, I will make coffee for you,' said Riyad.

The drink was too sweet and strong, so as Riyad prepared it in a metal pot David made himself an instant coffee.

Then they sat on plastic chairs and set their daily meal of unleavened bread, chillies, tomatoes, processed cheese, cucumbers and onions, onto a plastic table.

He relaxed and was pleased that the fine meshes over the windows were welcome barriers to the mosquitoes.

'David, are you married?' asked Riyad.

'Ana la mareed,' replied David. It meant 'I am not sick!' They laughed.

'You know, Abu Walid, has two wives and is now looking for a third!' Riyad continued laughing. 'But he must save up.'

'How many wives can he have?' asked David.

'Well, Muslims can take many brides, Muhammed had maybe even eleven, but we definitely don't do this now.' Riyad sat forward. 'But we have a joke in the village. A Christian woman saw a Muslim woman washing her sheets every day. She asked, "Why do you have to do so much washing?" The woman replied, "We Muslims must wash our sheets every time we lay with our husbands." So the Christian said, "How do I make my husband a Muslim?"'

Only Riyad laughed, then there was a long pause.

'You know, the problem here is that people are superstitious. That is why the Muslim family blocks the church roof with their garden. They believe the old stories about the church. They are worried about monsters from the cave.' Riyad leaned back, smiling to himself. 'One evening the grandmother saw the garden moving and cried out "Djin! Djin!" Her sons ran down to the church with sticks and found Abu Azmi there, covered in soil, trying to poke the garden through with a long pole.' David laughed with Riyad. 'The local Imam made him apologise to the family. He was not happy.'

David stopped laughing as he imagined Abu Azmi's face. He began to play with his lower lip, unsure what to think.

-

David sat under a tree with Abu Walid. He unrolled his tool bag, chose one of his tungsten tipped chisels, and started to cut a block of limestone, quarried from the local hills. He was carving ashlars for the doorway of the church. The sound of his hammer and chisel mixed with the rhythmic tak, tak, of the old man's adze. Neither spoke, as they worked.

He gazed from the desolate courtyard, across the valley, to the rough tractor road up into the hills. That afternoon, after work, he would head up the road.

It was an effort to walk up the hill, even in the late afternoon, and the rough road was longer than it had looked. It entered into olive groves, whose gnarled old trunks twisted upwards in the harsh sun, and at the top of the hill, where the leaves rustled in a cooling breeze, it narrowed to become a path.

Here the red and yellow flowers were miniature works of beauty that burned on the retina. Insects gently buzzed between them and darted around the splendour as David jumped onto a limestone rock, careful not to damage the delicate geometries of its rich algae. He hopped onto another large rock and crouched down to a bright yellow flower growing in a crack. As he bent forward he felt the heat of the sun warming the sweat on his back.

The scent of the flower filled his senses and he was engulfed by the perfection of all that he saw, felt and heard.

This was God's creation, alive and happy. The birds and crickets were singing and chirping in a celebration of life. The ephemerality of the flowers contrasted the permanence of the rocks. But all was splendour, even his own fleeting presence here. He hoped that somehow this experience could last, that it would become more than just a memory, that it would be a lasting part of his soul.

He continued to walk, mesmerised by the landscape, wandering westwards, over the range of hills. At a high point he stopped and gazed north, across the flat plains, to the distant Tiberias, the Sea of Galilee. He imagined Assyrian, Roman, and Crusader armies massed and setting up camp, rallying and then marching over this broad green expanse of land.

The blue and white sky began to fade into the gold of the sandy atmosphere so he began the long walk back. Coming from this direction he now noticed, behind a copse of small trees, scaffolding was built around a deep hole. In the middle was a pole, most likely for a drill to reach the water table. This was an activity strictly prohibited by the Israelis, who wanted compete control of the water supplies. He peered into the cool, dark hole then continued, traversing the ridge of hills that surrounded the village. It was getting late so he dropped down into a gentle valley that cut between a farm house and dense olive groves.

As he neared the village the groves led into fields of chickpeas, "tubus". In one field a figure waved from a red tractor in the setting sunlight. It was Riyad, working on the family farm. Riyad jumped down and walked towards David finding him a branch of chickpeas. David copied Riyad's actions and began to shell and eat the fresh crop.

Resting on the rubble of one of the old stone walls dividing the fields, he drank from his battered plastic water bottle, the last, orange glow of twilight on the horizon.

Stars slowly began to appear, bright in the deep blue sky and as Riyad still drove the tractor around the ancient groves David drifted into sleep. He dreamt of stars filling an infinite universe and felt pure contentment, pure happiness, in this dimly lit world below. As he awoke there was no gap, no seam between this dream and his waking life. All was perfect like the stars that now stood out in the blackness above.

They drove back to the apartment on the tractor and there David opened a note that had been pushed through the door. He shook his head as he passed Riyad the note.

'Ohhh, Daveed, Abu Azmi has been here. You were supposed to go to his home tonight.'

'Oh no, I forgot. Is it too late to go now?'

'No, I will take you now, but we must go quickly'

Riyad led the way with a torch and they made the short walk back to a bungalow on the outskirts of the unlit village. They fumbled with its metal gate and then Riyad left David in the darkness to tentatively step down the long garden path, towards a lit porch.

Abu Azmi opened the door. He was dressed in a suit. David made profuse apologies and after the traditional greetings Abu Azmi welcomed David into a lounge. Abu Azmi turned down the volume of the English speaking Jordanian news on the television. An icon of Christ hung on the wall besides it.

They sat together on a low couch and David's late arrival was soon forgotten.

The rest of the house was in darkness, apart from the light that shone from behind bead curtains over an open kitchen doorway.

'Would you like a drink? Coffee?'

Keen to have neither the potent coffee, nor the syrupy tea he asked for 'Chai bidoon sucre, min fadlik,' 'Tea without sugar.'

'Juliana!' called Abu Azmi.

A lady with long dark hair, perhaps in her late 40's, drew back the kitchen curtains. She was slim with long black hair. 'Here is my daughter.' She smiled and said hello. She was tall and slender like a model, straight out of a magazine. The instructions were given, she smiled and withdrew.

David understood that single women were kept indoors, out of sight until they were married. They were protected and cherished, like jewels in a ring, like flowers in a vase. But they were also locked in, like prisoners.

Then, with a framed photograph in hand the elderly man showed his real pride. 'I am Abu Azmi, father of Azmi.' He pointed at his chest as he lent close to David. 'This is my son, Azmi.' His palm turned to show the framed picture. 'He works at the Strand Hotel, in Jerusalem, Quds. He brings people on tours around Palestine, to Nablus and Sabastiya.'

David nodded in approval. 'A good job.' David found a point of interest. 'Does he also take people to visit the Samaritan Temple in Nablus?'

'Yes, on Mount Gerizim. He brings the tourists in coaches to see sacrifices, every spring.'

Juliana returned, bringing tea with fresh mint. She sat quietly as they drank. Then the conversation turned back to a focus on their families, their mothers, fathers, brothers and sisters, what they did and how many children they had.

Silence finally descended and Abu Azmi offered to take David back to his apartment.

As they were about to leave Abu Azmi was quick to add. 'You were in the woods today.'

'Yes,' replied David.

'You must ask me first.'

'Don't worry, I'm safe, I have been walking in the hills in England many times.'

The mayor's face became hard. 'No. It is not permitted.'

David was beginning to feel hemmed in.

12. Return to Jerusalem

The weeks passed and finally they were ready to use the hand held pneumatic chisel. The red air-compressor outside, that fed the chisel, growled and hissed whilst inside the Iconostasis shook under a constant hum as the hand held chisel. Its blade, the size of a normal chisel, cut at high speed, cracking the concrete away, without using heavy force. But it was a delicate operation. Apply too much pressure and the stone would be damaged and the fragile Iconostasis shaken apart.

As they worked David learned that the concrete he was removing had been put on 30 years ago, by Abu Azmi, who was still unsure what the problem was. For him it was a job well done as the concrete clearly supported the flimsy iconostasis and protected the monuments.

Once the back of the Iconostasis was exposed they grouted the rubble coring and re-plastered over it. They re-pointed the joints and made mortar repairs to the damaged stonework, using mortar to match the original stone, mixing the white, lime putty with different sized sand.

All was going according to schedule, ready for the inspection by the Dutch government, all except the Throne. Its seat was still was missing.

Hanan was supposed to design this but hadn't come up with any drawings. Everyone was concerned and, remembering Rockschild's lack of faith in Hanan, David decided to find a design himself. He would go to the library of the Orthodox Patriarchate in Jerusalem. And, he was feeling claustrophobic so this gave him a good reason to leave the village.

-

The bus journey from Burqin was bumpy and winding. The old seats were hard leather and the windows were covered with dust. But on the bus there was space to relax and watch the scenery, space to get away, space to be alone.

The young ladies that boarded the bus caught his eye. They sat two rows in front, on the opposite side. He could see them clearly and here he was free from the constraints of the village, no one was watching him. God watched, but surely God was more sympathetic, surely he understood his frustrations? He meant well. Burying his head within his hands, he prayed that he might overcome his desires as the bus lurched around the corners. He stared at the worn vinyl floor. He'd had enough, he would pray later, just now he needed to look at them, to admire their beauty. But they didn't pay him any attention.

Outside Nablus, near to the tank base, the bus stopped. An Israeli soldier got on, carrying a rifle and barking orders in Arabic. All the men got off, but David remained.

The soldier shouted at him, so he pulled out a battered, burgundy, British passport. The soldier took it, looked, tutted and handed it back with disdain. The young ladies looked admiringly. Now they had noticed him.

The men returned to the bus and sat putting their papers away. The lady kept glancing at David. He began to smile and she smiled in return. A man flicked the back of David's head. They both turned away from each other.

On arrival in Ramallah, he headed to see Hanan, to ask, for a final time, for the design of the chair. As he walked along one of the back roads at the top of the town he heard music blaring from a shop selling brightly packaged cassette tapes bearing the naive faces of Palestinian stars. He was surprised, it was an American song that he recognised. R.E.M.'s "Losing my Religion."

Despite all the messages that he had left Hanan was out. So David turned from the grey, three-storey offices of the Ministry of Tourism & Antiquities and crossed the busy roads. He weaved between taxis, past the central roundabout in Ramallah, and caught a "Service" to Jerusalem.

-

That evening, in his room at the British School of Archaeology, he shaved his beard then headed to the New City.

It was Saturday, the Sabbath was ending and people were going out to enjoy themselves in the restaurants and cafes. Everyone seemed to be dressed in black. David wore it too as he wandered the busy streets, past the Jewish bakeries and shops selling clothes and jewellery. These traditional European shops were mixed in with American stores, modern art galleries, kosher burger bars and kosher ice cream parlours.

Just down from the central square tanned girls were hanging out on the street, in short skirts and revealing tops, beneath a large London Transport symbol, it was "The Underground" nightclub. David entered and headed towards a muffled wall of noise. Double doors opened onto a mass of people dancing under flashing lights and the heavy throb of disco music.

The music blared out as soldiers danced with rifles slung over their shoulders. David tried to catch the eye of the girls but they just turned their heads away.

He bought an orange juice from the bar and jostled to position himself within sight of a pretty girl. His attention was obvious, but there was no interest, she looked at him with disdain, crossed their legs and focussed her attention across the room. He followed her line of sight to a tall, well-built, young man with slicked back hair and a gold chain over his tight t-shirt. David felt crushed. The young man noticed him looking. David wondered if women weren't interested then maybe men were.

He continued to look and the man now pretended not to notice, but couldn't help breaking into a self-satisfied smile, pleased at the attention, interpreting it as admiration. The girl cast a furious glance at them both.

David felt ashamed that he'd created a triangle of desire, for no other reason than to soothe his vanity. He retreated to a corner where a pretty girl leaned against the wall, her drunken friend behind her. He couldn't believe it, but it seemed that she wanted to talk to him. He turned and mustered the courage to speak. He didn't know what to say so the conversation was short.

'Hi. I'm David.'

'I'm Ruth.'

'What do you do?'

'I'm a business student at the Hebrew University. What do you do?'

He couldn't betray himself. 'I'm an archaeologist, working with the Palestinian Department of Antiquities.'

She turned away in disgust, blanking him. Her friend was more open but David didn't find her attractive. 'Do you want to go into the bushes outside with me?' she asked. She was drunk and at first he didn't understand what she was offering. She kept repeating it and he kept ignoring her. Finally she turned to a European man, wearing a pony tail, who stood near them with a bottle in hand. She made the same offer to him. He smiled and they left together.

When David built up the courage to talk with another girl he was surprised as she began to smile at him. He told her that he worked in archaeology and she was interested, encouraging him to tell her more until a tall Israeli sat down next to them. The man let out a snort of disdain at David's words, trying to grab the girl's attention. David didn't know how to fight it, but his conversation was slowly stolen.

Here was the paradise of girls that he desired but he could not compete with the men who knew how to speak with them. He had no small talk. His brain was paralysed with a mixture of lust and religious fervour. He wanted to stay, just in case he met someone, but soon realised it was futile. He gave up and left.

-

The next morning David made his way, up stairs near to the Church of the Holy Sepulchre and through a series of passages, to the offices of the Orthodox Patriarchate of Jerusalem. It was busy with bearded priests wearing black, cylindrical hats and serious expressions. A young priest took him to a narrow, wood panelled library filled with tightly packed shelves. In a small reading area a priest sat in thick glasses.

'Hello, I'm David Wolfe.'

'I am Father Theophilus. How can I help?'

'I'm working for the Palestinian Department of Antiquities at the Church of Saint George, in Burqin. We are looking for the original design of the Bishop's Throne there.'

'I know the church at Burqin but I am afraid I cannot help. We have no records of its history.'

'Nothing at all?'

'No, we have records on Jenin, but there is very little on Burqin.'

'What about general documentation about Bishops' Thrones?'

'We have very little about any of the relics in our churches. You should try the Palestinian Department of Antiquities.'

'I already have. Maybe you know of other Thrones with serpent arms? Maybe there are some in Jerusalem?'

'I am sorry, I do not know any like this.'

David's curiosity was deep. 'What about the serpent arms on the Throne? Could you explain about them?'

'I do not know. The only thing similar is our Pateritsa, the Bishop's Pastoral Staff. It has two serpents turned to face the guiding cross of Christ, the shepherd.'

'But isn't the serpent a symbol of evil?'

'Yes, in general. The serpent tempted Eve to eat the apple so God cursed it to slither on its belly and to bite the heel of man.'

'So why have it on the staff?'

The priest's brow furrowed. The question seemed petty. 'It goes back to when God told Moses to make a staff with a bronze serpent on it. This was to protect the Israelites from being bitten by the serpents in the wilderness. But King Hezekiah destroyed the staff in the 8th century B.C.E. after the Israelites began to burning incense to it when they began to worship Baal.'

Then, before David could ask another question, the priest held up his hand. 'I'm sorry but I'm a busy man.' He stood and offered his hand to David. 'It has been good to hear of the work you are doing in Burqin. I wish you the best with your work.'

-

Riyad stopped speaking with Abu Walid as David entered the courtyard. 'Oh David, how are you? Your beard is gone.' Riyad smiled in his sun glasses. 'You look better without it.'

'Hanan was not there, so I went to the Patriarchate library in Jerusalem, but they had no information.'

'We know you David. You go back to Jerusalem to...,' he rubbed his left index finger with his right index and middle finger then laughed, '...illab bikalak. To play with your uncle.'

David spoke over the laughter. 'No, I visited a number of Orthodox churches to look at the seats so I could come up with a design. I've got the drawings, all I need is to get the wood to carve it.'

Riyad put his arm around David's shoulder. 'That will be no problem. We have the wood in the village.'

They talked as they headed out of the churchyard, but Abu Walid turned and stood with his back to them. He was facing the rock wall just to the side of the church. 'Ohh, Abu Walid!' called Riyad.

David didn't know what to say when he realised Abu Walid was urinating. Then before he could speak Riyad patted his back. 'Come. We go to my mother's for tea.'

They left the sacrilege behind and climbed onto Riyad's tractor. Riyad turned his baseball cap around and they lurched forwards.

David gripped the metal seat as Riyad drove the tractor up the alleys then around the village. Riyad was celebrating the return of his friend. It sped around the tracks and the villagers waved. They liked him. They knew that the regeneration of the church would bring tourists and that would mean jobs.

From his vantage point David admired the village with its half ruined Ottoman houses on street corners, next to concrete homes. The tractor threw up dust as it passed the arched entrance to the mosque, its tall minaret dominating the village. Five times a day the calls to prayer filled the air, announcing over the birds of the morning, the bustle of noon and the dusk at the end of the day. 'Allah Akbar' - 'Allah is Most Great.' But for now the air was filled with the laughs of Riyad and the sounds of his tractor.

They turned one of the many rubble strewn corners and stopped, back in the town square, under the shadow of the minaret.

Men stood outside the shops, around the local Imam, who sat with his prayer beads. A group of young boys called out greetings whilst they jostled each other. 'Daviid, Daviid. Hello, hello.'

The Imam shouted towards them and Riyad translated the words. 'He says he has been keeping a close watch on you and asks if you are now a Muslim.'

David shook his head.

The Imam smiled and shouted again. 'So he says that he is sorry for you, as you will go to Hell.'

The Imam continued to smile so David returned a grin then waved to the boys as the tractor swung around in the square.

From his high seat he noticed a young woman behind a barred window of a simple whitewashed house. It looked like a prison and he became eerily aware of how few women were out in the village and how those that were out all wore scarves. The woman disappeared from view and they passed Abu Azmi's before free-wheeling down the main road, out of the village. It was like a big dipper ride as they sped into the drop, past the turn to Jenin, then rolled up the other side. The momentum took them to the top of the rise and a burst of the tractor's engine pushed them onto the final straight. They slowed shortly after as the road worsened.

Turning right into an orchard of perfectly spaced olive trees, they drove up a deeply channelled track. They began to bump, roll and lurch along a tunnel of branches that spread over them. Finally they climbed from the tractor and headed through the grove, in the midst of which was the farmhouse.

Children rushed out to say hello and an elderly lady smiled demurely, bowing her head.

'This is my mother,' said Riyad.

Her face was cracked with the lines of the sun and her body was bent from working in the fields. It looked like she was once beautiful but was changed by the premature ageing of childbearing and working in the fields. It occurred to all the ladies in the village, generation after generation.

Riyad sat on the veranda and rocked back and forth, his arms behind his head. He was pleased with himself as his mother served them tea.

Riyad's nephews were busy around them, chasing each other and play fighting. They ranged from five years old to the teenagers that sat with them. They had little English but the eldest suddenly called David's name. David turned to face him, only to see the young man pointing a pistol at his head.

Everyone went quiet.

David challenged him with a stare in the eye that said 'do it then!' The boy lifted the pistol and smiled. Riyad pushed him and slapped the back of his head, 'La, la,' sending him back into the house, embarrassed.

A silence fell and David felt an attack of paranoia. The cup he held, the ground he stared at, the people around him. All grew close, stifling, oppressive. No one knew he was here, in the middle of the West Bank, on a farm. He was exposed, vulnerable. He wondered about what he'd drunk. Had he been drugged?

Riyad smiled and lightened the tone. 'Daviiid, Abu Azmi is interested for his daughter to marry you. You are interested?'

David began to return to normal. He hadn't realised that Abu Azmi had been planning this, but it was probably true. There were not many Christians in the village and it would be a source of shame for Abu Azmi if his daughter married a Muslim.

'No, I'm not looking for anyone.' David bit his lip. If she had been younger then maybe he would have been interested.

'Ohh, Daviiid,' Riyad lightly punched his arm, 'are you sure?'

'Yes, I'm sure. But what about you? What do you do? Do you go to the disco in Ramallah?'

'Ha, the Ramallah disco is for married couples only. But I will marry one day, In Shallah.'

The conversation now became polite, but stilted. David pitied Riyad, who needed to make money in order to be able to marry. But with so few opportunities for him to work in the West Bank he would probably end up marrying a cousin. However David pitied himself more. He could not find anyone even when he was working. And at least Riyad could have a suitable marriage arranged for him.

Riyad's mother brought out a roast chicken, flanked by four roast sparrows and surrounded with rice mixed with nuts and sultanas. With his head bowed David tried to explain he was vegetarian, that he didn't eat meat.

He just ate the rice and they became quiet as they shared their evening meal. They left soon after eating.

-

Weeks later he neared the church, late from oversleeping after a restless night. Riyad squinted without his sunglasses. 'Hanan was here very early this morning. He wanted to make sure everything was ready for tomorrow's visit by the Dutch Government. He did not want to see you. He is very angry that you have made the chair. He says it could have been done in Ramallah.'

'He wouldn't have finished it in time.'

'I know, and it's like he's forgotten that we need at least one place for the Dutch to see good practice.'

'Did you show him the cracks in the ceiling plastering?'

'Yes, he said they would be filled on the next coat.'

David shook his head and stepped into the church.

Inside was Abu Azmi, Abu Walid and a group of villagers. They were here to watch the last part of the works being completed.

The chair was crafted to David's designs. It was a hinged seat with two gothic half arches as its rear legs. They fit neatly into the back of the Throne but David needed to do the final job. He needed to hammer two wooden plugs, to join the chair with the original holes in the front sides of the Throne. This would support the seat, replacing the need for front legs.

David was nervous. One side of the Throne was built against the springer of a Crusader arch, but if the plug missed the hole on the other, unsupported, side, then it would knock the arm away, and the front Throne would collapse.

The plug in the wall side took two hits until it fit in place. The Serpent on the arm seemed to mock that if the same happened on the other side then it would end in disaster.

Riyad propped against the side of the Serpent arm.

David stared at the open, reptilian mouth. It grinned at him.

He lined up the plug, then gave a mighty blow.

The plug fit with a dull thud.

Everyone clapped then shook David's hand. The Serpent Throne fit together perfectly. An order had been re-established. This was the culmination of his craftsman's training. He had been anointed and sanctified as a mason, an artist for God.

-

When everyone left for the evening and David stayed behind and sat in the Throne. The texture of its carved stone arms felt like a serpent's skin. His mind began to wander as he admired the space, piecing together the church's history.

In the ancient Canaanite village of Jenin they worshipped the bull God Baal. Later, when Jenin was a Roman city Mithras would have been worshipped in a Mithraeum, a Temple to Mithras. These Temples contained a small cave with a sanctuary and altar. In fact, their design was the same as that of this church.

He imagined that this site was a Mithraeum. Its ceiling decorated with a planetarium of constellations and its stone framed painting, of Saint George killing the dragon, replaced with an image of Mithras killing the primeval bull.

The rites of the followers of Mithras took place in such a cave and believers would eat the body of a sacrificed bull and would drink its blood as they ascended, like the Freemasons, through degrees of initiation, to Gnosis, the highest knowledge.

The air began to grow cooler and David rose from the Throne. He gazed at the painting of Saint George, the Roman soldier who followed Mithras before converting to Christianity. He was the perfect Christian soldier, a role model to gain Roman converts, and his slaying the Dragon, the Serpent, replaced the myth of Mithras slaying the Bull. Saint George became the example for Holy Christian warriors to follow, including the Knights Templar who bore his red cross upon their vestments.

It seemed so plausible. This had been a Mithraeum and was turned into a church, by Queen Helena, when the Holy Roman Empire was destroying all traces of Mithras.

David picked up his mallet and chisels, turned off the lights and closed the metal door for a final time.

13. Golden Gate

David left early the next morning, he would miss the inspection of the work, but it would let full credit go to the Palestinians. He took a bus from the village square, to the bus station in Jenin this time to take a "service."

To the side of the rows of buses was the taxi area. A small group had gathered beside an open shop. In front of them was an ochre coloured, Mercedes taxi. An elderly, overweight, grey jacketed, man looked up from drinking his shai. He stubbed out his heavy smelling cigarette and rose from the battered, leather, driver's seat.

The white Kafir fell in front of his face as he rounded up David's travelling companions. 'Ramallah,' he drawled. David threw his rucksack into the boot whilst a plump man, with moustache and glasses, sat in the front seat, and two elderly ladies, in traditional dress sat in the rear.

They headed out of the town, along the winding roads and onto the plains.

The wide taxi was luxurious when you sat alone, but not when cramped, pushed against the side door, by the spread of two large ladies. David did not enjoy holding onto the door handles, so that he didn't have to press against their sweating thighs as they turned right hand corners. But he preferred this to the left hand corners when they leaned against him.

The plains became hills that rose around them and the ladies began to sleep along with the front passenger.

They passed a donkey pulling a cart and David's mind turned to the Arab caravan traders who followed ancient routes, using camels to carry the arts of the nations.

The driver interrupted his thoughts. 'So where are you from?'

'Britain.'

'Ah, you are English? A Christian?'

'Kind of, but I believe in One God.'

The driver spoke his mind. 'For the sake of peace, In Shallah, we should try and live together. But people should know that the Qur'an was a revelation to Muhammed, from God, through the Angel Gabriel, and there is no poetry more beautiful. As the Qur'an says: "And if you are in doubt about what We have revealed to Our worshiper (Muhammed Peace Be Upon Him), then produce a chapter like it."'

There was no room to argue. David just listened.

'Mecca was the site of the Kaaba, where Abraham built a shrine to Allah, but the unbelievers had set up idols of Baal around it. Muhammed preached there for ten years but was persecuted for telling the truth, so he left for Medinah, in 622 C.E., then returned to conquer Mecca with an army of believers, in 630 C.E., smashing the idols and false gods of the unbelievers.'

92

There was silence until the parts   clicked together and David began to think out loud. 'Maybe the development of the religions of Abraham is like our own development. We start off with laws for just ourselves or our own tribe, like Judaism. Then we fight other people, other tribes, and need forgiveness to create peace, like Christianity. Finally when there is peace, we work out new laws for all people, like Islam.'

The driver was silent, his face blank to David's words, concentrating on the road. But when the "Service" taxi stopped at a junction the driver turned around.

'What do you know about Islam?' His index finger jabbed close to David's chest. 'What have you ever done to help the Palestinian people?'

David backed away in his seat. 'Well your chief archaeologist said I was the first person from Britain to help.' It was as if he had replied in another language. The others began to wake so the driver snorted and the journey continued in silence.

The Ramallah checkpoint was closed so they turned left, heading towards parched mountains that reached up, through a peach-red haze, into a deep blue sky. Their solidity constantly eroded by sand in the wind. Beyond these were the Jordan valley and the deserts of Jericho.

The sun was setting and the moon was rising. No poetry could capture the marvellous scene. Two perfect spheres flanked the mountains. Both were the same size, the same brightness. One glowed like dying embers, the other shone, a chill white. They were two gods greeting each other, or circling each other, ready for battle, above a "Holy" Land full of conflict.

David peered through the window. The darkening landscape was barren and primal, the sky was endless and clear.

His quest for truth had failed. He was back to a sense of nothingness.

He was tired of trying to understand why God, the architect of life, had created the world from this nothingness. But then he let his imagination go free, supposing that God's purpose was to be creative. And that God had made Himself and all His prophets to be artists.

He played with the idle speculation, Mohammed was a poet, Jesus was a carpenter and Moses was an architect, a Master Mason who had carved the 10 commandments into stone.

David imagined Moses climbing Mount Sinai, praying for God to guide him as he carried mallet and chisel, determined to set new laws in stone. His skilled hands were guided by the fire of God as he cut the words with precision. The chisel was a tool in Moses' hand, and Moses was a tool in the hand of God. He blew the dust away from the stone with the breath of God and when he stood back to read God's words he dropped his tools. Before him was the perfect work of art.

But when Moses came down from Mount Sinai, after 40 days and nights, he saw the people of Israel dancing around a Golden Calf, making offerings to the bull God, worshipping it. He threw down the tablets in disgust, breaking them upon the ground, then destroyed the Calf.

But he had to return to Mount Sinai, to find his mallet and chisel, to cut new tablets, the Laws that would be carried within the Ark of the Covenant.

On this long journey to Jerusalem David felt no sense of mastery. He was not like Moses. He had been denied access to the truth because he had followed lust, the bull God of fertility, more than God.

With his head against the window he began to pray. 'Oh Almighty God. I am a fool, I have sinned. In your justice punish me, according to your will, but I also beg you, in your mercy, please help me. Please remove the Devil from me. I am so sorry that I don't live up to your will. I want to change. I want to start again. I beg you, please help me to change. Thank you Lord God. Amen.'

As the taxi pulled into East Jerusalem his attention changed as he wiped the steamed up window to get a clearer look at two young ladies walking under orange street lights.

-

David decided to stay in Jerusalem, until 31st December, 1999.

On that night, Millennium Eve, he stood, at 11.30pm, facing the two floodlit arches of the Golden Gate, in front of the Eastern Wall of Jerusalem. This Beautiful Gate, through which Ezekiel prophesied that the Jewish Messiah would enter the city, was now sealed up and covered in graffiti. In front of it was a tomb, surrounded with a metal railing, and in front of the whole wall was a graveyard.

David was not just here to celebrate. He was on a pilgrimage to capture any spiritual change at the turn of the Millennium. He had a canvas rolled under his arm and a backpack full of paints. He was ready to receive, onto canvas, any inspirations, in the same way that Pollock and Rothko made their abstract expressionist paintings.

In different time zones around the world millions were being spent on firework spectacles created to dazzle and amaze. But away from the televisions, away from the bars and hotels, in the country of the man whose birth date had set the western calendar, there was no sense of occasion.

Here, in the Holy city of Jerusalem, Christians now made up just 2% of the population and the followers of other religions had different calendars, 2000 was 5760 for Jews and 1421 for Muslims.

The date was even contested by Christian scholars who believed that Jesus Christ was born in 3 or 4 B.C.E. and that the Roman calendar started at year 1 C.E. and not year 0 C.E. But the exact date did not matter, the dawning of the new millennia was still popularly held to be the Millennial anniversary of Christ's birth.

David waited in the cold, dark and strangely quiet air. His ears winced at the undulating wail of a police car, like a banshee shrieking in the night. Only four other people stood on the limestone path around the walls; a thin, young man, a middle-aged man with his young daughter and a small lady with dark hair.

The man spoke to his daughter 'You see the constellation Orion, up there?' he pointed between the clouds. '2000 will coincide with the highest point of its upward cycle...'

From behind her glasses and thick, fur-rimmed coat the small lady interrupted David as he listened in. 'You know, the Muslims sealed up the Gate in the 7th century to prevent the Jewish Messiah from entering. They believed that the Messiah would be from the Priestly Cohen, family so they also built a cemetery in front of the Gate, because Cohens are forbidden to enter cemeteries.' David nodded with interest and the lady held up a gloved finger. 'However the Messiah will be descended from the family of King David instead, so he'll be able to enter anyway.'

Placing his canvas under his arm, he rubbed his hands, blowing into them. 'Did you know this is being web-cast around the world by Messiah Cam?'

'You're kidding.' The lady's hand went onto his arm, her mouth wide open. 'Where's the camera?'

'It must be somewhere over there, across the Kidron Valley,' he gestured with his head, 'I had a look on the internet this afternoon.'

High up the side of the Kidron Valley, across from them was the large Jewish cemetery on the Mount of Olives, which Zechariah stated will be the site of the Resurrection of the dead into an earthly paradise, a "New Jerusalem," on the Day of Judgement. But this Jewish doctrine was rejected by Christians and replaced with a belief in Heaven, which came from the Greek, belief in the Elysian Fields.

The lady composed herself, 'but we don't need pictures of the Holy Spirit to know that He will be with us tonight.'

'I agree, but I'm hoping to capture the movement of the Spirit on canvas.'

She held him in an uncomprehending gaze. 'So you are an artist,' her eyebrow raised and she tilted her head, 'what kind of work do you do?'

'Mmm, all kinds of work, but in different art styles relate to different religious faiths.'

She shook her head and frowned, 'But there's only one true faith. All the others are false religions. Only Jesus Christ is Lord.' She turned and walked a short distance up the path, as if David might have a contagious disease.

He blew his hands a final time then carried the canvas up the earth banking and sat in front of the iron fenced tomb, directly in line with the Gate. In devotion he unrolled the canvas and spread it onto the rocky earth. He took paints, brushes and water from his backpack, arranged them neatly, then kneeled to pray.

He was readying himself to receive a vision of the Divine. He was waiting for the Messiah to be shown on canvas, at the Holiest site, at the Holiest time.

He could hear people arrive down at the main path. He concentrated and finally he was deep in prayer.

Just before midnight he stirred in the cold air, opening his eyes, in the glow of orange floodlights. His mind, like the canvas, was blank. He was ready to begin painting. There was no intention, no imagination, only reception of the Spirit within him, only guidance by its movement.

Lines, shapes, forms and colours gravitated together, coalescing into a vortex. With clarity he felt compelled to paint precise angles and arcs in the middle of the canvas. He felt an urge to express an explosive energy, almost to punch a hole through the fabric.

The vision grew clearer. A maelstrom of swirls was spinning before his eyes. Its four arms formed from iridescent rainbows, radiating from a central point. His heart raced and it all made sense. All had merged together. It was a Rainbow Swastika, a cosmic energy, splaying and exploding across his inner space.

'Lo, Lo!' A voice called down from above the Gate. David looked up, mouth agape. An Israeli soldier was waving a machine gun at him.

Half stunned, he shouted back, 'Ani lo madaber Evirt! I don't speak Hebrew!' He needed to paint but it was clear that he had to move.

He scrambled his paints together and gently rolled up the canvas before returning to the path. Israeli police arrived from the darkness, pushing between the small crowd of pilgrims, camera men and reporters that had gathered.

An officer in a navy blue bomber jacket, with fluorescent white bands across the chest, barked in English, 'Everyone, move!' He stood before David, staring at him, pointing at the canvas. 'What is this?'

'I was about to do a painting for the new Millennium'.

'Give it to me!' The officer grabbed it then shouted to the crowd. 'Move away!'

David took out his camera and shot some photographs as the crowd began to filter north, up the path, back to St. Stephen's Gate, the Lion's Gate. The flash was lost in amongst the flashes of the reporters.

The police officer remained and unrolled the canvas in front of his fellow officers. They looked at both sides. It was blank. The officer rolled it up, gripping it tightly, crushing it.

'What's in there?'

David held open his back pack and the officer glanced inside then checked David's passport against his list of suspected religious zealots and terrorists.

As they began walking away, the thin, young man now moved aside from the crowd and began to rapidly shout his rehearsed lines. 'The Anti-Christ will show himself as the beast. "His image will be set in the temple and he will demand worship as God. He will cause all, both small and great, both rich and poor, both free and slave, to be marked on the right hand or the forehead, so that no one can buy or sell unless he has the mark, that is, the name of the beast or the number of its name.'

The police response was also rehearsed. They moved quickly towards him.

'This calls for wisdom: let him who has understanding reckon the number of the beast, for it is a human number, its number is six hundred and sixty six." The Anti-Christ will appear at the Battle of Armageddon against the forces of Jesus Christ. Then the world will be destroyed in a holocaust. But if we repent now we can be spared.'

They grabbed him and he fell silent as they marched him up the path, to the Lion's Gate. There they bundled him into a small police vehicle that looked like a golf cart. He sat, wild eyed, in the front seat, as he was driven away, ignominiously.

The attention had shifted so David asked for his canvas back.

The officer returned it. David was obviously not a terrorist threat. They had done their work. They had made an arrest, and had kept the public safe from dangerous fanatics.

As David walked back along streets of East Jerusalem. A few fireworks cracked and spat, breaking the silence of the heavens. Their coloured lights exploded into view, then faded across the starlit sky. He had no need to paint his vision. It was etched into his memory.

14. Church Friends

David felt uncomfortable as Sebastian and Paul embraced him back in London. Uncomfortable because they had arranged to go out in Soho, not to celebrate his return, just to go there because Sebastian had something to tell them.

Their number 73 bus stopped on Charing Cross Road. They got off and headed down Old Compton Street. David noticed a nightclub called "Bar Salsa." He'd rather go somewhere like that but followed his friends.

Sebastian's thinning black hair, was slicked back and cropped closely at the sides. He looked like he was living in the 1920's dressed in a white jacket. Paul had tidied up his beard but still wore a fraying grey jumper. David was in his standard black.

They walked up a narrow side alley where shops sold red and black lingerie and studded leather suits. As David explored Sebastian called him back to a small door in an old building. Above it was a pink neon sign, "Pink Flamingo," and a rainbow flag hanging from the wall.

'What's the rainbow flag for?' asked David.

As they entered Sebastian explained. 'It's the flag of gay pride, all the different colours in unity.'

They walked downstairs, past rows of neon flamingos and Barbie dolls, into the busy club, where they ordered drinks. Sebastian had a double gin and tonic, Paul had a lager, David had an orange juice. They were lucky, a group left to go into the main night club, so they took the cream leather couches, under the green lights.

Paul looked out of place and David sat on the edge of his seat, ill at ease as he played with his glass on the Perspex table. Sebastian leaned back into the white leather, pleased, as the Wizard of Oz projected onto the white walls behind him.

David shouted above the disco beats. 'Visiting the places of the Bible, made them come to life.'

Paul turned to David. 'It doesn't matter where you go. You only get salvation if you accept Jesus Christ.'

'Yes but everyone there was just as passionate about their religion as you. But the nearest to God were those who wanted to live in peace with their neighbours. We can learn from all religions.'

Paul frowned. 'Sounds like the Jews and Muslims put you under spiritual siege. They are on the Devil's side. Only Jesus Christ can save you and there's no point pretending to people that they are alright when they aren't.'

It was clear that they didn't want to know about his viewpoints or his experiences. But he was tired of being on the receiving end of their way of thinking. He wanted them to understand what it was like. 'No, you're the ones under spiritual siege from the Devil. It's your kind of Christianity that's wrong.'

Paul held back his anger. 'The problem is that you're ready to believe anything but the truth. You're taking bits of false religions and making them into one big, new religion. But it's all just full of lies.'

'I love it here,' said Sebastian putting his arm around Paul, diffusing the tension, 'it's a safe place. You can feel free. People can just relax and be themselves.'

David stopped arguing. He just wanted their friendship.

'You've missed so many really interesting things since you've been away,' said Sebastian. 'Our church has under-gone a lot of changes.'

'What, you've renovated the room above the post office?'

Paul's ears twitched as he concentrated hard. 'A church is the people, not the building. You seem to be even more confused than before you went away.' Hands shaking, Paul opened his tin, and got out his tobacco and rolling papers.

'The pastor called us to his house,' said Sebastian, 'and started blaming us for what was wrong with the church. But he was just jealous that I was too popular, that I was doing naturally what he and his team of elders should have been doing.'

Sebastian looked, lovingly at Paul, smiled and squeezed his arm. 'But our friendship has become stronger.'

'Joint?' suggested Paul in response.

Sebastian rolled back onto the couch as he laughed. 'You can't do that in here Paul.'

But he still finished rolling the joint and lit it. Drawing deep he held the smoke within his lungs.

'Go on David, have a bit,' said Paul as he blew out across the table.

'No thanks.' David held his breath as the smoke dissipated. He was glad to be back with his friends, but didn't like their new faiths, Sebastian's born-again homosexuality and Paul's Evangelical dope smoking. But he loved them, and accepted them, and didn't want to lose their friendship.

The sides of Sebastian's mouth rose, along with his eyebrows. 'You said on the bus that you were given a swastika from God?'

'Yes. It was revealed to me at the Golden Gate, Jerusalem, on Millennium Eve. It's a Jewish swastika.'

'Jewish?' asked Paul as he held the smoke whilst looking at Sebastian, his smirking. 'How do you work that one out?' He exhaled.

'The swastika is a universal religious symbol and there are even swastikas in early synagogues.'

Paul laughed. 'That's typical of you, a Jew promoting a swastika.'

'It's a peace symbol for the new age, for the 21st century and in a rainbow form it's a sign that the Holocaust on the Jews won't happen again. Just like when God gave Noah the rainbow as a sign that the Flood wouldn't happen again.'

Paul shook his head 'Well I wouldn't be so sure about that. I wouldn't want to be a Jew in these times. Things are going to get a lot worse.'

David didn't understand what Paul meant. Music played over the awkward silence.

David stared into his orange juice. He felt very distant as he sipped the acid sweetness. Then he turned to Sebastian. 'So what did you want to tell us?'

Sebastian drank. There was a long pause. 'Kirsten wants a divorce.'

David wasn't surprised. Sebastian never seemed to be in love with her and they hadn't shared a bed for years. His late night drinking, frequenting of gay clubs and entertaining of "toy-boys" had all increased. But Sebastian was still devastated. There was a real shock, and it was not just to his pride.

'It's a really bad thing,' said Paul, 'Kirsten is just getting more and more screwed up. The scriptures say that she should follow the lead of the head of the household.'

'Yes, yes,' Sebastian nodded with closed his eyes, 'scripturally.' He sank another gin and tonic. 'The irony is that she was the one who wanted to get married in the first place. I was happy with an open relationship but she wanted more. I only married for our child. And now she's the one who's moved out to live with some boring bloke.'

'I'm sorry to hear it,' said David as he listened without judgment. He wanted to reassure Sebastian but didn't know what to say.

'Kirsten left me but then had the cheek to be annoyed with me for getting upset. Women are far more manipulative and cruel than men. I tell you, I can't stand them any more. It's far easier being a puff.' He paused as Paul stroked his back and Sebastian paused with admiration clearly in his eyes. 'Isn't Paul good-looking? He could make a fortune being a model.'

David didn't agree. He just sipped his orange juice. The conversation lulled so he tried to find something to say. 'I didn't meet anyone in the Holy Land.'

Sebastian drew on the joint as he stared back blankly. 'Stop being obsessed with trying to find a woman. Don't trust them. They just want more and more. It never ends. They're crap. But you respect them too much. They need you to dominate them. If you idolise them then they destroy you then despise you for being weak. Take a puff pill, it's much easier. I tell you, I'll never let anything like that happen again.' Sebastian's eyes were now glowering. 'Women are jealous of men because men are close to God. That's why they need their men to be like Gods over them.' He stubbed the joint in the ashtray and lit a cigarette. 'Come on, let's dance.'

Intoxicated, Sebastian demanded that they followed. He led them to the main dance area, onto the floor, full of men, shouting and laughing. David's cries of 'It's too loud!' were drowned out by the thumping disco beats. David had missed his friends, he was here to   be with them. And whilst there was no possibility for conversation, as they moved into the throng, he still felt contented.

But as they danced they drifted apart and when he turned to see Sebastian and Paul leave the floor, embracing, he felt abandoned. He fought it and forced himself to let go of his sadness, forced himself to become absorbed into the beats. Soon he lost sense of anything but the music. His body moved with the rhythms, sensual and complete. But when he stopped dancing he remembered his emptiness.

The next track started and he began turning and moving again. He could see the flashing lights even behind his closed eyes. He could still feel the bodies moving, in a warm sea round him. Opening his eyes he found himself surrounded by body builders, shaven and stripped to the waist. They all looked the same, all with the same chiselled features. They jumped in the air, arms reaching up, crying in unison. 'Freeee!' The breeze from their movements cooled David from the glow of their sweating bodies.

He didn't belong with them, he didn't belong here, he retreated to sit down. Next to him was a small group of thin young men in tight t-shirts. They were with girls who called themselves "fag hags," female friends coming for a safe-night-out. David imagined that he could talk to one of the girls, but before he could muster up the confidence Sebastian came over, with a young, blond haired man, and shouted in David's ear. 'This is John. We're just going upstairs. I'll catch you later.'

There were no girls around to remind David of his lack of love but he didn't want to be on his own. He searched for Paul and eventually found him by the bar. 'Sebastian's gone with some boy.'

'Aha,' replied Paul, 'I'll just go and find him.' He climbed from his stool and disappeared into the crowd. David ordered a drink. Then, after sitting alone for an hour, he left.

15. Exhibition

Blessed molten bronze poured from the crucible into the mould buried in the ground. Then the cooled metal was dug from the earth. Its encasing ceramic shell was cracked by the strike of the heavy hammer and the treasures of its shape slowly revealed.

A forehead, a nose, a cheekbone, a mouth and finally the eyes came into view. The head of the bearded Cherub stared out, as if awakened to return to dutiful guard over the Ark of the Covenant.

David had cast his Zoroastrian Icarus sculpture in parts, then welded the segments together. Now it stood, two metres tall, on guard at the oak and glass entrance doors to the Quaker Gallery.

Its bronze form shone and glowed. Its outstretched wings pointing the direction, for all who entered David's exhibition, past his sculptures on plinths and towards the far end of the gallery.

There an enormous photographic triptych. A print of the Golden Gate filled the wall. Flanking it were giant photographs of the police and crowd at the Golden Gate. But hanging in front of these was the center-piece of his exhibition. A painting covered with a veil. Sun from the skylight shone down on it.

David greeted the visitors and began an explanation of his work. 'This exhibition is a map of how different religions express themselves in art. And the final work is an expression of modern religious art.' There was a buzz of excitement and expectation from the crowd.

'The sculptures on the left show the mystical traditions, the dancing Shiva of the Hindus and a seated Buddha, using human forms to express their abstract spirituality. Contrasting these are the sculptures on the right which show the Monotheistic faiths. The Jewish geometrical carvings to celebrate the Divine and my designs around the names of "Allah" come from traditions that hold it is idolatrous to use icons and human forms to depict the fatherly figure of God.'

It was hard for the crowd to see the works in the busy space.

'Further into the exhibition, is my bust of Apollo, celebrating the beauty, youth and power of mankind. It is followed by my carving of Christianity, a religion that combined the Jewish God with the Gods of the Holy Roman Empire, creating Orthodox icons and Catholic idols of the human form.'

David now moved to the end of the gallery, amongst the photographs of police and the Golden Gate.

'But with the invention of the printing press the Bible was widely translated and distributed. As a result people began to make their own Protestant Christian interpretations of the scriptures. And with more books printed people grew further away from the traditional belief in God and this was the beginning of Modernism, with its science, rationality and abstract spirituality. And here, at the Golden Gate, that I made an experiment using Rothko and Pollock's method of Abstract Expressionism to see if anything would be revealed at the turn of the Millennium. And this is what I was given, a symbol of perfect spirituality, the swirling energies behind all religions channelled into one clear, perfect geometric form. The ultimate expression of Modernity.'

David raised his arm, ready to remove the veil from the painting. 'The Zoroastrian Icarus guards the truth which only the God of Monotheism can reveal. I submitted myself to Him at the Golden Gate, Jerusalem, on the Millennium Eve. These photographs show how God did not want an image of Him to be made. But at the same time He revealed a symbol of His Divine energy to me. That symbol is …' he pulled the veil and it came off beautifully, to reveal, precisely painted '…the Rainbow Swastika.'

As the crowd clapped David realised the hollowness his words. His ideas were brilliant, but they had no soul, they had no feeling.

As the crowd mingled, inspecting the artworks, Sebastian walked in, confidently. He was late but despite his confidence he was twitching in his blue jacket. His sun glasses crowned his head and his ruddy, bristled face was slightly swollen. He looked at the bronze, stroking it, tapping it to hear its ring. 'It's amazing!'

He hugged David.

'Oh, Paul's just round the corner. He says he can't come in. He thinks that your work is technically brilliant but he just finds galleries a bit nauseating.'

David knew how much Paul hated the air of pretentious arrogance that he found in galleries. But he struggled to understand that Paul's position was nothing personal.

Sebastian looked around. 'So this is your exhibition.' He stood, hands on his hips.

David noticed a watery sheen over his eyes. 'Yes, and there's the Rainbow Swastika I was talking about.'

Sebastian pretended to hide his amusement, preferring to stroke the head of Apollo. 'So have you had much interest?' David could now smell the pungent odour of stale alcohol.

'There were some reporters from the art press, but that was it.'

'Can I be honest with you?' He didn't wait for David to nod. 'Your sculptures are the only great pieces of art here, but they're not in fashion. Like I've said before, you have to change your work. It's too traditional. You need controversy, but none of that swastika stuff, you'll offend too many collectors. What they want is sex, violence and money. That's what they're interested in.'

'I'm not sure. My art's more a quest, a vocation.'

Sebastian's eyes were wide as he looked at David. 'You have to decide if you're doing religion or art. If you want interest in your work then you have to stop trying to ram religion down people's throats, it just gets their backs up. You need to get more involved in what the art-world is interested in.' His words began to slur. 'Look, I know lots of artists from Goldsmith's, the Royal College of Art and Saint Martin's. I know what I'm talking about. What school were you at?'

'I studied Philosophy at York then learnt stone masonry at Portland College.'

'Exactly.' Sebastian began to back out of the gallery, past the visitors. 'That's the secret in this town. It's all about who you know and what art-school you went to.'

David followed him. 'So do you know anyone who would help?'

'No one's sympathetic to religious work. That's why I've changed my paintings. Even the churches aren't interested in your faith. They only want to know you if you're famous for art.' Standing at the doorway Sebastian made his final flourish. 'Like I say, just a thought.'

David soon lost his career focus as he turned to survey the crowd of guests. Amongst them was a blonde lady with the androgynous beauty of a fashion model in a white shirt and black waistcoat. She stood, poised, 5' 6", slim, her face like David's head of Apollo, an ideal, classical perfection. She was looking at him, her eyes wide, her body lent forward.

His attention was absorbed and he did not have the shyness he normally felt with girls because his art had instilled him with confidence.

'Hi. What's your name?'

'Rachel.' They shook hands. 'I love your work.' She had an intelligent, kind air.

He wanted to impress her. 'I use art to explore and join all the different faiths.'

Her hand touched his arm. 'Yes, I heard, it's really interesting. I'm interested in the unity between all the different spiritual paths.'

'Oh, do you have a belief yourself?'

'Yes, I follow the rainbow spirit, Oshumare, and I wear this in honour to him.' She pulled a small rainbow beaded necklace from under her shirt.

David dismissed its significance but still feigned interest. 'Sorry, I've never heard of the religion of Oshumare.'

'It's not a religion it's a spirituality. I have a real problem with organised religions. They are too patriarchal and oppressive.'

David stood upright. 'I'm the opposite. I used to be spiritual until I experienced Nirvana. Then I realised that spirituality just runs away from the conflicts of life. Spirituality transcends the world's problems, so we need religions for the fight of good against evil.'

Rachel bunched her brow in confusion. 'It all depends on how you define spirituality. It sounds to me like you're just beginning your journey to unite your Enlightenment with your ordinary consciousness.'

'Ahh, but Buddha said you can't join illusion and Enlightenment together.'

Her face grew hard, her pupils contracted. 'So what's your answer?'

Her lips pursed. 'Religions cause all the problems in the first place. They just preach hatred and war. Look at you, your ideas are cold and unfeeling, they contain no love.'

Annoyed that she had lost her composure she made curt goodbye, moved between the remaining visitors whilst pretending to look at the exhibition, then put on her fashionable coat and left onto the busy street.

He was delighted and bitterly disappointed. He had met someone he really could talk with but he just couldn't get along with her. He couldn't compromise his basic beliefs. He couldn't pretend to agree with her.

When all the visitors had left he watched the busy street outside. He was excited that a few collectors had bought some works, but they were not big dealers with any influence in the art world. The exhibition wasn't the success that he had hoped for and Sebastian's words came back to him. He ignored the criticism that he hadn't been to the right art school, there was nothing he could do about that, instead he remembered that he musn't ram religion down peoples' throats. But how could he do that when he was more like a missionary than an artist and his exhibition was more like a religious shrine than a gallery.

Unsure what would eventually happen with his work he locked the doors and headed up the busy Charing Cross Road.

-

As he neared the stop for the number 73 bus a man's voice called across to him. 'Excuse me! Excuse me!'

David turned. A young, thin, shaven headed, black man, wearing an open shirt stood outside "Bar Salsa". The man smiled. 'Come to the church of salsa.' David returned a quizzical look but the man seemed serious. 'In Cuba everyone dances, its part of life, it's sacred.'

Beside the doors, a sign beckoned. "Learn To Dance". It was enough to raise his curiosity and draw him in. He paid the Spanish girl in the small wooden booth, and as he headed down the broad wooden staircase the city traffic became drowned out by the constant drum beat of the rising music.

The large dance floor was bordered with young and old dancers, mainly women, leaning against wooden railings. Most of the men were black and muscled, in t-shirts and vests, showing off on the dance floor, competing to make their mark. They were dancing better than the white men and when the music reached its finale they threw their partners into drop holds.

David blinked as the lights came on and a short Latino instructor, whose t-shirt bore the name Mushti, began calling everyone onto the floor. He lined up the cramped group, and started speaking into his headset. 'Side, together, side, together.'

It was hard to see and David couldn't get the hang of how to move his feet.

'Back, together, back, together.'

He started to watch the feet of the blonde lady in front of him but everyone was too close, he couldn't get the distance. But he could see that she was wearing tight black pants. He stopped concentrating on the dancing and cast a furtive look at her bottom.

'Okay. Leads find a partner and take them like this.' The instructor took a young lady, put his right hand on her shoulder blade and held her right hand in his left.

The lady in front of David was smiling as she turned to take his hands. It was Rachel. Her face dropped, 'Oh, hi,' but she still offered her hands.

'Hi.' He took them but didn't know what to say. 'Have you done this before?' he blurted out.

'Yes, I'm one of the teachers.'

David blushed, he felt like an idiot. 'I've never danced before, sorry. I won't be very good.' He looked down at his feet

'Don't worry, I'll show you.' She manoeuvred him so that he held her in the dancing position. He could feel her bare back. Her skin was smooth, like Carrara marble but warm and soft. 'You need to hold a little closer.' She pulled herself nearer and his blood quickened.

The instructor called out. 'Okay let's do the Mambo step. Forward and back, forward and back. Now let's do a turn.'

Seeing David struggle, Rachel passed under his raised arm, guiding him into the turn. As they began to sweat in the busy club, her body yielded to the touch, moving with the fluidity of water. He felt her scented hair in his face.

All the years without love melted away. This was the first time that he had been happy. This was the first time he had been in love. The rhythm engulfed him, taking him away from his constant thinking. The movement was joyful, it was bliss, but his analytical mind came back, he couldn't help himself.

'I didn't think that you'd be a dance teacher.'

'Actually I'm a consultant in management development, I just do this for fun.' They continued to dance. 'But my real love is literature. I'm taking a Doctorate, a PhD, at the moment.'

David was impressed. 'So what's your thesis going to be on?'

She raised an eyebrow. 'Thanks for showing an interest. I had you down as someone who wasn't a listener.' He wasn't sure what to think but she gave him a charming smile. 'It's on the relation of Salsa dancing to the writings of the German philosopher Friedrich Nietzsche.'

It was the philosopher that Rockschild had spoken about. He stopped dancing and gathered his thoughts. 'Is salsa an academic subject?'

'Of course.' She had clearly defended herself many times. 'For starters, did you know it comes from the Santerian religion?'

'The Santerian religion, I've never heard of it.'

She smiled as she flicked his arms like reigns to make him dance again. 'Santeria is "the way of the Saints" and it has millions of followers. It began in Cuba and is a mix of Voodoo and Roman Catholicism.'

'I'd no idea. But I thought you didn't believe in religion and God?'

'No, I never said that. I said that I follow spirituality and, like Nietzsche, I would only believe in a God who could dance. So I believe in Olodumare, the creator God, and his spirits, the Orishas, who are associated with the Catholic Saints.'

'Really?' David was surprised, but he was now concentrating on dancing.

'And my personal Orisha is Oshumare, the rainbow serpent who helped Olodumare create the world. He is the king of the rainbow and takes the shape of a snake. He lives in the sea and is like water, moving all the time, like the dance, constantly changing, full of surprises. He, she, is a man for half the year, a woman for the other half. Look.' She nodded at her t-shirt.

David tried to ignore the curve of her breast and to just look at the semi-naked figure in a billowing skirt, headscarf and necklace of snakes. He began to lose the beat so looked at his feet again, trying to get the steps right. 'Sounds like a religion to me.' He picked up the beat again.

'This is different, it's more the spirituality of dance than a religion. Christianity has always misunderstood dance, treating it as an activity of the Devil. Nietzsche understood it. He contrasted Dionysus, the Greek God of music, intoxication and ecstasy, with Apollo, the God of civilization and law. He said that Apollonian society sees Dionysus as evil but that the true philosopher must embrace Dionysus.'

David could no longer keep the beat. 'I've read some Nietzsche but I don't understand. Are you saying he'd have liked Salsa dancing? His writings influenced the Nazis. Surely they'd have seen Salsa as corrupt and degenerate.'

She shook her head. 'The Nazis twisted Nietzsche's ideas. In "Thus Spoke Zarathustra", he preached about a new breed of men, creative geniuses, Ubermensch, Supermen, beyond the petty rules of the herd. Hitler misinterpreted this as meaning that they could commit atrocities but for Nietzsche Zarathustra was a dancer who leapt, somersaulted and beckoned with his wings, ready for flight.'

Despite the fire of enthusiasm in her beautiful eyes David was not convinced. 'My bronze angel is called Zoroastrian Icarus and Zarathustra is another name for Zoroaster.'

She nodded. 'That was why I came to see your exhibition.'

He continued. 'How does Nietzsche's famous declaration that "God is Dead" fit with your Orishas?'

Rachel glared. 'In my theory the Orishas are not gods, they are more like his Supermen.' Her brow had lowered and her eyes penetrated his. 'But David, you are too serious. You must learn to laugh, you are too stiff for dancing.'

David realised he'd been talking too much. 'I know.' He wanted to be with this girl, but he couldn't let go in the dance. He didn't know how to.

She smiled as the couples moved around, but they had lost connection.

He found himself with a new partner, a petite lady. They exchanged greetings but she was even worse at dancing than he. Especially now that he was lost in concentration, thinking.

Nietzsche had used Zarathustra as a literary device to replace God with a belief in the "Will to Power," the "survival of the fittest" and the need for hardness, strength and cruelty. He saw Christianity as weak and the religion of the oppressed that came out of the Jewish religion, which came out of slavery in Egypt and Babylon. Instead he wanted the religion of the hero, and his Ubermensch, lords of the earth, who were even ready to destroy themselves to achieve victory. This was why the Nazis read his philosophy.

The couples moved around again and David mumbled 'Hello,' to each new partner and went through the moves, but was constantly thinking. Maybe Nietzsche's Zarathustra was more like Icarus, who fell from the sky for his pride.

Freestyle dancing began after the lesson and David saw Rachel with the instructor. He wanted to speak with her, but he couldn't compete with the instructor. Not knowing what to do next he decided that he should leave. He went over and said a quick goodbye. As she waved from her partner's shoulder he tried to imagine that she was interested in him. But he just couldn't convince himself.

-

"Bar Salsa" tempted David back and dancing became his release, his escape.

He lived for the evenings that he might see Rachel again, to dance with her, to hold her. But she was no longer there. And even if he saw her he knew would not have the courage to approach her. He couldn't face the prospect of her not being interested in him. He had picked on someone too beautiful to fall in love with.

So he began to practice and hoped that he could became good enough to be her dance partner. This fantasy became the relief he needed for his loneliness.

He struggled at first, but he was   determined. He had no partner to help him and only one elderly lady would dance with him after the lessons. The side step, the cuddle, the basic turn.

He started to meet the same people each week and as he picked up the skills he also developed the confidence to ask people to dance. He began with the worst dancers then built his way up to the best dancers in the room. And as he grew more adept at the movements he could read a person's character from the way that they danced. It was like having a relationship. Awkward and stiff, fluid and sensuous, impatient and quick to blame, or grateful and keen to learn. Often the most beautiful, slim and elegant women were the stiffest and most awkward dancers.

With his improved technique he was able to maximise on his partner's skills and enjoyment. He even had girls with no natural ability dancing well. Two turns out, hand up the back, eye to eye. A smile. A laugh. He would whip the partner into a spin across him, catch her and lean with her over in his arms. But showing them how to dance was never enough, however, when the dance ended he had no conversation, nothing to say. He couldn't even look them in the eye.

When the main lights dimmed and the disco lights came on he was transported from the rainy darkness outside and the personal sadness that he felt. Fake palm trees added to his illusion of escape as the large black lady danced beautifully, turning like a well-oiled wheel, spinning on the lightest of touches. He brought her arms over his head, again and again, he closed his eyes and in the sounds the sadness drifted away, far enough to imagine it was not there. It was washed away by the glorious harmonies of the music inherited from slaves who were free when dancing in the healing powers of the Santerian religion.

But its powers were for more than just healing. Old, young, fat, thin, black, blonde, curly, straight, rich, poor, all joined in the promiscuity of the dance of fertility.

There were always new girls, ladies and women to dance on the polished floor. David offered his hand. 'Would you like to dance?' he had no money but it was not a problem, he could dance. He had free reign. He was good and girls liked it.

He was trapped between God and his desires. Why did he have to wait for one of the virgins promised to martyrs in Heaven. The dance was not enough.

He would hold girls close to him in the final embrace of the salsa dance and they would melt into his arms, consumed by the thrill. He lost control and could not help it, his responsibility left behind in his state of lust, of compulsion and action.

But the more intimate the dancing became, the more his frustration grew, because he was never confident enough to make the final move. They knew that

he was interested in them and they   gave him opportunities but he was
waiting for someone else.

He smiled, reassured them, helped them to have a good time but he didn't
love them. They all reminded him that his dream of perfect love was slowly
fading. He wept inside. The more he danced the more it covered over his sense
of loss, his sense of grief. He had convinced himself that he loved the perfect,
timeless Rachel. And as far as he knew she didn't even want his love.

Only when carried away in an ecstasy of rhythm, as if possessed by the
Orishas, was there relief. There was no thinking as he swirled around, pushing
up his body and reaching up his arms. Exhilarated and invigorated he span with
arms outstretched then close to his chest. He stopped, his head spinning in the
engulfing luminescence of the disco lights, still connected with the rhythms. It
was as if he had entered one of Rothko's paintings. His body the brush and the
dance floor the canvas. But this ecstasy of Dionysus, the blend of the beats,
tunes and frequencies of the Orishas, was slowly consuming him.

He slumped into one of the leather couches that intruded into the dance
space. And across the room, in the dim light, amidst the noise and bodies he
imagined that he saw her with the Mushti. He sat forward, he had to let her
know that he loved her, but his heart relaxed when he realised it wasn't Rachel,
just Mushti's new partner, another blonde. She looked similar but now he could
tell that her attitude was very different.

As she danced with Mushti their aggression and vanity began to clear a
space around them. The muscled dancer span furiously, with his low centre of
gravity, on the shining wooden surface. Effortlessly he collected his balance
and launched his partner's lithe body into a series of twists and turns from
which she emerged with remarkable elegance. Smiling.

In Cuban salsa the partners came together in a sensual caress that was
never harsh. But this was New York Mambo style, where their warped pride
was destroying them, aided by the forces of the Spirits, the Orishas. Mushti's
new partner had worked her way up the ladder to be with the best dancer, to
have the best partner. Now she moved back and forth in aggressive, sexual
combat.

They pushed everyone out of the dancing space so that they could pose
and be the centre of attention. He was clearly hurting her as he forced her into
the moves. She had to be responsive and obedient. But above all she had to
smile. She had to pretend that she found the moves easy and pretend that she
was enjoying herself. In return he was supposed to make her look good but
instead he just showed off his own abilities.

The audience clapped as they finished with a drop hold and the space
filled with dancers again. David walked over to ask the girl for a dance. But she
looked him up and down then just turned away. Clearly there was no politeness
in this mating ritual.

16. New York

It was winter in New York. David had been invited to speak on art and religion at the New York Studio School of Art. Dealers said that his work was highly skilled but was too traditional, too classical, but this was his opportunity to convince people in the art-world that his work was "contemporary."

In New York he wandered in a daze, looking at paintings, sculptures and installations, exhibited in white room after white room, in a hundred galleries, nestled inside tower blocks and old dock buildings. The New York scene was seductively exciting. But it soon became clear that all this art-world really cared about was money, sex and power.

He ended his search in the prestigious The Rockschild Museum of Modern Art, a modern gallery overlooking Central Park. It was showing the work of postmodern artists whose work was clearly anti-religious. Andres Searing's "Piss Christ" 1987, a photograph of crucifix in urine, Herbert & George's "Shitty Naked Human World" 1994, a photo-print of a crucifix made out of excrement, Damien Heist's "Mother and Child" 1994, a dissected cow in formaldehyde, Chris Awfully's "The Holy Virgin Mary" 1996, an African Mary in blue robes surrounded by vaginas from porn magazines and surmounted with elephant dung. It was as if the artists had all made a pact with the Devil.

But the most celebrated works in the exhibition were by the New York artists, Robert Applethorn and Ron Atheyist.

Applethorn took black and white photographs of scenes of semi-religious devotion. But the devotion was to explicit, hardcore homosexual acts. A fist being shoved up a man's anus, a man in sadomasochists' leather clothing urinating in another man's mouth, a finger being pushed into the tip of an erect penis and a naked man hung upside down on an inverted crucifix. David wandered from piece to piece, embarrassed that the gallery assistant might be watching him. He stopped at two of the less extreme images.

In "Self Portrait" 1978, Applethorn had taken a photograph of himself from behind. He was dressed in a waistcoat and seat-less leather pants. His hair was in a wild abandon, as if allowing the unfettered flow of his desires, and sporting a goatee beard. He looked defiantly over his shoulder, at the viewer, as he inserted the handle of a bull whip, as if it was the Devil's tail, into his anus.

As soon as David had worked out the picture he turned away to the final work, a close up of Applethorn's face, "Self Portrait" 1985. Eyes, surrounded with eye liner, looked out, piercingly, behind dark hair that descended to the sensuous curve of his naked shoulders. But protruding from this hair were pointy ears and horns in the manner of Satan, Lucifer, the most beautiful, outcast angel.

David read the caption. "For   Applethorn the perfect, gay body was a manifestation of the divine. Here he is Dionysus, the God of intoxication and nature, who the Christians called the Devil because they did not understand him. Dionysus had two horns, one of life and creation, the other of death and destruction. Pleasure, pain and fear were the materials of Applethorn's art and he photographed acts of sexual punishment and martyrdom because bitter sweet sex was sacred to him. His aim was an ecstatic transformation away from the chains of the "civilised" world. Tragically, 4 years after this portrait, he died from A.I.D.S."

David shook his head. Art was about breaking down barriers, finding new materials new forms of expressions but this was just sadomasochism. The exhibition continued in the next room with the work of the inheritor of this tradition, Ron Atheyist.

On display were photographs of Atheyist's 2002, performance, the "Solar Anus." The naked, bald, heavily tattooed artist had spread the cheeks of his backside to show a black flaming sun tattooed around his anus. This was a black hole of darkness and he was pulling a string of pearls from out of it.

In another image he was sat upon a throne. Lifting a golden jester's crown, with hooks fixed to both it and his face. The hooks pulled his bleeding skin upwards as he crowned himself Sun King mocking the God Apollo. Then, in the final image, he had powdered his face and was sodomising himself, with dildos attached to his shoes.

David was now completely confused. This was just awful. He picked up an information sheet for an explanation from the art curators.

"In his "Solar Anus" performances the pierced, A.I.D.S. infected Atheyist is in pain. But the more pain, blood and horror that he creates, the more value he finds. The name, "Solar Anus," comes from an essay by George Bataille, who used erotic deviance and human sacrifice to overthrow the rationalism, science and materialism of Modernity. Bataille wanted to escape the world and to reach a sacred black star of chaos, the Solar Anus. In this ecstasy is the union of Death (Thanatos) and Love (Eros). Atheyist is overcoming his corruptible flesh, in the eternal ecstasy of Thanateros. Both Atheyist and Applethorn liberate their souls in infinite ecstasy."

A deep sadness filled David's heart as he left the museum. These dark visions were slowly leading him to despair.

He wandered, in the freezing air, past Central Park then began a long walk down the crowded Broadway, through Greenwich Village and along the west side of Manhattan.

He finally cleared his head as he reached the side of the River Hudson. He headed south down the promenade.

The sun still shone in the azure sky as he admired the beauty of the silhouette of the Statue of Liberty, in the distance, across the Hudson. It was late, time to find a subway, so he walked quickly. He stepped carefully on the ice and crunched into the shovelled snow that was hardening in the evening air. Further on he turned and headed inland.

He was overheating from the walk and was thirsty as he entered a Cathedral of empty space, devoid of buildings, with its centre fenced off.

Here was a site of devastation, of souls screaming out at him. He felt confused, unable to understand as a crane arm slowly swung to a halt. Yellow taxis roared across the road. The ground was icy, the concrete hard and the metal sharp.

The sweat around his chest began to feel cold. The surrounding skyscrapers were lighting up and echoed the Twin towers that collapsed here, on 9/11, with a hideously perfect precision.

With all the sick artwork that he had seen he began to wonder whether an Islamic extremist might see the films of the terror attacks, one tower smoking whilst a plane struck the second, as a work of Avant-garde art. There was no way that David could accept it. It was off the moral compass. So that meant art must have some kind of limits, but what were they and who set them. Why was the work of Applethorn and Atheyist accepted.

Tired and cold he steadied himself against a railing.

He felt a wet chill seep into his shoes from the snow around his feet. Looking up, past the branches of a sapling tree, into the empty space, he saw a twisting light spreading through his field of vision.

His heart raced as the spikes of light engulfed his vision. He was going blind. Mist had come down and he was dizzy. He felt sick, he was panicking.

From the centre of this terrible light a figure began to appear, riding out of the sky. It drew closer on a chariot with golden wings and whose wheels were spinning rainbows. On the chariot a child, with a shimmering nimbus of spikes, steered the horseless chariot with one hand whilst holding out a bitten apple with the other.

'Oh my God,' David said to himself, 'it's Elijah the prophet.'

David's reached out his arms and felt colours sparkle upon him. The vision became clear. It was a girl and around her waist was a skirt, on which was the Star of David and up on her bared chest was a rainbow swastika, dripping, as if blood. But her bizarre, silver, halo… was… a crown of disco boppers. It was absurd but upon his own head he sensed the same halo.

Looking down at himself, he now was dressed in the vestments and symbols of many faiths and around him were seven religious leaders; Buddhist, Hindu, Christian, Muslim, Jewish, Sikh and African. Each bathed in light a colour of the rainbow.

In his ears rang church bells, calls to prayer, prayer wheels turning, horns blowing, yogis chanting mantras and the singing of the word 'Messiah'. All mixed into a union, a cacophony, an epiphany.

The girl held out the apple in both hands and David reached to take it…

…his shoulder was shaken. 'You can't do this here,' said the large security guard.

David looked round in confusion. He was on his knees, hands reaching up. His head was numb.

'Sir, you're gonna have to leave.'

The sky had darkened and the moon had risen, it's light was overwhelmed by orange floodlights that streamed across Ground Zero. A helicopter approached, its sound was overpowering as it hovered onwards.

'Okay, okay,' mumbled David, as he collected himself together and took out his camera to photograph the scene of his vision.

'No pictures.'

'What?' queried David as he clicked the camera.

'No pictures!'

The helicopter flew overhead, watching him. The guard spoke into his handset.

David kept clicking images as he put the camera back in his bag. 'Okay, I'm going,' then stumbled away, numb, in search of the nearest subway.

-

David stood on a podium in front of smartly dressed ladies and unkempt students in paint stained shirts. He was dressed in robes and garments from different religions, surmounted with a halo of disco boppers. The room quietened as he reached aloft.

'Since coming to New York I've had a vision, and because of it I've thrown my lecture notes away. At Ground Zero, I saw the sacred and secular join together in a new art. In a Postmodern Religious Art.' The audience looked confused. 'This seems to be a contradiction, as the postmodern artists seem to hate religion, but this is because they are still at heart Modernists, with Modern prejudices.'

The audience now buzzed with interest. This was a completely new idea, and they thrived on the new.

'Pre-modern religions were weaved into every aspect of life. They were a way to explain the universe and a way to keep people controlled within a social hierarchy. The fifteenth century Renaissance began a period of rationality and the eighteenth century Enlightenment began a period of scientific progress. Together these led to a rejection of God. But science and reason were used for evil as well as good and the faith in Modernism was destroyed in the 20th century, with Nazi and Soviet genocides and with the use of nuclear bombs in Hiroshima and Nagasaki. Postmodernists rejected the authoritarian Modernist governments but at the same time they accepted that they could not escape corporate control, and that all of culture had become a series of brand names, images and thought patterns to trap people as impotent consumers.'

David held the turning switches   of the two slide projectors, like a pair of guns, firing slide after slide, like a disco show of Postmodern art.

'Since the late 1960's and early 1970's the Postmodernists wanted shock people and to wake them up, to make them think and feel in a different way. So they promoted dark, artists who used their own bodies in performance art to unite violence and eroticism, death and life. They broke-down the artificial moralities of the modern state and its power structures into a "formless" equality. But this rebellion was not just against Modernism, it was against the original authoritarian figure. It was against God, the "author" of the universe.'

The images of Atheyist and Applethorn had begun to create some discomfort in the audience.

'Cruelty, horror and sexual desire were used to humiliate and disintegrate the personality, to shock humanity into waking up from rationality, so that they could see their mystical core. A Gnostic state where opposites, like the sacred and the secular, are united. But what these postmoderns didn't realise was that the Modernists had already destroyed God, and reduced all the world's religions to a mystical core. True Postmodernism should encourage people to create their own religious beliefs, however bizarre, not force them to follow any single spirituality.' David's arm swept the air, red sleeve trailing.

'And because their spirituality was too elitist to be followed it created a vacuum and the love of money, the lowest common denominator, filled that void. That is why artists now use shocking images. It's just advertising, to grab attention for their work so it can be sold for a higher price. Damien Heist became famous for this, but he could not have done it without being promoted by the advertising mogul Charles Saturate. They were the High Priests of art who commodified animal sacrifices and nightmarish images of bloodletting, even mocking the divine by giving his dissected cows titles like "Mother and Child."'

David stopped to catch his breath. 'The only way of escape from this selfish consumerism is for God to liberate us by sending us each our own personal Messiah.' The audience began to murmur, unsure whether to be amused at his conclusion.

Now his slides were of scenes from New York. 'At Ground Zero, I had a vision that the prophet Elijah was riding out of the sky on a golden chariot. It was a girl, with a nimbus, a halo, of disco boppers. She was to bring peace between the religions of the West and the East and her halo represented a new unity of the sacred and the profane. In the vision I was dressed like this,' he gestured to his regalia, 'as the prophet of Postmodern Religious Art. So I became like a man possessed, wandering around the city, on a shopping spree for objects from different religions, trying to recreate the clothing in my vision.'

David stood in a spotlight to the side of the podium, unsure if he was a priest, an artwork or a fashion model. 'I bought these,' he pointed to the red silk Bishops robe, rimmed with gold ribbon, 'in a Catholic shop. And this,' he pointed to his black hijab and yashmak for his face, 'in a Muslim shop. I bought this prayer shawl in a Jewish shop. 'And this Hindu temple banner,' rimmed in golden swastikas, 'in a 1960's retro-shop. But finally, in "Greenwich village," in a shop full of rainbow flags, butt plugs, porno videos and fetish gear, I bought this rainbow coloured disco ball necklace and this pair of disco boppers.'

A gentleman in the audience stifled a camp laugh.

'To consecrate my vision I took a ferry to the Statue of Liberty.' He pointed his left arm up in imitation. 'There she stood, on her vast plinth, a green bronze lady holding aloft the flame of liberty. A statue designed after the Egyptian, Mother Goddess Isis and the Roman Goddess of Freedom, Libertas. Her head crowned with a 7-spiked halo of the sun god, Sol Invictus, Apollo.'

The murmuring audience grew quiet. Respectful of the statue he described.

'As I unzipped my bag on the grass in front of her I wondered why Monotheism had no room for such a Goddess. Now it was time for male religions must work with female spirituality to help solve the crises in the world. In my vision Elijah wore the Star of David on her skirt but she also had a rainbow swastika on her chest. It is a symbol of the mystical energy common to almost all the religions of the world.'

'So I prayed. "Oh Lord Jesus Christ," as I put on the robes, "Allah," as I put on the hijab, "Hashem," as I put on the prayer shawl and "Buddha, Krishna, Shiva and Brahma," as I put on the swastika banner. Finally, as I put on the disco ball and nimbus, the sky became electric.

The blades of a watching helicopter cut the air, filling it with sound, as I began to pray. "Please let this be for goodness and world unity. Please bring together the people of the world, sacred and the secular." A crowd gathered as a barely visible moon rose behind them. I repeated the prayer, maybe a dozen times, then ended, "Your will be done. Amen."'

'As I prayed I could hear someone say. 'It's a performance. I like it, its got contemporary attitude.' At the same time another person said, 'I think its kind a creepy.' Another said, 'He's like the Devil.' On those words I had a sense of dark foreboding. I wasn't clear if I was an enemy or an ally. The boppers were like the horns of Dionysus and I was dressed in red and black, like some kind of emissary of the devil. I needed saving, from myself and from the consumerism that I am trapped within. I was a prophet of Postmodern Religious Art, customising the miracles, signs, prophecies, scriptures, rituals and icons of religion, into my own personal religion.'

David now looked at the audience, seeking an answer. 'But can a religion just be created?' He nodded and the boppers rocked. 'Yes, because we need them, because they are all we have left. We need faith that God can wake us out of the authoritarian governments and corporate empires that control us.'

He had their interest again. 'I   propose a new community, where children are taught how to become the creators, the "artists," of their own religions. This is the new religious consumerism that is evolving in Western Society. If it is allowed to flourish then we will have true democracy and social justice. Why? Because people will only reject fundamentalism when they are free and wealthy enough to be artists of their own religions.' His talk had reached a crescendo. 'Then there will be heaven on earth.'

Polite applause filled the room before it emptied into silence.

David took a question from a heavily bearded man, who spoke slowly, deliberately. 'If I was being generous I'd say your vision was of the Jewish Shekinah, the female presence of God. However it's more likely that it was from the Way of the Chariot. Most visionaries who follow this way go insane. Do you think you might be insane?' The man smiled.

David managed to smile in return. 'They say that there is a thin line between prophecy and madness. In fact, most religious traditions have the idea of a Holy Fool, who looks mad but really just holds up a mirror to point out the hypocrisies of society.'

The man breathed deeply. 'It's a shame you think it's funny. I, for one, don't like your pic 'n' mix attitude to religion and, frankly, find it offensive that you are wearing a swastika over a prayer shawl.' He spat the words at David as he raised his heavy frame.

It seemed as though any reply would just anger him more. So David just watched the man leave the room. Some sheepishly took it as an opportunity to follow but a lady near the back, with greying hair, called out.

'You said you had a vision had a Star of David and a Swastika. Did you know that the emblem of the Theosophical Society, a movement founded in New York in 1875, is a swastika above a Star of David?'

There was a stifled laugh in the audience. Then David responded, 'This is exactly the kind of Divine coincidence we need to be open to. I knew the Hindu based Theosophists influenced the modern art of Pollock and Rothko, but I didn't know about their symbol.'

The lady lifted up a silver necklace from her black jumper. 'I have it here. At the top is the Hindu sacred AUM, the vibration sound from which the Universe was created. Beneath it is the swastika of energy and beneath this is the Star of David, of heaven and earth. Surrounding this is the serpent of eternity, biting its own tail.'

'Yes, but isn't the serpent, a symbol of evil, deceiving Adam and Eve, into biting the apple of knowledge?'

The lady had become impatient. 'That's a very child-like interpretation. The Masters tried to help Adam and Eve evolve. But the Demi-urge, the God who traps mankind in the world, wanted to prevent their evolution.'

'No way, it was the Devil trapping them, not God!'

'Think what you like, but if you   are serious about finding the Truth then heed your vision, and listen to your Masters.'

When the lady had finished shouting an uncomfortable silence in the room. It was broken only by the tutts of people shaking their heads. They didn't want to listen to ideas about radical religion. So David finished the lecture to more applause. But as everyone filtered out of the hall he wondered if any had understood his new faith.

17. Dancing Gods

Back in London, down the broad stairway in "Bar Salsa", the music played. Boom, boom, click, click-click. Boom, booom, click, click-click. The sound of the clave.

The club was softly lit and behind the bar the pink and blue neon tubes flickered. The floor was full of dancers, possessed by a dangerous musical energy, by the movement of the spirits. Those who were not careful let their egos consume them. They let arrogance flow around their veins. The men dominated the women, who flaunted their sexuality, advertising themselves as objects to be lusted over.

The better that David became at dancing the more he had to compete with the aggressive vanity of other dancers, coming into his space, showing off. It depressed him. Why was he still dancing. The reason that he had begun to dance had left, she was no longer here. He had given up on seeing her again.

As he crossed the floor to ask someone to dance he felt a tap on his shoulder. His heart almost stopped. It was Rachel. He had walked past her. His focus became acute. He had to speak with her, but he had nothing to say. She continued to put on lip gloss as he stood embarrassed. Her blonde brown hair flowed perfectly, cut into a symmetry that accentuated her soft shoulders beneath.

Holding out a hand he mouthed the question, 'Would you like to dance?'

She smiled, raising her eyebrow, 'I'm out of practice.'

He proffered his hand again, and with a reassuring look from his deep brown eyes, her resistance melted.

His confidence was now strong on the floor and as he held her body with his right arm they began to sway. Their soft fingers caressed in a gentle hold as they merged with the coloured lights and the music, in a smooth and comfortable union.

He led the dance with a left-brain logic and she reacted with a right-brain, intuition. The dance was a language, a vocabulary of steps and the music was its grammar.

They turned in time to the music. And with sensuous creativity they carved each supple movement into the space, defining new shapes of perfection.

The intimacies of the dance had finally flowered into romance. A cuddle, a gentle rock, a push and pull together. He held her close, 'David,' she sighed, 'your dancing is amazing.' He leaned back to admire her face, her freckles. He was captivated by her beauty. They both smiled in blissful happiness.

He breathed in her hair as his face rested against her smooth neck. He was lost in the trance as his hips rolled and he swept Rachel into a circle. They twisted and turned, always finding the correct step, the movements ingrained, second nature, led from a deep memory. He now seemed guided as if by an invisible force.

The crescendo was continuous, a sustained release of pure pleasure, building to a fever pitch until she span and he caught her in an embrace. They stopped, sharing the wonderful experience, pausing in a mutual gaze of love, intoxicated on a wild ride. They were held in ecstasy, within the all embracing arms of the God Dionysus.

As the music climaxed he felt compelled to kiss her. Her mouth yielded and the soft velvet caress of lips became his home. His fingers left trails of pleasure as they sensuously slid down her moist skin. The energies of wild abandonment were straining to burst.

The music ended and they became self-conscious. They moved awkwardly from the floor and sat to talk. Rachel reapplied her lip gloss.

'It's good to see you again. Where've you been?'

'I had to work abroad, for the New Bank of Manhattan, in New York.'

'Really, I've just been there to give a talk about my artwork.'

She raised her eyebrows, impressed. As she brushed her hair from her face David noticed her wedding ring for the first time. 'Are you married?'

'Divorced. I keep it on to get rid of unwanted attention.'

'Children?'

'No.' He looked concerned, so she felt a need to explain. 'My marriage wasn't very happy. My husband was an Investment Banker who drank too much. I didn't love him but he pressured me into marrying him. Maybe that's why I started working in Management Development, to help people reach their full potential. It's so important.'

'And how's your PhD?'

'Work's taken over, so I've had to defer it. I'd been researching the Orisha, Oshumare, remember?' He nodded. 'In fact he reminds me a bit of you. I mean, look at you now, you're a brilliant dancer.'

He blushed.

'And how is your art?' she continued.

He became animated. 'I just installed my Zoroastrian Icarus in the grounds of Leyton Hall. It's in a small orchard. It looks fantastic.' She smiled, happy to listen, until he glanced around the room, just curious who else was there.

She squinted, 'Do I look alright?'

'You look fantastic.'

'But I don't make an effort like other women.'

He laughed but looked kindly into her eyes. 'What do you mean? What about the lip gloss you've been putting on?'

'That's just to be presentable. But I don't make any real effort.'

'You don't need to. You're classically beautiful. You've got the figure of a model. Women would kill for your looks.'

Rachel looked mournfully at him, 'But you're such a good dancer now. All the girls want to dance with you.'

He gazed into her eyes. 'Listen, you're more important to me than dancing. I'd give up dancing for you, I'd even give up art for you.'

They kissed.

-

Glitter balls hung from the ceiling of Sebastian's basement. He put on another CD of electronic world music, It soothed out of the stereo, relaxing his guests.

A male manikin wearing only boxer shorts and a construction hat stood in the corner. It was a guardian of his new kitchen units.

'People are so narrow minded, I put George in the window and instantly the neighbours came round to complain. They're so narrow minded and hypocritical. They probably went home and watched something far more outrageous on TV.'

David sat at a frosted glass dining table, upon which was a white vase, tastefully arranged with red and yellow tulips. He leant back on a retro white plastic chair. It seemed as though he had never been away. The only difference was that Rachel was now with him, tentatively sipping her tea, suspicious of the smoke filling the air.

'I'm just getting changed,' said Sebastian. 'I'll see you in a minute.'

Paul sat in the corner of the room. He had stubble around his small goatee beard and his hair was longer than usual. 'How's your art going?'

'I've had some breaks but the art-world just seems corrupt. It seems like religion is a dirty word.' David began to study his coffee cup.

Paul looked directly at him. 'I wouldn't worry about it. Like I say, the quality of your work is excellent, but it makes me feel nauseous. However, the problem is that your work needs to be even worse, more like Damien Heist's.' David felt like Paul was gloating at his failure.

'I'd rather be unknown than do work that's all about sex, violence and money.' David drank his bitter coffee. 'Heist has sold his soul to the devil. His sliced cows are like the Golden Calf and he even gives them religious names, like "Mother and Child, Divided."'

Rachel took David's hand, holding it tightly. 'What gets me is that he's not even that original.'

Paul put his hands behind his head. 'Stealing ideas is rife in the commerce, its very naïve to think that art is any different. It's just like supermarkets squeezing out corner shops and like corporations taking-over small companies.'

'True enough,' said David. 'Heist's work expresses the triumph of the free-market. He was promoted by the advertising mogul Charles Saturate, the guy that led the advertising for Margaret Trader's election campaign, promoting the free market "ethic," and the guy that helped Lionel Scarota get appointed, by Margaret Trader, as the Director of the Sugar Galleries.'

Paul had lost interest but waited for David to finish. Then he sat forward and continued with a zeal that he normally reserved for theology. 'The free-market was meant to increase the wealth of everyone, but it just increased the gap between rich and poor. The corruption of the free-market was mirrored in the lies and spin of Blar and Bash in their reasons for going to war in Iraq. They lied to us that Sadam Hussein had Weapons of Mass Destruction and that he was linked to Al Qaeda, and was somehow responsible for 9/11. But he was a secularist who the US had put into power and if anyone had links with Al Qaeda it was the US, who trained them to fight the Soviets in Afghanistan.'

'Sadam Hussein was a dictator who committed war-crimes,' said Rachel. 'He needed removing. That's why they went to war?'

Paul continued. 'But there were plenty of other dictators as bad as, or worse than, Sadam and they didn't invade them. Everyone knows the real reason was to gain control of Iraq's oil reserves, to secure US energy supplies and to make a US base in the area. They say it was done in the name of Democracy but that's just media propaganda.'

'And their example has affected society,' added David. 'People are far ruder and more aggressive to me than ever. They think that might is right and keep trying to mentally impose themselves on me.'

Rachel's voice was smooth and reassuring. 'I'm not sure I know what you mean?'

David tried to explain. 'Well it's hard to describe, they just seem to want to assert themselves mentally, its almost telepathy.'

'You mean like body language,' said Rachel. 'I guess it just shows how much you threaten their egos.' She shook her head and squeezed his hand. 'Society is getting worse and worse. People get jealous when they see someone who is confident. But you're never arrogant. One of the great things about you is how sensitive you are to other people, but you've got to just ignore it when they don't like you.'

Paul leaned his chair onto its back legs. He'd hardly touched his coffee and was aloof from the conversation. 'It's the same when you have faith in the Lord. People try to undermine you.'

David sat forward, seeking Paul's sympathy. 'But I try to ignore them and to forgive them, but they keep trying to get an upper hand, until I end up getting annoyed. Then they're pleased, because I stoop to their level of aggression.'

Paul's chair returned to the floor but Rachel replied before he could speak. 'The last thing you should do is fight back. You don't need to. Just remember your own self-worth, all your positive qualities. Remember that if they weren't jealous then they wouldn't want to try and put you down.'

Now Paul leaned over the table. 'No, the only way to deal with it is to remember that your real worth comes from God.'

David rested his elbows on the table and brought his hands to his head. 'I've tried thinking about my good points and thinking that everyone is equal under God, but none of it works. They still attack me.'

Rachel squeezed David's hand. 'Well, everyone is equal up to a point, but if they work hard and become something like a doctor, or a scientist, or an artist, then surely that makes them more valuable in some way?'

Paul's finger stabbed down on the table. 'Talents are a gift from the Lord, not yourself.' His chair went back again. 'People are misled by the Devil if they think anything else.'

Rachel's hand left David's thigh as she turned towards Paul. 'I don't think you can bring the Devil into this when there's a simple psychological explanation. When society leaves people with no respect or control in their lives, they become "little Hitlers" who want to have power over those around them. So what we need to do is help people develop to their full potential.'

Paul rose from his chair and moved to the kitchen. 'No, we can never reach full potential without Christ. The Devil just wants you to think that you can become "top dog" and be happy, but true happiness only comes if you put trust in the Lord, not in yourself.'

David paused. 'Isn't that just as domineering? Calling on a powerful God instead of your own fists?'

'People will always worship the "top dog" whether movie stars, footballers whoever. But only God is worthy of worship. And only God can unite us against a self-obsessed society.'

Rachel shook her head. 'What makes you think that faith in God will unite people when all the religions just fight one another? They use missiles, tanks and suicide bombers to blow-up innocent people, all in the name of God.'

Paul folded his arms. 'That's because "religions" like Islam and Judaism follow laws, like "An eye for an eye, a tooth for a tooth," but the Christian faith is based on God's Forgiveness and tells us to "turn the other cheek". And that's because Christ was a sacrifice to pay for mankind's sins. It's just that people, like David, don't follow His teachings properly.'

Rachel played with her hair, thinking.

'But none of that makes sense,' said David. 'How could Jesus die for our sins? You couldn't get someone to go to prison in your place.'

'Jesus Christ took on all mankind's sins, and destroyed it when he died on the cross. But he tricked the Devil and rose again and ascended to be with his Father.' Paul's tone was now patronising.

'Yeah but that's the doctrine of the Trinity. A theological trick invented of Saint Paul. It mixes up Jesus Christ, making him die as Jesus the man, with the world's sins, and then resurrecting him as Christ the God, without them.'

A smile formed under Paul's goatee beard as he stretched his arms slowly back. His smooth but hairy waist was showing. His barbed words were carefully directed. 'You Jews always found Jesus' sacrifice hard to accept, probably because you were responsible for killing Him.'

David's jaw jutted forward. 'Look, if Jesus died for your sins then he was sacrificed for you, not for the Jews! So it must be you that killed Him!'

Rachel thrust her arms into the space between them. 'Stop it! I thought you were both against fighting over religion.'

'I'm sorry. I'm just standing up for my position. Paul only respects the Bible and because I'm questioning the Bible, it's like you said, it threatens him and makes him aggressive.'

Paul folded his arms around his waist and began to stroke his goatee. 'Mmm.' He raised an eyebrow.

David's had no idea what was occurring inside Rachel's mind but his heart leapt as her eyes moved rapidly, up and down, admiring Paul's face. She turned to David. 'You've many talents, but if you want people to listen to you then you have to nurture what they value.'

Paul placed a hand upon David's shoulder. 'It's like if you want to become a pastor. First you have to understand and forgive your own failures. Only then can you understand and forgive those you lead.' Paul seemed gleeful as he made his excuses and smiled at Rachel as he left for the toilet.

David looked her in the eye as he spoke over the table in hushed tones. 'This is what I'm saying. Paul's been trying to dominate me. He's been trying to beat me in an argument and been trying to get you to flirt with him. And it's been working. Because women desire strong men and you think he's won the argument.'

'I don't know what you mean.' Rachel was angry. 'You know I love you. I'm always supportive of you.'

'I'm sorry,' said David sheepishly. But he was apologetic because he'd heard someone coming down the stairs and did not want to cause a scene.

'I'm really hurt by what you said,' replied Rachel with intense annoyance. Yet when Paul returned into the room her gaze stayed away from him.

Paul had left victorious but returned vanquished. He put the kettle on and sat back in his chair, observing, calculating as Rachel spoke. 'I thought about what you were saying. People need to know that their leaders understand and value them. So if David understands and values people more then they will stop attacking him.'

David was earnest in his reply. 'Maybe that's why people try to undermine me, because they feel rejected, because they know I have all the qualities of a leader but also that I don't want to lead them.'

Rachel nodded and this was followed by a long pause. It was broken by the boiling of the kettle.

Paul had his back to them as he made the drinks. He handed David his coffee and Rachel her tea. 'I'm surprised that you don't have children?' said Paul.

'It was never really the right time,' replied Rachel.

David bit his tongue. But as he left the argument he wondered if it was also time to leave the friendship.

At that point Sebastian came down the stairs. He had bathed, changed and applied copious amounts of aftershave. He clearly needed attention. He lit his cigarette, drank from his gin and tonic and went to change the CD. 'I tell you, I'm bored with this town.'

'Maybe it's because you've tried everything London has to offer.'

Sebastian turned. 'Actually, it's because my new boyfriend, Jim Rockschild, has broadened my horizons.' Paul shook his head but Sebastian continued. 'He runs a finance company and he's also a collector of art and antiquities. He's bought some of my new Rothko-meets-Warhol style works.'

'Is that Dr James Rockschild?' asked David.

'I don't know, they might be related. We're flying to his second home in Nice on Friday.' Sebastian made sure his words were clearly heard, then continued drinking. 'He's very sweet, he just paid for my new kitchen, so I can sell the house and get something smaller, now that Kirsten's gone. '

Paul continued to shake his head.

Sebastian turned to Paul. 'What? My relationship with Jim has been the deepest and best relationship of my life.'

Paul stood up, put an arm around Sebastian's shoulder and squeezed. 'I just want what's best for you. We've both been backsliding as Christians. So I've brought you a CD, by Jerry Fulwell, I want you to listen to it.'

Sebastian laughed. 'You mean the Evangelist who was caught with a prostitute. Look, I'm tired of supporting other people. That's all I did in the church.' He turned to David. 'How's your art?'

'Well, my sculpture won first prize in an art competition. The awards ceremony is on the Thursday. It would be really good if you could make it.'

Sebastian's face dropped. 'I'm not sure. I think I might have a street party to go to in Belgravia.'

'Well you could come after, or before.'

'I don't know. But anyway, apart from that, have you got a dealer yet?'

David didn't reply.

'Well I'll ask Jim what he can do. It's people like him and his friends who decide what is art.' Sebastian took out a small silver pill-box. Inside was white powder which he dished onto a mirror   with a small spoon. 'I showed him your website and he wants to buy one of your heads of Apollo. It will be ideal surrounded by pink neon on his garden roof.'

'Sorry?'

'He throws parties there for his clients.' Sebastian chopped the powder to make it fine, then separated it into 2 rows. 'Would you like a line?' He offered them all his rolled up £20. 'Everyone I know takes it. It's completely normal.' Each declined in turn. 'Suit yourselves.'

Sebastian snorted both lines of coke.

As the drug took hold he began to leap around the basement, dancing whilst boasting of the premieres he'd attended in London and the money that he'd spent in the casinos of Monte Carlo.

The balls hanging from the ceiling span as the stereo played Patrick Hernandez's 1978 disco hit "Born, born, born… Born to be alive."

As David felt their friendship fade he thought that he heard it saying "Born to be a liar." But he wasn't sure if it accused Sebastian, Paul, or himself.

18. Legal Case

David and Rachel stood with their backs to the Thames, facing Sugar Modern. Its tall tower reaching from a wide rectangular base into the sky. This converted power station, with its beautiful angles, was a piece of art itself, a monument to a long gone British industry.

David had just given a talk on his Postmodern religious art, in the gallery, as part of a conference on "Heaven and Hell." Despite inviting the director of the gallery, Sir Lionel Scarota, and his curators, none attended. 'Why didn't they come? It's such an important topic.' He turned and leaned over the railings, staring into the polluted river.

Rachel's arm slipped under his. 'I don't know. I can't understand why they aren't interested in your work.' Her hand was on his back.

'They aren't open to art about God. They only allow art that whips up hatred, like the blasphemous cartoons of Mohammed, that reinforces their beliefs that religious people are fanatical.'

'What are you going to do?'

The sound of a passing boat made him pause. He gulped. 'I have to fight them over this.'

'I thought you were against fighting?'

'I need to stand up for myself, to stop them walking all over people like me. Everytime I submit work to them they turn me down and refuse to give any reasons. But religion is the most important issue in the world today and the nation's main public gallery should show art addressing it. They need regulations for how they select art but they're completely unaccountable.'

'But isn't art all subjective. You know "Beauty is in the eye of the beholder" and all that.'

David traced the deep frown marks on Rachel's brow to her nose, to the gentle freckles on her face, then to her lips. 'There is a consensus amongst scholars about the principles of classical art. And now, even though modern art is about ideas as well as beauty, it can still be systematised. But rich people don't want a system. They want to be free to pick and choose art on a whim. I tell you what we need are state regulations to ensure fairness, and I'm going to campaign for them.'

'Great, but don't expect to make any money.'

He turned from her. 'I don't care about the money. I'm a religious artist. I make art because I want to express the truth in a beautiful way.' They began to walk past the Sugar, toward the footbridge across the Thames.

'Yes, but you have to survive.' She played with her rainbow necklace as a gust of wind blew her hair across her face.

'I know, I know, but until things   are fair, I'll never make a living from my art.'

Her posture stiffened. 'Okay, but the Sugar is run by big businesses and if you want them to change then you'll have to speak to them in a language they understand.'

'So I'll teach them the benefits of religion in business and then they'll want to listen.'

'Great idea, but how would you do that?' They headed across the bridge, towards the gleaming white Portland stone of St. Paul's Cathedral, avoiding the rushing, unyielding, tourists whose heads were down, determined to reach the gallery before it closed.

'Well, I don't want to do it as a lecture. It needs to be a performance as some kind. Maybe as some kind of "Business Messiah" that incorporates religion into business structures.' Rachel was completely attentive.

'Brilliant.' She clung tightly to his arm as they crossed over the waters. 'Oh, I'm quite excited by it.'

The Cathedral faced them. Around it was "the City", whose glass and steel office blocks now seemed accessible. 'Yes, art has become about money, so what better way to show that religion is needed in art than through a business presentation.' He was now staring into the sky. 'I can show them how to increase their market share by moving towards religious management models and religious products.'

'But is it art?' she seemed frightened to question him.

Blood filled his cheeks 'Yes, it's performance art. And one day my ideas will be recognized, because religion will rise just as surely as the Thames will flood.''

She stopped as they reached the other side of the bridge. 'But what if they just steal your ideas, like Damien Heist?'

'I have faith, that's all I can have.'

-

The hotel door slammed and clicked. He lifted his black trolley, loaded full of case notes and tribunal regulations, and strained to lower it gently down the steps. It landed with a thud.

David looked handsome in his beard. Instead of his characteristic black he now wore a navy blue suit, with a light blue shirt and pink tie. Rachel carried a shoulder bag, she was in a formal trouser suit and white shirt. Their shoes clicked against concrete paving and their trousers flapped across their shins. They began the day's journey, down the drab and dirty street, into the city.

Rushing workers pretended not to notice his suit. His tie patterned with religious symbols, his golden Buddha tie clasp, his silver cross cuff-links, his ring set with gems representing the twelve Tribes of Israel, and his lapel badges, on one side a golden Allah and on the other an enamelled Rainbow Swastika.

They strode forwards, past tall grey Imperial offices. And as he pulled the trolley, its wheels scraping under the slight buckling, his neck was clammy and his heart tight felt tight as his chest expanded. There was no fear or excitement, just the need to be punctual.

Heading down the steps from Blackfriars Tube station they passed along the Thames Embankment, with its pillars and lights on black iron stands.

He had begun a case at the Employment Tribunals, claiming that Sir Lionel Scarota, the Director of the Sugar Gallery, was guilty of religious discrimination against him for not showing his work. He argued that the gallery only showed art that was offensive to Christians. He also argued that as the Prime Minister, Mr Timothy Blar, was responsible for employing the Director so was also guilty of discrimination.

David turned, to look the way they had come, and pointed beyond Blackfriars Bridge, across the river, to the tower of Sugar Modern. 'Look how close it is.' Then pointed down the river, to where it bent around to the left. 'And just beyond there is Parliament.'

He was under no illusions. He had no naïve belief that the judicial system was fair. He knew that pressure would be brought to bear to exonerate the Director and the Prime Minister. He knew that this was a battle against corruption, like Christ against the Pharisees. But he had faith, against all odds.

They waited for a break in the rushing traffic. Black cabs, white vans, black saloons, white vans. Then they crossed the road, towards a stone and red brick Georgian building. A brass plaque announced that this was the "Employment Appeal Tribunal."

They entered, under a carved and painted Royal Coat of Arms. The golden lion and white unicorn held a red shield, embossed with golden lions. It stood upon the motto. '"Dieu et mon droit," "God and my right." But whose God and whose right hand?'

At reception they were greeted with a board that stated, "BOMB THREATS – THE STATE OF ALERT IS NOW HEIGHTENED". They signed in and were brusquely instructed in procedures by a receptionist with unintelligible English. David didn't want to ask her to repeat herself. He sensed that she would accuse him of being a racist. He took the power back by asking for a room in which to pray. It was a new request for her and she had to think quickly, knowing that it was her duty to provide one.

-

Dust floated through the sun rays in the small, stuffy room. The dull growl and whoosh of traffic bounced off the white walls and was damped by the ribbed nylon of the grey carpet. David sat upright, the fabric on the chair clinging to his suit, and breathed deeply. He needed to compose himself.

'Can we pray?'

Rachel nodded, taking her necklace to Oshumare in her fingers.

He scratched his beard and then they bowed hands clasped. 'Oh Lord God. I am not a good man, but please, God, help me with this case. But whatever your will, I will accept it. I know that...'

Before he could continue there were muffled foot steps in the corridor, a knock and the door was opened slowly.

'Amen.'

'Mr Wolfe, the Tribunal is ready,' said the clerk, a grey haired man with a beard.

They grabbed their things and were led down corridors until they were ushered into the bright, sunlit, Tribunal Room. Then they were directed to sit facing a raised wooden table at the end of the room. The sunlight did not touch this end of the room, where a plump Asian lady sat, preparing her notes. The clerk took his seat to her left.

On the other side of the room to David was the slick barrister, Tim Showhard, of No 6 Chambers, and the large eyed Laura McCarthey, of Beast, Swell & Wraithbaite, solicitors for Sugar. There was a light whisper of conversation between them.

David parked his trolley to the side and sat, with Rachel at his side, methodologically getting out his papers. As he was shuffling industriously through his notes the clerk called, 'Court rise.'

They all stood and the Chairman entered, with prematurely aged white hair. He took his place in the central chair then looked down his spectacles, at his notes.

'Please sit.' His tone was surprisingly relaxed. 'Today's case is to determine whether there has been discrimination within the Employment Equality (Religion of Belief) Regulations 2003. Mr Wolfe, the Claimant, will represent himself, then Mr Showhard will make the Respondent's representations. The Claimant will then be able to make a final response before we hand down our Judgment. Is that understood?'

David nodded, looking at his hearing notification, to double check the name of the Chairman. It was the Right Honourable Lord Justice Sir Stephen Steadfast of the Court of Appeal, Civil Division.

'Mr Wolfe, as you may need to give evidence you are required to take an oath. Which Holy Book, if any, would you like to use?'

David's continued to shuffle. 'Which do you have available?'

The Chairman closed his eyes as he took in the reply. He leant over to consult with the clerk then looked up sternly. 'The Bible, the Qur'an, the Bhagavad Gita or the Guru Granth Sahib?'

'I'd like to use them all please, as accords with my religion.'

The Chairman's tone was withering. 'Mr Wolfe, you have to choose just one, and we cannot proceed unless you take an oath.'

Every other sound disappeared as David paused for a moment, then repeated his words. 'I'd like to use them all, as accords with my religion.'

The Chairman stopped. There was a thud as he opened a heavy book of regulations. Its thin paper rustled whilst he referred to the law, thumbing leaf after leaf. Finally he stared at David. 'Right, Mr Wolfe, as you refuse to cooperate I will use the Chairman's right to get evidence from you by request.'

'I don't refuse to co-operate, I just want to swear an oath according to my religion.'

'Mr Wolfe. Do you want to end the proceedings?'

David shook his head.

'Then I will use the Chairman's right if I need to. Let's begin by dealing with who the correct Respondent is. Mr Wolfe, you have put Sir Lionel Scarota, but you have also put the Prime Minister, Mr Timothy Blar.'

'Yes, the Prime Minister appoints the Director.'

'But clearly the Prime Minister is not responsible for the choices of artworks at the Sugar, so you will have to drop Mr Blar or we cannot proceed.'

David's mouth went dry. He looked at the jug of water. 'But the Prime Minister is pivotal. He appoints the Director, who selects the discriminatory art that the public "should" appreciate.'

'Do I need to repeat myself? If you insist on including the Prime Minister then I will call an end to these proceedings. You will be able to appeal my decision but if you are unsuccessful in your appeal you will be liable for full costs.'

Clearly pressure had been brought to bear. Clearly the Prime Minister didn't want anything to dent his faith credentials. The Tribunal was beginning to have the same stink of corruption as the art world.

David had waited 2 years for this Hearing, pursuing the case from the Employment Tribunal to the Employment Appeal Tribunal. They had tried every trick in the book to dismiss his claim rather than let it go to a full hearing. He had outsmarted them at every turn but now, at the final stage, they had him in a corner. If it went to appeal he would be bogged down in red tape for another year.

There was only one reply. He poured himself a glass of water. It was luke-warm. 'Alright, I agree to drop the Prime Minister from the case.'

There was a sense of relief from the Chairman. 'Then we will amend the Respondent to just Sir Lionel Scarota.' He scribbled some notes then leant forwards. 'So let's begin. Why exactly do you think there is discrimination against you Mr Wolfe?'

David handed out copies of his skeleton argument, which set out the information in the correct legal manner. 'I sent a proposal to Sugar Modern to put on a "Business Messiah" artistic performance, based around my religious visions. This proposal was rejected.'

'Yes, but why was it religious discrimination?'

David's reply was calm. 'The statistics clearly show that the works presented at the Sugar are atheistic, express some kind of vague mysticism or are directly offensive towards Christianity. "Religious" art is not included and this means that the curators are discriminatory against religious artists and their art.' He flicked through his notes, carefully organising the information. 'At best they show the spirituality of artists like, Jackson Pollock and Mark Rothko. At worst they show anti-religious works like Herbert & George's "Shit Christ", Sarah Lucas' "Christ made out of Cigarettes," and Chris Awfully's "The Holy Virgin Mary" surrounded with pornographic images. And none of these are even original. They are just derived from Andres Searing's "Piss Christ," a 1987 photograph of a crucifix in urine. What next? Tampon Christ, Mucus Christ, Semen Christ?'

'But surely this selection isn't discrimination, it's just artistic preference.'

'No, it's not a preference, it's bias, and it's been getting worse with the violent work of artists like Damien Heist. He mocks religion, with his pretend Satanism, slicing cows in half as sacrifices to the God of money. The works are evil.' David felt a bristle in the room, he had overstepped the line or had he just struck a deep nerve. 'But you aren't allowed to say this to the liberal art-world. They say his art makes us look at the world with fresh eyes. But society is just being manipulated and infected with Heist's "values".' David was aware the Chairman was writing none of this down. 'The galleries are socially engineering people into being anti-religious. They pretend that they show avant-garde art but they censor any real protest because they are dictated to by corporate collectors who only want art that celebrates brutal, selfish capitalism. Religion is banned.'

'We understand your disappointment Mr. Wolfe, but surely selection is just based on artistic preference. And surely the best art has always been commissioned by the rich.'

The Chairman watched, aloof from David's deadly earnest expression. 'That's the problem. The system of the rich selecting art hasn't changed since the times of the Medici family in Renaissance Italy. And the Medicis were worse than the Mafia. They murdered and cheated their way to the top and even put their own corrupt Pope into power. But no matter how much money you give to a talented artist, if they have sold their soul to money then they will never produce truly religious art. The best religious art is done by poor monks and devoted believers. And this is the kind of work that the Sugar refuses to show.'

'We understand your point Mr. Wolfe.' The Chairman finished making a note. 'But I don't think it is proof that the Sugar galleries have a deliberate bias against selecting religious art. I think we can move onto your next point now.'

David didn't see how he could be any clearer, but he had to move on. There was no arguing. He composed himself as he looked through his notes. 'Curators need to be held responsible for the decisions they make but because there is no regulation of the way that art is chosen all kinds of discrimination occurs.'

'Mr Wolfe, you can't possibly regulate subjective choices.'

'No, that's a fallacy. They aren't subjective. Classical art has formal "standards" based on originality, draughtsmanship, composition, form, tone, perspective, brush-stroke, colour, light, narrative, meaning, etc. And Modern Art kept many of these standards but now they've all been over-ruled by the whim of rich, white, male collectors.' David stared the Chairman in the eye. He had struck another chord.

'But regulations would just destroy creativity?'

'No, regulation would ensure maximum creativity occurs, because it would stop the same old ideas and styles of work from being regurgitated and passed off as original and would mean that the creative contribution of all kinds of people would be valued. But racist, sexist, anti-religious art continues to flourish because the art world is controlled by bankers and the corporations who are against regulations.'

The barrister dropped his pen emphatically. He looked at the Chairman, as if to ask, 'Aren't you going to stop this farce?' Then he spoke. 'Might I just add a note of explanation, to help clarify Mr Wolfe's confusion?' The Chairman nodded and the barrister continued. 'As a public gallery the acquisitions of the Sugar merely reflect the interests of the broader art world.'

'And that's the problem,' replied David. 'This broader art world is run by oil corporations and financial institutions who use art as a way to culturally dominate us. It's the same as the way that Adolf Hitler used art as propaganda to promote Aryan purity. He exhibited classical German Art and only put on exhibitions of Modern art to show that it was the "degenerate" art of Jewish profiteers. These were his unregulated, "subjective" choices.'

The Chairman's brow furrowed. 'Mr Wolfe. What is your point?'

'My point is that regulations would have prevented the Nazis from selling art-works, stolen from Holocaust victims, to US collectors like the Rockschilds. But there were no such regulations because many of these collectors were linked to companies that had business dealings with the Nazis.'

'To be honest Mr Wolfe, I've listened to your arguments and they appear to be speculation with no relation to the case at hand.'

'Okay, let's look at the facts.' David began to read from his notes. 'The works are now in the collections of patrons like the Rockschilds' New Bank od Manhattan and from corporate sponsors, like Petroleum British and the Switzerland Union Bank (SUB). The Sugar displays these works and this both enhances the sponsor's corporate image and boosts the value of the art. And when Rockschild lends his paintings by Andy Warhol, Mark Rothko and

Jackson Pollocks their value goes up   by millions. Then, when they donate artworks to public galleries, they get a 50% tax back for the overvalued work. None of this is regulated, which is no surprise, because the whole art system is corrupt.' David poured a glass of the lukewarm water and continued. 'And dealers and buyers bid for their own works from their own auction houses to artificially inflate their prices.'

The Chair put down his pen and settled into a calmer position of consideration, clearly pleased with himself. 'I'm sorry but I just don't see how your unproven allegations and your personal objections to the high prices paid in the art world are relevant to your claim.'

David realised his face was glowing so took a deep breath and returned to a steady pace. 'It's all background to my main point, that the world of finance is dominated by corrupt businessmen who make discriminatory choices. Take the recent Chairmen of the Sugar Trustees. They have all worked for the Rockschild banks, and the Rockschilds recently worked with the Prime Minister to raise funds to purchase US art for the Sugar. And when the Prime Minister leaves office his new job will be with a subsidiary of the Rockschilds' Bank.'

'Mr Wolfe, if you don't stop mentioning the Prime Minister I will have to suspend the Hearing.'

'Sorry. I wanted to show that corporations use art sponsorship for financial gain but they also use it for cultural domination.' He looked through his notes to find his place. 'Sugar Modern put on an exhibition of Chinese Contemporary Art and shortly after this the China Investment Corp put a $3 billion, 10% stake, into a Rockschild Private Equity group. At that point the Rockschilds donated £5 million to the Sugar. The exhibition was a sweetener to get the Chinese to do a deal with the Rockschilds but it was also a part of a plan to change Chinese culture, by encouraging Chinese artists to join the corporate collectors in their Satanic program, of celebrating sex, money and violence. Chinese artists now made photographs of Gods worshipping mobile phones, Christ crucified on cans of coke, and Christ with his genitals hanging out.'

David paused to check he still had the Chairman's attention. 'The Chinese, the Saudis and the Asian countries have financial reserves earned from manufacturing and oil sales and the Western financial firms opened these reserves up, getting the countries to invest in their Private Equity firms that sell high risk loans whose values are artificially hiked because they are based on projected returns. They're just like the artificially high art prices.'

His throat was dry. He had another sip of the unpleasant water. 'And just like the art market, the value of these companies is based on a house of cards. So when it collapses these countries will lose heavily. This whole agenda is corrupt and my performance at the Sugar was to show how faith in God could provide a new model for a global economy.'

David now straightened his papers. 'In summary, my religious artwork should have been accepted by Sugar Galleries. Instead I was discriminated against because Sugar is controlled by the banks and oil companies who want to create a climate of greed and selfishness.'

The Chairman raised his eyebrows to check that David had finished, then sat upright. He looked at the Sugar's team then returned his gaze to David. 'I have listened carefully to your presentation, Mr Wolfe.' He folded his hands on his desk. 'But I'm afraid to say that you have not submitted concrete evidence over any of these points so I will not be able to consider them in my final Judgment. The only evidence we have is that you submitted an application to put on a performance and that this was rejected.'

David's stomach sank. 'But when I requested an order from you to make Sugar disclose evidence you denied that it was relevant.'

The reply was casual, off the cuff. 'Then you should have appealed against my decision.'

'I couldn't, because at the time Sugar's legal team was bullying my web-host into taking my website off-line.'

The barrister stabbed his pen into the page then spoke in a well-educated drawl. 'That was because Mr. Wolfe infringed our client's copyright. Using their logo in one of his so called artworks.'

The Chairman interrupted before David could defend himself.

'Thank you Mr Wolfe. I will take into consideration what you have just said when I make my Judgment. Now Mr Showhard, if you would like to present your arguments.'

The barrister rose to speak. His pinstripe suit looked shiny, slippery. His tone was deferential. David paid close attention. 'Sir, our response to Mr Wolfe is brief. Crucially, we contend that he is not even covered by Employment Discrimination Regulations. The law says that if there is no offer of work then there can be no application for work and therefore there can be no discrimination over work. Mr Wolfe sent a submission to my clients but they had never put out an invitation for proposals for work, at best they just had an open "encouragement" to submit ideas but never any offers of work. So Mr Wolfe is not covered by the regulations.' David was scribbling notes, considering how he could reply.

'Furthermore,' continued the barrister in a patronising tone, 'it is clear that Mr Wolfe is a second rate artist who has engaged in a cynical publicity stunt against our client. His motives are frivolous and vexatious and we believe that he should pay the full costs of our client, around £50,000 in barristers' and solicitors' fees.' The barrister sat back, arms folded, hiding a smile.

'Thank you Mr Showhard,' said the Chairman. 'Mr Wolfe you now have an opportunity to respond, but please make it brief.'

David responded to each point. 'My case is not a publicity stunt. It's done to establish the right of artists not to be discriminated against. As a barrister for the Sugar it is only natural that Mr Showhard thinks that all artists are vain and cynical. But as a religious artist I'm against that kind of art. My art is not for my own glory, it's for God's. Besides, my case cannot be a publicity stunt as the corporate newspapers refuse to report on it.'

From the corner of his eye David saw the barrister's chest rising and his breathing quickening. The barrister contained his anger by folding his arms around his rigid frame.

'It's also ridiculous to say that I did not apply for work. "Encouragement" is the standard way that Sugar recruits artists for work and should be covered by employment legislation because encouragement to terrorism and encouragement to murder are legally punishable offences.'

David indicated that he had finished his response and the Barrister half rose from his seat. 'If I might just clear up the Claimant's confusion. My clients at the Sugar want unsuccessful artists to feel included. That is why they are "encouraged" to submit ideas but there is no real offer of work.'

'Thank you Mr Showhard. That's a useful point.'

David could almost hear the scribble of the Chairman's pen as he tried to object but the Chairman held a hand to stem his words until finally the Chairman spoke. 'The parties will please take a moment whilst I retire to consider all the points before returning to hand down my Judgment.'

The clerk stood, calling, 'Tribunal rise.' They all rose and waited until the Chairman left.

Then David straightened his notes and Rachel put her hand on his shoulder. 'You did really well.' She squeezed. 'It's clear to anyone that you won.'

-

David didn't want to talk as the time passed slowly to the artificial ticking of the electric clock. The room felt claustrophobic.

He began to pray as they waited for the Chairman to return, to deliver the Judgment.

When he opened his eyes the sky had clouded over and they were now bathed in the radiance of strip lights. The heaters were breathing out, drying his lips and he was sweating under his collar.

He cooled his hands against the table top as the clerk called, 'Tribunal rise.'

They rose as the Chairman entered.

'Please sit.'

There was a long pause. 'I have considered all the merits of the Claimant's case, including his request for evidence to support his allegations. In this instance I rule that his claim fails on the grounds that a gallery is free to encourage the submission of proposals for work without needing to have any work available. As a result there was   no true offer of work and so there was no application for work. This means that there is no jurisdiction to hear his claim. However, I would like to add that even if a true offer of work had been made and that discrimination in the selection process, would be too difficult to prove.'

The Chairman now looked at the barrister. 'So I find that the Respondent, Sir Lionel Scarota, did not discriminate against the Claimant in any way.' Smiles of relief broke on the faces of the barrister and solicitor. The legal system had given them the answer that they required.

He turned back and showed David a stern face. 'Full written reasons will be sent to both parties in due course. You have leave to Appeal to the Royal Courts of Justice within 14 days of this Judgment but please note, Mr Wolfe, that if you do then you will become liable for the Respondents full legal costs.'

David nodded that he understood and the clerk called again, 'Tribunal rise.'

Everyone rose in disciplined obedience and the Chairman left with an understated sense of ceremony.

As each party began to shuffle out of the doorway the barrister offered David his hand. David shook it whilst catching the smug grin of the solicitor. Her face changed to a fake smile and she offered him a limp hand.

-

Stepping out into the fresh air, onto the steps of the Tribunal, they avoided the photographers and reporters who were jostling a young Muslim girl and her legal team. He heard a reporter asking, 'So you say you were discriminated against because you weren't allowed to teach in a veil?'

David shook his head. Why were they reporting on this new case and not his ongoing battle for artist's rights.

The tower of Sugar Modern mocked from across the road, from across the Thames. 'I don't want to go that way,' he said to Rachel. He pulled his trolley behind. Rachel held his hand. She was beautiful, a consolation.

They walked in silence, until they found a café that overlooked the river.

They sat on aluminium chairs around a metal table. A waitress came. David thanked her as she cleared the table and took their order. But he didn't look at her.

'So that's it then,' he said. 'My case was thrown out on a spurious technicality.'

'So what are you going to do? Will you just let it all end there? Aren't you going to Appeal to the Royal Courts of Justice?'

'It's pointless. I'll become liable for the £50,000 costs that Sugar was hounding me for. Then they'll really hammer me. Besides I put my faith in God and it seems like He doesn't want the   case to progress, so I should leave it. Maybe He has something else for me.'

'But it's so unfair!'

'The whole system is and the Chairman was just someone the government could trust to reach the "correct" decision. Incidentally, he was recently criticised for proposing to put profiles of the entire population onto a national DNA database. He's also Jewish. Along with Scarota, Saturate, Rockschild.'

Rachel raised an eyebrow. 'That's interesting.' They became silent as the waitress returned with their drinks.

'But I don't want to go there. It's dangerous anti-Semitism,' said David. 'And, after all, I'm Jewish as well.' He blew on his strong latte as Rachel sipped her tea.

Her fingers followed the line of the chair. 'Well at least they haven't managed to get you for legal costs.'

'It's still cost me enough. If I hadn't started teaching salsa dancing to top up my income I'd be completely broke.' He drank the bitter coffee.

'But don't forget that you've brought about some important changes. Last week you told me that the Sugar Gallery announced that it was addressing the discriminatory balance of the work in its collection.'

'Yes, but they've made it into an issue of sexual discrimination, using it to promote female artists already in their collection. And the religious art that they are starting to show has to be by young Muslim women who make works like "How to decorate a bomb."'

'How sick.'

'Yes, but like with the Chinese, it's all a way to make Muslims feel included in the "art game." So they can sell art to rich Saudis whilst maintaining a climate that makes fun of religion. I just pity everyone still caught up in it. I'm not going to do any more art. The whole system is too corrupt.'

'You say that, but what's your next art-work going to be?'

He folded his arms then stroked his head with his right hand. 'No I mean it. That's it. My art career, 15 years of my life, finished. Paul was right. Doing art was a big mistake. I ended up dressing like a madman, half possessed by the Devil. I compromised myself and I'm still in a bit of a daze.'

'Don't worry. You'll find what you want to do. You always do. That's what I admire about you.' Her hand stroked his shoulder.

They both stared across the Thames, for some time.

Then Rachel began to pull her fingers through her hair. She kept looking at him, for reassurance, then finally broke the silence. 'David, can we talk about the salsa?'

He shook back into ordinary reality. He'd gone over this before. He looked down at his coffee. 'Don't worry about it.'

'I know but it's different now. If   you aren't going to do art any more, well, what are you going to do instead.' She straightened the knots, pulling, combing hard. 'You wouldn't leave me for a better dancer would you?'

'No, I said, our relationship is far more important than dancing.' He put his hands on her knee.

She let him hold her hand. 'But we have a problem. I've even been praying to Oshumare, asking him to stop you from taking the dancing too seriously. Why can't we just keep it as a bit of fun?'

'I try to, but it's something I can do, something I'm good at, and it's easy to use the dancing to escape from my failures.'

'You aren't a failure. But the energies of the dance are dangerous. They can take you over if you aren't careful. Sometimes you frightening me, when you start spinning and turning so fast.'

'I'm sorry, it frightens me as well. It's like a ride. I don't know how to get off.' David knew that he had allowed the dance to become an obsession. In the orgiastic dance of the nature god, where everyone danced faster and faster, in a crescendo, until they reach a peak of ecstasy, he had unleashed the power of the Hindu god Siva, a trickster, who led the dance of creation and destruction.

He put his head onto her shoulder. 'My life's a mess.' A tear fell down his cheek.

'I'll help you.' She squeezed his hands.

'Thank you.' David stared across the Thames and sighed. 'Is London beautiful?'

Rachel stroked his hair, 'Not really.'

'So why are we here?'

'Maybe we should move.'

'Maybe.' He continued to stare across the Thames. 'Maybe we should move to the Lake District.'

'And live together in a cottage. I can get work as a management consultant up there. I can make enough for us both to live on.'

'Mmm, but I still like teaching salsa.'

Rachel snapped to attention as David's eyes momentarily strayed towards the waitresses tight black trousers.

'Look at the way you just looked at her! You keep doing that, looking at other women.'

He replied in a hushing tone. 'I don't.'

'What's wrong with me?' Her eyes pleaded into his.

'Nothing.'

'Why don't you look at me in that way?'

'I do.' He sat up, drank and looked away.

'No, David, you don't. And what about that girl the other night. The good dancer.'

'What girl?' He knew the one. He'd enjoyed himself. She'd moved fluidly and gracefully. A better, younger dancer. He knew at the time that Rachel had been studying his face, his reaction. But he couldn't stop himself.

'I was watching you. I saw the way you looked at her. Why don't you dance with me like that.'

'I do.' He picked up his cup, but he'd already drained it.

'No, David, you don't. You say you do but you never do.'

'I do.' Now they had entered a completely different reality. His case, his art, his religion, all forgotten.

'Look at me. Tell me to my face that you love me.'

'Please don't make a scene.'

'See, you don't love me.'

'I do. It's just you're putting me on the spot again, in public. You know I don't like to discussing personal matters in public.'

'Just tell me you love me.'

'Please don't raise your voice.'

She grabbed his arm. 'Tell me. Please.'

He twisted free and stood up, pushing back his chair. 'That's it, I'm going.' He headed away from the cafe.

'Noo, please, I'm sorry, don't leave. Not like this, please, please.'

An elderly couple hid their pleasure at seeing them squabble.

'I just need you to make a commitment David,' said Rachel, the desperation in her eyes welling into tears.

As far as he was concerned they were married and he wanted to stay together with her. Yet even though she was perfect for him, even though she was beautiful, slim, and sexy, even though he loved her, he still lusted for other women.

'Can I have a hug?' she pleaded, as the tears fell.

'I love you,' he said as he embraced her, trying to ease her sadness.

She searched her shoulder bag for a handkerchief, dried her eyes and then began to paint her lips, gently and precisely, without a mirror. Her mouth glistened with a pink gloss. It was full and soft. Her pupils widened, framed behind running mascara. 'David, can I have a kiss.' She moved close, her lips pursed.

He moved away and she slapped his chest. 'What's wrong with me? Why am I so damn ugly to you?'

'You're not, you're not. You are beautiful on the outside, but even more beautiful on the inside.' His hands stroked her sides. 'I just don't feel like it at the moment.

-

That evening he gently pushed her onto the bed. Kissing, caressing, firmly arousing her thighs, her breasts. They built into a passion, a frenzy of love and lust. Stripping their clothes, flinging them to the floor. He mounted her cool, smooth body as she grew wet. Then thrusting between her moist thighs, penetrated her gently, again and again, then deeper, longer, harder.

Locked in the embrace of her legs she panted, as if gagging, giving out deep moans, flushed scarlet. He pounded, again and again. A cry breaking up her moans.

She was his ideal, but now they were in an animal union, his erection dominating her, pushing into her crotch, bringing her into orgasm again and again. But when they peaked, his power was spent, his energy destroyed. But her capacity for love remained endless, and she yearning for an emotional whole. He felt vulnerable to her. Had he satisfied her? But the way that she kissed him and stared into his eyes answered his questions.

'Hold me tight.' She asked as they curled up in bed. She wanted him to protect her, in everything. He held her. 'What are you thinking about?'

'Nothing.' He didn't look at her.

She spoke softly. 'No, you are. I can tell. Please tell me.'

'I'm just happy that you still love me.'

'Of course I do. You are the most wonderful person in the world.' She hugged him tightly. He felt her sensitivity, her love.

'I love you too.' They kissed and she snuggled into him. Soon she was asleep.

But as she lay, in his arms, his last feelings of divine protection ebbed away. Her body felt too hot. Lifting her arm he freed himself to pray, 'O God, please save me from corruption!'

He condemned himself. 'You are corrupt! You are eternally corrupt!' Why had he been obsessed with gaining recognition in the artworld. Why didn't he have more faith in God? Why hadn't he looked after the people that he loved.

He stared, wide-eyed, from his pillow, as he realised that he had lost his way. Deep down he didn't care about love. Everything he'd been doing had been about himself.

19. The Prophecies

On the 7th day of the 7th month of the 7th year, 7.7.7. David knelt on a large, flat rock in the centre of the ruined chapel of St. Patrick, on a rocky outcrop overlooking Morecambe Bay.

The ancient sandstone chapel dated to the 8th century C.E. but was from an older consecrated site that dated back to 1000 B.C.E. It was built upon a rock that was sheer on three sides. And now its walls were half surrounded, by tall trees.

In front of David, to the west, six human shaped tombs were cut out of a large, flat rock. The bones that they once contained were removed long ago.

As he kneeled he noticed patches of moss on the stone beneath him. They seemed to be conscious of being alive. The rays of the lowering sun glistened on the grains of silica in the sandstone and a long shadow cast behind him, between the ruins that flanked him.

To the north, to his right, was the last remaining full wall. Through its semi-circular archway was a sheer cliff edge dropping to the beach and a stretch of sea, that crossed the bay to the Maitreya Institute and the Lakeland Mountains beyond.

The wind blew, rustling the trees and stroking the grass. It buffeted his ears, mixing with the sound of the sea against the shore far below.

A dog barked as birds trilled, and seagulls laughed as he gazed forwards, from the pinnacle of rock, the centre of the chapel. He let himself feel the wind blow away the impurities of his past as cloud half-covered the sky whilst dazzling shards from the sun still reflected on the sea. For a moment they blinded his view of a horizon that was once limitless, but was now fenced with rows of windmills. To the south of this wind farm was Heysham nuclear power station. A concrete cathedral to nuclear energy.

A splash of rain fell upon his head and upon the black cover of his book. He opened it. Another splash darkened the paper.

His legal case had been his most religious artwork, closest to the "logos," to the "word" of God. The prophets may have been artists but their real art lay in words. The New Testament, the Torah, the Qur'an, the Guru Grant Sahib, the Bhagavad Gita. All were the words and laws of God.

He realised that he needed to write a religious book. Not a work of "modern" literature, whose vain writers were greedy for fame. No. A Holy book, where the writer was the voice-piece for the Divine.

He had come full circle. Once again he knew that religion was more important than art. He'd grown further from God than ever, trapped in vanity and lust, nourishing his soul in the gratification of his desires.

He prayed for forgiveness and direction, promising to exorcise himself of the demons and spirits that had infected his mind and had "possessed" him.

He wanted to cry, for his tears to mingle with the drops of rain upon the page, but the wind had blown his eyes dry.

As the clouds cleared an opening all he could hear was an unquestionable, essential voice. 'Man on earth, write this book.'

He looked down at the unfathomable blankness of the page.

'Oh Lord God. I am sorry for things that I have done. Please forgive me, on this sacred site. Grant me, please, your clear revelation. Thank you God. Amen.'

He continued to pray. This time upon the page. He didn't know what drove his hand but his pen moved with quick, defined, irreversible strokes.

The words, the commas, the final stop.

Page after page.

7 prophecies.

Each rapid.

Each finished with "7.7.7."

The flow stopped. He became aware of his own writing.

This was where he would find his answers. For the first time he began to feel fulfilled.

By God's grace "The Book" would be his second chance.

"7.7.7."

Part II – The Auditors of God

Prophecy 1

The World will be consumed in greed. The leaders of the faiths will meet to fight this greed.
7.7.7

The serpent was calm and still. It was familiar, comforting. Slowly it began to move and David felt invited to stroke it's under belly. He was surprised how dry it was to touch. It writhed and coiled around his arm, like he was gripping a rope. Its red tongue darted, and a hissss issued forth. The faint odour of sulphur made his tongue twitch, but then it became almost soothing.

The serpent began to leave his arm, heading towards his leg. The crusty skin began to moisten in his sweat. Its rub now aroused him. He twitched, a spasm of revulsion at his own desire. The serpent turned to face him. Hissss.

Startled awake he called out the name of Jesus Christ.

-

David entered the first floor room of a large, white Georgian terrace at Lancaster Gate, London. He was dressed in black, with a Cross inside a Star of David on one lapel of his black suit and a Rainbow Swastika on the other. His beard now thick, his brow furrowed and on his head was a skullcap. His mixture of faiths gone. He now followed a Messianic group, called Jews for Jesus, who tried to get back to the original Jewish teachings of Y'shua, Jesus. Rachel was behind him. She wore a creamy white silk chiffon head scarf.

Through the doorway about twenty faith leaders were gathered around a large oval table.

Standing in his way was a short Chinese man in a suit and round glasses. Hands clasped the man nodded. 'Mr Wolfe, I am Jintao, Zhang, from the Chinese Ministry for Religious Relations. I have been sent by Chang Qing.'

'Hello, I'm David.' He offered his hand to the man.

'A word of advice. When you meet Chang Qing you must say, 'Wo jiao Wolfe, David. First name second.'

'Wo jiao Wolfe, David.' He smiled and then tried to get past.

'Yes, yes.' Zhang Jintao blocked him. 'Also, no hands, just bow your head. Only in business use your hands.'

He smiled, 'This is business,' and bowed his head. He passed and then met with the firm handshake of an elderly man with a large beard, in a black turban and beige robes. It was the Shia cleric from Iran, Waheed Khomeini.

'Ah, David. I just read your old critique of art. I agree with you. Our museum in Tehran has billions of dollars of art collected before the Islamic Revolution. Picassos, Pollocks. It is all Satanic.' David blushed as the cleric led him to the podium at the far end of the room. It was part of the past that he'd moved on from.

The leaders turned to face him as he walked the length of the room. Near to him were the Christians, across the table were the Muslims and the Jews. At the far end of the room was a podium and behind this was a large Georgian Window that was flanked by lilies in vases. Bright sunlight flooded in and net curtains blew in the breeze.

Nearest to the podium was Alex Wilber, a tall, shaven headed American Buddhist in orange robes and Swami Dr Kailashnath Bandopadhya, a plump Hindu Brahmin, clean shaven in light peach robes.

His old acquaintance from Jerusalem, Rabbi Shmuel Jacobs, the Reform Jew, was there, with a small kippa positioned on the back of his head, over a thinning area of ginger hair. The Rabbi, an expert in corporate law, now exuded the authority of a person of both financial and political power. His beard was heavy and his voice was sharp, but he was also laughing demonstrably at loud comments from Jerry Fulwell, the American, Evangelist. Fulwell was dressed in an expensive suit, an open shirt and light reactive glasses that were dark as the sun shone in his face.

Rachel sat as David spoke. 'Welcome to you all. Thank you for attending. Our meeting today has been generously supported by Sheikh Abul Qasim Muhammad.' David pointed to the Saudi Arabian, a Sunni Muslim who wore orange tinted glasses and a white kifr headscarf, held by a black coil. This was another man that David remembered from Jerusalem. 'We have received apologies from the Unification Church, Shintos, Bahais, Jains, Rastafarians, Zoroastrians, Quakers, Jehovah's Witnesses, Seventh Day Adventists and Scientologists. The full list of names is before you.'

Only a Sikh gentleman, with a pointed black beard and orange turban, studied the papers in front of him.

David continued. 'Before we begin, please take a moment to pray in your chosen manner.' David rang together two finger sized cymbals and a high note resonated through the room.

The room was silent but the air felt warm and thick with thoughts. After a few minutes David rang the cymbals again and the room slowly stirred.

'I would now like to introduce our main speaker, Ricky Brands, of Version Enterprises.'

Brands had grey shoulder length   hair and a close cropped beard. With a youthful spring he took the stand then gripped the sides of the lectern.

'I'd just like to say how delighted I am to see you all here. And I'm sure you'll all be very interested in hearing about the religious business innovations that I've been involved in with David. But first we need to look at how our new business model has developed. In the last century brands like Microsoft, Coca-Cola, Nike, Virgin, Disney, gave consumers a myths and role models to live by. But people have grown tired of shallow consumerism and that's why ethical trading, in organics, fair trade, recyclables, have become a growth industry. But now the ethical companies have been bought out by big corporations who have eroded their original ethics. And religion has begun to go the same way. Corporations have begun to use religious references in their products. Here are a few recent examples; "Heaven Scent" perfume, "Sacred Chocolate," "Nirvana" holidays.'

From the far end of the room the long haired American Indian, Robert Gist, called out. His eagle feathers shook and the beaded leather pouch around his neck rattled. 'Once we were astonished that the "White Man" could think he "owned" our sacred land. Now your religion is being bought and sold in the same way.'

'Precisely,' replied Brands, 'but I'm not against this. With 2 billion Christians and 1.5 billion Muslims in the marketplace their interests cannot be ignored.' By now Brands' had wafted his expensive scent into the room. 'And this is why I have worked with David. Together we have divided my religious business department into tightly focussed sub-branches. My goal is to make a Version Islam and a Version Hinduism and to buy up stakes in the 50 key achieving companies that have a strong identity to each religion. I've currently got shares in religious papers like the Jewish Chronicle, Muslim News and the Hindu Times. And as each enterprise grows I will give, annually, 10% of its returns to charity and reinvest the rest into each group. I've already started with this and my company's growth has consistently out performed the markets.'

The delegates began to murmur a mixture of interest and mirth. The Sunni Sheikh stared hard, his protruding nose matching the curve of his bearded chin. 'But aren't your religious sales just a pious fraud.'

'No, the key to their success has been David's independent assessment of our corporate governance. He sent his people to my Annual General Meetings, to ensure that the correct items were on the agendas and that I didn't deal with companies making weapons, destroying the environment, or violating human rights. But the problem we now face is that to become more successful we need each sub-branch to be endorsed and run by faith leaders.'

David piped up. 'And that's why we're here. We need your help.'

Rabbi Shmuel Jacobs responded in his New York accent. 'I don't understand what you're saying.' The tassels of his prayer shawl swung beneath the rim of his jacket.

Jerry Fulwell filled him in as he eyeballed Ricky. 'He's trying to create a monopoly. He's trying to take over our Christian Music and television Channels.'

The 70 year old Anglican Archbishop of Nigeria, The Most Revd Peter Kwashi broke into a sharp laugh. His shaven head reflected sunlight, like his round glasses, like his chubby cheeks and boyish grin. 'I don't think you should be too worried Mr Fulwell.' He turned and continued with a low, Nigerian accent, bringing his hand down repeatedly. 'What you are both doing is wrong. But at least you don't sell religion like it was some kind of shampoo to wash sins away.''

David swept his hand over the table, offering it, palm up. 'It's not just about products. It's about services as well. We provide the Rabbis, Imams, Ministers and Priests for all the stages of life. Christenings, bar-mitzvahs, weddings, healthcare, funerals, blessings.'

Brands leant forward. 'Let me make it clear. Because of our success, less scrupulous companies are copying us, selling religious services, and if we don't work together then true beliefs might be wiped off the face of the earth.'

The Hindu, Dr Bandopadhya, laughed out loud and called down the table in a thick Mumbai accent. 'Rubbish. We can stand up for ourselves.'

Brands put forth a hand. 'Please, unless we work together, on a long term strategy, then we will be lost. Believe me, we are against the complete dumbing down and commercialisation of religions.'

Fulwell the Evangelist sat back, hands in pockets. His voice boomed across the table. 'Let the free-market take its course. It increases the wealth of everyone. And you'll find that in the end people will naturally choose the best religion.'

Brands had an unexpected fit of coughing. He drank from a glass of water, turned the page on his notes and resumed. 'We used to believe the same thing at Version,' said Brands, 'but it just doesn't work. The religions they chose hasn't stopped the number of people in poverty increasing by millions each month. It hasn't changed the fact that the world's richest 500 people have more wealth than the poorest 500 million.'

Fulwell shrugged his shoulders. 'Corporate charity programs help those in need.'

The Archbishop raised his eyebrows. 'Window dressing! In the Niger delta Western oil companies got fat whilst our people had to survive on less than a dollar a day.'

'Exactly,' continued Brands, 'the world has become a feudal state, with an international nobility who don't pay taxes and who don't help the poor. The poor are forced to work in sweat-shops, making luxury goods and crops for this Global Elite. And when they are caught breaking the law they pay $1 million fines, tiny amounts to them, and then just carry on the same. Governments can only afford to help their citizens by selling off state assets, like healthcare, industry and even clean water. And governments are controlled by this Elite who run the unelected International Monetary Fund, the World Bank and the World Trade Organisation. They offer loans when interest rates are low, then put interest up so the countries default on their debt repayments, and have to sell off more of their assets.'

Fulwell sat up. 'That's just conspiracy theory.'

'Conspiracy fact,' said the Archbishop. 'It's been going on for decades. In the 1970's OPEC, the Organisation of Petroleum Exporting Countries, raised oil prices and created economic collapse. The Saudi oil sheiks got extra profits and paid huge amounts to the financial institutions that advised them. These institutions bought up the collapsed African companies, then revived them, making huge profits whilst our people starved.'

The Sunni Sheikh held up his hand. His beige suit showed beneath his brown robes. 'The past. We were misled by kafirun.' He smiled nervously.

David interjected. 'Please note that today's meeting has been made possible with the generous assistance of Sheikh Abul Qasim.'

Brands took the lead and continued. 'The point is that the actions of companies caused people to starve and the companies won't let them have surplus food and medicines because it would harm profits. To make matters worse, the companies spread deserts, remove forests, drain ground water, push half of the world's species to extinction and cause global warming by burning fossil fuels. They destabilise countries and war results. A fraction of military spending could be used to prevented famine, but war is big business.'

Shmuel checked his watch. 'We've heard all of this before. So what do you suggest?'

'Well it's pointless to demonstrate. Look at history. 50,000 people demonstrated against the World Trade Organisation in Seattle in 1999. In response the riot police charged the crowd. Millions of people protested against the invasion of Iraq and it still went ahead.'

A South American priest, with short black hair and white collar, spoke. 'Sorry for interrupting. I am Father Emilio Rodriguez, president of the Pontifical Council for Interreligious Dialogue and Papal Envoy from Rome.' He paused. 'I must tell you, that protest still works and it is the only way that we can deal with what Saint Paul refes to as "spiritual wickedness in high places." That is why it is such a very dangerous activity for many of us. In my home, El Salvador, they wake protestors in the middle of the night, drag them from their houses and murder them. I have seen it happen many times.'

'Yes, we're faced with the same unjust systems that the prophets of our religions arose against,' said David, 'and we can't afford to be divided. We need to find the beliefs that unite us all and to work with Mr Brands to promote our faiths.' He pushed his papers further onto the table.

'But there aren't any shared beliefs,' said the Sheikh, emphatically folding his arms. 'Take this meeting. You knew I am Wahabi yet you still put me in the same room as this woman', he nodded towards Rachel, 'who is not under the veil. Is it an insult? Should I leave?' The Sheikh looked around the delegates. 'Why should we listen to you,' the Sheikh looked David up and down, 'the dancing Blasphemer.'

Everyone knew his dancing days were long gone, but they laughed, enjoying his embarrassment.

'I'm sorry for my mistakes, but please, wait, until you hear what we have to say. We can be united in belief.'

Shmuel squinted. 'Naaa. It can't work. We've too many conflicting values. We drink wine but Muslims ban alcohol.'

The Shia took pleasure in contradicting him. 'Although neither of us eat pork.'

Dr Bandopadhya replied. 'Eating meat makes people aggressive, and you Muslims are aggressive to us.'

Fulwell announced. 'I agree. Islam is an aggressive religion, with its suicide bombers.'

There was silence, then the voice of the Sunni dropped to whisper a final comment. 'Radical Muslims got the idea of suicide bombers from the Tamil Tigers, who were Marxist atheists.'

Brands clasped his hands together, as if in prayer, to distract them from starting a new quarrel. 'Please remember, we are all here as a men of peace. Like the Qur'an says, we are all "People of the Book." The title given to Jews, Christians and Muslims.'

'What book? Whose book?' asked Shmuel. 'The Muslims changed whole chunks of the Jewish Tanach.' Then he nodded at the Archbishop. 'And they changed your Christian Gospels as well.'

The Sikh spoke. 'Yes, and do you "People of the Book" allow Sikhs into paradise?'

The words were drowned out by the Sunni, who had stood up. 'Your so called "original" Torah of the prophet Moses was invented hundreds of years after his death.' He turned to the Archbishop. 'And you turned the prophet Jesus into a Pagan God.'

Fulwell the Evangelist dramatically pointed at the Sheikh. 'Whore of Babylon!'

David stood, banging his hand on the table. 'Stop fighting! Our enemies are the Satanic Corporations, corrupted by money and power.' His face glowed red. He now had their complete attention. His voice quietened. 'Please listen to what Mr Brands has to say.'

'There is a long history of religion being closely linked to business,' said Brands. 'The Benedictine Monks laid the seed for modern factories in their mediaeval monasteries…'

The South American priest interrupted, 'And the Catholic Second Vatican Council said there should be no separation between business and religious life, that we should see the world as a single family and we must use our profits to provide our fellow humans in food, clothing, housing, medicine, employment and education.'

'This is true,' said Jintao, 'and Confucius wrote that the harmonious family is the model for an ideal society.'

Fulwell spoke out. 'But if the Catholics believe in family then how come our Pilgrim Fathers only won their freedom after years of persecution. I'll tell you how, because God rewarded their hard work and industrial innovation.'

'What. By letting your ancestors steal my people's land,' said the Amerindian.

The Nigerian Archbishop continued. 'And take millions of my people for their slave trade.

Fulwell threw his hands in the air and turned his head from the table. 'You're both hypocrites. The Cherokees owned slaves and the Africans enslaved other Africans for years.'

But the Sunni Sheikh continued the attack, pointing to the Reform Jew. 'And your American Jews took the land off the Palestinians.'

Unexpectedly the elderly Rabbi Solomon Cohen, of the Orthodox Jewish Hasidic Satmar group, arose. He was unsteady on his feet and wore a tall black hat, a black suit, white shirt and black tie. He had a long beard and a large curved nose, upon which were black rimmed glasses. He spoke in a quiet voice and held his hand up to stop the Reform Jew from replying. 'And this should not have happened. The establishment of a Jewish state is divinely forbidden until the coming of the Messiah.'

Whilst Shmuel was trying to push the arm aside, Fulwell shouted over the table at the Sheikh 'Whadya mean? You Muslims ran the slave trade in Africa.'

'Please,' begged David, 'think about what unites us, so we can protect the world and the poor. When God created the world He declared all creation to be "good." Surely he wants us to look after His planet and all His creatures.'

The Orthodox Jew picked up the line of argument. 'The Psalms tell us that "The earth is the Lord's and the fullness thereof, the world and they that dwell therein." But Hosea warns us that when there is no acknowledgment of G-d in the land' then 'all who live in it waste away.' Then the solution will only come with the Messiah who will bring a time when, as Isaiah says, there will be joy and peace. Then "the mountains and the hills will burst into song, and all the trees of the field will clap their hands."'

Jintao nodded. 'The Tao Te Ching says that when man interferes with the Tao, the sky becomes filthy, the earth becomes depleted, the equilibrium crumbles, creatures become extinct.'

'In the Qur'an,' agreed the Shia, '"The creation of the heavens and the earth is indeed greater than the creation of mankind," and Humanity are the Khalifah, the trustees of Allah on earth.'

'And for us Hindus Nature is   sacred. If you damage the sky, the earth or the sea then you also damage yourself.'

'You see,' emphasised David, 'this clearly unites us all against the big businesses and their empty promises to do something about pollution. We need strict, religiously enforced quotas to prevent pollution.'

'But,' said Fulwell, 'the Bible says that God gave man dominion over the world. Our workers' have a right to their jobs in the mines and oilfields.'

The red lipped Dr Bandopadhya furrowed his brow, emphasising his orange tillac mark. 'And what about our farm workers? They also have a right to their jobs, but your climate change is destroying our agriculture. We are running out of fresh water.'

David pushed down on the table with his index finger, looking around the delegates. 'God wants us to grow but we need to know when to stop. But the Bible tells us what the real problem is. It says that you cannot serve God and Mammon and that the "Love of money is the root of all evil." It is the banks and their usury, a practice condemned in all our scriptures, that encourages people to be greedy and to over-work the land.'

'Usury is only half condemned,' said the Orthodox Jew. 'When Ezekiel said that those who charge interest and take increase, shall not live, it only applied to Jews. Because Deuteronomy tells us that "Unto a foreigner thou mayest lend upon interest,"'

Jintao interrupted. 'But you surely agree with the Tao Te Ching, that "when rich speculators prosper while farmers lose their land … it is not in keeping with the Tao."'

The Archbishop shook his head. 'And for Christians, all men are brothers, so all usury is bad. In the Sermon on the Mount Jesus says 'Sinners lend to sinners, to receive as much again. But love your enemies, and do good, and lend, hoping for nothing again, and your reward shall be great.'

'You know as well as I,' declared Fulwell, 'that Jesus condemned the unfruitful servant who did not get interest by investing his master's money in the bank.'

The Shia looked amused at the division over Christian scriptures. 'In Islam it is very clear. Usury is prohibited. Interest, "riba," cannot be charged and wealth can only be generated through legitimate trade.'

David quickly outlined more. 'Only 3% of financial speculation concerns real market exchanges. The rest is speculation that makes money out of money.'

The Shia gave a soft nod of concurrence. 'and this speculation is gambling.'

Fulwell looked overwhelmed. 'You've gone too extreme. There's a difference between acceptable interest rates and abusive interest.'

'No, we Shia have reviewed this matter. All interest is usury.'

'So what are you suggesting,' scoffed Fulwell, 'that everyone should have 0% interest accounts and never borrow any money?'

'No, profit can be generated through Sharia compliant trading, not through banking.' As the Shia spoke he looked at the Saudi Sunni.

The Saudi Sunni looked embarrassed then fired a furious look back at the Shia. 'I do not bank my money for financial gain. I do it to support the work of the Lord Almighty.'

Brands had been listening from the podium, startled by the disagreement. 'We all know that western banks lend to companies who deal in alcohol, pork, pornography, arms and other "Haraam" forbidden activities. So the City of London set up Islamic finance as a way to get hold of all the Middle Eastern petrol dollars.' Brands rocked forward onto the podium. 'But the problem is that most Islamic accounts in Western banks are just a kind of religious money laundering. The first bank sells the money to a second bank who then gives the original amount back to the original bank after gambling with it on the stock market. Only the Jews can be bankers who lend with interest. But this must only be to non-Jews and not to each other.'

Then Shmuel glanced up, looking surprised. 'You aren't going to win friends this way. That's not going to go down well with the banks.'

'That's the point,' countered Brands. 'We're in a financial Holy War against the Elite.'

Shmuel wagged his finger. 'Are you sure that you aren't just being anti-Semitic.'

Brands countered again. 'I know there are a lot of Jewish bankers, but it's nothing to do with being anti-Jewish. We're just against unfair banking.'

Fulwell folded his arms and rocked back in his chair. 'So what's in it for you?'

'Just like Sheikh Abul Qasim,' said Brands, 'I'm not interested in the financial reward. I used to be in my youth, but now I realise that God's work is the "bottom line." I have no personal money, I reinvest it all into the business.'

'Wise words,' agreed the Catholic. 'Jesus led a simple life and said "It is easier for a camel to go through the eye of a needle, than for a rich man to enter into the kingdom of God."'

'Wooah. Easy there. It's alright to be wealthy and follow Christ.' The Evangelical shook his head and held out a hand. 'The "eye of the needle" was a small gate in the walls of Jerusalem that merchants would get their camel through when the main gate was shut. It's difficult but it's not impossible.'

David knew the line of thought. 'There's no archaeological evidence to support your theory about the gate. The story implies that it's impossible for rich men to get to heaven. It's the same as in the story of the rich man and the beggar, Lazarus. When they died, Lazarus went to Heaven and the rich man went to Hell. It's teachings are clear.'

The American Buddhist tried to explain. 'Buddha's teaching is that all fortune is the cause of misfortune.'

Shmuel laughed. 'Okay, so how   come a Buddhist like Rajneesh set up sex communes in 1970's California and had a fleet of Rolls Royces.'

'He was Hindu, from India,' clarified the Buddhist.

Dr Bandopadhya interrupted. 'This is true, and I find myself disagreeing with you all. The money of Lakshmi, the Hindu Goddess of wealth is to be used, not just hidden away. Money is not the problem, It is the attachment to money that is the problem. But then attachment to any desires is an impediment to Enlightenment.'

The Archbishop gazed tiredly. 'I agree with Swami Dr Bandopadhya. We have come full circle. Like Christ said, it is the love of money, not money itself, that is the root of all evil.'

Brands' soft features grew stern. 'And the main point is that we must promote genuine religious belief in business to overcome the rampart greed that is destroying the world.'

'You just sound like a management "Guru,"' said the Reform Jew. 'I've seen them before.'

'No, no,' objected Brands. 'Management "Gurus" preach about developing businesses through positive thinking. They use spiritual techniques but still act like ruthless cut-throats. No, we want to transform companies into genuinely religious organisations.'

'I don't buy it,' said Shmuel, 'like I said, you're just a New Age "Guru."'

'Please, we're not preaching a New Age, mystical unity between religions,' clarified David, 'we want a coalition of believers who will follow a shared set of rules, to fight corruption.'

At that point the Sikh, Mr Jasbir Khangura, stood up. He wore rimless rectangular glasses and his beard was closely cropped. Around his waist was a small dagger, the Kirpan. He pointed to the symbol on his orange turban. His English was impeccable. 'These two swords represent our self and our responsibility to others. Only with these together can we be surrounded by the circle of God. If you show me how you provide these then we will follow you.' He sat down.

'So, then here is the solution,' said the Sunni, 'and you are free to follow this as you please, for as the Quran says, "there is no compulsion in religion." The Qur'an, the Hadith sayings of the Prophet and our Shari`ah law give clear guidance over all aspects of life.'

The Orthodox Jew's hand chopped onto the table. 'Sharia only has jurisdiction over Muslims. We will not follow a Shariah court.'

David noticed the rising anger around the room. 'Look, our foundational texts and traditions contradict each other in their details. But we all have a relationship with God and we all share the same enemy, the Global Elite, who hate religion because it preaches equality.'

Brands ran a hand across his hair. 'And remember, a Jewish company has more in common with a Muslim company than it does with a corrupt corporation.' He looked at Fulwell. 'So people need to start buying from their own religious communities. And we need to market ourselves in the mosques, temples, churches and synagogues, as being the only force left to fight against the satanic corporations.'

The Sunni stopped stroking his beard. His eyes widened. 'Here is a shared rule. The Qur'an says how the prophet Jesus summarised God's commandments. We must love God with all our might and we must love our neighbours as ourselves.'

The Taoist nodded enthusiastically. 'This is like the "Golden Rule" of Confucius. "Do unto others what you would have them do unto you."'

David felt a surge of uneasiness. 'It's too general.'

The Sunni continued speaking forcefully. His kindly manner was tempered by years of annoyance at servants who did not follow his orders. 'So here is a third solution. When Muhammad fled from Mecca to Medina he established a nation of equals and the Jews joined this new society and between them the "Covenant of Medina" was signed in 622 C.E. And for more than eight centuries it was the basis for the Muslim treatment of non-Muslims. Its terms were that Muslims and Jews had to live as one people. Each party kept its own faith, and did not interfere with the other's beliefs, customs, and laws. But if one was attacked the other must help and all had to be involved in any peace deals.' The Sunni's Jaw tightened. 'Now we are all attacked by the "democracy" and atheism so either we stop it, or it stops us.'

The Orthodox Jew gave a stiff nod. 'We can agree with you on that.'

'It is the same for us,' the Archbishop's deep voice resonated.

Shmuel's response was impatient. 'Without democracy we would have no declaration of human rights.'

'Those who follow the Qur'an have cleaner hands,' said the Sunni flatly.

Shmuel locked horns with the Sunni. 'That's ridiculous. Just look at the repression of freedom in Islamic states. Look at the way you treat women.'

The Sunni stalled in his anger so the Shia replied to the pointed question. 'My friend, your "Woman's Rights" have destroyed families and increased sexual immorality.'

The Sunni followed this with a furious look but realising his anger the Sunni calmed himself and smiled. 'We respect our women and for this they are happier than yours,' his eyes twinkled, 'who you treat like prostitutes.'

Shmuel's brow furrowed as Rachel recoiled in disbelief and spoke for the first time. 'I can't believe what you're saying!'

The Sunni raised his eyebrows above his tinted glasses and looked around the table. 'David, control your woman!' Half the leaders laughed.

Rachel looked incredulous 'I'm not standing for your power games. Every day your people force young girls into marriages with old men or kill them if they refuse.'

The Sunni turned sharply. 'You   kill children when you give women abortions.'

Her eyes darted like a cornered animal and she snapped back. 'You beat women and throw acid in their faces for not covering their heads!'

The Shia, now smiling, interrupted the Sunni's reply. 'Wait, she is right. Women in the Quran are equal to men. Superiority only comes for piety and righteousness. Let us not forget that the Prophet's first wife was a businesswoman for whom he worked.'

'But women need guidance,' pressed the Sunni.

The Orthodox Jew, had listened intently and now ventured his opinion. 'Controlling the lusts of women is a duty to G-d.'

At which the Archbishop announced to the full room. 'I'm glad this has been raised. Before we commit to anything I think you should know, David, that we believe you to be living in sin.'

The Sunni understood and continued. 'The Qur'an says "Ye that are unmarried shall marry." Do not let this woman corrupt you. Do you understand?'

The room went silent. They all starred at the couple. David was red, sweating. Rachel loved him, gave him deep down unconditional respect but all he could say was, 'Yes.'

Rachel's voice was now a whisper. 'I'm stunned.' Everyone waited for more. 'Are you saying that our relationship has been wrong? Don't you know what these people would do to your friend Sebastian?'

They smiled and moved in their chairs as David replied. 'Sebastian? I haven't spoken to him since he became a friend of Jim Rockschild.'

'Well I'll tell you,' said Rachel. 'They'd hang him for being gay.'

The Sunni frowned with deadly earnest. 'The irresponsible actions of gay men cause sexual diseases. What they need is the stick of the law to mend their ways and protect society.' The other faith leaders nodded in agreement.

'They deserve to be executed,' added the Shia.

With confidence Dr Bandopadhya added. 'Homosexuals should be fined, whipped and stripped of their caste.'

The Archbishop said abruptly. 'I wouldn't go that far, but the Episcopaleans in America who support gays are not true Christians.'

'And what about you David?' The Sunni exhaled, savouring the moment. 'What do you think?'

David felt a rising uncertainty. His throat was tight, his eyes swimming. 'We must not twist scripture to mean whatever we want.'

'David!' Rachel called. He turned, head down. Her voice was nervous. 'I love you more than the whole world but I can't take this. Don't you love me?'

He gave a calm look of apology. 'I have to love God first.'

'You only love yourself!' She turned to the delegates. 'You can keep all your religions and spiritualities. The lot of you are full of hate!' She pulled her necklace and threw it onto the table. The rainbow coloured beads spilled all over the polished wood. Her hand went over her mouth as she rushed out of the meeting.

'Rachel!' ordered David, surprised at his tone, but the door banged shut. The curtains fluttered. There was no sympathy around the table.

He drew a deep inhalation. The faces stared, unduly stern. He was preparing to be reprimanded. 'I'm sorry, I'll speak with her.'

The brown eyes of the Archbishop locked on. 'Sorry is not enough. You must marry her.'

'But I can't.' David's voice felt hollow. 'She's a divorcee.'

The Archbishop sighed, tired. 'No, David, it is allowed, if she was abused by her husband.'

David looked away for a moment. 'Yes, she was.'

With a concerned expression the Orthodox Jew added, 'it is better for a couple to divorce than to remain together in a state of constant bitterness and strife.'

The Sunni stared dead ahead. 'The same holds in Islam.'

The Catholic took a deep breath. 'Sorry, but Paul states, "if, while her husband liveth, she be married to another man, she shall be called an adulteress."'

The Sikh scribbled some notes. 'I'm also sorry. She can only remarry if she is a widow.'

Dr Bandopadhya just shook his head.

David was shaking as he stared at the table. 'Please believe me, I am truly sorry to God, for living against His Laws.'

The Sunni's low speaking voice filled the air with presence. 'David, we believe that you are sincere. If we didn't then we wouldn't be here. We are here because we want to know what you have to say.'

David looked up and the leaders nodded. He sat upright but he stammered. It felt like all the warmth and kindness of Rachel had been wrenched from him. 'The… Covenant… of Medina is a good pact, but it is not enough. So we need to return to the older prophets, who we know the Qur'an respects.'

'Yes,' said the Sunni.

David thought of Rachel as he continued. 'Well a Covenant was also given to the Prophet Noah after the Flood.' Water fell onto his cheek.

'Yes. Prophet Nuh.'

Dr Bandopadhya noticed the tear and tried to hide a smile. He prodded David further, in a sympathetic voice. 'Sorry, can you explain about this Prophet Noah and the Flood?'

Words escaped David. 'Rabbi… please… would you explain.'

The Orthodox Jew took over. 'G-d saw that the world had become full of wicked unbelievers. But in the midst of them was one righteous man, Noah. So

G-d told him to build an ark, into   which he took his family and two of each of the beasts of the earth. Then G-d sent a deluge to Flood to destroy all life on the earth. When Noah returned to dry land the Holy One made a Covenant with him, that He would never flood the world again. And the sign of this Covenant was a rainbow in the clouds.'

Dr Bandopadhya gave a wry smile. 'So why are we faced with another flood, if God said he wouldn't send one?'

David swallowed hard. 'Global warming is not God's doing. It's mankind's doing.'

Dr Bandopadhya paused, musing. 'But this Covenant is hardly a law for us to share.'

The Orthodox Jew patiently explained. 'The Talmud says that G-d gave Noah 7 laws to pass on to all his descendents, to all mankind. Any non-Jew who lives according to these laws is regarded as one of "the righteous among the gentiles." There is 1 law for each of the 7 colours of the rainbow.' He counted on his fingers. 'No idolatry. No blasphemy. No murder. No theft. No sexual immorality. No eating of meat that contains blood. And last of all. Men must establish courts of justice, and a righteous government, to police these laws.'

David looked around the room. 'Our religions all agree with these 7 laws.' He hesitated, feeling uncertain, as Dr Bandopadhya's eyes bore down on him.

The Sunni nodded. 'Islam does,' then he turned his gaze to the Brahmin. 'But what about idol worship?'

Dr Bandopadhya ceased staring at David and shook his head, caught out. 'Our statues are not idols, they are just images to aid worship.'

The Sunni's eyes twinkled. 'Is that what your villagers think when they feed them.'

Dr Bandopadhya opened his mouth to explain, then his face dropped and he dismissively wafted his hand at them. 'You are right. We will not sign this.'

The American Buddhist lifted his chair and moved it slightly away. 'Nor will we.' He said, flatly.

Encouraged Dr Bandopadhya now added. 'And we will not sign up to David's sexual immorality.'

The Sikh placed his palms onto the table. 'Despite his relationship to a divorcee he is a man of God and there is no alternative but to side with him.'

The Chinese man nodded. 'Wolfe, yes.'

The rest looked at each other, expressionless.

The pause was broken by the Amerindian. 'We wish to hear more before we decide.'

David began again, with renewed confidence. 'The responsibility for the legal requirements of each religion, like Jewish Kosher or Muslim Sharia, will remain with each religion. But I propose that a central judiciary, called the

Auditors of God, will ensure that the Noachide laws are followed. They will be a religious order that will take a vow of poverty so that it cannot be manipulated by corporate interests.'

His suggestion resonated.

'These Auditors will be religious teachers from each faith and will ensure that businesses, health agencies, educational establishments, the media and governments all follow religious practices. They will treat white collar crime as severely as any other crime and ensure that investments do not make a quick profit at other people's expense. A computerised register will ensure that Audited companies are encouraged to work together, and not with the enemy.'

The leaders listened intently.

'Our Auditors will go to the shareholder meetings to make sure that major companies tithe to charities and enforce labour standards, environmental safeguards and community building. They will also require each company to produce an annual report and only if the company complies with the Audit will they get a stamp of approval, just like the religious stamps for Kosher, Halal, and Fair Trade.'

Fulwell did not look convinced. 'You'll make things too strict for businesses. There needs to be some leeway!'

'Yes, I know,' said David. 'That's why they will only need to be 51% correct in their trading. As long as they repent and confess a list of their failings, for all to inspect, then they will get the stamp.'

Shmuel probed further. 'What if people repeatedly fail?'

The Catholic, elbows on table, fingertips touching, as if in prayer, tilted forward his hands towards David. 'Perhaps they could face excommunication.'

'Yes,' said David, 'if they do not try to change.'

The Shia's eyebrows arched with intrigue. 'This is interesting, but what is banned?'

David's eyes shot round the room. 'We will meet again to create a list, but no doubt it will include abortion, experiments on human embryos, usury, pornography.'

'Then we are interested in a covenant of Auditors,' said the Shia, nodding towards the papers.

'And we are interested,' added the Orthodox Jew. 'Providing we all remember that the ultimate Auditor is G-d'

David felt a bristle. 'We must remember God and make sure our congregations only purchase from Audited businesses. But it won't just be the Auditors that will keep the companies in check. The ordinary believers, the secretaries, the clerks and the customers will point the finger at any who breach the Audit. And these believers will also have a "Personal Audit" in order to be blessed.'

Shmuel rolled his eyes. 'That would be impossible to enforce.'

David continued. 'Each believer will have a book for coupons, for heating, transport, food, clothing etc, to prove that they have used Audited companies. If they successfully fill this for a year then they will get a stamp of approval from their religious leaders.'

Shmuel looked sceptical. 'But people can't afford to buy just religious or ethical products. They are in the hands of the supermarkets and the megastores.'

David's eyes shone. 'The Audit makes it inexcusable not to remember God. Believers will have to choose between comforts and excommunication.'

'I'm convinced,' said the Sikh. 'For too long I have put business first. This idea will allow people to be proud to be good Sikhs again.'

Now Shmuel cringed. 'Don't you think the governments and corporations will stop all this?'

Brands replied. 'The governments protect the super rich, but you Rabbis, Priests, Ministers and Imams can work with my Audited religious companies to make people too powerful for the government to stop. One by one the banks, the media and politicians will be transformed. Maybe the Auditors will even end up replacing the governments that fail the Audit.'

Those inspired were moving in their chairs, the rest looked troubled.

The Sikh asked suddenly. 'What will your stamp of approval look like?'

Jintao pressed. 'Yes, I was also wondering this.'

David explained. 'We propose to use four curved rainbows, to represent the four corners of the earth, joining together in the Noachide covenant. It forms an almost universal symbol of good luck and energy. A Rainbow Swastika.'

Shmuel's face dropped. 'That's a Nazi symbol for Christ sake!' His face went red as everyone stared at him. The Archbishop tutted.

David challenged back. 'The Nazis used it wrongly. They thought it was an Aryan symbol, taken from Europe to India, but they had no archaeological evidence to support that.'

The shock on Shmuel's face was genuine. 'Couldn't you choose something else? A circle or something.'

Dr Bandopadhya became enthusiastic. 'It is the emblem of Lord Shiva.'

The Buddhist added. 'And of Buddha.'

'Swastikas are also used by our Falun Gong,' explained Jintao.

The Amerindian nodded. 'And Navajo blankets were woven with swastikas.'

This was followed by the Catholic. 'It was also amongst the first Christian symbols found in the catacombs in Rome.'

The Shia smiled. 'And some of our mosques have this design.'

David hesitated, he needed to win over the Reform Jew, 'Some of the synagogues in Israel were even built with swastika mosaics.'

Shmuel began to patronise with the accent of a child. 'Look I've heard it all before. I even know Coca-Cola and the Boy Scouts used the swastika. But that was all before the Nazis and their genocide of the Jews. The Nazis stained the symbol forever, you can't bring it back.'

Anger welled up in the Shia. 'But if we banned all religious symbols that were associated with genocides then you would have no crosses, no Star of David. Besides, you think that the only genocide of importance is your Holocaust.'

David cringed and gestured to distance himself from the Shia. 'I'm sorry, Rabbi Jacobs, but you have to understand. We need a sea-change, a shift against the usury and greed in Western culture. It was a negative symbol for a brief moment in Western history but this obsession with the Western perspective that we are trying to get rid of. Besides, the Rainbow was God's sign that he would not Flood mankind again, so the Rainbow Swastika is a sign that we must never let genocides happen again.'

The Shia interrupted in a dangerously defiant tone. 'Usury is the cause of the world's problems and your Jewish bankers promote this most.'

'What!' gasped Shmuel. He turned, appalled, and looked at David.

David's heart was pounding. He took a quick breath, then tried to reassure the Reform Jew by correcting the Shia. 'It's not a Jewish problem. It's a problem with the Western corporations.'

'Nonetheless our nation must change,' shrugged the Orthodox Jew, adding fuel to the flame. 'Isaiah says that our mission is to be "a light unto the nations." We must set the example "Not by might, nor by power, but by His spirit." We must end usury.'

The Chinese man nodded. 'A nation centred on the Tao, that nourishes its own people and doesn't meddle in the affairs of others, will be a light to all nations.'

Shmuel stood, in shock, in anger. 'You can't talk. Look at all the Tibetans China has murdered.'

The Chinese man yelled back. 'Past instabilities! Our leader, Chang Qing, now bring… harmony… to country!'

Shmuel pushed away his papers and the leaders muttered as he marched angrily to the door. He held the door. There was silence. 'I knew I shouldn't have come here. But before I go, let me tell you, that it was John D. Rockschild, a Jewish banker, not a Muslim or Hindu, who gave ½ billion dollars to charity.' His intent gaze bore down on David. 'He was more a man of faith than ever you will be. You're just a Jew hating Jew.'

The door slammed behind him.

Prophecy 2

The heart of the greed
will be laid bare.
This heart will know
no shame and will
try to seduce the
leader of the faiths.
7.7.7

David now stood before the impressive tower-block of the Rockschild's New Bank of Manhattan. The clouds passed above the sunlit pinnacle of this modern obelisk, this bank, that had failed the Audit and whose chief executive had asked to meet David.

The sleek interior was whitewashed, like an art gallery, and David was overwhelmed by the grandeur of the abstract paintings that hung in its four floor high atrium. The hard marble floor and the unyielding designs reinforced the hierarchy of the corporate ladder. As did the aloof receptionist who directed him to a glass elevator.

Slick businessmen peered at him from their offices as it rose. And the higher it rose the more their curiosity turned into envious sneers. David turned in prayer, hands held over his briefcase handle, asking God to forgive them.

The doors hushed open and he was "greeted" by a human bulldog in a pin-stripe suit. Short and broad, he was in his fifties with a grey crew-cut. He stood in front of strong black chain railings, behind him, through glass, was a dizzying drop into the city. He gestured for David to head down a beech panelled corridor.

It was lined with Jackson Pollock's most brutal canvasses, splashed in red and black gouges of paint. Interspersed with these were Applethorn's glossy black and white photographs of scenes of sexual violence. The decadent art all looked the same, a repetition, like the panel reliefs in the courts of the Kings of Ancient Babylon and Assyria, displayed to impress approaching clients and to instil fear in executives.

The luxurious soft crush of the thick carpet invited him to like the works, to sign up to the ideals, to fall in line with the hierarchy. He shook off the temptation as he passed through the open doorway.

Wide windows revealed breathtaking views of the Manhattan cityscape and the Hudson River as Wagner's opera Parsifal played.

Sun raked into the room, lighting one of the two tanks of green formaldehyde that dominated the room. Each contained a half of a bull and David had to walk through the gap between them, through the sliced middle, to reach the now elderly Rockschild who sat at the far end of the office. He had put on weight, and his feet were on the desk.

'Hello David. Please make yourself comfortable. It's good to see you again, after so long.' David raised an eyebrow as Rockschild continued. 'As you can see, I finally had to take over my father's empire?'

He shook Rockshild's hand. It felt like lifeless clay. Rockshild's thick curly hair and permanent tan made him look young, but his unnatural skin, corrected with cosmetic surgery, stretched across wizened features, gave his age away.

'Do you like my collection? Selected from my father's Museum of Modern Art. Along with the CIA he helped make Pollock famous. They promoted his abstract art because it helped us in the "Cold War." His expressions of freedom and individualism were the perfect antidote to Soviet art, with all its kitsch pictures of workers and party leaders. But that was another era.'

The leather chair creaked as David sat down in front of Rockschild. He felt its smooth texture and its smothering comfort.

'And I bought this Heist sculpture to impress private equity investors. To let them know that we will take them on the bull-run and stampede anyone who gets in our way. That our business is to cut other businesses in half and then sell them on.'

David shook his head. Rockshild put his hands behind his head.

'I'm not sure what I did with Sebastian's work but don't worry, I still have your head sculpture on my roof. However, the loveliest part of my collection of works of beauty is your former partner, Rachel. She's now head of our management development programme.'

'I was hoping to see her.'

Rockshild gave a proud nod. 'I'm sure you were.'

David now struggled to be courteous. 'You're playing Wagner's music. Wasn't that Hitler's favourite?'

Rockschild cast a scathing look and dropped his fake hospitality. 'I hear that your religious banks have aligned with communist countries to try and take-over some of our banks.'

David stared back. 'All our Auditors are doing is removing corruption and fighting the West's unfair trade tariffs, created in your so called free market.'

Rockschild replied impatiently. 'Well, you might control some countries, but our "Corporations" own the World Bank, the International Monetary Fund and all the Central Banks.'

David felt a chill, then anger. 'Banks that have ruined the economies of the developing world.'

Rockschild feigned that he was hurt. 'We are the victims of irresponsible borrowing. The developing countries took our credit in good times and invested it as they saw fit. When the bad times came they defaulted on payments and we were left owed millions.'

David groaned in disbelief. 'You gave poor nations loans at low interest rates then increased the rates to collapse their economies. You took all their billions in reserves and then bought up all their devalued assets. And you did the same with poor people, forcing them to become bankrupt, repossessing their homes. Your usury was illegal and no one should pay you back. They should owe you nothing.'

Rockschild pulled his feet from the table and sat forward. 'This attitude of yours has begun to be a bit of a problem for us.'

'A problem for you?' David shook his head blankly. 'You want to control the prices of commodities around the world, playing with market prices, creating booms and busts, dragging down smaller economies and picking off any investments you like. You tried to get the Chinese to bail out your banks with the reserves that they were stockpiling, to protect themselves against an economic crash, like the one that you created in the Far East in the 1990s.'

Rockschild sat back with surprise then leaned onto the desk. 'You're too cynical.' Rockschild's voice was hollow. 'We can't just collapse the economy of China. For a start, they're too strong.'

'They were too strong,' replied David. 'But they lost millions that you owed them and had to write off the debt.'

The old man shrugged his shoulders. 'China played a cunning game. They tried to get us into a 1930's style economic crash, to force us to export our best weapons systems to them, so they could copy our weapon's technology. But we've been holding out because eventually arms manufacturing is the only industry that provides sustainable growth.'

David felt shocked.

'I'll level with you.' Rockschild's expression was grim. 'You've become China's pawn. They opened up their companies to your Audit to enjoy privileged trade relations with Third World countries. But meanwhile they're getting ready for war. We need you to fail them. It's your national duty. Join us. You could work with Rachel. We need someone to lead our new way.'

He felt a pulse of excitement as a vivid picture of Rachel flashed in his mind. He still felt betrayed, that she worked for Rockschild. He pressed his lips together, and composed his reply. 'I don't want to keep people ignorant and brainwash them believing in your selfish and ruthless market ideology.'

Rockschild gave a sneer of contempt and a quiet wave of dismissal. 'I prefer to call it social engineering. We just give people what makes them feel good. Our global surveillance society has so much data that our computers can predict what trends people will follow before they know themselves. We keep them happy and we keep society strong.'

David eyed him. 'But you forget, we also check on you.' He opened his briefcase and took out a thick document. 'And your misuse of personal data has failed our Audit.'

Rockschild slammed his palm onto the table, then regained his composure. 'We are in control.'

David didn't flinch. 'No, God is in control.'

'What's the difference?' Rockschild stood up. 'We are God! We control the media, CCTV, the police. We can get people to believe whatever we want.'

David kept his focus. 'We are exposing your corruption. This is now the era of religion, not the era of your Elite.'

Rockschild looked impatient. 'Religion is a fairytale for hypocrites. Look at the Catholics abusing children, the Muslims beating their wives. At least we give people what they desire in this life, not in some fantasy afterlife. Glamour and wealth are more important to people than God or morals. The weak and ugly use religion to attack the powerful and beautiful because they are jealous. Join us David. One day we will make everyone strong and beautiful.'

'As scripture says, "there will be no poor among you if only you obey the voice of the Lord your God..." I'm not interested in your way.'

Rockschild's eyebrow arched as he peered at David and then smiled. 'I know your weakness. Your vice is pride. You want to be a great religious leader. Join us and all your prophecies and ideas will come true, just in our way. But I tell you, if you don't we'll drag your name through the mud. We'll label you a lunatic.'

David's voice was firm. 'You preach some vague "world spirituality" so you can turn Westerners into sheep while you create wars between religions and sell arms to both sides.'

'They'd fight anyway. We just control the conflict, and as countries pay for arms we take control of their assets. Our aim is to control the world economy,' Rockschild began to sound like some kind of visionary, 'so that we can force governments to surrender their arms and nuclear weapons to our United Nations. And then war will be removed.'

David spoke hurriedly. 'You mean anyone who disagrees with you will be killed. It's global fascism. No different to Nazism. Our Audits on your corporations are damning. In fact many of your corporations helped put Hitler into power and supplied him throughout the war.'

'That's ancient history,' retorted Rockschild.

'It continues through, embedded   in your corporate culture. Your CIA was formed under the control of bankers and lawyers who looked after the US affairs of companies working for Hitler.'

'David, that's just the nature of international finance. Many directors of banks used by the Nazi were also directors of London and New York banks.'

'But the CIA also helped smuggle billions of dollars stolen from Holocaust victims into Swiss bank accounts and they even had a "rat line" for Nazis to escape to South America.'

Rockschild nodded absently. 'Good research and a neat little theory. But why did America fight against the Nazis if they were in collusion?'

David held an intent gaze. 'The Nazis were your pawns. You wanted to make money by selling arms to both sides of the war and only came into the war late, after sufficient profit had been made. You even allowed Hitler's genocide of the Jews because US companies helped build the concentration camps and provide the services to run them. But you also allowed this because you needed to create a Jewish homeland, so that you could have a strategic base from where you could oversee the taking of oil from the Middle East.'

Rockschild sat on the desk. 'You're simplifying the situation.' He picked up a pencil and began playing with it as David continued his flow.

'And it's the same with 9/11. You orchestrated Osama Bin Laden's al-Qaeda terrorists to crash into the World Trade Center as an excuse to launch the war for the oil of Iraq. Even though Al-Qaeda had nothing to do with Iraq, and even though Saddam Hussein had no weapons of mass destruction. You waged a war.'

Rockschild snapped the pencil. 'It's true that Saddam had nothing to do with 9/11 and although he was Sunni he was not Al-Qaeda. He'd been useful in keeping the Shia of Iraq from joining Iran's Shia. But he got out of hand. He attacked Kuwait and threatened our Saudi, Sunni, allies. So, yes, we needed to get rid of him but we didn't plan the 9/11 attacks.'

David ignored the denial and pressed again. 'You planned them and then invaded Iraq because the control of Iraqi oil was worth 10 times what was spent on the war.'

Rockschild looked out of the window. 'Oil is the life blood of our nation and our dependence on Iraqi and Iranian oil goes back a long way. Without it we would be destroyed. In the 1950's the Iranians democratically elected a government that overthrew the Shah and then nationalised their oil industry, taking it away from us. So the CIA then helped the Shah regain power. But then the Shah was overthrown by the Shia Ayatollahs. So we financed Saddam in a war against them.'

'And you armed both sides of the conflict, just like you did with Hitler. Sadam, like Hitler, had been useful. You sold him weapons until he got out of hand. And that's why you knew Saddam had the parts for weapons of mass destruction, because you sold them to him.'

'Like I said,' the old man began to look tired, 'Saddam got out of hand and we needed to get rid of him. But we didn't plan the 9/11 attacks. That's just conspiracy theory.'

David felt a pulse of excitement. He was getting to the truth. 'But it doesn't just make a neat conspiracy. It also fits with Biblical prophecy. Your media diverted attention away from the Millennium, so that people would not be saved, in the Rapture, when Jesus returned in spirit. That's when Israel's period of tribulations began, with the troubles from Lebanon and the Palestinian uprisings. And in this time your new world leaders arose. And they began a period of world chaos.'

Rockschild shook his head. 'How does anyone take you seriously?'

'But what is next in store?' David stared at Rockschild. 'The prophecies say that many will be martyred and that your Anti-Christ will make a covenant with Israel to rebuild the Jewish Temple. Aided by a False Prophet he will defeat an army that invades Israel from the North and will become the World ruler, demanding that all nations worship him as God.'

Rockschild now looked perturbed as David continued, with a wild stare, reeling off the information. 'The Anti-Christ will receive a death stroke but will recover, and show himself as the Beast. He will destroy the real church and his false church will flourish, until Babylon falls and Christ returns in glory, to defeat him at the battle of Armageddon. Then the world will be destroyed and the new Kingdom of God will begin.'

Rockschild shook his head, then whispered, as if in secret, mocking. 'So who do you think our Anti-Christ is?'

'Revelations says that the number of the beast is the number of a man; Six hundred threescore and six, 666. But any name can be made to add up to 666 using computers. Number the letters A=100, B=101, etc, and you get H+I+T+L+E+R as 666. But you can make George Walker Bash into 666. Even the name of Jesus Christ can be made to add up to 666.'

'Yes.' Rockschild nodded eagerly. 'Everyone has it in them to be an Anti-Christ.'

David ignored the contribution. 'The Beast, the Anti-Christ, isn't one single person. It's whichever world leader is being backed by your rich and powerful kingdom of Satan.'

Rockschild offered his hand. 'I knew you thought like us. We are alike in so many ways.'

David was now confused, then felt a chill as Rockschild held up his fist to show David his skull and crossbones ring. 'The Skull and Bones Society. My college fraternity at Yale University.'

'You are a Skull and Bonesman?'

'You know it?' He turned the ring on his finger.

David nodded as his thoughts churned. 'An elite "club" that follows Thanateros and is run from a Tomb. Initiates kiss a skull and lie naked in a coffin whilst masturbating. Then they're brought before a "Grand Knight" who stands between the Pope and Lucifer, to symbolise there is no difference between evil and good. Afterwards they eat a meal with some of Hitler's cutlery. An initiation into hypocrisy.'

'You exaggerate. Our members include George W Bash, his father and grandfather and the former heads of the CIA.'

'Exactly, people whose companies helped the Nazis war machine.'

Rockschild's eyebrows raised. 'Our Bonesmen are respected financial leaders.

David shook his head in disdain.

'Look, David.' Rockschild was licking his lips. 'Don't get stuck in the past. Recognise who our real enemy is. Look at this.' Rockschild pressed a button.

A blind lowered over the view, the lights dimmed and a panel opened in the wall behind the desk. There, behind a glass screen, was a skull, covered in diamonds, lit with halogen, sparkling brilliantly. '"For the Love of God" by Damien Heist. 'Amazing artwork isn't it? But every time I see it I feel angry because the Chinese now control all the African diamonds sales. The Chinese are the enemy.'

David scowled. 'Your Bonesmen are the enemy. You run Wall Street and the CIA. Now you are trying to run religion. Bash was your Anti-Christ and Timothy Blar was your False Prophet. Blar helped you go to war and then you gave him a job with one of your banks, made him a lecturer in religious business at Yale and made him your Middle East peace envoy. And your new leaders just took over where they left off.'

'You're such a self-righteous prig.' The old man's hoarse voice now cut the air. 'Call them False Prophet and Anti-Christ if you like. Anyone in power knows that to do great good then you must do great evil. That's the deal. This is the initiation for world leaders! Hitler, Saddam, Bash, Blar.'

'Is that how you groom your "Anti-Christs?" Tell them they have to commit atrocities to get world peace? Is that what you do with all the Presidents?'

'There is no light without shade, no beauty without ugliness, no black without white. Kabbalistic numerology teaches that the value of the Serpent and the value of the Messiah, are both 358. They are one and the same person. Lucifer, the god of light, and the Demiurge, the god of evil.'

For a moment David remained silent, uncomprehending. He stared at the crack of light coming from the shuttered window. 'Lucifer, the Devil, the great dragon, the Serpent from the Garden of Eden, the King of Babylon. How can you call him good when he was cast from heaven for rebelling against God?'

Rockschild simply shook his head. 'Lucifer in Latin means the "light-bearer." Only you Christians see him as evil. He is like Prometheus, the son of Zeus, who was punished for bringing fire to mankind. Punished by your evil

God, the Demi-urge, who trapped the   spirits of mankind in his creation. Lucifer gave Eve the secret wisdom for how mankind can escape the Fallen world, but to save the whole world there must be a new balance. The Demi-urge must unite with Satan to bring about the New Age.' Rockschild pointed towards David. 'This is why the final Christ will be the Anti-Christ.'

David felt a knot tighten in his stomach as the old man exhaled and lowered his voice. 'The Babylonians gave the Jews a Serpent Throne as a symbol of their rule over Israel. It was a set in the Jewish Temple and there the High Priest sat, overseeing the ritual sacrifices…'

David interrupted. 'It's still not too late to side with me. You made some wrong choices in the face of overwhelming temptations. That's when the Devil had you, but it's never too late to side with me. You can be forgiven.'

Rockschild raised an incredulous eyebrow, paused and spoke slowly. 'The Babylonian Priests sat watching the sacrifices in the caves that became the Mithraic Temples of the Romans. Constantine adapted these rituals to the Christian communion…'

David felt himself suddenly reeling back.

'…but the new Anti-Christ will restore the Serpent's Throne. There are very few of these left. But you conserved one of the most important, the one at the Church in Burqin. The place where Saint George slayed the dragon, conquered it by uniting with it. This is the initiation of the serpent biting its own tail, Serpens Candivorens. And you completed this initiation in Burqin. Since then we have followed the development of your ideas.'

David's reaction was of complete disbelief. Followed by contempt. 'You are in league with the Devil!'

Rockschild raised an eyebrow. 'Revelation 13 says that all, people "both small and great, both rich and poor, both free and slave, will be marked on the right hand or the forehead, so that no one can buy or sell unless he has the mark of the beast." Your Rainbow Swastikas, that people wear on wrist bands, caps, badges, veils, turbans. That is the "Mark of the Beast."'

Suddenly David could hear his own heart. 'No! The Auditors is a system for goodness.'

Rockschild lowered his tone. 'Don't worry. We find a gap in your system and then take over your Auditors' database. We'll use it to track people's religions, what street they live in, where they shop, who they vote for, what their tax code is, what groups they are members of, who their friends are.'

'No, you'll never get it from us. We are too strong. We are united by the Noachide Covenant.'

Rockschild sneered. 'The Noachide? As promoted by George Bash Senior in his 1989 Presidential Proclamation 5956. Ha ha?'

For a moment David was stunned. 'I don't believe you.' He looked at Rockschild in confusion. 'But we also have the Covenant of Medina and the Mahdi, the Prophet to unite Islam.'

Rockschild blurted out in disbelief. 'What another Shia backed by the Iranians?'

David caught his breath and his confidence. 'No, the real Mahdi, who will unite the Sunni with the Shia.'

Rockschild gave a long, forced laugh. Then his voice trembled with excitement. 'You can't unite them. The split between Sunni and Shia is worse than the split between the Catholics and the Protestants. It started when Muhammed died. The Shia said that Muhammed's son-in-law should lead the Muslims and the Sunnis said that Muhammed's follower Abu Bakr, should be the leader. The division grew when the Shia said that their first twelve leaders, Imams were divinely infallible whilst the Sunnis said that only Muhammed was infallible. Now they pray in different ways and destroy each others shrines.'

David could see hatred ingrained in the old man's brow. He collected his will and pushed back. 'Yes, but we have unity. The Shia believe that the 12th Imam will return as a leader called the Mahdi and we have found our Mahdi, it is a Saudi Arabian, the Sunni Sheikh Abul Qasim Muhammad. And this has been accepted by both the Sunnis and the Shia.' He spat the words onto the desk.

Rockschild was silent for a moment. He pressed a button and the wall panel closed over his diamond skull. The window shutters began to open and he grinned as light flooded into the room.

'I'm a busy man. It's been interesting with your guessing games about our Anti-Christs and False Prophets, but unfortunately you were a little too slow with your Mahdi. We already united the Muslims with our own Mahdi, also a Sunni. You may have heard of him, one Osama Bin Laden. You were right about 9/11. Al Qaeda's attack united much of the Islamic world in a Jihad against the US. This meant we could justify an attack on any Muslim country in our war on terror. So, we invaded Iraq. And, once we'd done that, then we funded the Sunni insurgents to orchestrate bombings to bring back sectarian divisions and destabilise the region. To keep Iraq and Iran divided. So we had a reason to stay there, so that Iran didn't gain control. We even got Al Qaeda to bomb the al-Askari shrine of the 12th Imam, the Mahdi, to fan the flames.'

The anger welling in David exploded. A picture of Jesus destroying the stalls of money lenders in the Temple flashed before him as he swept Rockschild's desk with his arm. Water spilling over the papers. Pictures and ornaments crashing to the floor. 'You're going to rot in hell you arsehole.' He breathed deep and hard. 'I'll expose your whole fucking conspiracy.'

Rockschild's smile was broad. He snorted a laugh. 'Who's going to believe you? We've got teams writing conspiracy theories as smokescreens to keep the public baffled. They are far more convincing than your "truth."'

David couldn't comprehend what he had done. He could only whisper. 'People will believe me.'

Suddenly Rockschild's demeanour changed. He straightened his tie and pressed a button on the table. 'If you'd like to come in now Rachel.' He turned back to David. 'I'm sorry. I've been playing with your gullibility. None of what I've said is true.'

Rachel entered in a formal suit. She was stunned to see the room in a mess and David's face red with anger.

He caught Rachel's stare and felt a surge of longing, as his eyes moved to the floor, in shame.

'Don't you think it's psychologically interesting, see what kind of aggressive man your former partner is.'

Rachel faked a smile.

'Take him somewhere to get cleaned up. He looks terrible. Try and get him on board.' He turned to David. 'I'm sure I'll see you again.' Then whispered in his ear, 'But don't flatter yourself too much. Whatever we made you, Anti-Christ, Christ, Mahdi, it wouldn't even be close to the awaited one.'

-

David and Rachel entered the elevator. As they descended he stared out of its glass sides. The heaviness of his body beneath him. His eyes drifted out of focus and his mind followed. The crooked lines of concentration leaned up his brow. He was not ready to give up the fight. But he broke down and wept uncontrollably. 'I'm so sorry.'

He'd comforted Rachel so many times before, but now she had to bring him back to his feet.

Prophecy 3

The Temple will be restored where the sacrifice has continually been.
7.7.7

David stood in white robes, transfixed in prayer, in the centre of the ruined Basilica at Tell el-Ras, on the plateaux top of Mount Gerizim. The wind blew the shrubs around the ruins at Gerizim and blew through his beard, filling it with the faint smell of smoke. A crowd of religious leaders, of Jews, Muslims and Christians, were gathered behind him. Beneath his feet, under the church, were the remains of the ancient Temple of the Samaritans.

The Mediterranean coast lay to the distant west, the Jordan Valley to the east and Jerusalem to the south. In the twilight David looked across Nablus, the Palestinian city that dropped into the valley below, to Mount Ebal in the north. Ebal, whose barren slopes were strewn with grey rocks.

Evening shouts came from the nearby Samaritan village of Kiryat Luza and the dull sound of cars and sirens drifted up from Nablus. The noise was drowned by a sudden cold wind that pushed his robes to the side, and he remembered the wedding, his marriage to Rachel.

Now, at last, he was fulfilled.

-

David had become a "Jew for Jesus", a Jew who believed that Jesus was the Messiah, so the ceremony had all the features of a typical Jewish wedding.

The ceremony was held on top of the hill, the Tel, of the ancient city of Megiddo, which stood in open plains on the main road from Nablus, to the northern town of Jenin. It had been the site of many battles and was an ancient trade route between Egypt and Assyria. But the greatest battle was still to occur, as foretold in the New Testament. At the battle of Armageddon where the forces of light, led by Jesus Christ, would fight the forces of darkness, led the Anti-Christ.

They were hot in their traditional clothing. He wore a long black coat and hat, and she wore a white bridal gown, symbolic of the practices of cleanliness she had adopted. They had been shielded from the glare of the autumn sun by a marriage canopy of embroidered, royal blue, velvet. Date palms grew around the hill and a crowd of thousands had gathered on the arable plains before them. The masses were like fans at a rock concert, here to celebrate a wedding that would be transmitted around the world and televised on a giant screen behind them.

'Baruch habah! May he who cometh be blessed! He who is supremely mighty, He who is supremely praised, He who is supremely great, May he bless this bridegroom and bride…'

Deep, resonant Hebraic melodies wafted through the air as the canopy moved gently in the breeze. They had come, after days of prayer, to make a commitment, greater than their own love, a promise to work together to serve God and those around them.

But the marriage was also political. It was the final seal of the Auditors of God, televised to show the closing of the last gaps in David's own Audit trail. It was a condition imposed by the Mahdi and had to be fulfilled before he would save the Auditors from financial collapse.

David's hands trembled whilst he inserted his bride's finger into the engraved gold ring. The cameras filmed as they exchanged vows under the soft roof.

The hushed reverence gave way to whoops of joy and the trilling of Arab ladies. Their tongues oscillating as they wailed and cried, celebrating the union made good. Then the Rabbi hushed the crowd, waiting for quiet.

Finally they partook of the Kiddush cup and broke the glass to joyous exclamations of, 'Mazel tov!' as the crowd roared and cheered.

The cameras continued to film as they kissed.

Amongst the wedding guests on the Tel were the chief Auditors and representatives from many faiths. The Chinese Auditor, Zhang Jintao, sent by Chang Qing, the Shia cleric from Iran, Waheed Khomeini, the Orthodox Jew, Rabbi Solomon Cohen and the Sikh businessman, Mr Jasbir Khangura.

David accepted that the Most Revd Peter Kwashi of the African Anglicans and Swami Dr Kailashnath Bandopadhya of the Hindus refused to attend on a point of principle, that Rachel was a divorcee. But at least they were still united in the Audit.

He was deeply disappointed that Rabbi Shmuel Jacobs, the Reform Jew, and Jerry Fulwell, the Evangelical Christian, were also absent. They said that it was due to the unfolding political situation, but they had also failed their Audits, the third year running.

But these absences seemed inconsequential compared to the absence of Brands. He had seriously failed the Audit. He didn't see why the Audit had to be extended to cover all his different business branches. But he no longer mattered. He had been replaced by the person, everyone was waiting for, the one who overshadowed the event, Al-Shaykh Abul Qasim, the Mahdi. All waited for him to return from pilgrimage, to descend from Mount Arafat in Saudi Arabia, to make his announcement.

-

When the evening celebrations began the guests sat at a long festival table that had a commanding view of the floodlit plains. The plains were crowded with perhaps 10,000 men, all dancing. And on the periphery the women looked on, covered with headscarves and hats.

The Shia, Waheed Khomeini, nudged David and pointed to a bearded man seated on the left of the stage. 'He is one of the leaders of the new Intifada!' Then he gestured, with disdain and suspicion, towards a young bespectacled German. 'Who is that?'

'He's from the Bahai faith,' replied David.

The Shia rose from the table and walked over, to the Bahai. 'Only the Mahdi will save us, not your false prophet.'

The Bahai stared back. 'I support all faith leaders, but you must respect that Bahuallah, my Prophet, is my true Mahdi.'

The Shia had his answer waiting. 'Ah yes. A Sufi heretic. But the Mahdi will lead you back to the true practice of Islam.' The words just bounced off the Bahai's glazed expression. So the Shia prodded his chest. 'And in these last days he will fight with Jesus against the Dajjal. So whose side are you on?'

David tugged nervously at his beard then took the Shia's arm and steered him to face the crowd. Keeping the Shia by his side David managed to kiss Rachel and then led him down the hill to join the Palestinian dancing circle. The leader of the new Intifada got up to follow them.

A crowd gathered around them as they joined the throng and hands rained down to touch David's head. Rifles were pointed in the air and shots were fired. And soon they turned and twisted as the focal point of this people united under the Audit.

When the dance moves became too complex they broke away and stood to the side, watching the rhythmic movements. It was beautiful, the community uniting with God, but he was broken from his reflections as a group of Palestinian men mobbed him, patting his shoulder, his head, his back. He was being pushed around, then, in the commotion, he could see his old friend from Burqin reaching towards him. Riyad's face beamed as he shouted and cleared a space amongst his friends. He bent down. 'Come David.'

David climbed upon his shoulders then, supported by Riyad's friends, they arose, unsteady. Riyad's frame was thinner than David remembered. But slowly they rejoined the mass, where other dancers followed suit, until a group of thirty, also on shoulders, danced around him. Getting used to the movement they turned and whirled as Riyad laughed.

The Intifada leader also had a mount, and before David knew it they were dancing, on shoulders, face to face, the leader now wielding 2 pistols. David hid his surprise and just smiled, moving his pointed fingers up and down to mimic the pistols, whilst rifles were shot into the air.

From his vantage point he could see the dancing horses caught in the edge of the floodlights, beyond the crowd. He admired their brightly decorated saddles and the feathered headdresses. But they were rearing. He dropped from Riyad's shoulders. 'When will the horses start dancing?'

'They won't dance now. The guns have scared them.'

He began to feel agitated and trapped. People were smiling at him but he was ready to leave, he needed to get back to Rachel.

There should have been a week of celebrations for their marriage, from Shabbat to Shabbat, but the night before his wedding, there were reports of Israeli tanks on the Northern plains, heading towards Jenin, from the Sea of Galilee.

It was the escalation of a conflict begun by the Israeli Government. For years the corrupt Palestinian government, supported with UN funds, had been ineffective against the expansion of Zionist Settlements.

Finally the expansion grew too great and a ramp was built up to the Al Aqsa Mosque in Jerusalem. It collapsed the Southern Wall of the Temple Mount and destabilised the Mosque. 2,000 soldiers were deployed to "protect" the Islamic Shrines with teams of armoured Israeli bulldozers. It was clear what was happening. The Mosque and the Golden Dome looked certain to be destroyed and replaced with a Jewish Temple. World leaders protested. The King of Jordan along with the other Arab nations threatened invasion. Yet if the Arabs fought they would be defeated, more land would be taken and the Temple would be built anyway.

The situation escalated when a small pro-US group in the North of Iraq, the Yazidis, had offered support for the recreation of the Temple Mount. This support had been blown out of all proportion by the world media and the Yazidis were demonised in the Muslim community.

The Yazidis were already seen as a Satanic by the Shia. They had grown from a 12th century Sufi order that venerated fire and believed the world was ruled by 7 angels, like the 7 Yazatas of Zoroastrianism. Their Highest Angel, Melek Taus, had refused bow to Adam when God instructed him to. For his wisdom God made him the leader of all the angels. But the Muslims believed that Melek Taus was Satan, cast from Heaven for his sinful pride. A story echoed in the Christian accounts of the fallen angel, Lucifer.

Al Qaeda massacred the Yazidis for supporting the Israelis. It was genocide. All that had remained standing in Lalish, their place of pilgrimage, was the large statue of a rearing snake that guarded the town.

The Israelis claimed that this was the final straw. Tanks and jets were now poised to invade northern Palestine, poised to fight at Har Megiddo, a swift response from the US backed Israeli forces.

The view of the Muslim community, the Umma, was unanimous. They distanced themselves from the genocide of the Yazidis but described the Israeli and US forces as belonging to Satan and the Dajjal, the false prophet described in the Hadith. This Dajjal was the Anti-Christ who would promote himself as God, would gather an army against the righteous army of Jesus and would bring rivers and fires in the final hours. The Umma was not clear who he was, but it was known that he would be a short, bulky man with crooked legs, a red complexion and thick, twisted locks of hair. Most telling was that he would be blind in an eye that was swollen like a grape. But whoever he was, it was clear that the Western leaders were in league with him.

Rachel had descended into the crowd. She caught David by the arm and spoke in rapid bursts. 'Those men were whispering obscenities at me!' She tried to point to them in the crowd. They had vanished.

'Don't worry, I'll look after you,' he said, hugging her.

She took a deep breath. 'I'm frightened for the women here.'

'Don't worry, we are all believers,' he responded calmly.

She pushed him back and stared at him as if he were crazy. 'I wish your real friends were here.'

David shook his head. 'Like Sebastian who became a "coke-head" years ago, and Paul who was never friendly after I started the Auditors.' He felt guilty as he saw the sadness in her face.

Suddenly there was a silence.

The giant screen flickered blue, then the Mahdi's face appeared.

The quiet was eerie as the Mahdi surveyed the crowd. Then he began to speak in classical Arabic. His deep, guttural voice, translated in English beneath.

'My friends. Iranian Shia, Lebanese Hezbollah, Palestinian Hamas, Saudi Wahabi and Taliban. All of us, together, a people truly Islamic in our Umma. No longer centred on our individual nation states we are centred around God alone. Friends, do you accept me as your Mahdi?'

'Naam!' The shout of assent came with military precision.

There was a satellite delay in his response. Then his voice reverberated over the night air.

'There is only one group that stands outside our Umma. Al Qaeda, who want our House of Saud to be removed. It is this Al Qaeda that was funded by the US to try and scare us with the Devil's catastrophes and to keep us dependent on the US for help. When sanctions were brought upon me for supporting the Auditors of God I transferred all assets from US banks to Islamic finance. But the Dajjal's banks tried to infiltrate our Sharia finance and we had to fight. But we freed ourselves from their economic grip.'

There were cheers from the crowd.

'Now the Dajjal has threatened you with invasion. So I persuaded for Iran to threaten Israel, saying they would use nuclear weapons to protect you. But Israel threatened to use their own against Iran.' There was a pause. 'So I prayed,' he paused again, 'and was granted by the highest,' he pointed upwards, 'a revelation.'

There was a cheer.

One of Rachel's bridesmaids, looking troubled, grabbed her to speak. Rachel turned to David but he hushed her, annoyed at the interruption. She snorted and disappeared into the crowd.

The Mahdi's eyes went wide as he continued. 'I dreamt that the Dajjal had raped the earth and like a lion he drank her black blood. He tore out her heart, and growled and mauled at any who come near to her rotting carcass.' He flashed a triumphant smile. 'This is his weakness. He desires our oil, no matter what the cost. So I froze our supplies to the US and set on fire the oil pipelines throughout our lands. I told them that their precious oil will burn forever in our deserts unless they withdraw.'

The cheer grew louder.

'And now they have agreed to withdraw.'

There was a roar of the crowd. 'Now even you, brother Shias,' he smiled, 'must agree that I am your Mahdi.' The Mahdi beamed. 'Learn from this my brothers and sisters. In Shaallah.' Then he gloated over his final words. 'Tonight we have defeated the work of the Dajjal!'

The crowd went wild, ecstatic. Whilst the Mahdi smiled, as a father to his children.

He patiently waited for the cheering to subside. 'Now we must take our struggle to its conclusion. As the Prophet, Peace Be Upon Him, said, "Make ready whatever you can to terrify the enemies of Allah."'

It was 10 minutes before the storm of approval passed. The Mahdi's image had long gone and the music had returned with fervour.

The Shia spoke to David. 'That was indeed the Mahdi. But David, does that make you the returned prophet, Isa?'

His blood went cold. He hesitated, trying to find a way from the current of thought. 'I may be a mouthpiece for the spirit of Jesus but I'm not Jesus.'

The Shia nodded and then his expression grew serious. 'What you are doing fits with prophecy. It makes sense. Jesus will come with the Mahdi to fight the Anti-Christ in Israel.' The Shia stared him in the eye. 'You are the Second Coming of Isa in the end times, the times of the Unbelievers.'

The crowd had begun chanting. 'Isa, Isa, Isa, Isa!'

'David,' he continued, 'they are calling for you!'

David couldn't believe his ears. He went hot and began to sweat.

He was worried how far this hysteria might spread. He needed to make some kind of speech to diffuse the crowd. As he was forming his ideas Rachel returned with one of her bridesmaids. His relief to see her was only momentary as she pleaded. 'No one has seen Anita. Ruth here says that she was dragged off by some young men.'

'Adjust your headscarf sister,' interrupted the Shia dismissively.

David stood silent. He didn't know what to do. He was afraid. He could see Rachel was astounded. 'Are you going to let him criticise?' she snapped.

The Shia shrugged her off and smiled at David. 'She is strong, like Abraham's wife, Sarah. Even in Sarah's old age God blessed her with children.'

'Rachel, we'll sort this out, I promise. I just need to calm everyone down.' But instead he turned and walked beyond the floodlights and into the darkness.

It was his wedding night and victory had been announced but he had lost control of his life.

-

Now, on Mount Gerizim, the sun was setting and the beige, red stones of the hills lit in its golden glow as clouds streaked the blue sky, breaking and fragmenting in their slow drift across the moon.

David was surrounded by Sunnis, Shias, Orthodox Jews and Christians. He was to perform a ritual sacrifice of a bull. It was to be a seal of the new covenant between the faiths. The factions of the Holy Land had been brought together with the help of the Samaritans, a dwindling, inbred population with joint Israeli and Palestinian citizenship. Their land rights were ignored by both and they now lived in small houses in the narrow streets of Kiryat Luza, a village just beneath their Holy summit of Gerizim.

Their Temple at Gerizim was older than even Solomon's Temple at Jerusalem and was believed to be where Noah's ark came to rest and where Abraham offered to sacrifice Isaac to God.

Like the Jews they believed that, four thousand years ago, Abraham migrated West, from southern Iraq to Canaan, and that, several generations later, Jacob and his twelve Sons migrated further West to Egypt until, in 1453 B.C.E, the twelve tribes (descended from the twelve Sons) were led out of Egypt by Moses, in the Exodus. Like the Jews they also follow the "Five Books of Moses", and keep the Passover, still sacrificing a lamb in spring. But unlike the Jews they believe that Moses ordered that the original "Holy of Holies" of Israel be established at Mount Gerizim. Then, when another Temple was later built in the south, the Israelites split into the Northern and Southern tribes.

In 722 B.C.E. the Assyrians conquered the northern Kingdom of Israel, assimilating with the ten tribes and sending many into captivity. 100 years later these tribes were allowed to return to Samaria and reinstitute their Temple and then, in 586 B.C.E., the Assyrians conquered the Southern Kingdom. The Southern tribes were exiled into Babylon and 70 years later, now united as the

Jews, they were allowed by the Persians, who had conquered the Assyrians, to return to Judea and to rebuilt their Temple in Jerusalem.

When these two Kingdoms were under occupation by the Greeks the Jews revolted in 167 B.C.E. and gained power over all of Israel, destroying the Samaritan temple. After this the Romans gained control of the area and by 70 C.E. had destroyed the Temple in Jerusalem. But around 135 C.E., the Temple of Gerizim was rebuilt and lasted until the 5th century C.E., when it was destroyed by Zeno, the Christian Byzantine Emperor and replaced with an Octagonal Basilica, dedicated to Mary, Mother of God. In whose ruins David now stood.

It was clear to David that the Israelis only had a claim to the southern Kingdoms of Israel. And that any claim to the Northern Kingdoms clearly belonged to the Samaritans.

The Auditors had redrawn the map of the Holy Land to include Samaria, reinstituting the Samaritan's claim. But as history told the Samaritans to trust neither Jews nor Palestinians, they had agreed to let their land rights be owned by the Palestinians but on condition that it was administered by the Auditors. And to seal the contract David was to perform an animal sacrifice to coincide with the Muslim festival of Eid-al-Adha, the festival that related to Abraham's near sacrifice of his son. Ishmael according to the Muslims, but Isaac according to the Jews, Christians and Samaritans.

David stood in the excavated remains of the Basilica at the northernmost peak of Gerizim.

Around them were the remains of the Greek Temple to Zeus Hellenios. Its 60 metre wide platform, with Corinthian columns and a giant staircase, had been stamped upon the 6th century B.C.E. Samaritan Temple. This was a simple, square hall, cut from the bedrock. And though smaller than the Temple in Jerusalem it was here that Alexander the Great visited in the 4th century B.C.E. as he swept through the Middle East.

The old Samaritan High Priest stood in his green robes and white and red hat. He looked tired as he carried a staff as he led the Samaritans in their white robes and red hats. They took off their shoes as they approached. 'Here is the spot where you will perform the sacrifice,' said the Priest in heavy accented English, through a grey beard. His eyes were hard as he spoke. 'We have chosen this church because you are a Jew, who follows the teachings of Christ, and also because beneath your feet is the sign of the Auditors of God.'

David looked down. He hadn't noticed, but within the mosaic floor were interlaced swastikas. The Christians who designed the Basilica hadn't stamped out the pagan influences, just absorbed them.

Smoke caught his nostrils as young boys, dressed in white, gathered tree branches to throw into a fire pit being stoked to the south of the ruins. This was for the burnt offerings. Four of the boys ran, half stumbling, through the crowd. They carried a long trough covered with black bin-liners and containing plastic buckets, then lay it before David. This   was not the altar he had expected. It was more like a vessel from an abattoir.

Palestinian politicians stood just beyond the circle of Samaritans. Beside them, watching, was Rabbi Solomon Cohen and his black coated Hasidic groups. These Ultra-Orthodox Jews avoided the Arab Christian nuns who jostled to get a clear view. David nodded in recognition of their support. They came from only 10 percent of Israel's population but they were its religious backbone, living in separate neighbourhoods, obeying their own courts and following a strict interpretation of Jewish law. And whilst they saw the Samaritans as impure their interest was to stop Zionist expansion because they believed that a true Jewish state should not be created by man, that it would only arrive when the Messiah appeared.

They also insisted on following the 3 strong oaths of the Talmud. 1, not to invade the Holy Land using force. 2, not to rebel against the governments of countries in which they live and 3, not to prolong the coming of the Messiah with their sins. Rabbi Cohen believed that the Zionists and the secular State of Israel had broken all 3 oaths, by invading the Palestinian land. He prayed for a coming Messiah, a new Moses, to restore the Temple and bring all the tribes of Israel back together.

The Samaritans also believed in such a Messiah, the Taheb. And it was by chance that a young shepherd boy found the signs of his arrival. He had squeezed under rocks, to rescue a lamb, and found a sloping passageway ending in large boulders. He continued to crawl between them, into a rock hewn cave and there, amongst bones, he found traces of decayed cloth, wood and bread.

Archaeologists dated them to within a hundred years, possibly left by another shepherd, but it didn't matter. The Samaritans hailed these to be the relics of the Ark of Covenant, the Staff of Moses and the Mana. The young boy was declared their Taheb and with the rediscovery of their relics they sought the restitution of their Temple on Tell el-Ras. But now the boy had disappeared.

Speculation ran riot in David's mind. Instinct told him that something was badly amiss. He looked again into the High Priest's eyes. They were hard. They yielded nothing as the High Priest called out. 'Four portions are to be created. One to the High Priest of Samaria, one to the Mahdi. one for the Auditors of God and the rest to be burned as offerings to the Lord.'

Priests surrounding a young bull led it, past grazing sheep, to the plateaux. The High Priest clapped his hands and parted his arms to move the crowd. They parted in a panic as the bull was brought before them. The beast snorted and jostled whilst two priests dragged it, by the horns, to the floor. They bound its legs, then lifted its head, pulling it back, exposing its neck over the trough.

The sun now set and the light fell from David's face as Jintao, the Chinese Auditor, shuffled forwards with a sacrificial knife for the High Priest to bless. The Chinese had quickly taken over from Brands as the main providers of religious goods and services and now even manufactured Samaritan ritual paraphernalia. They wanted religions to renew their society's morals as Jintao had once confessed that Communism destroyed his peoples' identity and capitalism had made them selfish and corrupt.

Jintao then placed the knife in David's hands. 'Xie Xie,' thanked David. The blade was square ended but sharp, so that the animal would feel no pain.

The High Priest began to read aloud from Deuteronomy. 'The word of Truth will penetrate and illumine the world, in which he will come to dwell. How great is the hour when one comes to hear the voice of God walking throughout the world, and all creatures shall be in order and bow their heads, their hearts will shiver and their eyes droop and their limbs shake from fear on the Day of Judgment. And the mouth of Deity will speak: "Now see that I, I am he!" '

A wild eye looked up at David, or was it into the sky as the Samaritans gathered around, until it was impossible for outsiders to see the ritual. Then the High Priest led the chanting and gestured for David to cut its neck.

In a surge of power the beast straightened its neck and bellowed. A ripple of fear ran down David's back and his nervous hands went weak with excitement. He was afraid that he'd enjoy what felt like a cowardly, ignoble act on such a magnificent beast. Alone the bull could kill him. He prayed for the spirit of the bull, then returned to his purpose. He needed to cut the wind pipe, the food pipe, the carotid arteries and the jugular vein, all with a single knife stroke.

A cold wind blew as his knife slid deep and quick. He pulled it towards him as the bull's eye continued to stare. It had no accusation, just fear. The pain had not yet reached its brain as the blade stuck in the middle of its throat. Tugging, the sinews gave way and the blade came out, splashing his robes with blood.

The animal's spasms began and the priests struggled to keep the neck and head pushed over the trough as the blood gushed from the animal's neck. The trough collected most of the running, spitting blood. The rest splashed onto David, the priests and the ground. Seeping into the mosaic.

It was hard to tell when the animal was dead, when its stare became empty, when its panic became nothing.

The Shia, Waheed Khomeini, in his familiar voice, had been reciting the name of Allah throughout the sacrifice and now called out. '"Neither the flesh of animals of your sacrifice nor their blood reach Allah – it is your righteousness that reaches him."'

The bull's eyes were glazed over.

Prophecy 4

The leaders of the faiths will turn to greed and the powers of destruction will be turned to the East. 7.7.7

David wore a heavy black coat as he walked down the Boulevard of Foliage and Water. The boulevard was designed to be in harmony with the landscape. He was in Astana, the capital of Kazakhstan, the ninth largest country in the world. A city that rose from the bleak West Siberian steppe and where freezing autumnal winds cut between modern mosques and white civic buildings.

Astana was full of money from the gas and mineral resources pumped thousands of miles away from the Caspian coast, from the flat landscape that still echoed with the memory of Soviet nuclear tests.

It was 7am in the morning and the boulevard was empty apart from the government gardeners, whose clothes seemed barely adequate to protect them from the cold. They were repositioning the hardy plants that had been blown from their beds by the high winds of the night. The city had to be kept clean and this daily ritual of perfection was regulated, as were the workers.

David had slipped out of his hotel to meet the chief Kazakh Auditor of God, Rakhat Nazarbayev.

Ahead of him the sun glinted on a landmark 100 metre high tower, an inverted pylon, topped with a giant golden ball. The faint sound of Opera music came from its pinnacle.

A short, thin, man approached from the roadside and waved to David. His fur hat, too large for his head, slipping down, almost to his bearded face. David stepped onto a grassy bank and broke a spell. The gardeners turned. The harmony must not be disobeyed, the rules must not be broken.

Beneath the calm rationality of the boulevard were the tortured cries of political dissent. Like the plants that had blown out of place, the inhabitants of the city's perfect apartments could be taken away at a moment's notice. Their apartments then replanted with new citizens, desperate to be housed and fed.

Rakhat greeted David with gloved hands.

'Thank you for coming here.' Careful to walk around the grass Rakhat steered David back to the official route. 'I trust that you are enjoying your stay.'

'Your city looks beautiful in the morning.'

'Thank you. Please sit,' prompted Rakhat. They sat on a stone bench, flanked by bushes. He gestured for David to cover his mouth with his hand. David complied. 'We have no freedom here. There are cameras everywhere. Our government gets arms from Western corporations and in return they get our oil and sites for their nuclear weapons. That's why no instability is allowed in the region.'

David gave a calm look. 'Keep working at the Audit and it will help you. It will free you again.'

'But the Audit here is in tatters.' Rakhat stared at David. 'The religious leaders have become corrupt.'

David looked away to regain his composure. 'That's why we've called a crisis summit here.'

'The people follow you David.' Rakhat spoke, with conviction. 'They know the leaders are puppets of the Elite, but they trust you because you are righteous.'

David continued with confidence. 'And we have a strong core. The Mahdi, the Chinese Chief Auditor, the Shia Ayatollah from Iran, the Chief Orthodox Rabbi of Jerusalem and Mr Jasbir Khangura of the Sikh corporations. We are united, and we are not corrupted.'

Rakhat looked him over. 'You must keep this position firm when we meet today at the Pyramid of Peace and Accord. Years ago President Nazarbayev built the Pyramid as a centre for world religion. But underneath it is a launch pad for nuclear weapons.'

David leant forward, shocked. 'What?'

'The glass pyramid is on giant steel bearings. This allows it to slide to the side, to open up a giant shaft, a missile launching pad, with nuclear weapons directed at China and India.'

David grew stern. 'It's twisted. Hiding warheads in a peace centre.'

Rakhat coughed into his hand and then continued. 'I cannot speak out to our media and no one would believe me anyway. People trust you. I will show you this place. Tell them about it.'

David put his hands on Rakhat's shoulders. 'Yes, I need to see it. But when? My itinerary is full.'

Rakhat stared at David's hands, letting him know to cover his mouth again. 'My man, Vladimir, will meet you in the opera house of the Pyramid of Peace, after the summit meeting. Before the meal.'

David hesitated. 'Can't it be another time? The meal is an important time of sharing.'

Rakhat frowned. 'No, we need   to take the opportunity when we can. I will make excuses for you.' He fidgeted, he seemed to have desperation in his face.

David stroked his thick beard and searched Rakhat's eyes. Then put his hands back over his mouth. 'What time?'

Rakhat exhaled in relief. 'Thank you. Just go there as soon as the meeting is over. Vladimir will be waiting. Please, though. Do not to take help from anyone else. They will be agents for the government. And the security guards in your hotel. They are also agents.'

David nodded, then Rakhat smiled as he rose from the seat. They shook hands. 'See you in the meeting!'

-

David soon found himself heeding the advice. A young Kazakh stood in his hotel doorway. He resembled any other citizen, with blue jeans, heavy jacket, beard and grey woollen cap. But as he headed down the steps, he veered into David, grabbing hold of his coat. 'Excuse me!' he exclaimed, then whispered, 'take this.' He grabbed David's wrist and passed him a piece of paper. 'Read it then destroy it. Come if you need help.'

David was still shaking from the encounter as he entered the Hotel. The two black suited Kazhaks were there to "greet" him. His nerves were on edge and he avoided their glare as he headed for the lift.

In their room Rachel sat on the bed, her long wet hair, blown by her hand packed dryer.

David kissed her, put a finger to his lips and pointed around the room. He was about to speak when Rachel turned off the hair-dryer. He turned it back on.

'What are you doing?' shouted Rachel.

His voice was just audible to her as he spoke. 'The room's bugged. The guards downstairs are here to watch us, not protect us.' Then he shouted, 'Just looking at a guide I picked up from the Tourist Office!'

He read the paper. On it was the address of a mosque, "Masjid Akmola." He opened a map of Astana then put a cross, not on the mosque, but on a church on the same road.

He went to the toilet and flushed the paper.

When he returned Rachel had switched off the dryer and sat upright, now alert to the danger. Wanting to make everything sound normal she commented, 'Isn't it great, room service brought me breakfast.' An elegant silver pot and china cups stood on the side. 'It's lovely tea, but I haven't had any breakfast yet. I thought I'd wait for you.'

'I don't feel like any at the moment. My stomach's churning.' David grabbed a bread roll and some cheese, wrapping them in serviettes, then gathered his notes into his briefcase.

Rachel picked up her creamy white silk chiffon scarf. 'I'm not sure of the point of doing my hair when I need to wear this?'

'Listen, I think you should stay behind,' said David, almost pleading.

Rachel looked incredulous. 'But I've travelled all this way, to go to the summit.'

David frowned and whispered, 'It's not safe,' then spoke in a loud voice, 'Yes, but you know the Mahdi doesn't like women to attend.'

Before she could reply she had put a hand over her mouth and darted to the bathroom.

He heard her being sick.

She returned to the doorway, looking confused. 'I don't feel well.'

He embraced her, soothing her back. 'I really don't think you should go. I'd rather stay and look after you, but I've got to go.'

'I'll be alright. You go. I just want to be with you, that's all. I love you.'

He held her hands, 'And I love you. But please, just wait here, lock the room, put the chain on. Don't let anyone in. Only open it when I'm back.'

'Alright, but please, before you go, tell me that I'm as important to you as your faith.'

He wanted to say that she was more important. But his official, religious conscience made him uneasy. 'I love you.' He hugged and kissed her. 'And keep your phone switched on. I'll ring to see how you are.'

She looked up at him and stroked his face. 'Please be careful. Promise me you'll be safe.'

He smiled and stroked the hair from her face. They prayed together before he left.

-

David refused to ride with the two security guards in the black BMW, so they insisted on escorting him, like a prisoner. They strode down the boulevard and passed the blue dome of the white marble President's palace, a gaudy version of the White House, that looked more like a bank than a state residence. The Auditors needed to keep this key, strategic location. At the moment the President was immune from prosecution and immune from the Auditors. But exposing the military complex would unseat the President's international standing.

Flanked by the guards, David felt powerless, as he continued his long walk towards the lone edifice. The Pyramid of Peace and Accord.

He calmed his mind as he approached, counting the five rows of triangular steel lattice frames. The penultimate row was bright blue stained glass. The final triangle, the apex, was golden. The Pyramid seemed so solid, but he had to prove the might and ambition that was beneath.

A crowd had gathered around the entrance and he almost grew grateful for the guards as they warded off the reporters that had begun following him, trying to grab an interview. A microphone would occasionally find its way in front of his face.

'Are the Auditors falling apart?'

'No comment.'

'What about the charges of corruption?'

'No comment.'

'Is a new leader going to be appointed?'

They were trying to goad him into a reaction. 'You will see.'

More press and cameras arrived and extra security guards joined them to help him pass through the swarm.

He kept his head held up, then, out of nowhere, a young Muslim reporter, in a hijab, skipping along, shouted to him. 'I'm from the World Religious Post.'

At last someone he could trust. He stopped and pointed. 'Yes. I'll answer a few questions.'

The reporters gave space for her microphone, their's joining behind it. 'Mr Wolfe. Will you excommunicate the faith leaders who have not followed the Audit?'

David felt a rising uncertainty as he replied. 'I'm not ruling anything out at this stage.'

She nodded, her eyes riveted on him. 'What is your position on the proposed American sanctions against China?'

David's eyes shot round the reporters, scanning them, mentally noting the names on their press badges. 'Points of irreconcilable difference of faith have been raised. We must use the scriptures as the basis of any agreement. Unfortunately the American faith leaders behind the sanctions have interpreted their scriptures too liberally.'

Then he clasped his hands as sign that he should not be interrupted. 'Excuse me now, I must pray before the meeting.' The guards formed a tight circle around him and led him onwards.

He kept walking, with eyes closed, trying to pray. He wanted to shut out the din of the crowd but his mind was racing, trying to understand why he felt confused, out of his depth. All he could do was repeat the Lord's Prayer, given by Jesus, taught to him as a child. 'Our Father, who art in heaven, hallowed be Thy Name. Thy Kingdom come. They will be done, on earth as it is in heaven. Give us this day our daily bread and forgive us our trespasses as we forgive those that trespass against us, and lead us not into temptation but deliver us from evil for Thine is the Kingdom, the Power and the Glory. Forever and Ever, Amen.'

Soon the steel framed pyramid dwarfed him. Its diamond shaped stained glass windows, depicted flying doves of peace, but he looked away. He could not bear to admire the beauty when it hid such hypocrisy.

A black granite ramp led to a dark entrance. There he adjusted to the light as men and women, all of faith, jostled each other, without manners.

The passageway opened out into a complex that was like a corporate shopping mall, adorned with hanging plants.

Hundreds of faith leaders had congregated here, filling the ground floor atrium. And walls sloped inwards, above them, reaching, like a Cathedral, to a circular ceiling. A blue and golden light shone through the hole in its centre. Such beauty.

The summit meeting would be held above this hole, in the upper room. It would not include all the leaders, only the heads of the different movements, but it would be relayed onto a large screen below.

David shook the hands of all who offered them as his guards steered him brusquely, past the delegates, to the lifts.

He tried to phone Rachel as he waited for the lift. No answer.

The lift opened onto the luxurious upper room, at the top of the pyramid. About 20 delegates sat on modern chairs at a white ring shaped table. In the centre of the floor was a hole to the atrium below. Surrounding them were the giant blue triangular stained glass windows, upon which were the photographic images of doves. These windows sloped to a golden glass apex of power.

The delegates were clearly divided. The Mahdi, Sheikh Abul Qasim Muhammad and the Chinese Auditor, Zhang Jintao, sat either side of David. Close by, supporting him, all in black, was the Shia, Waheed Khomeini and the Orthodox Jew, Rabbi Solomon Cohen. They were now joined by the Russian Orthodox Christian, Aleksandr Alfeyev. All wore the Rainbow Swastika lapel badge of the Auditors.

From the far side of the table the Reform Jew, Rabbi Shmuel Jacobs, and the Evangelical Christian, Reverend Jerry Fulwell, staring at David with superciliousness. Clearly they had become the ring leaders of an angry group. Their key followers were the Buddhist, Alex Wilber, and the Hindu, Swami Dr Kailashnath Bandopadhya. More key antagonists than David had anticipated.

They kept darting across the room to lobby the other faith leaders, right under his nose. They were trying to do deals with the Papal Envoy, Father Emilio Rodriguez and Mr Jasbir Khangura, the Sikh who now wore traditional silk robes. David felt betrayed, but kept his composure, controlled his anger under the hot, spot lights.

Between the two groups sat the Kazakh Auditor, Rakhat, who spoke into his microphone, introducing the proceedings and leading the opening prayers. But as soon as he had finished Fulwell launched his attack.

Dressed more like a salesman than a preacher, Fulwell's shouts cut the air. 'Before the meeting begins I want you all to know that we will be forced to leave the Audit if China remains within it. They have been investing in corrupt Islamic regimes in Africa, regimes that are committing genocide. And their industry is creating complete global environmental devastation.'

Only the authority of the Mahdi   could interrupt the tension. Smiling, he held forth his arm, white cuffs and golden cufflinks showing under his beige suit. 'The prophet said, in his last Sermon, that all mankind is from Adam and Eve. African Muslims are an equal part of our Umma, our Muslim community. They are our brothers, and if China is their ally then she is also our ally.'

'Let me clarify this matter,' said David pointing at the sheet in front of him. The delegates stared blankly. 'I understand your concerns. Groups that do not live up to the regulations required by the Audit, have 3 chances to comply more fully. China is doing this, but Jerry, your Evangelical Alliance has consistently failed in its requirement to support the development African nations. Now you are trying to throw up a smokescreen to paint those who follow the Audit as being corrupt.'

'Please,' Fulwell feigned courtesy, 'you're always too simplistic. Each year we give aid money to Africa but you just criticise how it is spent.'

'Because it is all spent on arms and luxury goods by corrupt African officials. None of it goes to the people. We've told you.' David brought his hand gently but forcefully down onto the table. 'Throwing money at countries doesn't help. Instead, you have to remove your trade tariffs, stop giving subsidies to your own farmers and stop giving all your big construction contracts to your own Western companies. Then you will pass the Audit.'

Jintao was nodding, then interrupted. 'We Chinese are not like this. We invest in infrastructures to get African countries working. We get a share in their profits, but also their losses. We guarantee them a good price for their goods, no matter how the market drops. This is fair trade.'

Shmuel's finger wagged as he spoke out in his New York accent. 'You call over-fishing, over-polluting and 100 million people in slavery fair trade?'

The Mahdi's low voice filled the room, commanding respect. 'Your private companies lend to African countries, then, collapse their economies, by playing with commodity prices and demanding high repayments. Once they have collapsed, then you buy up their devalued industries. Your usury, this is the corruption.'

Shmuel locked horns with the Mahdi. 'That's ridiculous. The corruption comes from the Chinese. They accumulate trillions of dollars worth of foreign reserves and prop up their cheap exports, to undermine our manufacturing whilst they steal our intellectual property with their fakes.'

'You are stupid,' interrupted Jintao. 'You forget history. In the 18th and 19th century, you Westerners imported Chinese goods but when we did not want your shoddy goods in return you sold us opium, getting our people addicted. It was the same in the modern age, with your stocks and shares, getting our people addicted to your gambling. But then you collapsed your banks and industries, leaving us owed trillions. Then you printed more money and devalued the dollar to reduce the value of debt it owed to us. We accepted on condition that we agreed on a new global currency, one that couldn't be devalued. But now the US is manipulating the value of global commodities and strangling our exports. You are forcing the Shanghai Composite Index to fall and our world stocks to plummet. You have sparked a mass sell off by investors. You have created a Chinese banking crisis.'

Shmuel folded his arms. 'Everything that we're doing is within international law.'

David challenged back. 'Whose legal system Rabbi? God's law says no usury.'

'Only our Islamic Banks are preventing complete collapse.' The Mahdi exhaled, impatiently. 'You played a skilful game, but we had Allah on our side.'

'Hogwash,' scoffed Fulwell. 'You're oversimplifying a complex situation. The bottom line is that the Auditors are biased against the Western economies. That's why you overlook Chinese human rights abuses and environmental damage.'

'We stand with Jintao and his leader Chang Qing. Rights are tied in with development issues.' David pushed down on the table with his index finger. 'What's more, you ignored the reports about global warming in the 70's and now you are just trying to shift the blame over pollution onto China.'

Fulwell threw his hands in the air and turned his head from the table. 'But they are poisoning the soil, the rivers, the sea and the air. They've got hundreds of thousands of coal fire power stations pumping out greenhouse gases.'

Stunned, Jintao began yelling, 'US citizen make five times more pollution than Chinese. We suffer most. Our people live in poverty. Shanghai is flooded and there are droughts in the mainland.'

David clapped his hands. 'Please! We need solutions. This is why we Audit each other.' He looked at Fulwell and Shmuel, with eyes pleading for reasonableness, then kicked himself for showing weakness. 'What do you want? Another chance?'

Shmuel pushed away his papers. 'As a young man in the 1960's I had a hippy idealism that the Age of Aquarius had begun. But we are still stuck in the Age of Pisces, the fish. The sea level is rising and the only way to stop this is to give up our dependency on oil.' He looked at the Russian Auditor and at the Mahdi. 'In particular, China must stop using oil and convert to nuclear.'

Waheed Khomeini, the Shia in black turban and beige robes turned sharply.
He feigned amusement. 'And employ nuclear companies owned by the Rockschilds?'

Fulwell laughed. 'Come now. China already has many reactors from Pakistan.'

The Mahdi fired a furious look at Fulwell. 'You prevented Arab states from developing nuclear technology and now you want to supply the world with your nuclear power. Why? To   restrict our sales of oil and to cripple our economies.'

Fulwell shook his head in earnest. 'Look, we will lose the most. Our companies control most of the world's oil supplies.'

Jintao pushed his glasses to his face. 'Lies. Our Chinese National Petroleum Corporation has won the struggle for oil. Our pipelines reach Russia, Iran, Pakistan, Uzbekistan and Africa. And now the Mahdi pipes his oil to us.'

David picked up on the lead. 'And what will you do with all the nuclear waste that your proposed power stations will create?'

Fulwell's face dropped. 'The deserts of Africa will be used for a safe, controlled depositing site.'

The Shia's eyes widened as his brow frowned with anger. 'So you want to turn Africa into a gigantic nuclear dump for the world, to bury your waste, like you bury your lies and corruption!'

'Wooah. Easy.' Fulwell sat back, looking unconcerned. 'Look, nuclear is safe, it's green. The waste disposal just needs to be responsibly managed.'

Jintao's fury pierced the air. 'In the 1970's your discredited nuclear power to maximise oil sales. Meanwhile you monopolised nuclear technology. Now you want to promote nuclear and restrict the use of oil. But I understand your plan. You will cause the price of oil to fall, then buy it up and when you are in control, then you will start using oil again.'

David tried to distance himself from the speculation. He wanted to reunite the delegates. 'Please, please. This is still a meeting of all the Auditors.' He turned to the Hindu Brahmin. 'Dr Bandopadhya, how do you feel about this?'

The plump old man had an air of wisdom as he delivered his words in a heavy accent. 'The law of karma allows us nothing for free. Even Mother Earth's Uranium resources are depleted and now we need to dig deeper and deeper to find them. But this may be our only alternative until we find a solution.'

As David heard the soft voice he couldn't help but speak out. 'Why does this stop you from rejoining the Audit? We need you.'

The red lipped Dr Bandopadhya laughed. 'But we cannot trust you. You betrayed us by sealing a key deal of the Auditors with the sacrifice of a cow, an animal sacred to us.'

David stared at the Brahmin. 'But the Elite will betray you.'

Dr Bandopadhya was confident. 'Our decision has been made. Pakistani Muslims riot on our borders but China has sided with Pakistan, so we must side with the US, and those you call the "Elite."'

Shmuel quickly backed him up. 'We aren't the Elite, we are the democracies. And it's the Chinese who need exposing. Their protectionism is destroying international trade. They're using all their reserves to prepare for war, stockpiling reserves, manufacturing weapons, training their army.'

Fulwell's face was now blank as   he spoke. 'There will be sanctions against all counties who refuse to open up their trade, and refuse to stop using oil.'

Shmuel continued. 'Look, the world's overpopulated, there's climate change and the US, Europe and India are poised for war against China, the Middle East and Pakistan.' The faces around the table were blank. 'Don't you understand? Unless we all change to nuclear then there will be a global meltdown.'

Jintao's eyes were furious. 'David, they are just trying to deflect attention from failing their Audit.'

Fulwell sat back, hands in pockets. 'The Audits in China, Russia and Iran are all controlled by organised crime and they do nothing to stop human rights. David, you are just their stooge.'

As Fulwell spoke the Catholic Monsignor was shaking his head, but the American Buddhist, Alex Wilber, spoke for the first time. His tone was flat. 'You have become too extreme. You have sided with the militants.'

David could not ignore the comments. 'Our Audits show that these nations are clean.' He needed to squash the opposition. They were like a wriggling snake, ready to turn and bite. But something stopped him from attacking. 'But I will forgive your slander.'

Fulwell's body was rigid, his contempt clear. 'I notice the Catholic Church is still in the Audit, despite their latest scandal of Priests abusing little boys. Have you conveniently forgiven them as well?'

The Catholic Monsignor took a deep breath. He held his hands in prayer and tilted forward. 'We are rooting this out, which is more than can be said for your scandals with prostitutes and your embezzlement of Church funds.'

Shmuel held out his arms between them. 'Stop. Catholics and Protestants are brothers.' He looked around the room, avoiding David's gaze. 'We are all brothers, and should unite here, in Kazakhstan.'

David's heart sank. 'What are you saying? We're already united under the Audit.'

Shmuel's callous gaze bore down on David. 'The old Audit has become an inquisition. It needs to be dismissed. We've brought everyone here today for the launch of the President of Kazakhstan's new 'World Council of Religious Harmony.' The Pyramid of Peace and Accord will be its centre.'

David sprang to his feet, about to shout but the Shia held out his arm. 'David! No! There is a Persian proverb. "When a wise man argues with a fool the greater part of the blames lies with the wise man."' He spat a look at Shmuel.

Stunned, David leant onto the table. But his spirits rallied as the Monsignor rose then stood beside him. The room was now evenly split between the two factions. Only the Sikh, Mr Jasbir Khangura, was undecided. 'How do you feel about this Jasbir?'

Jasbir thrust out his proud chin   and long beard. 'We do not trust these new ideas, but, like our Hindu brothers, your sacrifice of a cow was an insult to us.'

David had prepared for this problem. 'The First Mehl of your Guru Granth Sahib says: "Those who renounce meat, and hold their noses when sitting near it, devour men at night. They practice hypocrisy, and make a show before other people, but they do not understand anything about meditation or spiritual wisdom."'

Jasbir looked over to the Hindu Brahmin, then closed his eyes in prayer. Those in the room waited. He nodded and lifted the seat of his chair and moved it towards David, away from the dissenters. His support now clear.

The shock on Shmuel's face was genuine 'Don't you see Jasbir? He's made the Auditors a false religion.' He now turned his directly towards David. Anger filled his face. 'And he offends us all by saying he's the Messiah!'

David was quick to reply 'I never claimed to be the Messiah. This is hateful propaganda that you've invented because you failed your Audits.' He picked their documents up. 'Failed!'

Shmuel feigned a smile. 'True, we've failed.' Then his eyes flashed triumph. 'But we've only failed a program of inquisition, made up by a man guilty of bribery, tax evasion and embezzlement.'

David was stunned by the accusations but, before he could reply, Fulwell stood up. 'As God is my witness, it's David's Audit that has failed. It's the Audit that's dismissed. It is dissolved. This will be the first decision of our new World Council of Religions.'

David rolled up the Audits and pointed them at the group across the table. 'You are self-elected dictators.' His voice grew louder and his anger greater with each word. 'You have lost the support of your people. It is you who are dismissed. You are traitors every one of you!' He threw the Audits. The main wad just missed Fulwell, hitting the table. Pages separated as it flew, fluttering through the hole in the floor, down into the cavernous atrium below.

David grabbed his coat and stormed out of the room, the Kazakh Auditor, the Mahdi and Jintao running after him.

He was heading for the lift. The Mahdi smiled nervously. 'David where are you going?'

He was breathing heavily, his heart pounding. 'I have urgent business that will bring this all to a conclusion.'

The Mahdi's moustache twitched. 'You must go to the banquet or they will take all your support.'

The Kazakh Auditor and two security guards held them back as David entered the lift.

Jintao clasped his hands. 'I must speak with Maitreya to discuss what action to take.'

David was confused by Jintao's words. He had not been told about a Maitreya.

'Press -1 David,' said the Kazakh Auditor.

David spoke over their arms. 'I'm sorry. I will contact you as soon as possible.

He reassured them with his eyes as the doors closed.

-

He was still incensed from his boardroom confrontation as the lift descended and its heavy doors opened. The deep reds of the baroque opera house immediately had a calming effect.

A large man with short grey hair and strong physique sat in the middle row of the seats. He wore a suit and his feet rested on the back of the chair in front. 'Wait there!' he said as he rose. 'I am Vladamir. You will follow me for security clearance.'

They shook hands. The man's grip was hard. His narrow eyes closed in on David and his equine nose flared.

'I will sign you in as a British engineer. I have documents for you here. Your name is John Smith.'

As they walked to the lift Vladimir eyed David with suspicion. David looked up. A hole in the centre of the ceiling let in a shaft of natural light from the atrium above.

'I can understand how the Pyramid can move,' said David, 'but how does this opera house move when it's already underground?'

'The floor moves with the seats, all of it, whoosh,' he gestured with his hand. 'Like a drawer.' Vladimir then inserted a card and the lift arrived. David tried to phone Rachel but again there was no reception.

Inside the lift Vladimir quizzed him. 'So, who is the Maitreya?'

It was the second time David had heard that. But he dismissed the question. 'I'm sorry, I don't know.'

They stared at each other as the lift came to a halt. There was no emotion in Vladimir's face.

The doors opened onto a short corridor whose concrete floor was painted gloss red. Ahead a sign on a mesh gate read, in various languages, 'Authorised Persons Only,' and beneath it, 'This Gate Must Be Locked At All Times.' Next to the gate a guard sat in a small booth. His peaked cap was pulled over his eyes as he spoke into the radio on his lapel.

Vladimir muttered some words of Kazakh and the guard surprised David by speaking in English. 'All visitors, must book in and out of the building.' A standard lamp shone down on the security book.

David shifted his coat to under his left arm and signed the book. "John Smith."

CCTV followed them as they   passed through the gate and beyond a bronze relief of the head of the President of Kazakhstan. They proceeded, down the white walled corridor to the sound of patriotic Kazakh music playing through a network of speakers. They passed doorway after doorway, and finally entered 'The Regional Commissioner's Secretariat Conferencing Room.'

A man in a uniform with a gold trimmed gold cuffs turned and saluted, fingertips touching his peaked hat. Behind him the wall was covered with a world map, divided into continents by strong white lines. The map was split into zones and lights flashed for different states of alert and officers from ten or more nations watched their computer screens.

They walked behind the officers and left through a side door, emerging in a corridor where aluminium ventilation pipes snaked overhead. David looked for security cameras. There were none. A fire-extinguisher stood next to massive coding units whose lights flickered green, red, orange and yellow. Besides this was a bank of grey steel cupboards, gauges and switches. 'Danger Electric Shock Risk!' 'Keep Out!'

Vladimir turned to face him. 'So, who is the Maitreya?' his voice had become more assertive.

'I told you. I don't know.' The hair on David's neck bristled, but he didn't want to ask why Vladimir needed to know.

They continued in silence, past more doors, then a new corridor. David became aware of the flash of red wall lights as the hum of machinery became an indistinct murmur.

A bell rang twice.

Through a glass window he could see yellow radiation suits with clear face masks and umbilical air-tubes. 'Danger, Restricted Area. No Admittance Without Authority.'

The air in the corridor grew cold and their footsteps now echoed like water dripping in a cave. The red lights grew further apart until they were on the verge of being engulfed in darkness.

David's heart was pounding. He knew something was wrong. He took a quick breath and tried to reassure himself. He just had to pretend that he hadn't realised. Then he might have a chance. He clasped his hands in silent prayer, too frightened to close his eyes. 'Oh Lord God, please protect me, please protect us all.'

His rigid body relaxed as they rounded the curve of passage. A side lit, heavy steel door marked the end. The guard placed his wrist over a sensor in the middle of the yellow and black hazard stripes. 'Microchip implant,' he said as the metre thick door whirred and slowly moved to the right. A crack of bright light widened as the door opened.

'Hurry. Don't get caught in the door.' commanded Vladimir as it fixed in place with a 'thunk' behind them.

Before them was a red railed balcony that went half-way around the green metal column of a missile. 'Radioactive' signs and white numbers were stencilled upon the weapon. The claustrophic hum of heavy machinery filled the shaft. He felt strangely compelled to try and touch the missile body even though it looked out of reach.

Vladimir spoke. 'This is an intercontinental ballistic missile, armed with ten thermo nuclear warheads. The arming unit and ground control unit are in the body. The impact sensors are in the cap.'

David looked up. Its red nose-tip was near the hazard stripes in the concrete roof. He looked down, through the grill flooring, where the body of the missile sank deep beyond at least two more balconies into the vast shaft. He took out his phone and turned it on so he could photograph the missile and its code.

'Switch off your mobile you idiot!' ordered Vladimir. 'These rockets are filled with liquid gas.'

David switched it off again, unsure how he was going to prove what he had seen. Then suddenly Vladimir pushed him. He looked down at Vladimir's hand and his chest rose in anger. He stared Vladimir in the eye. 'Who are you?'

'I ask the questions. Who is the Maitreya?' Vladimir pushed him again.

David batted the hand away but then Vladimir grabbed him, pulled him forwards, then slammed him against the curved concrete wall. The bang echoed round the wall and David's mobile flew out of his hand and clattered down the shaft. The wind was knocked from his lungs and his head seemed to split. Spiked stars flashed in his blackened vision. 'You piss me off you little arsehole.'

The guard had gone mad. David struggled against the grip, but he was no equal to the sheer brutality.

'My friend, I need to know who is the Maitreya,' screamed Vladimir, 'so tell me!'

David struggled as he was pulled from the wall, swung around and bashed against the railings. It felt like his ribs were broken and all that kept him from wincing into a ball was the terror of being manhandled over the railings.

Foul breath, hairs and sweat filled his face as Vladimir pressed down in disgusting intimacy, arching David's back onto the steel balcony. His skullcap fell from his head and in a flash of lucidity he imagined the fall, and the agonising death, his bones splitting and steel ripping through his organs.

He was going to fall and there was nothing he could do, not even pray. He was terrified.

'I despise you, you piece of shit', spat the Kazakh as he raised David up, pressing him on the railings. His back was going to break.

'Tell me or you will fucking die!'

He was being slowly lifted backwards. Looking round with the desperation of a cornered animal he grabbed for the railings. He couldn't get a grip. He saw lights on the walls   beneath him as he began to slide over the railings. There was an officer on the balcony below, with a rifle. He was going to fall. He careened his neck up. A voice on Vladimir's radio was calling in Russian. In a blind panic David grasped, then grabbed it. Vladimir raised a fist, ready to punch.

The back of Vladimir's head exploded a hole in his forehead streamed blood. He slumped on top of David, his weight bringing David back onto the balcony.

With hidden reserves of strength, David pushed the guard's body forwards. It thudded onto the floor, spilling blood and brains. His stomach turned as he started shaking. His eyes wide.

There were noises below. But he was trapped.

He grabbed the body's wrist to lift the hand up to the sensor. The arm was too short.

Horror and revulsion filled him as he hauled the warm body up against the wall. 'Please God,' he pleaded as he took the wrist and slapped the microchip implant against the sensor. The door opened with a 'thunk'.

He let the body slump into an unholy mess then stumbled down the corridor, into the darkness beyond.

He staggered, looking for somewhere to hide, passing the red lights, then stopping at the room with radiation suits. The door was locked.

He felt drained of life. He was confused, his body in pain and his hands cold and clammy. He gulped and then his instincts took complete control. He began jogging, then running softly, focussing acutely on what he was hearing.

He reached the corridor with the ventilation pipes. It wasn't safe, too obvious, too easy to find him here. Then he realised, he'd forgotten Vladimir's key card for the lift to the pyramid. But he couldn't go back.

He continued through another door and was back to the original long corridor. A security guard was at the exit and CCTV whirred as it fixed on him. The guard was shouting, running. David turned in a split second. Up a yellow stairway, grabbing black handrails. Left. Left. Left. He just kept going until he was at the top.

There was an emergency exit. It was bolted. A glass case covered the bolt. His eyes darted around in panic. There was a hammer to break it. But the guard was right behind him.

Which way? Double doors to a long corridor, or an open doorway right? He rushed through into a dormitory of bunks with grey woollen blankets. No room to hide under the beds. He rattled the cupboard doors. They were locked.

'Stop!' shouted the guard. He entered just as David ran out of its other doorway.

David was in another long corridor and the guard was right behind him. He turned a sharp left into a side corridor that ended with double doors. He charged through them, stumbling into a large kitchen, then skirted around the metal tables, sliding on the greasy floor. Chefs and waiters carrying plates all stood still and faced him. They blocked his way. The guard arrived, shouting behind him. David's adrenalin slowed, his head became dizzy. Two more guards arrived.

The sound of diners enjoying their meals came through a swinging door on the far side of the kitchen. It must be the restaurant area of the Pyramid of Peace. He was nearly safe. At the top of his voice he screamed 'Help!'

His mind went black.

-

David awoke in his hotel room. His mind was blank, his body numb, his head too painful to move. He touched it lightly. The hair was matted together with blood.

'Oh, my head.' He remembered now. Images of Vladimir's smashed head suddenly flashed before him. The adrenaline fired him into lucidity.

It was night time and Rachel lay next to him. He shook her and she began to stir. 'Ooh, whaat?'

She struggled to awaken but tried to kiss him anyway, then saw the dried blood on his face. Her hand went to his head. 'Ooh no. What happened?' She felt the back of his head.

He winced.

'I'm sooo sorry. You're hurt. We need to get you to hospital.' She tried to stand, eyes half open, but collapsed onto the floor.

David fought the pain as he struggled to rise enough to crouch and hold Rachel.

Her eyes widened in fear. 'What's wrong with me?'

'I don't know.' He looked around the room. It was as he had left it that morning. 'I don't know.'

She lay trembling, looking at David in horror. 'What's happening?' Her eyes began to roll as she curled into his arms. 'Please help me. Please.'

David's throat became tight, his eyes began to swim.

'I love you,' sighed Rachel. She stared into David's tearful eyes then slowly asked 'Can I have a kiss?'

His lips touched hers. The salty tears joined in the corner of their dry mouths. She was the most important person in the world to him and he needed her to know it. It was hard to get through. She was losing her consciousness.

'Am I dying?' Her voice was full of fear.

'I don't know.' He couldn't believe it, but it she seemed like she was.

'Will it hurt?'

'No.' He put all his effort into reassuring her.

'I'm not afraid of dying, but it mustn't be painful.' Her voice was now a whisper

'I love you, I love you, more than anything. I really do. I don't want you to go.' He was red, sweating.

Her heart beat fast and strong, her breathing grew quick. 'I don't...' she gasped '...want... to go.'

He was not sure that she could hear him cry as she started rasping and began convulsions. In less than a minute her breathing slowed and finally stopped. His whole body welled up, sobbing, rocking her in his arms.

He cradled her, giving every part of love that he could to her lifeless body. Giving every bit of warmth, hoping something would still reach her.

Through the blurring of the tears David saw blue flashing lights behind the thin curtains. The police had arrived.

Instinct told him that it was a set-up.

He lifted her body onto the bed and placed her hands over her lap. His tears fell onto her cheeks as he closed her eyes and kissed her mouth a final time.

He wanted to stay with her, but he had to go. He couldn't be found here, he would be accused of her murder.

He needed his coat. It was gone. He fumbled with the lock, began to panic. It opened. 'The map!' He turned back and took it from the table. He couldn't look back. He would never leave if he did. He staggered from the room, down the stairwell, controlling his sobbing.

The police had just entered the reception lounge and were talking to the security guards. He turned quickly, to avoid being noticed, and walked into the unlit dining room. The tables were laid for breakfast.

Slipping behind a curtain he tried to open a window. It was locked. So was the next. David kept repeating, 'Please God help me, please God help me.' Then he came to a wide window with a horizontal bar. It opened, not fully, but enough for him to squeeze through.

Hoping that no one would see him from the road he climbed through and began to lower himself, painfully, into the darkness. He let go and dropped the remaining few metres. He screwed his eyes tight with agony as he stumbled over, onto the frozen ground then arose and brushed himself down.

The police cars were near the hotel entrance so he quickly walked across the lawn to a side road. From there he turned the nearest corner and worked out a route that would take him to the church he'd marked on the map.

He could no longer run, so force marched until he reached the church. It was surrounded by modern apartments, fronted with lawns, but there was no Mosque. He grew cold as he moved from entrance to entrance over small walls. Sirens and flashing lights were now growing close. Then he came across a brass plaque in Arabic, "Masjid Akmola". Shivering he rang the bell.

Within seconds the young Muslim from that morning opened the door. This time in a light blue shirt, open at the collar.

'Help me,' croaked David.

The Khazak's face was like stone. His first words were 'Have you got your phone?'

'No,' replied David.

The Muslim's expression warmed as he pulled David in. 'Good, that is how they trace you.'

They walked up a flight of shabby concrete stairs to a flat.

'Here you go,' said the Muslim. In the room was a shoe rack and prayer mats upon a large arabesque carpet. Assorted cushions provided back rests against the wall. In the corner of the room was a framed picture of the Kaaba in Mecca. Beneath it was a computer.

As they walked into the room David saw his deathly reflection in the large window that looked out across the street. The Kazakh drew the curtains.

'Who are you?' asked David. But he didn't need to know. He just needed help, from anyone.

Abdullah passed David a heavy leather jacket. It was old and musty, but it was warm.

'I am Abdullah Aliyev. A true Muslim. The government only tolerates us while it suits them.'

David sat on a cushion and began to rock, uncontrollably. 'They killed Rachel. I woke up and now she's dead. Poisoned. I have to get hold of the other Auditors.'

Abdullah crouched in front of him and rested his hand on his shoulders. 'You can't be found in Kazakhstan. They will arrest you and blame you for her murder. So we need to get you out of the country.' He paused to think. 'But they will arrest you at the airport.'

David turned his head down, helpless. 'Will they torture me?'

Abdullah gave him an unsympathetic look. 'If they wanted to torture you they would have done it. They have torture cells, all over Astana. There they 'dry drown' people. Tie plastic bags over their heads until they suffocate. It leaves no marks.'

David felt a deep shiver. 'That's terrible.'

Abdullah looked annoyed. 'Surely you knew of all of this. Your Auditors in Kazakhstan had been told many times.'

David was now composed 'Honestly. I didn't know.'

The Abdullah looked straight at him. Then closed his eyes in disbelief. He rose to his feet. 'I will phone Vladimir and he will be here with a car, in minutes. Meantime, try to eat something.'

As Abdullah dialled David asked, his breath quickening. 'Why are they doing this?'

Abdullah eyed him incredulously. 'To discredit you and the Auditors.'

-

David drank water from a plastic bottle as they stood outside, hiding in the shadows as a police car passed by.

Moments later a black car with tinted windows drew up. They hurried down the path and the rear door opened. David stooped to get in then was pushed onto the back seat. He fell on warm leather and looked up with the surprise of recognition. It was Rakhat Nazarbayev, the Kazakh Auditor.

'We wondered where you were David.'

David quickly turned to the driver and front passenger. They were the agents from the hotel. Both held silenced pistols. One pointed at David, one at Abdullah.

'Where's Vladimir?' demanded Abdullah as he got in the car next to David. The agent touched a finger to his forehead and grinned.

David was confused and terrified. He felt a spike of adrenaline mix with his anger. 'Why did you send me down there?'

Rakhat looked uneasy. 'We needed to get you away from the meeting. But if we could also get you to rant to the world about our secret weapons, then you would be seen for the madman that you are. But we didn't know Vladimir had become a rebel, like your friend here.' He nodded at the steel eyed Abdullah. 'You should thank us,' smiled Rakhat. 'Abdullah here wanted to kill you.'

David now eyed Abdullah with suspicion.

Abdullah didn't turn, his eyes remaining fixed ahead. 'True Muslims hate you. You make deals with the unbelievers who corrupt Islam. Ahhh!' Abdullah winced and recoiled as an agent removed a syringe from his leg. The agent placed it back in a box and removed another syringe as Abdullah slumped.

'What are you going to do?' David was almost too afraid to ask, in case he prompted the wrong answer.

'It's been messy,' said Rakhat. 'You woke up too soon. Left the scene of the crime. Now there is a hunt out for you.' His smile turned into a mocking stare. 'Apparently you are a crazed killer.'

David stuttered in disbelief but Rakhat just shrugged off his surprise. 'We can't afford for you to have an accident. It's too obvious. The Kazakstan people would think that we killed you.'

David wanted to ram his fingers into Rakhat's eyes but jumped as the needle stabbed his leg.

'But unfortunately Rockschild has a new use for you.'

David passed out as Rachel's dying face flashed before his eyes.

Prophecy 5

The light will shine upon the history of the darkness, but the darkness will roar.
7.7.7

David awoke, in a haze, surrounded by a droning. It was like he'd been swallowed by a giant insect. He was shackled to the side of an executive jet plane that was buffetting in a storm.

A deep voice broke his trance. 'You are in a place with no laws. We keep you. We bury you.'

He had no idea who was talking as the drugs sent him back to sleep.

When he awoke again he was riding in a large black car. It reeked of new leather. Abdullah was beside him, unconscious. Autumnal picture-postcard scenery stretched in every direction. Open plains and woods. The road signs read North Rhine. He was in Germany.

Rain began to pelt the windows and he heard the spraying under the wheels. He closed his eyes and saw Rachel's face, gasping for life. He couldn't believe she was gone. As he wept, so sorry that he could not bring her back, he passed out again.

Next he knew he was being carried down cold, dark corridors by two men in black hoods and balaclavas. Helpless, he looked up, at brick, barrel vaulting, as he was carried into a small whitewashed cell.

As soon as they put him down the bottled up sadism in the guard's cruel eyes exploded and the nightmare took complete control. The men began ripping off his clothes with insane carnal haste. Struggling, writhing and kicking he made for the door.

Blows rained down from all sides.

'Get up!' demanded the guard.

David curled into a ball. No one knew he was here. He had no hatred, only fear.

'You are a little shit, a weakling to be squashed.'

David panicked. He was going to die. Only pain stopped his headlong descent into terror.

The guards shook him and dragged him across the room. He began to scream.

'I'm going to throttle him,' said   one guard.

'No, just do what we've been told,' said the other.

The wild eyed David was desperate and terrified, but in that moment he saw something in the eyes of the other guard that he trusted.

He didn't resist as they strapped him around the waist onto a slatted bench, his feet locked in with a wooden clamp. One end of the bench was raised, lifting his backside into the air, stretching his legs, straining his hip and knee joints.

They rammed a cloth into his mouth and he arched violently as they struck his backside and legs with a stick. The movement tore at his joints as the sound of wood on flesh absorbed into the stone of the small room. He screamed until the cloth was sodden, then fell into shock.

His whole rear felt like a gaping, exposed wound. It pulsed, in spasms, twitching, terrified of the next assault. When they poured salt solution down his straightened legs, it was like warm blood over his wounds. He squirmed wildly, involuntarily contracting. The excruciating pain was beyond screaming, but scream was all he could do, choking on the gag.

David was unbuckled and left face down on the device as the door slammed shut.

He was in constant agony, in the shivering cold and numbing darkness of the cell. The dribbling liquid grew cold in the draught and, as the pain dulled, rushes of panic swept over him, surges of abject terror.

As his body grew still he gathered his mind. 'Don't panic. Keep calm. If you panic you have no chance of surviving. Relax, bring breathing down as far as possible.' His mind cleared and he felt ashamed, humiliated.

His eyes adjusted and hobbling onto the cold, hard floor he staggered towards the door. Feeling the thick wood, he searched the side, but couldn't find a handle. A spasm of pain returned and he steadied himself against the door, panicking again. 'They're going to kill me!'

He stumbled back around the cell, eyes wide in fear, up against some cloth. It was his clothes. Shaking with cold he slowly put them on, with numb hands and in shooting pain.

He shivered into the warmth of his coat, rocking obsessively, and then began to pray out loud. 'Oh God, I'm so sorry that I have been a bad man. Please help me out of this. I promise to be good. I really, really mean it this time.' He repeated the prayer like a mantra.

The blood and water had dried under his trousers when the door finally burst open.

-

The light was blinding as the two guards entered. Their feral eyes, found their target, then cuffed his hands behind back and half carried him down the prison corridor, the noise of his dragging feet mixing with their hard steps.

The cold air was sweet as they entered a high walled, triangular courtyard. They headed, crunching over gravel, towards a small doorway in one of the towers. The expectation of death closed in on him, along with the narrowing walls, as they neared the thick, wooden door.

The guards opened it and dragged him through.

Inside was a round, marble hall. Dim light, from tall windows, and an iron chandelier, reflected on the polished floor and columns. A recording of a deep male choir played as they entered

Before him was Rockschild, wearing a pinstripe suit. David's heart both soared and darkened at the familiar face.

Rockschild stared deep into his eyes and spoke in a steely tone. 'We didn't kill Rachel you know.'

'Shhh.' David gasped in disbelief.

'It was that young Kazakh Muslim and his group of rebels.' Rockschild turned and walked into the middle of the room. 'I had thought you were a weakling so I was impressed when you escaped them. That's why I brought you here,' his eyes hardened as he turned back to face David, widening his arms, 'to the "Hall of Supreme Leaders," our centre of power. Dedicated to the genius of all Western empires.'

David's legs trembled but his fear left as he felt a fury rising from deep within. 'A centre for scum.' The guard punched him in the stomach, beating the air from his lungs. His wrists were cut by the handcuffs as he bent double.

'We are the "Black Nobility!" Descended from the original Venetian bankers and the Royal Houses of Europe. We run the armies, the banks, the United Nations, the world's secret services.'

David was still struggling to breathe.

'And this is Wewelsburg castle. It was Himmler's Camelot for the SS, built by concentration camp workers. I hope the guards went easy on you. I told them not to give you the full experience of one of the workers' punishments.' The concern rang hollow and was followed by an ominous pause.

'Listen, it's Wagner's opera "Parsifal." The scene where that knights mourn their dying King in the Hall of the Grail.' The low operatic voices reverberated in the cathedral-like acoustics of the large room.

David wasn't listening. His mouth was bone dry, his lips cracked. Hunger turned his stomach. Pain bit his legs. He swayed on his feet, then slumped onto his knees.

Rockschild offered his hand with its ring, a sardonic skull. 'Kiss the Death's Head.'

David just kept his head slumped, until Rockschild nodded and the guards lifted him, supporting him until he could stand alone.

Rockschild poured a glass of water. David couldn't resist. The cool liquid soothed his throat and withered body, but the guard snatched the glass before he could finish it.

Rockschild leaned into David's face. 'Himmler understood that the Crusader Knights, were holy warriors, remnants of the Roman Empire, and the last followers of Mithras. And beneath your feet is their secret symbol.' David looked down. He hadn't noticed the chamber floor, with its mosaic wheel radiating twelve SS lightning bolts. 'It is our victory rune, a twelve armed swastika. A symbol of Time, the God who rules over everything, and a symbol of the star from which the Aryan race originally came. They lived in Hyperborea until your Demiurge flooded the world in the time of Noah. Then they took refuge in the Himalayas, from where they travelled over Bifrost, the rainbow bridge, back to the stars.'

'Only Noah survived the F-flood' stammered David as the pain welled up inside him.

Rockschild began to circle behind David. 'The story of Noah is just derived from older Babylonian myths, where your Semitic races survived but so did our Aryan Masters. Their teachings were passed down through history, by the Mithraists, the Gnostics, the Knights Templar, the Kabbalists, the Freemasons. All branded as heretics by your old false, religions. The goal of our Masters is to return from the stars, in the New Age, and we prepare the way for them, by removing your false religions.'

David felt a shiver from Rockschild's evil. He wanted to get away from the words, away from the castle. He had no idea how to respond, but the reply just came, automatically. 'You are a Jew hating Jew.'

Rockschild looked smug as he retorted. 'You should know that the highest Jew renounces his Jewishness. Our families have been trying to dilute the blood and beliefs of the Jewish race, fighting to change their genetics, to get rid of their worship of the one God and to get them to follow our Masters' mystical teachings. We even encouraged their expansion in Palestine, to turn world opinion against them, so that one day they might be wiped off the face of the earth. Then, when the earth is pure, our evolution will be complete. Humanity will accept the "gnosis," the knowledge, of our Aryan Masters, the One, true, race of light.'

David knew there was no point replying to Rockschild's insane ranting.

'We worship Zurvan, the God of infinite time, whose children were Ahura Mazda and Ahriman the Gods of Good and Evil, Light and Dark, Life and Death.' David approached as Rockschild continued. 'The Jews made Ahura Mazda supreme and called him Jehovah, who we call the Demi-urge, the jealous God who trapped our souls in his prison world and stopped us from returning to Zurvan. But beneath Jehovah were the 7 angels. One of whom was Mithras, Lucifer, the bringer of Inner Light. He is the one who shows us how to awaken our spirits from this vile,   cruel world. Through rituals of pleasure and pain.'

David felt a surge of profound fear. His hands suddenly sweating. 'Satanic rituals.'

'You don't understand. You only see Satan as evil because you are not fully evolved. His darkness is needed so that we can have light. Our Master is working to evolve the earth towards a final unity of darkness and light in the Oneness of Zurvan.'

David eyed Rockschild with incredulity. 'Your Master?'

Rockschild's eyes brightened. 'Yes, the Angel of Wisdom who Buddhists call Maitreya. His Roman name is Lucifer. His Greek name was Prometheus. But in your Bible he was one of God's angels, a Seraph, a fiery serpent who opened the eyes of Adam and Eve. For which your jealous God expelled them and threw the Seraph down from Heaven.'

The accusation offended David deeply. 'No. They were expelled because they disobeyed God. He told them not to eat the...'

Rockschild snapped back. 'He was malicious. He didn't want them to have immortality from the Tree of Life.' His hand moved heavenward, his voice rose. 'Look, it's in the stars. The constellation of the Dragon coils around the Pole star in the centre of the world. The World Serpent who takes man to the highest truth of the heavens.'

David was weakening but a flash of fear brought him clarity. 'Revelations 12:9 says that the great dragon, the old serpent, the Devil, Satan, he deceiveth the whole world.'

Rockschild did not flinch. He held his anger in check as he gazed at David. 'Your Demi-urge is the true deceiver. The one who imprisons our spirits in matter.' As he spoke Rockschild reached into his pocket. Then David's mouth fell open as Rockschild dangled a twelve branched swastika pendant in front of him, the same design as on the floor. Only in a rainbow form.

'You gave us the key when you used the rainbow swastika as the symbol for your Auditors. You have reintroduced the swastika for us, and your rainbow brought our twelve armed swastika to life. Now we will carry our new swastika across the world, as the new symbol of our World Council of Religious Harmony, our replacement of your Auditors.'

Rockschild nodded and the guards bent David forward as he tried to ceremoniously place the pendant onto David's shoulders. Feverishly, David yanked his head back, his whole body rigid, but the guards pushed him down. Rockschild whispered as he leant forwards. 'It symbolises the star of our "Master" Lucifer, who will return to complete our planet's evolution to the New Age.'

David's emotions went reeling as the pendant was placed upon him. His heart was in his stomach, he was ready to spew. His hands strained in his cuffs.

The pendant mocked him from upon his chest. Crestfallen, he stared at Rockschild. 'Lucifer is the Devil. You are evil.'

Rockschild tutted and shook his head. 'You still haven't understood. Now is your last chance to join together your good and evil sides,' David drew breath to protest, but Rockschild continued, 'your last chance to become worthy of your Master. The one the world will know as Maitreya, the World Teacher.'

David was dumbstruck. 'But Maitreya is the future Buddha.'

Rockschild continued shaking his head. 'There is so much you do not know. Alexander the Great called himself Mithras, to secure peace in his conquered Persian Empire. He joined the Babylonian Mithras with Mitra, the Hindu God of Light. And Mitra became known to the Buddhists as Maitreya.'

Rockschild pressed home his point as he observed David's reactions. 'You see, all our myths interlink. Even the Babylonian, prophecies about Mithras found their way into your Christian book of Revelations. There God sits on a throne in Heaven, with a rainbow and lightning behind him, along with 7 Seraphim, the angels of fire who will destroy the earth. One of these will be the light of our spirits, the bright Morning Star, Jesus Christ. You see, this passage originally refers to the 7 Yazatas and to Mithras, the fallen star, Lucifer!'

David had a slow sinking sensation. His foundations were being undermined. It made sense on some profound level. He wanted to reply but just sputtered in shock. He pulled away and shouted in desperation. 'I don't want anything to do with your twisted religion.'

Rockschild gave an unpleasant laugh. 'It's too late. It's in the stars. Your old religions of the Age of Pisces are dead, flooded out, and the Age of Aquarius, the water bearer, has begun.'

David's knees trembled as he looked down at the floor. 'I don't believe in the stars.'

Sensing his guest's weakness Rockschild held David's shoulders, looked into his eyes and spoke gently. 'After the Great Flood, in 4000 B.C.E., the Age of Taurus began, when man was at the complete mercy of the sky bull, the God of the Jews and Babylonians, the Demiurge who trapped men's souls in the material world.'

'In 2000 B.C.E., in the Age of Aries, the Gods of war slayed the cosmic bull with their weapons of iron and freed mankind into the world of Spirit. Alexander conquered Babylon and the Demiurge but the Jews still remained believers in the Demiurge. Constantine fought its resurgence in the form of Jewish Christianity in the Age of Pisces, in 0 C.E. But he couldn't win and had to let it dilute the religions of Rome. Mankind became enslaved again by the weak spirit of Christianity, a religion of slaves. Eventually the Demiurge was fully resurrected in the restrictive religions of Islam, Christianity and Judaism, and their followers have held science back, misusing it and allowing the world to be Flooded again.'

David pretended not to listen   but Rockschild gripped tight, startling him into attention. 'Throughout this time our warriors preserved the secret teachings of Mithras and in 2000 C.E. we have resurfaced in the Age of Aquarius, the water carrier. Our Master, will save the world, by containing the flood waters. But brutality is needed to bring about change and our Master, is ready for these hard decisions. The Anti-Christ will unite with Christ and the Earth Mother will unite with the Sky God, in the war to end wars. Then the Master will free mankind from the mortal world, even if he must sacrifice the world in the process. Only then will men fully evolve, as true Aryans.'

The words bore down upon David. He was being smothered. He fought back the fear and blurted out. 'You're mad. It's nonsense.'

Rockschild paced. 'No, the world is overpopulated, there are limited resources and we have environmental devastation. Our Master has returned to adjust population levels with a global war. China is growing the fastest so we have tried to strangle their energy supplies, but they are propped up by the Saudis. So Maitreya must lead a war against them.'

David couldn't believe it. 'But our chief Chinese Auditor, Chang Qing, has not told me of any Maitreya.'

Rockschild laughed as he drew near and put a hand on David's shoulder. 'The time must be right to gain full support. There have been too many false Maitreyas throughout China's history.'

David looked away, and began to pray. 'God will guide us. God is our shield and sword.'

Rockschild held firm. 'True holy warriors, like Alexander and Hitler knew that peace only comes with the total destruction of the "old order."' He was interrupted by a loud scraping from the floor below. The awful noise chilled David's heart.

Rockschild held David's arms like a trophy, shaking him in triumph. 'Hitler began this task of destroying the old Gods.' He let go and paced back into the room, turning sharply. 'He knew that the cleansing fire was needed to make way for the Age of Aquarius.'

David now seemed unable to tear his gaze from the colourful pendant around his neck.

Rockschild gave David's arms a gentle squeeze. He spoke softly. 'Below us is the crypt of the eternal flame.' Rockschild took out a pistol then nodded to the two guards. They put a black, cloth hood over David's head.

-

David staggered around as Rockschild led him out, into the courtyard, crunching the gravel as they walked.

'Down here.' said the old man. David felt Rockschild's aged hand place his arm against a curved wall, to guide him down the stone steps.

The ground levelled as he hobbled along a damp path. Leaves rustled as he stumbled over branches. Twigs bent and snapped. Beneath the breeze, he could hear faint music.

Rockschild pressed the pistol to his back and whispered. 'You are my Parsifal.' David felt too wary to move. The gun was pressed deeper into his back. He kept moving as Rockschild continued, 'the knight who healed the dying King of the Grail Knights with the Spear of Destiny. The spear that the Roman Soldiers, followers of Mithras, used to pierce Christ's side during his crucifixion. I wish to show you this relic from our museums.'

David shook his head. It was hard to accept that Rockschild believed these bizarre myths with the vehemence of the fanatic. He replied automatically, without thinking. 'Probably a fake.'

An uneasy silence fell.

'When Hitler saw the spear he had visions of his destiny unfolding before him.' His riled voice developed into a crescendo. 'His Nuremburg rallies, his blood red sea of swastikas, his ceremonies to the Master's glory! But Hitler served his purpose and now we have found a new World Leader!'

The gun stabbed into David's back and he couldn't help it as tears broke down his face, wetting the bag already moist with his breath. 'I'm sorry!' David choked out as he stumbled onwards. The operatic music grew louder. 'What do you want me to do?' he said with words that came from a voice beyond his control.

Rockschild's laugh was an eerie chortle. 'Join us David, be initiated tonight!' Then he became perversely friendly. 'Your Master has chosen you. You must submit to him.'

David shook his covered head. But he was weakening and wanted to submit.

Wagner's harmonics resounded as he was led down a musty stairway and into an open space. But there were other noises that he couldn't quite make out as his heart pounded wildly. Rockschild began circling him. 'We prepare the world for evolution to a consciousness that is beyond good and evil.'

David straightened his back defiantly. 'Not even God is beyond good and evil.'

Rockschild gave an unnatural laugh and yelled out. 'We are the Gods!'

David spat words into his hood. 'You are monsters.'

Rockschild drew close to David, whispering, sensually, 'Join us,' stroking a hand down David's chest.

David felt his loins stir with desire. He violently shook himself. 'Never!'

Suddenly a group of men began chanting all around him. David drew a startled breath.

'Leader, my Leader, given to me by God, protect me and sustain my life forever!'

The singing drew closer and David turned his head wildly.

'You have rescued Germany out   of deepest misery, to you I owe my daily bread'

Their chanting seemed directed at him, willing him to join in. 'Leader, my Leader, my belief, my light'

They were nearly upon him. 'Leader my Leader, do not abandon me'

The chanting stopped as he was pushed, jostled and clawed by frail, bony fingers. His cuffed hands, feet and forehead washed and anointed with pungent cedar oil.

The oil seeped through his hood and stung his eyes. He could hear the music slowly building with waves of the horn and drums, carried by strings and wind instruments.

His cuffs were released, relaxing his shoulders and wrists, until a pole was forced into his hands.

'Listen!' commanded Rockschild. 'Parsifal will heal the King with his spear and we will drink from the grail.' Then he declared triumphantly. 'Moving from dark to light, from ignorance to Knowledge.'

Wagner's choir climaxed their singing in unity, with the brass instruments as David's blindfold was pulled from his head.

Eleven old men stood in a shallow circular pit in the centre of what looked like some ancient cave-like temple. All wore black capes and in their midst was an abomination. It was Abdullah, crucified upside down, on a cross tilted over the pit. A shirt of skin hung off his face and arms. Beneath him, resting upon a golden Throne, a flame burned in some fake unHoly Grail.

Between the violent spasms of surging pain. He stared at David, begging for help. His eyes bulging above his gagged mouth, his muffled wail piercing with an urgency that David was hardwired to help.

But David's muscles seized with absolute horror. Then he dropped the spear and grabbed his stomach, wretching, tasting the bile.

Rockschild picked up the spear, offering it to him. 'Be an Aryan warrior. Be in communion with us.' The blood dripped from the crucifying Kazakh, sizzling onto the Grail, creating a sweet smell of death.

Rockschild's eyes narrowed with rage. 'He killed Rachel. He wanted to kill you. Pierce his side. Feel the pleasure of his pain.'

David's mouth froze in terror. He looked for a way to escape. His eyes climbed the old walls to sloping windows that were too high, to reach. And above these, at the centre of the domed ceiling, was a swastika.

The initiates shuffled closer to Abdullah and dropped incense onto the grail. Smoke rose and dispersed in a snaking body of grey. Only now did David notice that the Throne had serpent arms.

Taking the spear Rockschild held it aloft and shrieked 'This spear is a shaft of light, of male power! The Grail is the female vessel, the Midnight Sun.' Turning his back to David he stretched out his arms and his voice welled up like a volcano. 'We seek communion through Mithras who slayed the Cosmic Bull, and obtained the "blood" of eternal salvation.'

Lifting up the heavy blade end of the spear he lunged into Abdullah's side. The scream came from deep in the inverted Kazakh's throat, pushing its bloody way through the gag. Rockschild's eyes gleamed red, his words erupting. 'We drink of his blood and eat of his body!'

Then an initiate took a concave, jet-black knife, and slit the Kazakh's throat like a beast. The blood gurgled from the deep, wide cut, gushing into the grail and onto the Throne. The chalice overflowed, its flame extinguished.

No orderly queue formed, in this unholy communion. Removing their robes the naked men clamoured into the Serpent's Throne to let the blood drip onto their heads and to drink from the cup. They embracing each other in a butchers' orgy whilst Abdullah thrashed until he slumped, lifeless. Their wizened bodies writhed in this mass of red.

Rockschild cried out. 'We flay his skin and offer his entrails to Lucifer, the serpent, who shed his skin in immortality.' He turned to David and heaved a sigh. 'Your last chance David. Be initiated tonight. His flayed skin can be your new skin!'

It was a moment of blind rage, of blind panic and power, David yanked the Rainbow Swastika pendant from his neck and stabbed it deep into Rockschild's eye. He reeled backwards, slipped on blood, then fell with a sickening thud as his head struck the bottom of the pit. Blood seeped from his head and ears.

Time froze in the stone chamber as David staggered in bewilderment and panic.

Snapping out of his shock he span around, pushing his way against the stone until he found the entrance, then sprinted up the stairs. 'Don't look back! Don't look back!'

He was out, in the open, in the mist, in the fresh dusk air. His body was hot, sweaty and trembling in the chilling wind.

'God, God, help me, please help me. Run, Run, Run.'

He wanted to scream as he ran down the dry gravel moat, around the nightmarish castle. Its walls coming down upon him and its leafless trees closing in on him. He ran under an arched bridge, the gatehouse above. Now excruciating pain stabbed his legs. He had to stop. But he needed to keep going, so he hobbled, heading for the silhouette of a church spire.

He felt condemned as he neared a dead end, a high wall. Then he braced himself, back against the wall and feet against a tree, and shimmied up, until he reached for the top, where he scrambled to pull himself over, staggering, through the undergrowth, onto a pathway.

Beyond exhaustion, he passed a low, concrete building, its small, square windows staring at him like the hollow sockets of a skull. But by now the adrenalin was fading and the pain was increasing. He could only just keep going, heading for the spire of the simple, stone church. By the time he reached the churchyard the pain was too much. Excruciating, unbearable, more than he imagined possible.

He slumped against the locked church door. But realised there was no one that he could trust, not even the Priest. But he couldn't go any further.

So with his last, inhuman effort he staggered amongst the damp grass and the tombstones until he found a broken tomb. He pulled the smallest half of it slab as far as he could. The stone scraped on the stone until it moved, just enough. Then weeping, from the core of his being, he squeezed through the gap, into a shallow grave.

Slumped, hidden inside a tomb, he pleaded, 'God, help me.' He didn't want to be found and crucified. But he wasn't ready to die. He had made so many mistakes and wanted to do so much more with his life. He pleaded again, 'Rachel, I love you, help me.' He wanted to be held and loved like he had held and loved her.

He lay motionless, curled, foetal. His mind and body had given out but was kept awake by instinct and fear. His ears strained and at the slightest sound his eyes stared wide. And in the brief moments of comfort from the cold he tensed his muscles to quell the gnawing hunger in his stomach.

But the air still held a sweetness to his painful delirium. And in the frosty, darkness he could almost forget the pain until the clouds cleared and the cold night bit through his coat. Then he imagined he could hear sadistic laughter, again and again as he looked, through the crack, at the clear, cruel, distant stars above.

-

The church bells woke David to the deep aching in his damp bones.

The dark sky was melting into the morning light, dragging him into a hope that he might survive. As colours returned to the trees and sky his body relaxed, but his mind was still acute.

He ignored the beautiful sounds of the dawn birds as he strained to hear the approaching cars and people. It hurt all over when he began to move his foetal body but he had to get up.

With his last reserves of life he crawled from under the tomb, lifting himself like a zombie from the grave, slumping onto dew soaked grass. Then, pulling himself up onto a gravestone, he cried out involuntarily before staggering to the church porch. From here he peered across to a car park, outside the castle walls.

The morning light filtered down, through the autumn leaves, bathing the car park in a golden haze. Around him the rocks and moss in the churchyard lit up a bright, rich green.

He was confused to see that cars   and tourist coaches had arrived. Two drivers stood, talking in loud German, as passengers descended, laughing, taking their cameras from their rucksacks.

The last of the elderly visitors emerged, scurrying out of their coaches, complaining about the cold weather. The drivers took them across the courtyard to point them to the castle.

Shaking from the cold, David mustered up some spit onto his grubby handkerchief and tried to clean his blooded face. He pulled his coat around him then set off, with a limp, heading around the side of the courtyard, trying not to be seen. He aimed to take cover behind a coach. Surely he was being watched but what else could he do. He couldn't think straight.

He sidled up, from the rear, between the two coaches. Maybe he could climb under the luggage door and hide amongst the bags. He reached down but could barely move his fingers as he tried to pull up the door. It was locked! Shit!

The drivers were still watching their passengers following signs to the castle "museum" so he climbed on board. Quickly, up the aisle, stumbling directly to the back. He looked for a seat where no one had been sitting, drew the orange curtain across the window, then hid beneath his coat.

His worries about being seen disappeared in the beautiful warmth. He wanted to stay alert but the comfort was overwhelming.

He awoke confused, heart pounding, mouth dry, hands and legs in pain. Passengers were boarding the coach. Chat filled the air, along with the rustle of carrier bags and the smells of perfume, food, and old people. The circulating blood renewed the agony of his wounds but he had to pretend to be asleep. David put his coat over his shoulders and face, then rested his head. If anyone came, maybe they would be too polite to wake him.

A man sitting in front of him looked like one of the robed initiates. He was still in a nightmare. He was about to jump up, to fight his way off the coach, when a plump, elderly lady looked down at him. She was about to ask for her seat when she recoiled in recognition. His flash of panic subsided as he saw her kind, intelligent eyes, the cross around her neck, the rainbow swastika on her lapel. She raised an eyebrow to see if he needed help and he shook his head.

When all the passengers were seated the driver made an announcement in German and everyone replied. The engine started, masking the noise of his gnawing hunger, and the coach began to move. It reversed, bleeping, then lurched slowly, around the corners.

As the coach wound its way down the castle road, David's stomach growled as the hunger bit deep. A gentle tap on his shoulder was followed by a bottle of water and some small packets of biscuits.

He couldn't look her in the face   as she whispered some words in German and he replied, 'Danke,' then tore his way through the packets, savouring the flavours of sugar, butter and flour.

He couldn't believe it, he had killed Rockschild but "they" were letting him escape. He would get help as soon as he could. He'd get off at the next town and phone the Berlin Auditors. They would give him some local contacts.

Then, as the distance grew, he broke down into silent sobbing. Rockschild's kind, Hitler's kind, had won.

Prophecy 6

The leader of the faiths will join with the East against the Greed. The darkness will be light. 7.7.7.

'Oh Jeshua, son of our Lord God. Please guide us,' said David, praying on his knees in the dukhang, the small, Tibetan Buddhist monastery hall. It was cold on the grubby carpet. He huddled into his thick, black waterproof clothing. His beard and hair were long and matted and upon his head was a Rainbow Swastika scull cap.

He slowly opened his eyes and stared straight ahead, at a brightly coloured painting, illuminated with the yellow light of candles. It was of the 12 armed, 3 headed, ferocious, black, demon-faced Buddha named Heruka. Wearing a necklace of heads and a crown of sculls he embraced his naked, female consort, ready to devour her.

The sun cast its pale, blue, morning light through small, square windows as David recollected how the media reported him as a wild, bearded madman, who had strangled Rachel. What was more, the Elite were now in full campaign to replace the Auditors with his World Council of Religious Harmony, using the 12 armed Rainbow Swastika on their identity cards.

He still couldn't believe that Rachel was gone. His Adam's apple expanded and grew hard in his throat, tears began to well in his eyes. He craved her soothing hand, her gentle smile. She had to be watching him, helping him. He frowned as he spoke to her. 'I couldn't forgive Rockschild. I killed him.' He had been so hateful. 'But I don't regret it.' His eyes squeezed tightly. 'I enjoyed it.'

He imagined her looking for the right words, trying not to disapprove. He could almost hear her comforting voice reply. 'You tried to forgive him, you couldn't help yourself.'

He nodded blankly then his head slumped into his chest, he was shattered. He had come full circle. He was empty. All his beliefs were just delusions. All he had left was blind hope.

-

David's mind drifted back, to the Auditors' last meeting, in a large, dark, wooden hall in Kathmandu. There was just six of them, sitting, tense, beneath an ornately carved and colourfully painted ceiling.

He was surprised how terse his voice had become. 'China wants South Tibet from India and India wants North Tibet from China. But for the moment lets us put this aside, remember the Elite are our common foe.'

The Chief Auditor of China, Zhang Jintao, removed his round glasses and put them on the table in exasperation. 'What do you mean "common foe"? India has taken the West's nuclear capabilities and trains their pro-Tibetan terrorists.'

Swami Dr Kailashnath Bandopadhya, the plump, old, Hindu Bramin looked pale with ill health. He sighed and looked across to the Mahdi, dressed in pure white, with a white beard. 'We have all dined with the enemy. The Mujahideen in Afghanistan, were CIA trained and even his Excellency sold oil to the Western Imperialists.'

The Mahdi shrugged. 'The past. Now they put sanctions against me for selling oil to China.'

Jintao subtly bowed. 'And we thank you and are at your service.'

The South American Papal Monsignor, Father Emilio Rodriguez, distinguished with greying hair and priest's white collar intruded in his strong, smooth, voice. 'And with the help of Brazil's resources we will also help defend the Chinese people against catastrophe.'

Dr Bandopadhya gave a quick smile. 'And since India's nuclear program is now free from Western control so we can provide you our surplus energy.' Everyone moved more comfortably as the tension dissipated, until the Hindu's eyes moved to the margins. 'But we are the ones who need help. We do not have enough clean water. The Himalayan glaciers that gave India half of its fresh water, have all melted and the upper Ganges is dry as a bone, all year, until the flash floods. Then she floods all Calcutta and bloated corpses float down her sacred course. In our myths Shiva caught the fall of the goddess Ganges in his hair so that she would not destroy the earth in a deluge. Now we need Shiva to save us again.'

The Mahdi grabbed Dr Bandopadhya's arm. 'The floods are because Allah is angry that you do not fight the West.'

Jintao leaned forward and pointed his finger at the Hindu. 'And do not forget, Shanghai is also flooded.'

Dr Bandopadhya slowly removed his arm from the Mahdi's grip and turned to address Jintao. Jintao did not allow him the chance. His eyes widened. 'Cyclones smash our homes and destroy our crops. We have famine. Our children are dying!'

The old Hindu recoiled before gathering his response. 'But you are the main cause of our water problems. You steal our Himalayan water so you can sell it back to us at overpriced rates.'

Jintao trembled with rage as he adjusted his glasses. 'We do not control the water. The West tricked us. They collapsed key Chinese companies, to undermine our economy, then bought up shares in our water industry.'

The Hindu shrugged and squinted. 'Maybe, but when our citizens riot in the streets see their families dying of hunger and thirst, they blame China.' Tension crackled. 'They riot in the streets and our police beat them. But we cannot hold them back forever.'

David threw his head back. 'No, no, no. Don't you see! It's not the "West". It's the Elite, the internationalists, who live in tax havens. They want the West and the East to wage war with each other because they want to sell weapons to both sides.'

Jintao put on his glasses and eyed them all. 'Together we have more manufacturing and can make more weapons.'

David could not believe his ears. He stood up, grabbing their attention. 'War is not the answer. The Elite would rather destroy the world than let us take over. In fact they want the world to be engulfed in the sea, because they believe that then the Age of Aquarius, the water carrier, will begin. It will be an Age that is all about who controls the drinking water and at the moment they have control of all the water companies.'

The delegates listened closely. Then Dr Bandopadhya, turned his head, eyeing David coldly. 'Whatever it is you propose, you had better hurry, because our refugees are heading to the Chinese border, looking for water in the mountains.'

David reassured Jintao with a glance, before pleading with the Hindu. 'Then we need to organise them into a peaceful Exodus, to turn their march into a symbol of unity between India and China.'

Jintao stroked his chin. 'It is unity that we hoped for from this meeting.' He paused. 'If the Indians denounce the "Western" Elite, then we will allow refugees over our borders to make a controlled refugee camp.'

David grasped the opportunity. 'And the Auditors can organise for food and resources to be dropped there.' He leant forward on the table. 'It can be a place for pilgrimage and prayer. A place to protest, to demand, that unless all India's and China's water needs are met then we will bring the world's economy to a standstill.'

All eyes turned to Dr Bandopadhya. But he remained silent, musing. Then a wry smile formed on his lips. 'Just like Mahatma Gandhi marched with the people of India, against the British salt tax, we will march to the Himalayas, in protest, against the "Western" Elite.'

Mr Jasbir Khangura, the Sikh businessman in a black turban, had been silent throughout the meeting. At these words his nostrils flared. 'Gandhi's protest worked a hundred years ago, but not now. You're too idealistic. We, the Khalsa, the Brotherhood of the Pure, we deal with the real world. We must enter talks with the Elite or expose their corrupt and fight them. Protest will not work.'

Dr Bandopadhya replied in a deliberate voice. 'Neither fighting nor diplomacy will work. Our only option is to just allow the people to do what they are doing anyway. This is their Karma, and the Karma of our planet. The world will balance through a natural cycle of Brahma!'

The Sikh shook his head. His warm brown eyes contracting into a hard stare. He spat words back. 'We must increase our number of sea water desalination plants and prepare for the worst. I say again, protest solves nothing.'

David held out a hand. 'Thank you Jasbir. But this is not just a protest. The Elite see global warming as the start of a prophecy about a global conflict and the end of the world. We must march to prove them wrong, to show people that these are not the end times, that we can work together and that God will provide for the righteous.'

As the Sikh shook his head the Hindu spoke further. 'The question is where in the Himalayas should we march to?' He looked up for inspiration, squinting, then declared. 'As Hindus we must return to our origins, to the source of the Ganges.'

'Good,' replied David, 'but Hindus originally came from the Indus valley, in 3,500 B.C.E., and only moved to the Ganges in 1900 B.C.E., when the Indus rivers dried up.'

The old man's eyes narrowed with rage. 'Do not "instruct" me in my own history! Remember we still have not forgiven you for killing a sacred cow.'

David breathed heavily and sat back in his chair, lifting his hands in admission of guilt. 'Again, I am so sorry that I offended you Dr Bandopadhya, but the sacrifice was my duty. In the Vedas it the Karma, the duty, of the Kshatriya, the warrior caste, to kill men in battle. And sacrificing the bull was my Karma.'

The Mahdi put a friendly hand on the old man's shoulder. 'Doctor, you drink milk don't you?' The Doctor careened his head back. 'Your cows need to calve to produce the milk. Well we Muslims are the ones who butcher the calves and eat their meat. If we didn't then you would have too many cows. You see, we must work together, because we have no alternative.'

Dr Bandopadhya pondered. 'Yes, you are right. We need cooperation. And there is another place for pilgrimage. I have been to many sacred places and I bow to them, but always less than I would bow to my guru. But to this place I would bow down the same. It is the pillar of the world, the center of the world Mandala. It is paradise and the destination of souls. It is Mount Kailash, the throne of Lord Shiva, and at its summit he resides, in perpetual meditation, along with his partner Parvati.' Then he pointed his finger onto the table. 'It is important for many religions. The Vedas say it is Indra's heaven for warriors and Buddhists believe that it is the home of the Buddha, Heruka.' He pointed again, 'Even the ancient, Tibetan Bön see it as the home of their highest deity, Demchog.'

Dr Bandopadhya looked around the table, 'It is in one of the most desolate places on earth but the four longest rivers in Asia flow from it. The Brahmaputra, Sutlej, Karnali and also,' smiling at David, 'the Indus.' He now watched Jintao very closely. 'It is the source of all power and life and is known as the swastika mountain.'

The Chinese Auditor nodded. 'It is an auspicious location.'

Father Rodriguez had been trying to speak and now pushed his palm against the edge of the table. 'We will pray for you in Rome, but sorry, this is not our pilgrimage.'

David gave a gentle nod of understanding then asked. 'What about the rest of you?'

The Mahdi smiled. 'It is a good idea for India and China, but I must speak with the Muslim Council, the Umma, before we give it our blessing.'

All the while Mr Jasbir Khangura had been shaking his head. 'What is Kailash to us?' He seemed genuinely confused. 'We Sikhs will lead a pilgrimage of our own people to Amritsar, our holy city.'

Dr Bandopadhya wrapped his robes around his shoulders. 'No, it must be Kailash.' All but the Catholic stared at the Sikh.

The Sikh businessman returned the stares with indignation. 'We will not change our mind.' They continued to stare until his brown eyes bore into them with rage. 'And if you do not also support our march, then we will leave the Audit.'

-

Weeks later the mass pilgrimage set off from Kathmandu in Nepal. It was winter, but the sky was still hazy, the soil still parched.

Garlands were thrown in front of the thousands of pilgrims as they sang and hummed their way along streets of empty shops. Coloured fabric and banners hung across the streets and draped down buildings. Everyone was excited to be together, sustained by their faith.

A Buddhist monk banged a gong at the head of the procession. His saffron robes cut a slow and steady pace through the grime and dirt of the city.

Ladies, in saris and shawls of purple, orange, blue and red, marched forward, jockeying for position amongst exotically clad religious figures. Boys jumped and shouted alongside middle aged Hindus, in suits and shirts, who proceeded in a calm and calculated way. Bespectacled Muslims, in round white hats, and a small number of Sikhs, in turbans walked with pride and certainty whilst the lead Buddhist just kept beating. It was a meditation.

The procession stretched for miles with motorcyclists' helmets bobbing about amongst elephants, decorated in red sheets, and cows with painted foreheads. Soon the crowd began to chant. 'The water is ours! The water is ours!'

Filmed from the tops of cars and buses, watched from trees, they passed the dried up fountains and pools of beautifully landscaped parks. Like rivers, joining seas, each road brought new pilgrims People joining it by any means possible, car, bus, train, scooter rickshaw and bicycle. Dust rose from their marching line, a convoy, a carnival of believers heading towards Chinese Tibet.

The procession stopped at a Hindu Temple, a Mandir, whose golden peaks and domes gleamed as they rose from creamy white towers.

The leaders walked through its limestone gateway, past dried up grass and towards the imposing marble stairway that rose to a canopied entrance. There Dr Bandopadhya was waiting. His cream silk suit reached to his knees and he was clearly too old and unwell to follow the whole walk. The leaders congregated at the foot of the steps.

Carved on the banisters and balustrades were swans' and elephants' heads, floral designs and geometric patterns. The temple itself was covered with Tantric carvings, scenes of embracing figures, wrapped around each other, making love. The Pakistani Auditors, Sunnis funded by the Mahdi, glared in their white suits and white hats. They approached David with a resolute stride. 'These carvings are wicked.'

David sized them up. 'Today we are all Mujahideen, in a Holy War against the truly wicked.'

The Pakistanis tutted and shook their heads whilst Dr Bandopadhya let out a loud cough and greeted them all, speaking with a monotonous, gravelly voice.

'Hinduism is the world's oldest living religion. It teachings, the Dharma are over 8,500 years old. The original Hindus, the Dravidians, worshipped the Nagas, the Snake Gods of the earth, and the spirits living in everything, the trees, rocks, animals, earth and sky. But our scriptures, the Rig Vedas tell us that Aryan conquerors then came, 4,000 years ago, bringing their sky Gods Agni, the God of Fire and Indra, the God of Thunder.'

As they walked up the steps David noticed that the filigree work on the golden doors contained a pattern of interlocking snakes, which formed swastikas.

'But the Earth Mother of India turned the Sky Father of the Aryans into her own Gods, Shiva and Vishnu. But now, male and female, east and west, sky and earth, all are needed to bless our pilgrimage. Without this unity we will fail.'

The doors opened and, leaving their shoes outside, they wandered into the sweet smelling room where a forest of white marble pillars was linked by undulating snake arches. Gods adorned the bases of the pillars and the floral detailing on the columns was superb. The pure marble floor radiated cool freshness and above them was an exquisitely carved dome, comprising concentric circles that were host to deities and ever smaller rings of flowers, receding into infinity. David felt invigorated.

But the red curtain, at the far end of the temple, was the focal point.

Dr Badopadhya continued his speech. 'We are united in our cause. As The Bhagavad Gita says "He is One in all, but seems as if he were many. He supports all beings: from him comes destruction, and from him comes creation. When a man sees that the infinity of various beings is abiding in the One, and is an evolution from the One, then he becomes one with Brahman." Let us sanctify our pilgrimage by meditating on the sacred word "Om", the first sound of creation, whose vibration connects us to the Divine.'

The incense smoke wafted, curled, into the empty air and the Pakistani Muslims left before the brief meditation. The rest remained. Then, as the bitter sweet scent pervaded the room, a bell was sounded. Its last resonance faded, the curtains opened and Darsha, receiving the blessings of the Gods by seeing and being seen by them, began.

There, revealed under a golden canopy, was a statue of Lord Shiva and his consort, Parvati. He wore silk robes, adorned with real silk garlands and his sky blue skin seemed to both absorb and give off light. She wore a silk shawl and orange garlands. Both wore the red tillac marks of marriage upon their foreheads.

The two Gods stood together, the perfect celestial couple, eternally in the raptures of their wedding day. Their eyes had been ritually painted on them, to awaken them with life, but they remained unmoved.

To some these were living beings but to others they were just a way to gaze upon "Atman," the eternal soul that is everything, the statues, the room, the faith leaders. To David they were a reminder of Rachel and her lifeless body in his arms.

In the Mandir the complex, intricate carvings represented the infinity, the fullness, of the universal soul that is in everything. This differed from the Buddhist doctrine that there is no soul and that all is emptiness. But the infinite complexity of the Hindu Gods and the elegant simplicity of the smooth golden Buddhas were just two sides of the same coin. "Infinity" and "Nothingness." Opposite ways of naming the same experience that was beyond the world of duality.

To encompass this duality Shiva also had another aspect. He will appear, at the end of time, in his most terrifying form, as the Lord of the Dance of destruction. With writhing snakes in his hair and his four arms twisting he will dance within a flaming cosmic wheel. Parvati will also be transformed, into the horrific, four-armed Goddess Kali. With sharp white teeth and dark blue skin, wielding the sword of death and wearing the severed heads of her victims as a necklace. All will be consumed by fire in the eternal dance of Shiva. But beyond even Shiva is Brahma, the God of Time itself, who existed before good and evil was created.

-

On the second day the parade of pilgrims stretched to the ends of roads, filling the air with excited chatter in many languages. Music pumped from the backs of old decorated trucks and dancers, in masks and costumes, enacted Hindu myths around the white and red holy cows.

On one wagon trailer cobras raised their heads, hoods splayed, hissing as their bodies reared. Writhing devotees showered the cobras, with rice and crimson powder, and offered them milk, silver and jewelry.

David looked confused. These Hindus were worshipping the serpents. He turned to Dr Bandopadhya who despite his frailty was still with them. 'Why are they worshipping snakes?'

The grey-haired doctor was pleased to help. 'They are sacred serpents, the Nagas, who have the power to both protect and destroy, bringing balance when good or evil becomes too strong. They bring the rains and are the source of the Kundalini, the divine energy. That is why Shiva, Vishnu and even Buddha are one with the Nagas. Look.' There on the side of the truck was Shiva, seated upon a Snake Throne whose seat and canopy were made from the snake's coiled body and raised head.'

A snake charmer wound a snake around a staff, its head resting upon the top, immobile. He held the staff before David's face, like Moses, then threw it to the ground. The snake re-animated and reared up, spitting, hissing. The charmer grabbed the back of its head but David's attention was wrenched away by a fever that gripped the crowd ahead.

He could swear that they were chanting, louder and louder, the name, 'Adolph Hitler.'

He pushed his way forward, through the of snake worshippers, and swept his way into a new throng. 'Adolph Hitler! Adolph Hitler!'

'What's this?' he demanded of a young man in an open shirt, who led the chant from a truck, decorated with swastikas.

The man looked at his guests, eyes afire with passion, then jumped down. 'We are the "Hindutva" Movement. We follow Savitri Devi Mukherjee who has told us that Adolf Hitler was an "avatar", an incarnation, of God.' David stammered, overwhelmed, as the young man continued. 'He proved that the Aryans conquered all Asia.' David pushed the man in anger, but he sprang back, supported by friends, and grabbed a tight hold of David's jacket.

'He made contact with Buddha, Shiva and all the "Masters" and they will return, with Hitler, to bring in the New Age he prophesied.'

David wrenched his jacket free and shook his head in disbelief. Dr Bandopadhya looked bemused. 'You did not know this?' His voice was tinged with irony, his manner diffusing the tension. 'These young men believe that Hitler will return as Kalki, the final incarnation of Vishnu, at the end of the world. He will ride a winged horse and will destroy the demon of corruption with his sword. Then the earth and the heavens will also be destroyed, returning into the eternal and uncreated Brahman.'

David backed away from the mob. 'They're dangerous. They're turning lies into racist myths.'

The young man jostled between them. 'Be careful that you do not blaspheme us. We know that you are a Jew!' David was numb with disbelief as the young man climbed back onto the truck, triumphant. 'The new incarnation awaits.' He reached out his arms to lead a new chant. 'Adolph Hitler, Adolph Hitler.' Then started grinning at David. 'Kill the Jews. Kill the Jews.'

David twisted his head to the Old Hindu but Dr Bandopadhya had turned away as the procession swept them along, in a relentless march.

-

David stared at the painting in front of him. The 12 armed, dark blue, wrathful Buddha, Heruka, stood, with the ferocious look of a dragon, surrounded with flames, ready to destroy, gnashing his sharp teeth. He stared from his three eyes and held a 'thunderbolt.' Flames came from his crown of skulls and he wore a tiger skin around his waist and a snake around his neck. In him the darker side of Buddhism was "perfected".

David's eyes drifted from the deep blue skin of Heruka to the dawn light from the small square windows. Behind the painting, beyond the plain brick wall, were dishevelled, desperate pilgrims.

-

Hindus from India and Nepal, Muslims from Xinjiang province and Buddhists from Western Tibet, had arrived by any means, bus, truck, land cruiser, car, bike, foot. Now all were in convoy over the flat plains.

David sat in the back of a shiny black 4 x 4. His Tibetan driver watched him through the rear mirror. 'In pilgrimage you must subject yourself to ardours to forget who you think you are, and find out who you really are.'

David sighed, half asleep, irritable. 'This isn't about finding myself. It's a mass protest.'

The reply was terse. 'My people know about protest. When China invaded in 1950, they killed a million Tibetans and destroyed thousands of monasteries. Now they have built roads and dragon gates over our sacred places and plundered our mineral resources. What good has protest been for us?'

David was tired, he was not listening as an ambulance sped past them. He turned on a small screen to catch up with the news.

The Tibetan shrugged away his annoyance but continued, in a louder voice. 'Kailash is the source of all possibility but her holy rivers no longer flow and you know who is to blame?'

Suddenly David's heart leapt into his mouth. It was Rockschild. Maybe it was an old program, but no, the swollen eye and scars of reconstructive surgery were clearly discernable under heavy make-up. 'Listen.' He snapped, turning it up.

The gravel voice polluted the air. 'China's unilateral pollution is undemocratic. This is a last warning to China to reduce their emissions, to turn to nuclear energy.'

The broadcast cut to another report. A crowd surged behind a lady for NBC. 'Following the death of 75 people in a stampede at a Hindu Temple in Kathmandu an estimated 6 million Indians, desperate to escape the floods, are being led by the murderer and disgraced former leader of the Auditors, David Wolfe, to the desolate Mount Kailash. He is irresponsibly leading them into a humanitarian disaster zone. The U.N has been dropping aid parcels but these are being confiscated by his rebel army and nothing is getting through.'

The driver jumped as David banged the off button with his fist. 'Their aid is a farce. It's all our aid.'

'They lie,' said the Tibetan, 'but we will win, with Demchog's help.' Before the words had all left the driver's mouth David began to pray. 'Oh Yeshua, please help us,' His prayers continued until the night faded and the outline of a mountain range came into view.

As they drew closer abandoned vehicles littered sides of the road. Closer still and streams of pilgrims filled the road, heading towards a well lit Chinese gateway in the foothills.

The driver stopped by fields full of parked cars. 'This is where you get out. Just follow everyone to Dira Puk Monastery. It is easy to find.'

David thanked him, climbed out and adjusted his backpack. But before he could say goodbye the automatic window raised and the wheels began reversing. Wrapped up in a heavy coat and gloves David trudged forwards.

The sun was rising but the air was still freezing so David put on a black baseball cap for extra warmth. The road soon became a wide path and the stones crunched underfoot. He felt invisible as he joined the army of people that surged forwards, in union.

The giant three-tiered dragon gate spanned the path. Its red columns on granite plinths supported ornate, golden roofs skirted with gilded filigrees of swastikas. Red, turquoise and golden dragons, sat, alongside CCTV cameras, perched on gable ends, watching.

Passing beneath the structure were wealthy Indian pilgrims in all manner of gaudy, synthetic jackets, hats and fleece scarves that competed for vibrancy with the traditional clothing of the Tibetans. Hindu Gurus walked with stylish sunglasses on their foreheads whilst venerable monks were pulled in tent-like golden carriages, decorated with tassels.

Distinguished Tibetans travelled by horse as quad bikers raced up and down the pathside, ferrying people and supplies, the Chinese flag waving high on their aerials. Short, swarthy, brown skinned Tibetan porters stared from under baseball caps, through permanently squinted eyes, as they carried over-laden baskets strapped around their heads and backs. Beside them the yaks, hairy cows, carried the heavier loads, and sheep followed, their bells ringing.

Everyone's target was the halfway point around Kailash, the 13th century Dira Puk monastery.

As the sun rose higher David put on his sunglasses. Everything went into a brown tint. A panting dog ran under his feet as a group of Tibetan women passed him in wide black hats and red striped skirts. They sang happy Chinese melodies whilst coating their faces with cream to protect their skin. But David was light-headed with the altitude. The rocks here were rough and sharp, the landscape was desolate, like the moon, and the air was hard to breathe.

The route was punctuated by a long lines of prayer flags, fluttering from poles stuck into rock cairns. Beneath these the pilgrims had left tattered clothing, yak heads and goat horns. A Hindu Saddhu, with long hair and beard, sat nearby, ash covering his body, from head to foot. A large brass sacred Ohm symbol was on a cone of red garlands that rocked upon his head. He called out in an American accent. 'Discard your old life, leave your belongings here.' David stopped to take off his coat and forced it into his rucksack. He drank, but still felt parched. He was overheating but the wind chill soon froze his arms. He had nothing to leave with the Saddhu so he just bowed and continued.

The crowd moved at different speeds as they followed the dried-up Lha Chu River up the empty valley. High, steep cliffs towered above and it looked as if boulders would roll down onto them. Faster walkers grew impatient at bottle-necks in the rocky path. Suddenly David found himself overtaken by a group of Orthodox Jews, wearing long black coats and long white socks. Their tassels and beards bobbed under furry hats as they negotiated the large boulders. He was delighted. At least Rabbi Solomon Cohen's followers were still with them. He wanted to call after them but his throat now began to feel like sandpaper. He was not acclimatised to the altitude of the Tibetan Plateaux.

When he caught a glimpse of the west face of Kailashhis excitement was mixed with a sense of unholy tragedy. The black granite mountain that dwarfed the mountains around with its sharp, perfect point that reached into the sky, had all but lost the snow from its famous peak.

The river-bed continued up a narrow canyon, leaving the awesome sight behind. And as the path grew steeper he tied his fleece around his waist and resolved to keep going. He looked down, and kept moving, one foot at a time. Every step felt like ten as waves of fatigue swept over him. He needed to take increasingly frequent breaks and each   time he stopped it became harder to get started again.

The day dragged on as they travelled around the Mountain. They were a mob that almost crushed the Tibetan Bon who came from the opposite direction. The Bon, who made full body prostrations, were walking, hands reaching upwards in prayer, then kneeling, bowing and lying, arms stretched forward, before getting up and repeating the steps. All the while they chanted. David's heart sank as the crowds began to laugh at them, resentful of the way they interrupted the flow of traffic. They were going anti-clockwise around the swastika mountain because their swastika rotated in the opposite direction to that of the Hindus and Buddhists.

The path narrowed, levelled and progressed over low dry grass. The sun beat down from amongst the sparse, white clouds, silhouetting the snow melted ridges against the sky. David had a headache, fatigue, dizziness. He was getting mountain sickness. He couldn't concentrate, he had to drink, he had to walk slower. He needed to find a cool, shaded place, but it was bitterly cold when he stopped for too long.

He only managed to continue, along the valley side, by being buoyed up by the masses. His lips cracking with thirst as they crossed a bridge over the dry river where the rocks were rough and sharp.

When he drank he was bumped by an Indian traveller, jealous of his cool, sweet water. Water fell from his lips, to the floor, and David noticed the yellow flowers for the first time.

-

David walked until the sun cast long, raking shadows up the vast valley plains. Before him were dark brown hills and beyond these was the sublime mountain, a great pyramid, a stunning yet terrifying sight. The late sun reflected on the remnants of snow on its peaks with dazzling brilliance.

Tired to a standstill, and coughing with lungs which told him that he was above 20,000 feet, he could see base-camp stretching up the wide valley. Thousands of tents filled with more than a million protestors and refugees. As the cloud began to gather in the sky he found the extra stamina, for the final push.

Many of the tents and shacks, along the central path through the camp, were new but as many again were made from blue plastic sheeting and empty food parcels. In the middle of them all was a 100 foot flag pole, supported with four ropes covered in flags. The pole fought in the wind struggling to keep standing.

In the middle of the camp were Tibetan monks, in red headdresses and red robes. They chanted and played drums, bells and horns for dancers who wore golden masks and whose long wigs trailed as they whirled and wailed, whilst the prayer wheels kept turning.

White necked vultures circled in the remnants of light as shouts of parading militia came from across the valley. It would be dark soon and he still hadn't found Dir Puk. Then he noticed a Rainbow Swastika flag, high on the side of the valley, and beside it, amongst the rocks, was a building.

He sweated as he headed towards the modest looking structure. His breathing was short and each slow step measured. He needed to keep going, but only the call to prayer encouraged him onwards. It came from rocky outcrops where Muslims kneeled and prayed.

Pushing his way further, he was pleased to see a camp of Sikhs sitting around old, triangular, orange tents. At least some were here to show support. Soon the shade had overtaken him. He continued amongst the rocks until he had lost all direction.

A scrawny ginger dog looked up at him in expectation of food. He dropped the last of his bread and the dog swallowed it whole. Then he continued upwards, resting amongst a group of well dressed devotees who had lit Yak dung fires around an iron trident, sticking up from a pile of rocks. They chanted to the glory of Lord Shiva as the fire glowed in their faces.

The believers surrounded a group of Hindu Sadhus who sat in complex Yoga postures, balancing on their hands and heads, invocating Shiva and chanting his mantras. People queued, waiting to be cured of illness, whilst the ash covered gurus pierced their semi-naked bodies, faces and tongues with skewers. They were trying to channel spiritual energy up through their bodies, to jolt themselves into enlightenment.

A proud man explained, in clear English. 'The trident of Shiva represents the energies of enlightenment at the summit of the head, but for those who are not with us, the same trident is for punishment.'

David did not want to talk, but when he heard the dog giving out a sickening yelp from somewhere behind him, he felt a deep urgency. 'Please. Where is Dira Puk?'

The Hindu just nodded the way.

Nestled between large, split rocks, painted with Sanskrit prayers, was the small, rectangular, red brick, building, Dira-puk. To the side, part obscured by tents, were hundreds of white stupas on two, low stone walls. Beneath their golden peaks, painted eyes stared out towards the tents that littered the other side of the valley. Beyond these was the massive north face of Kailash, now deep red. David needed to lie down but the view was mesmerising. As he stared at the peaks he was sure that he could see a scull.

The prayer flags and stupas became silhouettes as the sounds of the camp died away. Clouds rolled down past them, submerging the lights in the camp below, making the mountain peaks look like islands jutting from a bloody, celestial sea. David stood in these   heavens, watching, until the sky gave way to darkness.

Freezing he turned and headed for the entrance of Dira-puk where a robust monk, in orange robes and carrying tea, rushed to the doorway. 'David, I am Lama Tenzin Namjer. We have been worried where you were. Please drink.'

Pausing, David saw his reflection in the metal cup. Under his brow, in deep sockets, his sunken eyes had become like the painted eyes of a statue. He drank. Then coughed violently into the metal cup.

'You must get warm. Please follow me.'

Tenzin led David inside, into a small prayer hall, full of monks meditating on a carpet laid over a dirt floor. Before them rested a Thangka painting, of the twelve armed black Buddha, Heruka, surrounded with candles.

David looked surprised at the room. Tenzin stamped on the floor and laughed. 'For Tibetans this is normal.'

He offered David a bowl of hot soup. 'We feed people this in the large tents. Yak butter tea, mixed with flour. It is nutritious.' As David drank he started to feel some relief from the dehydration and exhaustion.

Then Tenzin put his hands onto David's shoulders. 'But before you sleep we have duties to perform. The crowd is thirsty and we have no more drinking water. So we must pray to Heruka. His magical Sanskrit name means the bliss of union with the emptiness that blows through everything.'

David was slowly led to a large cushion, his body shaking with fatigue, whilst the monks around him kept up a steady chanting, clashing symbols and beating drums.

'Om Shri Vajra He He Ru Ru Kam Hum Hum P'hat Dakini Dzala Shambaram Soha.'

'This is the mantra of Heruka,' said Tenzin.

David was keen to remove his boots and ease his sore feet but instead they prayed for hours. Pilgrims came and went, offering scarves and small denominations of money before him. He blessed their heads and handed out string necklaces from a pile by his side, until he slumped asleep.

-

David stood in a desert. A snake hissed and slid up the side of his leg, sensuously coiling around his body, onto his shoulders and around his neck. Squeezing, squeezing, until his swollen face split and his head burst, raining blood over the land.

He awoke, terrified. His legs agonisingly stiff from the cold. He was wheezing, coughing in his sleeping bag. Only the pain stopped him from panicking as he heard the wind hurtling down the valley, filling the crevices, passing over, like the hand of God. Shouts mixed with the gale that rattled through the canvas outside, and whistled through the walls of the monastery. He prayed to God that they would all be protected.

Then, with a flash of sheet lighting and a peel of thunder, the massive downpour fell.

He was in pain, his eye lids swollen, but he had to get up from his mattress. He jostled to the doorway, his feet numb with cold. He had to see what was happening.

Sleet and rain battered down as the wind blew away tents. As people scrambled to secure their shelters they slid on icy mud and rocks. Around and below, in the valley, he could hear cries of confusion and anger. Old and young, people and animals, gathered together, abandoned in a writhing mass of misery.

He set off to help in the camp but Tenzin put a restraining hand on his shoulder. 'Your duty is to pray.'

David asked out loud. 'Why has God let this happen?'

Tenzin led him back to the doorway, out of the gale. 'It is the final turn of the Wheel of Dharma, the whole of this land has awaited Heruka.' Tenzin pointed inside to the painting, 'the Highest One, the final Buddha. He sees everything and devours all of his lovers in the Supreme Bliss beyond opposites. His name in the Bon religion is Demchog, the wrathful high God. Kailash, the swastika mountain, is Demchog, and Lord Shiva, the destroyer. And tonight began their dance of destruction.' The monk's eyes were now as cold as the stars in the sky.

In the monastery, shoulder to shoulder with monks, David's hands numbed with the cold. He felt like he would freeze as he sat, staring at the painting of the 12 armed Heruka David slowly realised, with horror, that Heruka was the twelve armed swastika.

The storm eased and the shroud of the night finally lifted, the warm light of candles drowned out by the cold blue of morning. David struggled to stand on his stiff knees and was the last to leave the hall. The sun was rising and the rain had almost completely cleared. Beyond the Stupas a faint rainbow formed over the chaos in the camp, where tents and prayer flags had all but collapsed. But behind all of this, across the valley of devastation, there, presided Kailash.

Around the monastery a crowd of Chinese Taoist priests, in high-collared black, silk robes and with round, vertically rimmed hats, spoke in Mandarin with the Tibetan monks. They ignored David and he suddenly felt alone.

An air ambulance lifted from a rocky plateaux and as its loud drone faded, a piercing whistle blew, setting off a relay of whistles throughout the camp. It was time to move on.

David set off amongst the throng, to make the two hour walk to the Kangkyam Glacier, at the base of the north face of Kailash. The ground had turned soft and the main route from the camp was trampled into deep, squalid mud. Quad bikes and yaks were getting stuck as they tried to leave.

The sound of the wind joined with the sound of the water rushing over yesterday's dry river bed. It was more rain water than had been seen for years. Creating sweet and tempting streams that gushed down the gullies, spilling from their course and trickling over the paths that thawed beneath the pilgrims' feet. Up the valley, past lines of flags, the jostling crowd fought to drink from the fast flowing rivers. Further upstream others washed their muddy boots near to sheep that lay dead in the water.

David filled his bottle and watched the exodus of cold, dishevelled pilgrims snake up the valley to another Dragon gate. Beside it was a Chinese military outpost, where soldiers watched the masses pass over the icy skree. The wind blew between two mountains that flanked the gate like pillars supporting the heavens, on the approach to Kailash itself.

David was neither hot nor cold when he reached the top of the rise. He removed his sunglasses and breathed deeply. 'It's amazing!' he said aloud. The mountain stood as a God before him. Behind him the sky was now exquisitely blue. In front, around Kailash, the grey storm clouds gathered, fighting with the sun.

From here the quad bikes could go no further as the path narrowed and dropped steeply into the valley below. As he descended, Kailash seemed to push higher and higher into the sky and despite the distance it seemed so close that it might fall upon them. The sun shone briefly, as a crown on its peak, but was soon eclipsed as he stepped, lower and lower, into the deep arena. He looked up at the silhouetted mountain and above them buzzards were circling, their call interrupted only by passing helicopters.

It was wet underfoot as the sprawling mob crossed the natural amphitheatre in front of Kailash, heading for what was left of the Kangkyam glacier, at the foot of the giganormous mountain.

Hopping between rocks, careful not to slip on the ice, David assembled with the crowd in the vast area where much of the glacier used to be. The glacier was now in the distance, up the sacred slopes, descending as melt water that ran quickly between the grey rocks, creating small waterfalls flowing under beautiful, glistening icicles.

David put on his gloves as he grew cold in the valley shade. He watched the Chinese soldiers who guarded a generator and large speakers. These were either side a huge rock outcrop a giant buttress that jutted out from the base of the giant Kailash that rose behind.

Camera crews set up as people were ordered into rows by whistle blowing marshals. But no one would inform him what was happening.

For two hours the crowd waited with high expectation. Then Tibetan monks, wearing tall golden hats, with a crest running from front to back, assembled at the base of the outcrop. They sat behind long, deep horns and the sense of anticipation grew.

By early afternoon the clouds   began to break and the welcome sun moved around the mountain, hitting them with a raking light.

As they waited a helicopter caught his eye, its windows glistening, its red light flashing. As it grew closer he could see that it carried a giant statue of a red dragon with a golden Buddha. Traversing the air, it displayed its cargo to the crowd, then lowered the statue onto the ledge of the sacred outcrop. The supporting strap was released. Then the helicopter circled, and descended, scattering the crowd, with its chopping blades.

'It's Chang Qing,' said David, instinctively. But no one listened as he set off in a daze, weaving his way through the staring masses. The scree rocks slid under his feet as he passed between boulders split by glaciers, freshly painted with Sanskrit prayers. Pushing through the crowd he reached the base of the outcrop.

A figure dressed in golden, yellow robes turned from the Taoist priests beside the helicopter and walked towards him.

Chang Qing was not as David expected. Chinese, Tibetan, Mongolian, Nepalese, Indian. All the features coalesced, but what surprised David most was his swarthy bulk. A strength and power filling every muscle, every vein, channelled and magnified in the almost physical glow of his benevolent smile.

Chang Qing bowed and introduced himself. 'Ni hao David.'

David fired back. 'Tell me, Qing, why do you use my first name?'

Chang Qing stared at David. 'Out of courtesy to your tradition.' Then he laughed and raised a hand adorned with gold rings to quell David's anger. 'Please though, you should use my true name, Maitreya.'

David was stunned. His eyes narrowed. 'What are you here for?'

Maitreya grinned. 'I seeded the clouds to bring the rain, and now I bring a political solution.' He headed up towards the outcrop. 'Come.'

David scurried after him, trying to question him, trying to keep up, striving not to look old and weak. He was furious. Why hadn't he been told what was happening. Why weren't people in the camp warned about the rain. He called to Maitreya 'You're going off the pilgrim route! The mountain is sacred.'

Maitreya turned and cast an arrogant gaze over David. 'Let nature take its course, follow the current of the unknowable Tao, the essence of the universe.' Maitreya continued over the virgin land, up to the outcrop.

David followed, fearing that he would be left behind. He scrambled and climbed, to keep up with his destiny, finding his way up in the cracks in the rock face, avoiding the patches of ice and snow. He was gripped with a fear of falling to his death but driven upwards by a fear of failure.

Buzzards flew close as he climbed. He panted as his legs ached.

Near the top, he began to panic. Then he saw another flower, beautiful, yellow, alive, growing from a crack. He grabbed hold, destroying the flower, as he desperately scrambled to lift himself up.

At that moment loud jeers came from the demonstrators below. Maitreya had reached the edge of the outcrop and was standing as Master over all that he surveyed, in the sight of the Most High God, his sparkling gold and red statue beside him and the mountain behind him.

When David climbed over the final ridge and reached the ledge Maitreya turned, with angry brow. His eyes pierced David, demanding an explanation.

David no longer knew who was in control and he was too tired to fight. He had to work with the Maitreya. 'They still blame China for the drought. I will try to speak with them.'

'Take this.' Maitreya reached into his satchel, removed a microphone headset and thrust it into David's hand. Then he turned and began to remove the straps from the 2 metre high, 4 metre wide statue. It was a red, horned dragon coiled around a Buddha with polished gold robes and a matt gold skin.

Nearing the edge of the rock David stretched out his arms to quieten the solid, throbbing mass of people that stretched for as far as he could see. All became still, silent. The wind blew against the microphone.

Then, on Maitreya's cue, the Tibetan monks blew long and hard into their horns. The deep sound reverberated like the drone of a fleet of aircraft. The jeers subsided.

David called up the valley plain, 'Fellow believers in the Truth…' then waited for the loud speakers to broadcast translations in Hindi and Mandarin, '…we must listen to the Maitreya. He brings us water.' David took out his bottle. 'Take out your bottles. Hold them. What does it feel like to have water? Drink it. What does it taste like?' David drank. It was fresh, sweet. 'Do the same with his words.'

Then David handed Maitreya the microphone. The Maitreya spoke slowly, to control each sentence's power. 'Wo he shui. I drink water. Just like all of you.' He pointed, as if to each member of the audience. 'Put your hand on your stomach.' He placed his own hand on his hard abdomen. 'Here is the centre of our energy, our Chi, our "life force". And the symbol of Chi is the swastika, the symbol of the unity of the East.'

He raised his finger and stretched out his arm. 'China is sorry for its many mistakes in the Cultural Revolution.' He opened up his palm. 'We tried to remove religion but now we have studied the ancient Chinese art of Feng Shui, of "Feng" the wind and "Shui" the water. The two powerful elements which shape mountains, valleys and rivers.' Maitreya swept his arms in a martial arts movement. 'When man is in harmony with these then everything, in heaven and on earth, flows in unity.'

Maitreya now turned to the statue. He stood beside the Dragon. 'The most powerful Chi energy comes from the breath of the Dragon. It brings good fortune and good luck.' Then he took a long pause. 'Our dragons are your sacred serpents, the Nagas and our Chi energy is your Kundalini.' Maitreya now cupped his hands and brought them in front of his body, forcing his energies upwards. 'The Kundalini power of the snake rises up and becomes the Dragon.' He reached into the sky.

David grew disturbed as the crowd began to murmur. They were impressed, excited, hopeful. The powerful speaker thrust his chin forward and frowned. 'Treat the Dragon with respect then the ancient rivers will flow and life giving rain will come again. However, if you cross them then they destroy with floods, tidal waves, storms and droughts.'

Maitreya then took two paint brushes and pots from his satchel. 'I paint the Dragon's eyes to bring it to life.' He crudely painted in the dragon's large eyes. Two large blobs of white, then two smaller ones of black.

The Dragon now looked fierce and the crowd hung on every word as Maitreya pointed into the air. 'Yesterday, we seeded your clouds so that you could drink again. We fired pellets into them to get rainfall.' Maitreya expected a cheer, it was absent.

So he moved to the other side of the statue and spoke softly. 'Buddha carries gold, to bring good fortune to your families. He also carries a water gourd, to bring you good health. We in China, bring wealth, health and good luck for everyone. This is our pledge of peace. The Buddha and the Dragon are One. We want to give everyone clean, fresh water. But the Western companies tricked us out of our Himalayan waters.'

'But we must listen to the wisdom of the ancient Chinese general Sūn Wǔ. He instructs us not to be tied into fixed contracts, but to adapt our strategies to changing situations. We are a peaceful nation but only the warrior has the wisdom to truly understand peace. Sometimes the sword must come first. Our new leader must be a warrior who unites peace and war, creation and destruction.'

Waves of change washed over the crowd. They became unsettled and began moving, chattering, murmuring.

Maitreya folded an arm, rested his chin in his fist and cocked his head to the side. 'We must use necessary force.' His arm shot out to the Muslim area in the crowd. 'The Muslim supreme leader, the Mahdi, has stated that greed and corruption are his enemies. These are our enemies also. He has chosen to join us and we have made weapons for him.' The followers of Islam cheered.

It spread to other sections of the crowd. They began to cheer but Maitreya now shouted what they needed to hear. 'The West wants war! So we will give it to them!'

He seized on their excitement. A cloud had cleared above the mountain and he turned to face it 'Behind us is Kailash who to Hindus is Lord Shiva, who sits upon a serpent throne, a Dragon throne. But to Buddhists it is Heruka. When the last Dalai Lama of Tibet ceased his reincarnations he opened the way for the Buddha Maitreya, the "Most Loving Bodhisattva," committed to the enlightenment of humanity.' He stood, hands on hips, laughing, then thrust his face forwards, peering at them. 'Were you expecting Maitreya to be sitting on a lotus?' He continued even more deliberate words. 'I am Maitreya, the Buddha who is Heruka, Demchog, Kailash itself. I am Shiva, I am Vishnu, I am Kalki and we will bring peace by destroying the enemy. We will cut him down and bring unity to the planet. And to do this we must bring down the energy of Kailash, the swastika mountain!'

A realisation spread like a wildfire as the crowd called out a cacophony of saviours' names. 'Maitreya!' 'Heruka!' 'Demchog!' 'Kalki!' 'Shiva!'

Maitreya raised one hand and the crowd joined into his one chant. 'Kailash! Kailash! Kailash! Kailash! Kailash!'

Finally Maitreya held up both hands and the crowd roared.

Then he gestured for David to join him, in an embrace but David was shaking his head, in shock at what he had just heard. As David came close he grabbed the mouthpiece, shouting, 'Don't listen to him!'

But the microphone was switched off and the roar of the crowd even drowned his shouts from his own ears. Maitreya just embraced David and locked his arms in an immovable grip.

David stared at Maitreya, horrified, his knees weak and trembling. 'How did you win them over?'

The leader laughed and released David as he walked back from the edge. 'It is not me they follow. It is the Master that they follow.'

He sat on the flat rock and gestured for David to do the same. David remained standing. 'This is the centre of the world. This is the true garden of Eden.' Maitreya leaned back onto his elbows. 'I have seen your sculpture "Zoroastrian Icarus," your Cherub. But the highest angels for you Jews are the Seraphim.' He gazed up as if he had seen a vision of glory. 'They are fiery serpents who sit in the presence of God. They are the Dragons who live in the fire of mystical union. You are a Cherub and I am a Seraph.'

With a quiet smile Maitreya sat up and pulled a piece of paper from his pocket. He opened it and then began to refold it. 'I am Mithras the bringer of light, the Seraph, the Yazata that rebelled and freed mankind.'

'No,' David shook his head.

Maitreya continued to fold. 'I am Agni of the Vedas, Lucifer of the Romans and Prometheus of the Greeks. I am the God of divine fire, the God of Light.

'No,' David was still shaking his head.

'I am Lucifer and the Demi-urge. Anti-Christ and Christ. The opposites are united in me. In Maitreya, the laughing Buddha.' Maitreya began to laugh. 'The Buddha who extinguishes himself and the world from re-birth. The Buddha who returns us to the Divine fire. I am the one Rockschild told you would come.'

'No!' cried David.

Maitreya looked at the origami model in his hands. 'But do not be afraid. We must live as a sacrifice. Have without possessing, act without expectation. These are the supreme virtues of the Tao.'

Maitreya held a small winged model in his fingertips, flying it like a child. Then offered it to David. 'Ta jiao Tienshi.'

'What?' barked David, angry and afraid.

Maitreya placed the precisely folded figure on the rock. 'It means "She is called Angel."' Next to it he placed a metal cigarette lighter. 'It is a Chinese custom to burn origami at the graveside of relatives. This is for Rachel, a winged angel to help her in the afterlife. I know you still love her.'

A heaving grief swept over David as tears rolled down his face. Everything was lost. He crouched to stop himself from collapsing. Then, under a strange compulsion that overpowered his will, he came close and lit the paper.

He could not see the flames in the raking sunlight as the dark burn line crept up the figure. Its wings of fire spread out like Icarus and the paper crumpled into ash behind. He could see Rachel's face as she spoke her last words. 'I don't want to die.' The ash blew away.

The lump in David's throat grew large and hot. It made him gulp as the tears blew dry upon his face. He didn't wipe them away. The salt on his cheek carried his love for Rachel within it.

Maitreya took a rock and scratched the floor. A rising stroke from left to right. Then halfway along this a downward stroke to the right. 'Ren, means men.' Through the middle he drew a horizontal line. 'Da, means big.' On top of the character he now drew another horizontal line, as if a hat. 'Tian, means sky.' Maitreya laughed.

David looked up and saw a bright object travelling across the sky. It shone like metal, glinting with colours, reflecting in the deep blue above. A crescent moon was faint on the horizon, next to it was the small, bright, evening star. The crowd beneath them was silent. The moment was timeless.

David murmured, without thinking 'Now I undertstand.'

There was a flash of light. Everything went brilliant white.

Prophecy 7

Thank you God.
Amen.
Amen.
Amen.
7.7.7.

Lightning Source UK Ltd.
Milton Keynes UK
22 November 2010

163262UK00002B/23/P

9 780956 158703